From here to
ETERNITY

A.L. Jackson
www.aljacksonauthor.com

Cover Design by Qamber Designs
Cover Image Michelle Lancaster Photography
Editing by SS Stylistic Editing
Proofreading by Julia Griffis, The Romance Bibliophile
Formatting by Champagne Book Design

MORE FROM

A.L. Jackson

From here to ETERNITY

NEW YORK TIMES BESTSELLING AUTHOR
A.L. JACKSON

Chapter ONE

RIVER

THE SOUND OF THE TATTOO MACHINE WHIRRED IN MY SHOP. The day had long since set, and darkness closed in at the windows. The light in my station shined bright, illuminating the enclosed area as I worked a fucking immaculate piece onto my client's shoulder.

It was close to ten, but I tended to make my appointments late when it was quiet out and there were fewer people loitering around.

I leaned in close and concentrated on getting the shading just right. It just so happened my client was also one of my oldest friends, Trent Lawson. He was on his fourth session where we were working on covering an old skull with a portrait of his wife.

"Piece is going to be fuckin' sweet," I told him as I paused for a second to wipe up the excess ink and blood seeping from the design.

He tossed me an arrogant grin from where he sat in my chair. "That's because my Eden is fuckin' sweet. Couldn't turn out any other way..." He arched a flippant brow. "Unless your ass jacks up her pretty face."

A rough chuckle skated out of me as I leaned back in and started sweeping the needle across his skin. "Think you wouldn't be sitting in my chair if you thought there was a chance of that." I'd been tattooing

Trent for years. Since all the way back when we were both running the streets of LA.

Dude was covered now, head to toe, and almost every tattoo on his body was compliments of me.

He was a few years older than me, and me and a couple of my crew had ridden with his MC back in the day.

He'd saved my ass a time or two, same as I'd saved his. It was the way of that life, and I'd be a liar if I said I didn't owe him mine, and he was one of the few I trusted with it.

He was also one of the few outside my inner circle who knew the true details about who I and my crew had become. What we did.

My shop, River of Ink, was little more than a cover for it, even though I had a two-year waitlist for someone to get the chance to sit in my chair.

I loved my work and took pride in the fact people came from all around the world for a chance to get inked by me. Tattooing was my peace. The only time when my mind would drift and some of the anxiety that knotted my guts would drain away. When the ghosts didn't scream so loud.

Somehow, the constant flow of the needle bringing art to life gave me a moment of reprieve.

Completely unearned considering I deserved none of that.

Peace.

Not when I was a purveyor of destruction. An agent of ruin.

Sometimes I wondered what kind of person it made me that I didn't feel an ounce of shame over the blood on my hands. My soul tainted and my heart stained.

When I'd confided in Trent what was going down, he'd encouraged us to make our way up here to Northern California where we could live low. Hide out and fly under the radar.

Moonlit Ridge was a small town about an hour outside of Redemption Hills where Trent and his family lived.

Angling my head, I focused on a deeper pass as I worked to get a lock of her hair just right.

Eden was a fucking knockout and a sweetheart to boot. Didn't blame him a bit for immortalizing her on his skin.

Trent winced.

"You goin' soft on me?" I razzed.

Ridiculous since the guy was intimidating as fuck. There wasn't a goddamn thing soft about him.

He grunted. "You fuckin' wish, man. Think you're just getting a little aggressive with that heavy hand."

Amusement had me shaking my head.

"Don't know, brother…you are getting old."

He grunted again. "As long as I'm doing it with Eden, Gage, and Kate at my side, then you won't find me complaining."

"Have to admit, family life looks good on you," I said, meaning it. Dude had been nothing but a beast before he'd met his wife.

Air huffed from his nose. "Blows my mind every day that I got lucky enough to call them that, so you can bet your ass I'll never squander it."

He hesitated before his tone shifted. "What about you? How are you guys…handling things?"

Unease rippled through my consciousness. Made me fuckin' itchy when it was brought up in a setting like this, but Trent would always have my back, dude more like family than anything else.

Betrayal wasn't in his vocabulary.

"Otto is delivering a package as we speak," I told him.

There were five in my crew. Years ago, we'd become brothers, even though we didn't have the same blood running through our veins.

The five of us had made a pact. We lived on that pact, and we'd die on it, too. Each of us with different responsibilities although the mission was the same.

Strange how it could be the one good part of me, and it still made me wholly corrupt.

Trent hesitated before he pushed, "Shit's dangerous, man."

"You wouldn't expect us to do anything else, would you?"

Once we knew? Once we got started? There was no going back.

A sigh pilfered out of him. "Guess I can't, but you have to know you have more important things to worry about."

My chest clutched. There was no question what he was referring to.

I warred, pausing the pass, before I leaned back in and started sweeping the needle over his skin again.

"You know I'm careful, brother," I muttered under my breath.

He started to respond, except we both stilled when the security system dinged when the front door opened.

It was late, but it wasn't like it was rare for one of my brothers to come sauntering in at this hour.

I leaned back in my stool so I could see out through the opening of my station to the front door of the lobby.

Only it wasn't one of my crew.

It was a woman.

A woman I'd peg to be in her mid-twenties, nervous as all hell as she glanced around and fiddled with her fingers, clearly feeling ill-at-ease and out of place.

Pin-straight chestnut hair cut in a long bob and parted in the middle. She had this heart-shaped face that made her look so fuckin' innocent I felt guilty just looking at her.

She was tall and all goddamn leg, wearing a pair of white shorts and a white jean jacket with a red tank underneath, white tennis shoes on her feet.

She kept gnawing at a plump, cherry-kissed bottom lip that even in the distance I was sure was ripe for sucking. A bolt of lust hit me from out of nowhere, my dick kicking at the tantalizing sight.

Fuck me, she was delicious.

A lost little lamb who'd stumbled into a demon's den.

The last thing she needed was to be hanging around here, so I didn't take the time to stand when I called, "We're closed."

I started to turn back to the task at hand when a sultry, breathy voice hit the air, and in my periphery, I caught her lifting her phone and waving it in front of her. "It says you're open until ten. And the door was unlocked."

She said it timidly and with full of question, but with a fierceness that lingered underneath.

Trent angled his head toward the lobby like he didn't mind the interruption.

"What?" I mumbled at him.

His eyes widened in emphasis. "Why always such a dick?" He muttered it low enough that there was no chance she could hear. "Wouldn't hurt you to see what she wants, yeah?"

I knew Trent wasn't going to let it go, so I blew out a sigh, mouthing, *fine*, as I stood, and I took two steps to stand in the opening of my station.

Unfortunately for me, it only brought her into better view.

Eyes the color of melted caramel and dappled with cinnamon widened when she got a good look at me, and I could feel a fragment of fear roll through her system, anxiety radiating from her and riding on the air that had grown heavy.

She looked behind her at the door like she was contemplating walking right back out of it.

Yeah, she probably should run.

I hitched my shoulder on the jamb. "You want to schedule an appointment with one of my artists?"

She kept chewing on that damned lip, though she subtly lifted her chin. "I was hoping to get a tattoo tonight."

There was nothing I could do to keep my attention from roaming over her tight little body, searching every inch of exposed flesh, and my mouth was suddenly salivating because even though I couldn't see much, I was getting the hunch that this girl had virgin skin.

Not a trace of ink.

I was the twisted fuck whose fingers itched at the idea of marking her for the first time.

I needed to get her the hell out of there. Put fucking five miles between us and do it fast. Knew better than to even consider letting myself get near a girl like that.

A girl who oozed vulnerability.

A sweetness that I could scent and wanted to eat up like it was mine to take.

But there I was, opening my mouth and issuing an invitation I knew better than to speak. "I'm with a client right now. You'll have to come back tomorrow."

Nah. I didn't mention that I had a two-year waitlist.

Disappointment flashed across her face. A face that was too fucking soft, delicate to the extreme, though there was something harrowed that underscored her features and left me antsy. Maybe that was what had me anxious to look closer. What made me want to concede and tell her I'd do any-fucking-thing she needed.

But I didn't fucking do close, and I goddamned needed to remember that.

Before she had a chance to respond, I felt the stirring behind me, and I glanced over my shoulder to find Trent pushing to standing, all six feet of him filling the confined space, though he was still two inches shorter than me.

He snagged his tee from where he had it tossed on the back of a chair and dragged it over his head.

"What the fuck do you think you're doing? We're in the middle of a session."

He shrugged the same shoulder I'd been tatting, paying no mind that it was oozing ink and blood. Dude never would take care of that shit no matter how many times I'd threatened him that I wouldn't do his work any longer if he didn't.

"Seems someone needs this spot a little more than I do. Besides, my arm's on fuckin' fire. Need a break. I'll text you next week to set another time."

He gave me a look like he was doing me a favor.

I sent him a scowl because the last fuckin' thing I needed was to be boxed in this space alone with this girl.

"Yeah, and that's going to be two years from now," I grumbled at him, part of me wanting to argue him leaving and the other part sure I couldn't get him out of there fast enough.

Chuckling, he clapped me on the back. "Ah, I think you'll make time for me."

"You've got to at least let me wrap that," I told him, and he sat back down, lifting the sleeve of his shirt. I did it quickly while he sat there grinning like the asshole knew something I didn't, and the second I had the piece covered, he wound around me and sauntered all kinds of casual across the lobby of my shop.

Uncertainty swirled around the girl, her gaze swinging between the two of us, no doubt thinking twice about traipsing around town so late by herself.

Didn't matter that Moonlit Ridge was tucked in the mountains by itself. That the area was secluded and gave off the vibe of being safe.

Bad shit happened everywhere.

No one knew it as well as me.

"He's all yours, sweetheart," Trent said, punting me a knowing look before he tossed open the door and strode out.

The door clattered shut behind him.

The second it did, the atmosphere glowed, taking on a hazy aura as I stared across at this girl who stood there staring back, toiling brown eyes doing wild things.

That gaze ran down my body like she was trying to discern every element about me, and I could tell she was reconsidering what the hell she thought she was doing here.

Though there was something that kept her pinned, shifting on her feet, an energy that struck in the space that separated us. It was something that shouldn't be tangible, but even from across the room, I saw it skitter across her flesh.

Alive and palpable.

Didn't know what the hell was wrong with me because I liked my women hard and fast and one-hundred-percent without strings, and she was clearly not any one of those things, but my fingers tingled with the urge to peel her out of her clothes to find out exactly how bare that flesh really was.

Hungry and depraved, knowing I would tear right through her.

She watched me like she was both terrified and intrigued.

"You been tattooed before?" I asked, voice low.

The shake of her head was slow. "No."

My back teeth ground. Just like I thought. Virgin skin.

"And you want to change that tonight?" My voice was grit.

"That's what I'm here for."

I peeled the gloves from my hands and tossed them into the trash, pushed from the jamb, and strolled across the lapping wisps of light that played through the lobby.

Those wild eyes got wider the closer I got, her breaths coming short.

When I was within a foot of her, I got smacked in the face by the decadent scent coming off her flesh.

It wasn't floral or feminine.

It was warm—cinnamon and clove—just like those eyes—and it hit my tongue like the first sip of an old fashioned.

I forced myself to keep the foot between us. "What happens in here, you can't take back. You sure you want to stay?"

Something intense filled her caramel gaze, and her response nearly knocked me on my ass. "Every choice we make is one we can't take back."

"Which is why we should consider them carefully." I wasn't sure which of us I was warning.

Her nod was short. "I know…and this is one I need."

"Alright then, gorgeous, it will be my pleasure to give it to you."

Then I reached over to the door and turned the lock.

Chapter
TWO

Charleigh

THE SOUND OF THE LOCK CLICKING INTO PLACE RANG THROUGH the tension-slicked air, and my chest squeezed in a way that made it difficult to inhale.

I realized then that it was his aura I was breathing.

That fiery volatility that scraped up my lungs and left my throat raw as I struggled to draw in air as he stood staring at me.

The man was cut like a blade and carved like a shadow.

Eyes the color of pitch with hair to match. His face was slashed in harsh, beautiful angles. His skin was pale, and his lips were ridiculously full and pink.

"So we don't have to worry about getting interrupted," he explained as he let his hand drop from the lock.

I thought he maybe said it to give me some sort of comfort, but it still rolled through me like a threat.

My mouth went dry, and my heart battered violently at my ribs.

Clearly, I should run. Rip the door back open and get the hell out of here because there was something about this guy that left me unsettled.

I held back the scoff at myself.

Unsettled?

My knees were knocking, and I wasn't quite sure why.

Maybe simply because the guy was terrifying. Terrifying in a completely hypnotic, spellbinding way.

He swept his tongue over his bottom lip as he took me in, his head cocked to the side as if I were prey and he was gauging the best way to attack. "How long have you been considering this? Don't like being a part of the impulsive, especially when it's your first."

I could almost taste the danger that oozed from his being, though I didn't miss the care in his rough voice, the man a stark contradiction.

"I've been trying to get the courage to come in here for the last four months." The confession shook, but I figured there was no reason to try to hide the truth from him.

Those inky eyes toiled like a dark sea, softening as if he understood.

"All right then. Give me a minute to clean up and reset my station. Make yourself comfortable."

"Okay," I managed, and he gave me a jut of his chin as he turned and strode back across the lobby.

I couldn't look away as I watched him go.

He was tall and his body was thick. Muscles bulged from beneath his black tee and fitted black jeans. Every inch of skin I could see was covered in tattoos, so many that I couldn't make out the designs, except for the row of five tiny stars that followed the right side of his hairline at his temple.

He ducked into the little room where he'd been when I first came in. There were a row of them on that side of the tattoo shop, each with their lights out except for his that was closest to the window.

He started rustling around within it.

Once he was out of sight and it was possible to look somewhere other than at him, my attention swept the area. The studio was both industrial and posh. A plush black couch and two chairs sat beneath the window that overlooked the trendy main street of Moonlit Ridge, situated around a metal coffee table stacked with what I assumed were portfolios. The walls were covered in art, and in the middle of the lobby was a horseshoe display case.

I eased forward, peering down through the glass at the hundreds of different styles of body jewelry. I had to bite down on my bottom lip to keep the blush from spreading when I realized what some of them were for.

My nerves rattled, and I wasn't sure I'd ever felt so out of place.

But I didn't have a *place*, and I was trying to find one, and being here was a little piece of that.

I jolted when I felt the overpowering intensity suddenly whip through the room again, and my gaze jumped to the doorway of his station. The man leaned there, blithe, though there wasn't a single thing about him that seemed casual.

"You ready for me, or are you having second thoughts about me marking up that pretty skin?" It scraped the atmosphere like an omen, like maybe when he tattooed me, he was going to leave a piece of himself written in my skin, too.

"No second thoughts," I forced out, inhaling as I straightened and moved the rest of the way across the lobby until I was standing in front of him, though I froze two feet away.

His head cocked. "You sure?"

"Yes."

Arrogance twitched across his too-full lips. "Brave girl."

If he only knew that I was barely standing.

I shifted a bit to the side so I could squeeze by him, though my hand brushed his as I passed.

An electric current ran up my arm, and I nearly tripped. His presence slammed me like a shockwave. I steadied myself with a silent reminder of why I was there. Of what this moment represented.

"Have a seat." He gestured at a big leather and metal chair that looked like it could be contorted into a bunch of different positions.

I followed his instructions, awkward as I uneasily settled on the edge of the seat.

He pulled up a rolling stool close to me and sat on it.

It left him eye-level with me, and his massive shoulders drew up as he rubbed his hands together like he needed to press the energy out of them. His voice was low when he muttered, "Name's River."

"I'm Charleigh."

His nod was slow. "Want you to be comfortable."

I choked a small laugh, and I tried to put some lightness into my voice. "Says the purveyor of pain."

He blanched in surprise before the smallest grin tweaked the edge of his mouth. "Don't you know there's beauty in pain?"

"I think I've heard it a time or two."

He looked like the poster child of it.

He cleared his throat. "So, where's this tattoo going to go?"

I gulped around the thickness in my throat, and I twisted out of my jean jacket, trying not to meet his gaze as I did, then I lifted my left arm and ran my right index finger along the lower inner portion of my bicep. "Right here."

His nod was appraising. "And I take it you have something in mind?"

"Just a phrase," I whispered.

A dark brow arched, and the stars on his hairline danced. "Yeah? And what's that?"

"I have a drawing of what I want." My hand was trembling as I unzipped my purse and pulled out the folded piece of paper where I'd written it, and I was sure he could feel my insides quaking when he took it from my hold.

He glanced at me once as he unfolded it, and I swore my throat closed off as I imagined what he would think reading the phrase. I felt raw and brittle, like I'd peeled myself back to expose what was inside.

It was something I never did.

But I knew coming here would make me vulnerable.

I thought I saw his muscles flinch as he studied the words, or maybe he just thought me cliché and dramatic.

In grief we must live.

But they were my words. My truth. And he might be the one marking them on me, but I was the one who had to carry them. The one who had to believe them.

In an hour, I'd walk out of here and I'd likely never see him again, so it didn't matter what he thought.

He stared down at the paper for the longest time before he reached up and scratched his cheek with a tattooed finger. "You know what font you want?"

"If you can leave it hand drawn like that?" I wanted it in my handwriting.

His eyes flashed to mine, and it was then I noticed there were sooty grays mixed with the black, like the sky during a monsoon. A shiver ripped down my spine.

"Yeah, we can definitely do that. Give me a minute to get a stencil printed up. Fill out this information while I do."

He spun around and grabbed a tablet from the counter behind him and passed it to me so I could fill out my information and waiver, while he turned the stool and wheeled himself over on the heels of his boots to a lower section used as a desk.

His back was to me as he worked, a baited silence all around us.

After a few minutes, a printer whirred to life, and then he was back, spinning around and using his heels to glide himself close as he held out the stencil.

I could hardly breathe.

"Lay back and lift your arm above your head."

Shaking, I did, and he leaned in close, setting the stencil against my skin in the exact spot where I'd indicated. He glanced at me with those stormy eyes. "Good?"

I gave him a jerky nod. "Yeah."

He carefully pressed it against my arm, meticulous as he transferred the design before he pulled on another pair of black gloves. He already had a tray set with inks, and he moved some things around, squeezing the darkest black into a tiny pot, then he flicked on a machine.

He leaned in close, his mouth nearly brushing the lobe of my ear, his potency swallowing me whole.

Coarse words muttered there, hitting me in a way they shouldn't. "Last chance, gorgeous, before I mark up this bare, perfect skin."

But I was already scarred. He just couldn't see it.

So, I murmured, "Do it."

Chapter
THREE

RIVER

I LET THE NEEDLE BRUSH HER SKIN, MY STROKE AS FUCKIN' LIGHT as I could get it.

She gasped a throaty, bottled cry at the contact, body arching as a lick of pain whispered across her flesh.

"You okay?" I asked, barely able to get the words off my tongue as I struggled to grip whatever the fuck it was that I was feeling.

This stranger had me twisted.

Was bad enough the way I'd reacted when she'd first come through the door. It was an entirely different thing when I'd read the statement she'd had written in her pretty handwriting on the piece of paper.

In grief we must live.

Had nearly demanded that she tell me exactly what that meant, but I'd shoved it down because I didn't have any space to get stupid like that. Wanting to know the details of her life when I knew there was no chance that I could care.

"Yeah," she breathed, and I turned my attention back to the design, and I started sweeping the needle over her flesh that was blooming pink.

Could tell she was trying to hold her breath. Doing her best to ignore the burn that erupted on her skin as I marked her deep. Cutting into the lines and filling it with ink.

She squirmed and whimpered, and fuck me, my dick strained.

A twisted fiend who was eating up that little bit of pain. Consumed with the fact that I was causing it and wanted to soothe it at the same time.

Loving that I was the one etching her permanently. That she was going to walk out of here and forever carry a piece of me.

I edged back, wiping up the excess ink and the bit of blood with the towel before I leaned in and blew across the heated skin to give her some relief.

Yeah. It was a line I crossed, so goddamn irresponsible and against protocol I deserved to lose my license, but it was a whole lot better than dipping all the way in and swiping my tongue over the wound like I wanted to do.

Depraved, disturbed urges hitting me from all sides.

She whimpered a soft sound, and I murmured, "Just relax, I've got you."

She gulped and kept watching me as I pressed the needle back to her flesh, wild eyes raving as I worked, woman so fuckin' distracting with that heart-shaped face and those cherry lips that I was lucky I didn't slip.

Pausing for a beat, I glanced up at her, and those lips parted, air rushing up her throat as our gazes tangled, and I wondered if it was from the pain that she was gasping or if she might be imagining the same salacious things as me.

Me peeling her out of those little shorts and dragging her tank up so I could get to those sweet, tiny tits.

Sinking my cock deep into the well of her squirming body.

Fucking her right here on my chair, something I'd never done before because it was fuckin' unprofessional.

Yet there I was, itching to get shady.

That deviant part of me that wanted to devour her, anyway.

The tattoo didn't take long to complete, and in less than an hour, the phrase was forever imprinted on her skin. I sat back to appraise my handiwork, chest glowing for a beat because I was fuckin' pleased. Pretty much was every time I completed a piece.

"What do you think?" I asked her.

And fuck, the girl had moisture glinting in her mesmerizing eyes, and she bit down on her bottom lip as she whispered, "It's beautiful."

"Worth it?" I asked.

A smile tipped down at the edge of her mouth. "Yeah. I needed to feel it. I need to remember it."

Heaviness swam in my chest, thick and sticky as she looked at me with all that innocence, but carved beneath it was a sorrow so bleak I was slammed with the need to wrap her up and hold her in my arms.

And that was the most twisted urge of all.

Should keep my mouth shut and my hands to myself, but I was reaching out and running my thumb along the curve of her cheek. "It's the only thing we can do. Live. Put one foot in front of the other."

"That's what I'm trying to do." Her voice was soft, and I wanted to lean forward and inhale a bit of it. Her belief. A fucking glutton because I knew the only thing I would do was destroy it.

I cleared the roughness from my throat, and I applied the ointment and bandage. Peeling off my gloves, I ran through the care instructions with her then gave her the sheet that reiterated them.

"Do you have any questions?" I asked.

She slipped off the chair, coming to stand a foot away from me, gnawing that lip in uncertainty. Then she seemed to shake herself out of whatever trance she was under and grabbed her jacket from where it hung on the arm of the chair. "I think I've got it. How much do I owe you?"

There was no resisting the impulse, and I reached out and brushed the pad of my thumb over the divot in her chin. "How about you do exactly that—live—and we'll call it even?"

Heat rushed, and her cheeks pinked. "I don't like owing anyone anything."

"Told you tattooing you was going to be my pleasure. I meant it."

Redness swept her chest and rose up to her cheeks, and that

energy swelled. The two of us were trapped, the already cramped walls of my station closing in.

Somehow, I came to my senses, and I managed to grit out, "Think you should go before I ask you to spend the night with me."

Surprise widened her eyes, those eyes that rolled with whatever this insanity was that thrashed between us.

Something familiar.

Like she was someone I was supposed to know.

For one fuckin' second, she looked like she was contemplating it.

"Go," I grunted through the greed, and she blinked a bunch of times before she hurried to toss her jacket over her forearm like she'd just realized the treacherous path she'd been toeing, then she turned and headed for the doorway.

Only she paused, looking back with that stunning face that could convince a wicked man to do good things. "Thank you," she whispered. "For taking care of me. I'll forever be grateful."

Then she ducked out, leaving me inside my station, my hands curled into fists as I forced myself to remain standing and not go after her to see where this night might take us.

I listened to her light footsteps as she moved through the lobby, before I heard the scrape of metal as she unlocked the door, then the beep when she pulled it open.

She took that energy with her when she left, leaving me stunned.

"What the fuck was that?" I mumbled once she was gone. I scrubbed the heels of my hands in my eyes like it could break up the need she'd evoked in me.

Emitting a long sigh, I focused on cleaning up my station, doing my best to put the girl out of my mind, stamp it out, and do it permanently.

Once I was satisfied my tools and the room were clean and sterilized, I grabbed my things and headed for the door, though I slowed when I was passing by the display case and saw the stack of hundred-dollar bills sitting on top. I picked it up, seeing there were five of them.

I rumbled, "Shit," under my breath as the smallest smile hitched the edge of my mouth.

Sweet little thing wanted to do me in. Drive me out of my mind.

But I didn't mess with women like that. I saw what was in her eyes, the same as I understood what I'd inked on her flesh.

Grief.

This girl? She wanted to live.

And a monster like me would only destroy that.

Chapter
FOUR

RIVER

I STEPPED OUT INTO THE COOL OF THE NIGHT. THE SUMMER DAY had been close to hot, though with the darkness, the air had ebbed close to a chill. I locked the door to River of Ink behind me, giving it a tug to make sure it was secure before I stuffed my hands into my pockets and strode down the wood-plank walkway that ran along the buildings that lined Culberry Street, the main drag that cut through the middle of Moonlit Ridge.

The small town was situated around an expansive lake, and on the far side of the lake was a vast mountain range. People came here in droves to experience the awe-inspiring beauty and peace.

We'd come here a little over four years ago, setting up shop, purchasing legitimate businesses and sliding into normal positions.

Right up front and center without giving anyone a reason to look any deeper.

It was close to midnight, and a frisson of anxiety billowed through me since I still hadn't heard a word from Otto. He was always late. Asshole was going to send me to an early grave, though one of those had been coming at me for a long, long time.

There was next to no one out, the only sounds the faint strain of music coming from Kane's, the bar one of my crew owned and ran about a mile from here.

I was halfway to where my bike was sitting at the side of the building when my phone vibrated in my back pocket.

I hurried to pull it out, scanning the text that had just blipped through.

Otto: It's done.

I was quick to tap out a reply.

Me: No issues?

Otto: Package is safe.

Didn't know if it was relief or anger that pulled my chest tight. I guessed it would forever be a little bit of both.

Me: Thank fuck. Was getting worried.

Otto: Stuck around a minute to make sure everything was good.

I could almost hear the reticence in his voice. Dude always got too close to the job, and getting attached was not something we could do. It was too goddamn dangerous, not that we didn't have that danger part down pat. Every move we made was perilous.

Reckless.

But we did it anyway because any consequences were worth it.

Otto: Why are you asking? Was your sappy ass missing me?

There was the lightness he always effused. Playing life like it was a game.

Me: Not a bit.

Otto: Ah, come now, brother. You know you love me.

Dude knew I did, even though I wanted to rein him in half the time.

> **Me: You on your way back?**

> **Otto: Yeah. It'll be an all-nighter.**

> **Me: Be safe, brother.**

> **Otto: Always. I'll catch you for breakfast. You owe me.**

He capped it off with about five-thousand kissing winky faces like the cheesy fucker he was.

Shaking my head, I tucked my phone back into my pocket, then rounded the side of the building where River of Ink and a teahouse were located. My bike was the only thing sitting on that side since the rest of the trendy businesses on this street had closed hours before.

I swung my leg over the low-slung seat, the motorcycle a custom piece of art created by Trent's brother, Jud. Every inch of it was matte black. A fucking beast of a machine that made me feel like a king.

I took the handlebars, my attention slanting to the tattoo that covered the back of my hand.

It was two stacked Ss with an eye in the middle.

All five of my crew had it in the same spot, though mine had a knife jutting through the middle of it.

A reminder of who I was.

I kicked the bike over, and the powerful engine grumbled to life. I edged out onto the side road, making a right at Culberry to head out to my place.

The metal vibrated below me as I traveled through Moonlit Ridge, my hands fisting the bars. I only passed a couple cars, the only activity the packed gravel parking lot out front of Kane's as I passed.

And fuck me if I wasn't in the mood for an old fashioned, thirsting for a little spice on my tongue, but I forced myself to keep going, the wind lashing across my face as I traveled.

I rode all the way to the end of Culberry where it came to a T at Vista View. I made the right onto the two-lane road that wound along the lake. Here, the extravagant cabins were tucked beneath soaring pines and oaks. Most of their lights were cut, the windows nothing but blackened squares.

The moon hung low on the horizon behind the jagged, pitched peaks of the mountains, and silvered rays glittered over the stilled surface of the lake.

Air breezed across the water, and I inhaled the fresh scent of the woods, doing my best to clear out my senses since they'd been on overdrive the entire night.

Trying to eradicate the buzz that still pulsed beneath my flesh.

She was just another client.

Another canvas of skin.

In the far distance at the top of the lake, I could see the lights glow from The Sanctuary, the motel that Theo, another of my crew, owned.

I slowed to take the next right onto the small road into my neighborhood. My bike rumbled as I wound up the winding two lane before I made the left onto my driveway.

My place was done cabin-style like the rest of the houses in this area, two story and fronted by dark wooden planks and accented in chunky brown rocks. There was a wraparound porch, also in wood, and I pulled my bike to a stop before I clicked into my phone to lift the garage. I pulled in and parked next to my SUV, killed the engine, and blew out a sigh as I kicked out the stand and swung off.

I was ready to fuckin' call it.

It'd been a long-damned day, and I was drained. There was nothing I wanted more than to faceplant onto my mattress.

Well, except for sinking into that sweet, tempting body. Go back and erase the choice I'd made to just let her walk out the door, but I could be sure that decision was for the fucking best.

Tapping the button to close the garage, I quietly eased open the interior door. I kept my footsteps light as I crept down the short hall that led to the main area of the house.

A dim light burned from the opening to the kitchen, and I stalled when I rounded it and found it wasn't empty.

Raven stood at the sink with her back to me.

"What the hell are you still doing up?" I grumbled.

Shocked, she whirled around, dark hair whipping around right as the glass she'd been drinking from slipped from her hand. Glass shattered as it hit the floor.

And...well...fuck.

She slapped her hand over her chest, gasping for breath. "What the hell is wrong with you, River? Sneaking up on me like that? You scared me to freaking death."

I don't think it could ever be said that my baby sister wasn't dramatic.

"You do realize I live here and was probably going to be coming home sometime tonight, yeah?"

Striding deeper into the kitchen, I tossed my keys to the island.

Raven narrowed her eyes that were the same color as mine. "And you were supposed to be back like...three hours ago. Did you really think I would be able to sleep while I was worried about what might have happened to you? I mean, you could have been dead in a ditch somewhere for all I knew."

"I sent you a text that I was going to be late."

Her brows rose. "Um, yeah, and someone totally could have taken your phone and sent that."

"You think that's the way things would really go down, huh?" Amusement infiltrated my voice. The girl's imagination was wild. Seven years younger than me. Sweet as fuckin' pie and a giant pain in my ass.

"Well...you never know. People are crazy out there."

She wasn't wrong.

"Don't move," I told her rather than addressing her antics, and I stepped around the massive island that was topped in a thick chunk of whitewashed wood. When we'd moved in, Raven had insisted she'd do the decorating since I couldn't possibly be trusted.

The cabinets were a teal blue, and the floors were distressed planks of wood.

She'd dubbed it cozy cabin.

Opening the pantry, I grabbed the broom and dustpan then came all the way around so I could help Raven clean up the mess.

She knelt at the same time as I did, and I started swiping the tiny slivers of glass into the pan with the broom while she tossed in the larger pieces.

With my head downturned, I murmured, "You know I won't ever leave you. I won't ever let anything happen to me because I need to be around to make sure nothing bad ever happens to you."

She exhaled, and I felt her gaze burn into the top of my head. "I know. I just…worry about you."

Looking up, I reached out and tapped my thumb on her chin, something I'd always done in an effort to soothe her fear.

Might have felt like I was getting cut up by razors admitting it, but my sister was a fuckin' knockout.

Had to staunch the inclination to stab every motherfucker who went to gawking at her every time she walked down the street.

"Well, you don't have to," I promised.

Old wounds flared for a moment, those ugly scars that had kept her far younger than her actual age, before she stuffed the trauma down and gave her bright, blinding smile, acting like everything was just fine the way she always did.

"Um, yes, I do." She gave a playful shove to my shoulder. "Who else is going to take care of you?"

"Don't need to be taken care of," I grunted at her.

She fumbled around to grab the hand towel that was hanging from the stove handle while still remaining kneeling. "Wrong, big brother. You take care of me, and I take care of you. That's the way this thing works."

I pushed to standing and moved to pull out the garbage bin drawer where I shook all the broken glass into the container. "Fair, since you know I couldn't do this life without you."

I meant every word of it.

She soaked up the water from the floor then sent me a smirk as she straightened and tossed the sopping mess into the sink. "That's right, you couldn't. You'd be lost without me. I mean, you know how great I am, don't you? I even got asked on a date tonight, and I sadly had to decline since I'd already made a commitment to you."

She played it up like she'd given me one of her kidneys.

Rather than saying thank you like I should, I leaned back against the counter and crossed my arms over my chest. "Who the fuck asked you out?"

My sweet sister cackled, face upturned toward the ceiling as she let it go, before she gave a hard pat to my left upper chest. "Down, Papa Bear. You look like you're about to go on a rampage."

She'd never actually seen me go on a rampage. I made sure to keep her sheltered from that part of my life with everything I had.

"Just want to make sure this prick is good enough for you," I told her.

"Have you seen me, River? No one is good enough for me." She started to strut around the kitchen, and I was the one shaking my head.

God, she was a handful.

"You've got that right."

Okay, maybe I was only giving her shit, but the truth was, I couldn't imagine anyone on this earth being good enough for her. Couldn't imagine anyone who would take care of her the way I did.

Had nearly lost my life three times because of her, and I'd gladly do it all over again. She didn't need to know that, though.

"How'd it go tonight?" I asked, changing the subject.

"Good, but you might have a little surprise in your bed." She arched a telling brow. "He couldn't be swayed."

Pained affection pulled tight across my chest. "I better head up, then." I pushed off the counter, moved to my sister, and pecked a kiss to her temple. "Don't stay up too late."

She punted me a knowing grin as she peeked up at me.

Yeah, I'd likely never stop looking at her as a child. To me? She'd forever be that nine-year-old little girl who I'd run away with in my arms and had never fuckin' looked back.

"I think I can set my own bedtime, River."

"I know, Raven. I know. Thanks for being here for me. For giving up your night."

"Always," she told me, her loyalty just as thick as mine.

"Night." I turned on my heel and headed through the great room that was attached to the kitchen. There was a sweeping staircase off to the side of it to the right of the front door. I took them quickly and quietly. Hitting the loft, I turned right down the long hallway to my double doors at the end. I nudged open the one that was sitting partially cracked.

A light glowed from the bathroom, casting a wedge of it across my king bed that was done in a thick, black, velvet comforter.

He was nothing but a tiny bump beneath it, on his side and curled around a stuffed lion that was nearly as big as him. I crept forward, and I gazed down at the child as I ran my knuckles across his plump cheek, my heart a fucking bleeding rock in the middle of my chest.

My little dude refused to sleep in his own bed when I wasn't there, sneaking in here to be sure I got home safe.

Guess he had a whole ton of that caretaker in him, too.

I just prayed life would never carve him the same way as it'd done me. That he'd never know violence. That he'd never have to sink into the corrupt in order to survive. That he would find his way into the happiness he deserved.

The last thing I'd ever want was for him to dip his fingers into the wickedness the way I had, and that he'd never come to thirst for the sweet taste of vengeance.

I made a silent promise that he would never have to.

Because I would always be all those things for him.

Chapter
FIVE

Charleigh

IT WAS FIVE MINUTES TO FIVE WHEN I PLACED THE CHART FROM my last patient into the file cabinet, in alphabetical order, of course. The doctor I worked for was a bit old school, insisting that he still have physical copies of his charts, though we still had them updated electronically to comply with state medical record requirements.

The guy was close to seventy-five, and I was pretty sure he only conformed because he'd been forced into it, and he'd held out as long as he could.

But he was a good doctor. Cared. Took time with each of his patients. So, I didn't mind taking that extra step for him.

"I can't believe he still makes you do that."

I glanced over at Dr. Lingham where she was tapping something into her laptop as she strolled through the back office. She shot me a grin from the corner of her eye. Dr. Lingham was at least forty years younger than Dr. Reynolds, her ways a world apart, but their two styles complemented the other, and it made the small practice one of the busiest in the area.

"He says he doesn't want anything to do with one of those new-fangled things." A playful smile edged my mouth as I gestured at her laptop.

"I guess he gets along just fine, doesn't he? Hell, half the time he's running circles around me," she mumbled, balancing her laptop on one forearm while she typed with the other hand, her eyes jumping between me and whatever she was inputting.

"I think he runs circles around all of us."

"He does." A slight dent formed between her dark brown eyes as she slowed to appraise me. "How are you adjusting? Do you need help with anything?"

I'd been working here as a medical assistant for two months, getting patients to their rooms and checking their vitals, making sure Dr. Reynolds had whatever he needed. Plus, I organized files and basically did anything else that needed to be done.

I'd never imagined it would be a position I'd take, but I found that I loved it. Making a small difference in patients' days. I was still shocked that I'd managed to get the license. That I'd been brave enough to enroll.

To take the name Charleigh Lowe.

I'd been terrified of being discovered, but I knew it was the first step in carving out a path for myself. I'd had to be something more than just a girl on her knees.

"Well, I think I'm doing a decent job?" I couldn't help phrasing it like a question.

She let go of a soft laugh. "I don't think I've seen things run so smoothly in the six years I've been here, so from my vantage, I think you're doing great. But that wasn't what I was asking."

She quirked a brow, prodding me further.

I laughed a small laugh with a subtle shake of my head, my ponytail swishing over my shoulders. I forced any shyness away as I gave her what she was asking for. "All right, then, I think I'm doing awesome and am a huge asset to the team."

"Exactly what I want to hear," she said with a grin, back to typing away. "Just know you can come to me for anything. We're a family here, and we want to make sure every one of our employees knows it."

"I do. Thank you."

"Any time. Now get out of here before you get sucked into some task that can wait until tomorrow."

"All right, I'll see you in the morning."

"Have a nice evening."

I ducked out of the office and into the breakroom behind it, and I went to the little cubicle that was mine, grabbed my purse, and slung it over my shoulder.

Dr. Reynolds was shuffling down the hall when I stepped out.

"Oh, there she is. How was the day today, Charleigh?"

"It was really good."

He gave me a genuine smile. "That's great to hear. You keep up the good work. My patients have never been so comfortable when I come through the door, and that has everything to do with you."

He patted my shoulder in the fatherly way he always did. The man was always kind and sincere, and I gave him a smile of gratitude as I said, "Thank you. I really love working with them."

"I know you do. You have a good night."

He dipped his head, and I continued down the long hallway, passing by the examination rooms before I was pushing out the front. The lobby was empty, and the blinds had already been drawn. I pushed out one side of the swinging-glass doors and into the late afternoon light.

The sun remained high though it was sinking toward the west, the temperature still warm, and I followed the pathway down to the sidewalk that ran along 9th street. I'd rented a little apartment about three blocks away so I'd be able to walk to and from work.

I tilted my face toward the warm rays, inhaling a deep, cleansing breath, before I blew out the little bit of tension that always followed me through work.

The thing was, though, the second I did, it always ushered in the loneliness. It was the deep, dark kind. The kind that was always waiting for you in the silence. The kind that festered in the vacant well that was hollowed out within me.

Swallowing around the lump it lifted in my throat, I did my best to shove it back down as I headed in the direction of my apartment.

I wore my favorite light pink scrubs and a white, long-sleeved tee underneath it to keep my healing tattoo from chafing.

In an instant, the violent, beautiful edges of his face flashed behind my eyes.

Unstoppable.

Unavoidable.

God, I didn't even know the man. And still, these reckless, perilous thoughts of him had plagued me for the last six days.

A dark stranger named River who was haunting me at the edges of my mind.

I couldn't scrape the memory of the way that buzzy energy had swarmed between us.

It had made me feel as if I were being drugged.

Hypnotized.

Affected.

Wanting something I'd been terrified of for most of my adult life. To be touched.

Leave it to me that the first time I experienced that sensation it would be at the hands of a man who whispered of danger and malevolence.

But God, there'd been something tender about him, too. Something that was muddled by the ferocity that oozed from his being.

And here I was, being an idiot for even contemplating it.

Shoving those thoughts down, too, I tightened my hold on the strap of my bag and increased my pace, leaving the small medical plaza where I worked behind.

This area basically housed all the medical professionals in Moonlit Ridge and was the busiest section in town.

Two square blocks of roads that intersected, each boasting a light.

I crossed the street at the next intersection, and the more professional buildings gave way to restaurants and shops like Culberry Street flaunted, though here, they were more charming than trendy.

My apartment was in the middle of that block and on the second floor of a two-story building.

It was quaint and cute with white brick walls and blue shutters, and the two apartments had balconies wrapped in ornate black wrought-iron and overlooked the street.

The first floor was inhabited by a small café and a floral shop called Moonflower.

I went to pass by so I could round to the exterior steps that were on the side of the building that led to the landing of my apartment above, only I stalled out when I smelled the delicious scent of flowers wafting out through the white, wooden door that had been left propped open.

An A-frame chalkboard sitting out front read:

Sniffs are free—the rest are buy one, get three!

A bunch of flowers and swirls were drawn around it, and I couldn't help but smile as I shifted course and stepped through the door.

Inside, it carried the same quaintness of the exterior, a full country chic vibe with a splash of whimsy.

Two long aisles of fresh cut flowers ran down the middle, sitting in metal tubs that slotted into the wooden holes made in the display frames.

Along the two side walls were glass refrigerated cases with different bouquets in varying styles of vases, and a whitewashed wooden counter ran the back where the woman who owned the shop clipped fresh cut flowers and arranged them.

I'd been in a couple of times before, enough that when the owner stepped out from the back, a warm smile of recognition lit her face.

"Hey, Charleigh," she enthused, wiping off her hands on the apron she wore over a black denim jumper.

She had her long hair that was the color of the night sky in a braid that she then had twisted on her head, and a bunch of little white flowers were poked into the crown it made. She was probably a couple years younger than me, and I'd more than loved it when I found out she was the actual owner of the flower shop rather than just working there.

The first time she'd seen me pass by, she'd chased me down, following me halfway up my steps in an erratic bid to introduce herself. You could say she'd made quite the impression.

"Hi, Raven," I returned. "How are you?"

"Amazing! How about you? I haven't seen you in a few days. I was about to send out a search party." She quirked a teasing brow at me.

"Just have been busy and running around at work, but I definitely can't complain." Or at least, I refused to.

"But you have to be so exhausted after being on your feet at that clinic all day. And dealing with blood. Yick." She recoiled at that, her pretty face contorting in disgust.

I laughed with a soft shake of my head. "It's not so bad. It goes by fast. And we don't get a whole lot of bleeders, but when we do, it makes things interesting."

I waggled my brows like I was one of those who thrived in the chaos.

Not so much.

Thank God there was an actual urgent care just down the street from us, but every once in a while, someone came in with a bad cut that needed stitches. Since Dr. Reynolds had done those sorts of emergencies for years before the urgent care had opened, he still insisted on continuing to offer that type of care to his patients.

"I would literally pass out and die." Raven waved a hand in front of her face like she needed fresh air.

"Literally?" With a grin, I cocked my head at her.

Cracking up, she smacked her hand against the wooden countertop. "Okay, fine, maybe not die, but definitely the pass out part."

There was no stopping the way my smile spread. She was really adorable. Gorgeous in a way that could be intimidating if you let it, but there was something so kind that radiated from her that I doubted anyone would ever feel anything other than safe in her space.

An exaggerated gasp suddenly left her, and she lifted a finger. "Wait. I'm actually really glad you came in because I wanted to give this to you, and I totally forgot to get your number the last time you were here."

She pulled a flyer from a stack she had beside the register. "There is a big festival to raise money for the animal shelter coming up, because hello, the *puppers*."

Her voice turned to an *aww* before she continued on in a torrent of words. "So, pretty much all the small businesses are getting together to throw this big party. There's going to be a band and dancing and food, and it's going to be a total blast, so you absolutely have to come."

Her hands flew all over the place as she described the event. "I'm going to have a small booth, but I plan on having a little fun of my own, and I've been wanting to invite you to get a drink or something, so this would be the perfect opportunity for us to get together."

I glanced at the little flyer she'd passed to me before I looked back up at the eagerness in her expression.

Anxiety skittered through my body.

"Oh, I'm not sure that's a—"

"You can't say no! You just moved to town, and you need to get to know people. I seriously can't stand it that you're up there by your-self all the time."

She cupped a hand around her mouth, whispering the last while she pointed to the ceiling with the other like she was trying to keep it a secret that I lived by myself.

"I'm not alone all the time," I weakly argued.

That time, she was the one cocking her head. "Really?"

"Well, maybe I like to be alone," I amended.

"Really?" She challenged again before she dug her phone from her back pocket and tapped into it. "Here, give me your number so we can make plans."

"I—"

"Come on, Charleigh, it will be fun. I mean, unless you don't like me?" She feigned a pout and a whine, and I blew out an exasperated sigh before I muttered, "Fine."

I rattled off my number, and she squealed. "This is going to be amazing."

Then her eyes narrowed as she studied me from over the top of the counter. "What's your type?"

Confusion wound around me. I couldn't keep up with her. "Um...?"

She propped her elbows on the counter with her fingers still poised on her phone screen. "You know, who gets that cute body all hot and bothered?"

She shimmied her shoulders.

A surprised laugh gusted out of me because she was goofy and sweet and kind, and I didn't think I'd ever felt as welcomed as I did with her. My ribs clamped around my heart, in an instant adoring her without knowing her at all.

At the thought, that piece inside warned not to get close. No one could know me. Not really, anyway.

My head barely shook. "I don't really...date."

She made a sound of utter horror before she grinned. "I don't really, either, since my brother is ridiculously over-protective, but that doesn't mean we can't look, right?"

I did my best to keep River's face from flashing through my mind.

Because it was one guy.

One guy who'd ever had me hot and bothered.

I definitely wasn't going to tell her that.

"Um...sure?" I said it like a question.

"Get ready for an eyeful because my brother has *the* hottest group of friends." She groaned. "Just wait until you meet them..."

She was frantically typing something on her phone as she spoke, while a flare of panic lit in my chest.

"Oh, I meant it when I said I don't—"

My phone dinged in my bag, cutting me off, and I pulled it out since Raven didn't seem to be paying any mind to my refusal, anyway.

> Raven: This is Raven, your new bestie, you sexy bitch. Text me back.

Choking over a laugh, I peeked between her and my phone as I typed out a response.

> Me: You're kind of insane, do you know that?

> Raven: That's why you love me. Meet me at my booth at 5 on Saturday.

> Me: What if I say no?

Raven: Then I can't be blamed if I have to resort to desperate measures. I'm not above kidnapping.

I lifted my attention from the screen, a smile playing all over my face, a lightness in my chest I hadn't felt in forever. "Kidnapping, huh?"

"Oh, yeah." Her dark eyes were wide with the tease.

Air huffed from my nose. "I guess I don't have much of a choice then," I relented, though I was feigning the annoyance.

It felt…good. Good talking to someone. Good to be a part of something. Good that I didn't have to be completely alone.

But I had to remember it could only be surface. A semblance. A façade. Because real could never be *real* for me.

That vat of loneliness churned, bubbling up from the constant simmer. A burn that scorched my already charred heart. I pasted on a giant grin that I hoped didn't appear brittle. "It actually sounds really fun. Thank you for inviting me."

Raven smirked. "Um, of course it's going to be fun. You're going to be with me. As if I would ever dream of allowing you to have a bad time."

Fifteen minutes later, I left her shop with an entire armful of flowers since apparently for Raven's friends, it was buy one, get thirty free. Amusement still wobbled on my mouth as I climbed the exterior steps to the small stoop at the side of the building.

I turned my key in the lock and swung open the door to the stillness of my apartment.

It was small but cozy. The living area was right up front, and there were French doors that opened to the balcony. A tiny kitchen was off to the right of it, the cabinets whitewashed and the countertops butcher block. The appliances were old enough that it gave it character rather than just appearing dated, and the floors were original hardwood that had been refurbished to a beigy gray.

The bedroom and bathroom were at the back.

It'd come furnished, the couch a soft baby blue and the two over-stuffed chairs a matching floral, and I'd accented it with a bunch of pillows. A square dining table sat between the living room and kitchen, sectioning off the two areas.

I went into the kitchen, grabbed a vase, and filled it with water, then I trimmed the stems of the flowers and arranged them the way Raven had suggested.

I set them in the middle of the table, right in the path of the glittering rays of sunlight that streamed in through the French doors.

In the silence, I brushed my fingertips over the soft velvet petal of a pink rose.

I tried to stop it, but a rush of sadness slammed me.

As sharp as fists pummeling me in the gut.

I inhaled a jagged breath, and I pressed the back of my hand to my nose to try to staunch the burning of emotion. When I couldn't stop it, I crossed the short distance to my bedroom.

As soon as I stepped through the threshold, I peeled off the shirt of my scrubs. The long-sleeved tee followed it. I dropped both to the floor as I fumbled to the en suite bathroom where I flicked on the light.

Wearing only my bra and scrub bottoms, I lifted my arm so I could stare at the words that read backward in the mirror.

In grief we must live.

I shifted enough to the side so I could see the scars that scored my back, the skin puckered and forever red.

And the sadness I'd felt turned to rage.

To a hatred so fierce it made nausea curl in my stomach and bile rise to my throat.

Sorrow battered against it. A vicious storm that swelled and seethed from the darkest depths.

Why I tortured myself, I didn't know, but I grabbed my phone and searched his name.

Frederick Winston.

I knew what I would find. I always did.

His bright, shining smile that gleamed with straight, white teeth.

Salt and pepper hair and an expensive suit.

In every picture, he was shaking hands.

Schmoozing.

The entrepreneur.

The philanthropist, such a good fucking guy donating chunks of his billions.

The CEO of Pygus Software.

The man who had been my father's boss and the one who'd stolen everything from me.

And I'd never wished more that one person could be dead.

Chapter

SIX

Charleigh

Seventeen Years Old

"**M**om, it's fine." She tried to duck out from where her mother was fiddling with her braid from behind. Her mother watched her through the mirror with an anxious expression on her face.

"I know. This is just a big deal for your father. I want to make sure everything is perfect. It's not every day the big boss comes to your house for dinner."

Her mother had been fretting the entire day. The whole week really.

Frederick Winston was coming here.

"Dad's going to do fine," she said, smiling at her mother through the mirror. "He already has this promotion in the bag."

"I hope so, that is if I don't burn the chicken." Her mother gave a soft, ribbing tease at her own expense.

She wasn't known to be the best cook.

"It'll be perfect."

"You're perfect," her mother whispered, then she sighed out her affection as she held her by the outside of the shoulders. "Look how pretty you are in this dress. I can't believe how grown up you are. My sweet wallflower in full bloom."

Shyness splashed her cheeks, but still, she gazed at her own reflection, feeling that way in the floral knee-length sundress.

She had always preferred hiding in the corner of the library with a book, wearing an oversized sweater with her nose stuffed in the pages of a young adult fantasy, rather than having to sit at a big table with her father and his boss and carry on a conversation.

But it was important to her father, to her mother, to their family.

Her father had worked hard for this, and she was truly proud of him, so she'd be happy to do it for him.

But she didn't know…she didn't know.

None of them did.

"That was delicious." Frederick Winston rocked back in his chair where he sat at the head of the table sipping from a glass of the expensive red wine that her father had brought home that afternoon.

Her mother glowed. "Oh, well, thank you. It really wasn't a big deal. And Sweet Pea helped."

All eyes turned to her as her mother said it.

She fought the urge to crawl under the table and hide.

"I don't often get home-cooked meals, so it was a treat," Frederick Winston said, turning back to her mother.

"It was my pleasure to host."

"The pleasure is mine. It's great to spend time with you this way. Outside of the office." Mr. Winston lifted his wine glass, tipping it toward her father.

Her father adjusted his tie. "I'm grateful for the opportunity."

It was clear they were beginning to shift the conversation toward work, and her mother cleared her throat as she stood. "Let me get the table cleared so you two can talk. I'll bring out dessert in a minute."

She bit back the annoyance because that part seemed a little patriarchal to her, but she stood to help her mother, anyway, clearing the dishes from the table and carrying them through the swinging door that led into the kitchen.

Her mother released a ragged breath behind her. "How do you think it went?"

"Great," she told her, meaning it, because it truly had. Her mom had pulled off that stuffed chicken in a big way, and Mr. Winston had genuinely seemed pleased, engaged in conversation with all of them.

She had to give Mr. Winston credit since he'd taken the time to ask her questions about her goals for the future and had actually seemed interested.

"Really great. I'm sure he's offering Dad the promotion as we speak."

"God, I hope so. We need this. You're going to be going to college soon, and the raise would definitely help."

She playfully rolled her eyes as she set the pile of dishes into the sink. "You realize I will get a full ride, don't you?"

Her mother squeezed her shoulder. "I know, my smarty pants, I just want to make sure you have options."

"It's going to be great, Mom. Whatever happens. Why don't you take dessert out to them, and I'll do the dishes?"

A frown marred her mother's brow. "You don't have to do that."

"I want to."

"I don't know what I did to deserve you."

"I guess I'm just a gift," she teased.

Her mother swatted at her before her smile softened in sincerity, and she reached out and touched her cheek. "That's exactly what you are. A gift, my Sweet Pea."

Her parents had called her that since she could remember, and she doubted she would ever outgrow the nickname.

Her mother grabbed the cake she'd placed on a stemmed crystal platter and drifted back out the swinging doors, and she turned her focus on the dishes, loading them into the dishwasher and wiping down the counters, before she took the exit out into the hall that would wind her back to the stairs.

Only she stalled in the hall when Frederick Winston stepped out from the guest restroom. A casual smile was on his face when he saw her, though there was something about it that left her uneasy.

Boxed in the hallway with him like this.

"Where have you been hiding?" He gave her one of his big smiles, his teeth white and straight.

She swallowed around the nerves that suddenly thickened her throat. "I just finished the dishes, and I have some studying I need to do, so I was going to head upstairs."

His blue eyes appraised, and disquiet skittered through her nerves as his gaze drifted down her front. "That doesn't surprise me. You seem to have your future laid out in front of you. Quite the goal to go pre-med."

She nodded as a ripple of unrest flitted through her body. "I'm going to explore it, at least."

His head angled, a little too deeply. "I admire that, but it's people like you my company needs. Young adults who are smart and talented and driven. Why don't you come intern for me over the summer and explore that as an option?"

A frown pulled tight across her brow. "I don't—"

"I'm sure it would look good for your father to have his daughter be such an asset to the company."

She felt his words like a trap.

An indirect threat because she knew exactly what he was implying. As if her interning should have any bearing on her father receiving the promotion.

Still, the refusal got stuck in her throat, and at her silence, he nonchalantly stuffed his hands into his suit pockets.

"What could it hurt?" He took a step back, not waiting for her answer when he said, "I'll let your father know the good news." He paused for one moment as he rocked back on his heels, his smile shifting to a smirk as he winked. "Sweet Pea."

Chapter
SEVEN

RIVER

"**D**AD, DAD, OVER HERE! OVER HERE!" NOLAN WAS JUMPING IN the air, hands thrown high, his flop of dark brown curls bouncing around his adorable head. Skin pale with a dusting of freckles all over his chubby cheeks.

We were in the fenced-in backyard that was a huge expanse of green grass. Towering trees sprouted up throughout, their branches stretching wide to offer shade.

I'd put in a ton of shit for Nolan to play on, a fort, a jungle gym, and slides, but I'd left a wide section in the middle to ensure he had plenty of space to run.

I cocked back the small football, playing like I didn't know whether to throw the pass to him or to Otto.

Otto was currently acting the fool, dancing around Nolan in a bogus bid to block him, jumping right in front of the kid and waving his meaty arms in the sky. "Pass it to me. Pass it to me."

Nolan giggled like mad, and he gave Otto a big shove to get the brute out of his way. "No way, Uncle Otto! It's my turn, and I'm way more faster than you! Tell him how really fast I am, Dad!"

"Hold up. Did you just have the audacity to call *me* slow?" Otto rasped out the faked offense, pressing a tatted hand to his massive chest. "I'll show you just how fast I am. You'd better watch out."

A riot of giggles poured out of Nolan as he took off running, knowing Otto was about to give chase, and immediately my little dude was coming my way, tiny feet clad in his favorite blue cowboy boots eating up the lawn.

Mismatched tee and shorts since he'd been insisting on picking his own clothes for the last year.

Face pure, uncompromised bliss, a beaming fuckin' light that struck me right smack in the chest.

"Dad, save me! Uncle Otto is a monster and is going to eat me!"

Still nearly dropped me to my knees every time he called me that. Every time I looked at him, I wondered how I'd managed to steal this little bit of joy.

A thief who'd been given a gift.

The second Nolan got within reach, I scooped him up and swung him onto my side as I tossed the ball to him with my other hand. He caught it like he was making the pass of the century, hugging it to his chest and kicking his feet.

"Run, Daddy-O, run!" he shouted. "Leave him in the dust!"

Otto was still coming for us, lumbering along, so I turned on my heel and went sailing for the line of metal toy tractors Nolan had set up to indicate the end zone.

The second we crossed it, Nolan tossed his hands high again, this time with the ball over his head. "Touchdown!"

"Oh, man," Otto whined from five feet behind because I had, in fact, left his ass in the dust.

Nolan shook his head with a shrug of his shoulder, voice completely serious. "Guess you shoulda been faster, Uncle. Now you lose."

In defeat, Otto dropped to his knees, moaning toward the endless expanse of blue sky, and a chuckle was rolling out of me as I shook my head at the theatrics always spilling from my closest friend.

"Yeah, sucker, guess you shoulda been faster," I mimicked, laying it on thick.

"You wound me, River. Wound the hell outta me." He acted like he was being stabbed in the chest.

Nolan was completely aghast. "We would never hurt you, Uncle, because we really love you. Right, Dad?"

The kid looked at me for affirmation. Making sure he got in my line of sight so he could read my eyes.

My chuckle turned soft, and I ruffled my fingers through his hair as I set him onto his feet. "That's right."

"We help rather than hurt," Nolan stated, and he reached out a hand to Otto. "So, that means I gotta help you right up, Uncle."

Otto played it up as he let Nolan struggle and grunt and dig in his heels to help him onto his feet, and when Nolan gave him a giant tug, he popped all the way up. He dragged the back of his hand over his forehead like it was the hardest thing the two of them had ever done.

"Whew. You are a strong one, aren't you, young lad?"

"As strong as my dad," Nolan said with an emphatic nod. "Check 'em out."

The kid lifted both arms out to the side, flexing with all his might.

"Woo wee, I won't be tussling with you any time soon," Otto drew out with a whistle as he pinched Nolan's tiny muscles.

"You better not!" Nolan was all dimpled grins. "That would be the biggest mistake you ever had."

Otto shared a knowing look with me, his devotion to this kid nearly as fierce as mine.

"All right, Little Dude, go get your stuff, it's time to get going," I told him, knowing I was going to break a little of his heart. "I have an appointment with a client in an hour."

His shoulders sagged. "Oh, man, do we really have to go?"

"Yup."

"But I hate it at Miss Liberty's house." He whined right through what I knew was a flagrant lie.

I cocked a brow. "You just told me yesterday when I picked you up that you weren't ready to leave."

Then he'd hugged the crap out of his babysitter and told her he loved her. Pretty sure there wasn't any *hate* about it.

"But I'm having more fun here today."

"Doesn't change the fact that I have to work, so you're going to have to go."

Huffing, Nolan scuffed the sole of his little boot against the grass, grumbling, "Fine," before he went stomping across the lawn and up the three super wide steps that led to the backside of the elevated wrap-around porch. He slammed the door shut behind him when he went inside.

Otto laughed under his breath as he watched him go. "Looks like Little Dude has been hanging out with your surly ass for too long."

"Fuck you, man," I said, shaking my head, knowing even though Otto was busting my balls the way he loved to do, there was a shit-ton of validity to it.

Never in my life had I thought I'd be raising a kid.

Not after I'd taken care of Raven, terrified I was failing at every turn. Not after I'd seen the atrocities of this world. Not after I'd become who I had.

But I'd had little choice in the matter, and there'd been nothing I could do but stand up and do right by the little boy. Pray to fuck that I didn't mess him up.

Wanted to be the hope in his life when that hope had nearly run out.

Thought of it had regret obliterating my heart, nearly knocking me to my damned knees as talons dug into the gnarled, deformed organ inside my chest.

Otto clapped me on the shoulder like he'd read every thought that had just tromped through my mind. "You're too goddamn hard on yourself, River. Lighten the fuck up."

I grunted at him, and he grinned.

Otto was a fucking beast. Maybe an inch shorter than me and just as thick. Brown hair a bit on the shaggy side, scruff growing all over his face. Rough as fuck because none of us had come out of our pasts unscathed.

Loved the asshole to pieces, but most of the time, I wondered how the hell it was possible he was constantly sporting those easy smiles with the lot we'd been given.

With the pact we lived out.

Probably since the dude dipped his dirty dick in nearly everything that walked, fucking away all the strain and stress and grief. Never letting the weight of this sordid world hold him down.

Case in point, he squeezed my shoulder, mischief in his prodding voice when he said, "Seems to me, someone needs to get laid. Sink your fingers into some delicious cherry pie because you've been going hungry for too long."

That was all it took for my mind to go racing, traipsing right back to the girl who'd been splayed out in my chair last week. Woman clinging onto my thoughts and filtering into my dreams.

His grin widened like he thought he'd tapped directly into the problem.

He wouldn't be wrong.

"Things are slow right now, brother. Not a thing to be spun up about," he said.

Not a thing to be spun up about? I got his perspective on some level because his position was different than mine.

He got to be the white knight, while I succumbed to the call of the avenger. Not that I begrudged him.

Each of us fell into the pieces of the puzzle we'd been fated to match.

"Why don't you take this time to lay low and enjoy the more pleasurable things in life?" He didn't attempt to hide the suggestion. "You can bet your ass that I will be."

I was about to tell him he knew better than to get too comfy when a loud thunk then a crash reverberated from inside the house.

My insides seized for the flash of a second, and I shared a disturbed look with Otto in that beat, before I was sprinting across the lawn, taking the three steps in one, and ripping through the door.

That was just as a high-pitched cry reached my ears, and I was tearing through the living room toward where Nolan was in a ball at the base of the stairs.

Stairs that were hard wood. Stairs that I was constantly telling him not to run on because he was going to fall and get hurt.

"Nolan!" I wheezed, my heart a fucking mallet bashing against my ribs as I flew around the couch and into the foyer, dropping to my knees at his side just as he was rolling over and sitting up.

I tried not to let the clump of fear tear out of my lungs at the sight of the blood gushing from his mouth. No question, it would only wind him up more.

But fuck.

I wasn't equipped for this shit.

Didn't know how to handle it without freaking the fuck out.

Nolan handled the "freaking out" part for me, a wail coming out of him when he realized he was bleeding. "I *fink* I bit the big one, Dad!"

"It's okay, buddy, it's okay."

My gaze raced to take stock, muttering the whole time, "You're okay, Nolan. I've got you. You're okay. You're okay."

Fuck, let him be okay.

He looked at me with those giant blue eyes, tears streaming as thick as the blood.

"Can you tell me where you hurt?" I asked, trying to keep calm while my guts were tied in knots of dread. I ran my palm gently over the top of his head and down the back, praying to fuck there weren't any injuries there.

"My *mouf*." He poked his bottom lip out at me, giving me a glimpse of where it was split, plus a gaping hole where one of his bottom teeth was missing.

Ah shit.

"You think you can open up so I can see what's going on in there?"

He did, tipping his head back and making an *ahhh* sound like he was at the dentist.

Yup, one of his gapped baby teeth was missing, but I was breathing out the smallest bit of relief when I couldn't see any other injuries.

"Looks like you knocked a tooth clean out," I told him, letting a little tease slide into it, hoping to assuage him.

Only another wail tore out of him when I said it, and he smacked a hand over his mouth in blatant horror. "But I gotta eat, Dad."

Otto was behind me, trying to hide his chuckle. "Don't worry, Little Dude. You can't chew, I'll buy you all the milkshakes you want."

Nolan perked right up at that, grinning with all that blood gushing down his chin. "I like that idea!"

I cut Otto a look before I returned my attention to Nolan. "Do you hurt anywhere else?"

He flopped his arms out and wiggled his legs. "Nope. Not one little bit."

Relief pummeled me, and I murmured, "That's good, that's good."

I carefully scooped him into my arms and carried him into the kitchen where, one-handed, I filled a zippy bag with ice, wrapped it in a hand towel, and pressed it to his mouth since Otto had gone into the guest bathroom to get a rag and was currently wiping up blood from the floor.

"You hold that right there, yeah?" I told Nolan.

"I got it, Daddy-O. Don't you worry one bit," he mumbled around the cloth, now the one consoling me.

"Going to get him checked out just in case. Lock up, would you?" I called to Otto.

He gave me a salute. "Sure thing, boss. Text me and give me an update."

"Yup," I told him, then I was storming down the hallway and out the garage door and buckling Nolan into the backseat of my SUV.

"Where we goin', Dad?" he asked, the tears already melted away.

"Think we should have the doc take a look at that."

Chapter
EIGHT

Charleigh

I PUSHED OUT THE DOOR TO THE LOBBY, MY HEAD DOWNTURNED and my focus on the chart in my hand as I called for my next patient, a five-year-old little boy named Nolan Tayte.

My heart clenched in a rush of sorrow. A thousand regrets and *what might have beens* passed in that blink of a second, and the ink hidden on my inner arm burned like a brand, though I somehow felt comforted by it.

I had it controlled by the time the child's name rolled off my lips, though I swore the air shifted when I began to lift my gaze. Something dense and dark pounded through the atmosphere and hammered into me in a stark awareness.

In an instant, my throat closed off.

Still, I was blinking and trying to make sense of the sight in front of me as the man sitting on the far side of the lobby slowly rose from a chair.

A shockwave of intensity cut across the room.

A battering of energy that whipped and lashed.

I felt stuck.

Speared.

Staring at that vicious beauty that I hadn't been able to get off my mind in more than a week, like maybe he'd been inscribed in my being after I'd let him mark me, just like I'd worried he might.

Even from across the lobby, I could see the way his strong, carved jaw clenched and those stormy eyes toiled with unfound, violent things.

Attraction and greed spun like a tornado through the space.

Making me lose ground.

But it was the little boy in his arms that felt like I'd been delivered a sucker punch straight into my gut.

What knocked the air from my lungs.

Oxygen lost.

My knees wobbled, but somehow, I managed to get myself together enough to put on a form of professionalism. My reaction was absurd. I had no right to jealousy. No right to surprise. No right to *anything*.

But the last thing I'd expected was to see the man who'd been plaguing my thoughts and dreams holding the most adorable little boy that I'd ever seen in his massive arms.

A boy with dark brown curls that framed his cherub face. I struggled to remain upright as they crossed the room, and I leaned against the door for support.

My reaction was ridiculous, and I gave it my all to beat back the effect the man held over me. To lift my chin and act as if I'd left his shop and had never thought of him again.

Still, my gaze devoured him as he crossed the room. Again, he wore black jeans and a plain black tee, though this one was looser with a wide neck, showing off the swirls of color that curled up from his chest and climbed his throat. Heavy motorcycle boots ate up the floor as he took long, confident strides, though I still felt his approach as if he were moving in slow motion.

"Nolan Tayte?" I forced out when they got within two feet of me.

The little boy pulled the hand towel away from his mouth. His big, blue eyes were wide and eager as he sang, "Hey, that's me, right here!"

Dried blood was caked on his bottom lip and left cheek, and my spirit clutched as I took in the sweetest face.

There was a part of me that wanted to reach out and take him into my arms, carry him into the restroom so I could clean him up, soothe him, and whisper that he was going to be okay.

I blinked the impulse away, and the smile that climbed to my face didn't feel so faked. "Hi, Nolan."

"Are you my doctor?"

"No, I'm Charleigh, the medical assistant who's going to get you ready to see the doctor."

I refused to let that sting.

I glanced at his father who was watching me as if he didn't know how to process my presence, either. His big body vibrated with that severity that clouded my senses.

"Hey, Charleigh…" He issued it like a question, his voice that low scrape, and I wanted to stomp on the stupid flutter of glee that lit inside me that he remembered me.

"Hi." I managed not to stammer it like a schoolgirl with a crush. But that might as well have been what I was with the way he made me feel. A clueless, silly schoolgirl who didn't recognize when she was about to get maimed. "Come on back."

Forcing myself to go professional, I held open the door so they could pass.

Maybe I really had been hiding out in my apartment for too long. An hour interlude with a stranger who'd given me a simple tattoo should not make an impact.

Raven was right.

I needed to get out more. Interact like a normal human being so I didn't go around forming crazy attachments to people who didn't mean anything to me.

I cleared my throat of the rioting of emotion and did my best to smile, to act the same as I would with any other patient as the door swept closed behind us. "You're Nolan's father?"

The man hesitated for a second before he grunted, "Yeah."

I was an idiot for glancing at the chart, seeing if there was another parent listed.

Even more foolish was the relief I felt when I found that there wasn't.

God, I was teetering some strange, hazardous line.

I turned to the little boy and tried to keep my voice from shaking. "I hear you had a little accident today."

It only barely cracked.

I called that a win.

"I knocked my *toof* clean out," the little boy said, tripping over the words as he contorted his bottom lip so I could see that extra-large gap that had been left on his lower gums. I took note that his lip was also split where his tooth had likely made contact and was now purple and swollen.

But he seemed in good spirits, so I let my smile widen at the adorableness that was this child.

"Well, I'm sorry to hear that." I kept my voice light as I gestured for them to walk ahead of me. I held my breath as they passed, trying to avoid inhaling the aura of the man.

Leather and ink and wicked things.

"How did you do that?" I managed as I came up beside them to lead them down the hall. Each of the man's steps reverberated the floor, tremors beneath my feet.

Nolan grinned over at me. "Well, my dad was supposed to go to work so he can make some money because he's got a whole lotta bills he's gotta pay, and I had to get my bag with all my favorite things in it so I could go to Miss Liberty's house so she could take care of me, and I'm not supposed to be runnin' on the stairs, but sometimes I just gotta hurry because I'm always makin' him late."

It spilled out in a garble.

My heart panged in my chest.

His dad grunted, though somehow, it was an affectionate sound, and I stole a peek that way, getting stuck on the way River ran a tattooed hand down the back of the child's head.

Gently.

Tenderly.

"But you don't need to be hurrying so fast that you take a tumble, now, do you?" he said in his gruff voice.

The little boy tsked. "Whelp, I guess some days I just got bad choices."

River grunted again, and I slowed, waving a hand at the scale that sat outside the room. "Can he stand? I need to get his weight."

The chart only said he had a mouth injury, but I wasn't sure if he'd been hurt in any other way.

"Of course, I can stand. I'm already all the way five," Nolan cut in, tossing a hand with all five fingers spread wide.

A twinge of wistfulness swept in, a dull, bitter ache, and I blinked back the burn at the back of my eyes. Lifting my chin, I angled my head at the scale. "Well, you'd better hop on then."

His father seemed reluctant to set him down, glancing at me with those storm-cloud eyes, the gray toiling with the black, before he carefully placed the little boy onto his feet. He towered over him, like he was terrified the child might disappear if he let too much distance separate them.

My spirit thrashed, and there was a very stupid part of me that wanted to reach out and touch the horrifying designs that writhed over the bunching muscles of his arms, whisper my fingertips across his demons, and promise him I understood.

Nolan balanced on the scale, and the digital numbers hit the display.

"*Firty*-eight pounds!" Nolan shouted, thankfully stopping me from the dangerous train of thought. "I bet I weigh even more than my dad. Get on, Daddy-O, let's see!"

In what appeared agitation, River raked his fingers through the longer pieces of his hair. "Sorry, buddy, but we're not here for me."

"Ah, man, fine."

A giggle formed in my throat, and I tried to hold it back as I scribbled his weight into the chart before I used my pen to point at the room next to it. "We're going to be right in here."

I followed them in, and River sat in the chair in the corner and pulled the little boy onto his lap.

Nothing could seem so at odds.

The ferocity of the man, the enormity of his frame, the dark, swirling designs that spoke of the greatest evils and the deepest sorrows. Black hair and black eyes and black clothing. And sitting there on his lap was this tiny boy, a flop of messy brown curls on his head, freckles dashed across his cheeks and nose.

But it was the child's blue, mesmerizing eyes that stole my breath.

My spirit clutched again, and I grabbed the thermometer, thankful to have something to do with my hands, but it wasn't nearly enough to ground me as I slowly eased across the confined space so I was standing right in front of them.

Thunderstorm eyes clashed against mine, his massive arm locked protectively around the little boy's waist.

I couldn't look away from the man as I ran the thermometer across Nolan's forehead and to his temple, then I glanced at the number when it beeped. "Ninety-eight point six. Perfect."

Nolan looked up at his father with his wide, expressive gaze. "See, Dad, I told you that you didn't even have to worry one bit."

"Always worry." I got the sense that River was talking to me. "Can't hardly handle it when he gets hurt."

"I think worrying comes with the territory," I murmured. I tried to keep my attention on the child, but it kept getting dragged to the harshly cut lines of the man's face as I checked the boy's pulse.

"What time did this happen?" I asked.

"About twenty-five minutes ago," River said.

"And was he disoriented at all afterward?"

"No."

"Is there any chance he hit his head?"

The man cracked the smallest smirk, and my stomach tipped. "Nah, he was just upset that he lost a tooth."

He tickled the child then, fingers lightly digging into his sides.

Raucous giggles filled the room, and the little boy clutched his father's wrist as he squirmed and wheezed, "*Teef* are really important, Dad. You know what my dentist told me. I gotta take really good care of 'em."

"They are, but I think it's not going to be a big deal since it was a baby one," I assured him. "You just made room for the new one to come in."

I stepped over to the small desk attached to the wall and laid the chart on it. I scrawled the information and left it open for Dr. Reynolds.

Moving to the door, I opened it then paused to look back, feet stagnant with the thought of walking out. "He should be right in. I think you're going to be just fine, Nolan."

The little boy grinned as he leaned his back against his father's chest, his little arm looping up to hold the man by the back of the neck.

And God, it might have been the most precious thing I'd ever seen.

"I'm always fine, just as long as I got my dad."

Chapter

NINE

RIVER

I HAD NO CLUE WHAT THE FUCK WAS WRONG WITH ME, HOW I WAS being possessed by this compulsion, but it wouldn't let me go.

My guts tangled, cock steel, interest piqued.

Which was how I found myself easing up to the doorway of a small breakroom, gobbling up the sight of her where she stood facing away at the far wall, digging into a locker with her name written on a piece of tape at the top.

She had her chestnut hair in a short, fat braid, and she was wearing pink scrubs, her tight little body concealed underneath.

But I remembered.

Remembered the way she'd looked in those shorts and that fitted tank. Remembered her smooth, soft skin. Remembered what I'd inked on her that she now had hidden beneath the sleeve of her shirt.

I knew the second she felt me there, the way the energy shifted, and her spine went straight. Tension rode through her system and blew back into me. Didn't know which of us was radiating it most, this frenetic buzz that curled and twisted through the air.

Only thing I knew was I'd never felt anything like it before.

She finally peeked back at me from over her shoulder, those delicate features carved in wariness and uncertainty, though there was no missing the spark of attraction that flared in those wide, brown eyes.

"Where's Nolan?" she asked, peering farther behind me.

"In the restroom right next door. Saw you in here when I passed."

What really happened was I felt you in here and you stopped me in my goddamn tracks.

Wasn't about to admit that.

"Is he okay?" That sultry voice was a whisper and doing stupid things to me. I wasn't sure I'd ever felt a pull like this before.

Wasn't sure I'd ever wanted to fuck and taste and take the way I wanted to do with her.

Drag her right out of those scrubs and spread her out on the breakroom table and pound this need out of my body.

Didn't like being distracted this way. Thoughts wayward and errant.

Had too much shit in my life to keep straight without slipping up this way.

But fuck, this girl emitted some kind of gravity.

I crossed my arms over my chest as I leaned against the door-frame. "Yeah. Adult tooth is already right there, so he won't be going hungry any time soon."

The softest smile kissed the edge of her lips. "I thought I could see it."

She stared across at me. Awareness stretched on a taut, keening band.

"How's that tat?" I asked, voice rough with this unfound greed.

Redness splashed her cheeks, no doubt envisioning that night, the tension that'd strained, the suggestion I'd made right before she'd left.

She gave a slight lift of that arm. "It's almost healed. It's just a little flaky."

"Wouldn't mind taking a peek at it."

Caution marred her brow. "I don't think that's necessary."

But I was already pushing from the jamb and moving across the room, slow yet sure, unable to stop the urge from towing me across the room.

"Yeah, I think it is," I rumbled.

Because there was something about her that wouldn't let me stay away.

Chapter

TEN

Charleigh

WHAT WAS HE DOING? WHAT WAS HE DOING?

A sliver of fear rattled my nerves and his energy lashed, the clash of the two whipping the room into disorder.

Surprise and apprehension had me shifting the rest of the way around, defenses skyrocketing while the intrigue I couldn't shake flared. My breaths came short as I watched him cross the small breakroom, though he did it slowly, a panther that stalked its prey.

With each step he took, I pressed myself deeper against the lockers, the metal cold against my back.

Hitched there and unable to move.

He stepped up close to me.

Too close.

Close enough that I inhaled his volatility. The taste of violence and destruction on my tongue, though there was something about it that was dangerously sweet.

I wasn't sure how one man could appear so terrifyingly beautiful. Face hewn in sharp angles, lips pink and plush.

I didn't want to be afraid, but I couldn't stop the flutter of unease at his proximity, old wounds urging me to shrink inside myself.

But maybe I was more alarmed that the urge to sink into the heat he emitted was more prominent than any fear.

I'd thought of his parting words too many times over the last ten days.

"Think you should go before I ask you to spend the night with me."

There'd been one flash of a moment when I'd thought I might have said yes.

His eyes darted all over my face, like he was cataloging each line and dent and scar.

Searching.

Reaching into me as if he were seeking direct access to my thoughts.

My pulse ran wild, and I panted out a shocked exhalation when he reached out and took my left hand.

A firestorm burned through me at the contact.

"What are you doing?" I choked, the words barely a wisp.

His mouth twisted in a smirk that fluttered like warmth through my belly.

"Taking a look at this tat, like I said I was going to do." He said it simply. Like it was normal for him to have a stranger pressed up against a locker. And maybe it was for him, but I was so out of sorts, set so off kilter, I could barely stand.

He lifted my arm above my head, and he rested it on the cool metal of the locker. I could feel the material of the sleeve of my shirt skim my flesh as it slid down, exposing what had been written there.

River hesitated for a moment, attention flitting between my face and the tattoo.

"Fuckin' perfect," he rumbled.

I nearly crumbled when his palm slipped up my arm and he gently ran the pad of his thumb over the words, so light I wasn't sure if he was even touching me, though it felt like he might be marking me all over again.

A shiver rocked me, head to toe, and I knew that he felt it with the deep grunt that rolled in his thick, thick throat.

A throat that was written in his own words.

No mercy.

And I knew that I was right—this guy was undefinably dangerous. To my boundaries. To my sanity. Maybe to my actual safety.

I wasn't sure.

But still, I remained, willingly trapped.

A fool who was hinged on what he might do next.

He dipped in closer, so close that I panicked for a second that his mouth was going to press against mine, that he was going to kiss me, though he angled his head to the side and muttered, "Why's it I fuckin' love that I marked you?"

He kept brushing his thumb over the words, his eyes flicking between mine and the design.

"I'm sure you love making your mark on plenty of women." I didn't know where the rebuttal even came from.

Amused disbelief filled his grunt. "Always proud of my work, but this one hit different. Why's that?"

He was looking at me like I might be the one to possess the answer.

"I can assure you, there is nothing special about me." It was a defense. A wall. The need for him to look away because I wasn't sure I could stand beneath his attention.

He was the last kind of man I should want, not that I could ever trust *anyone* to hold me.

Touch me.

Wasn't sure I could ever expose myself that way.

But still, my stomach was in knots, a throb deep inside that I'd never experienced before.

His tongue stroked across his bottom lip, his gaze roiling with a dark understanding that made me want to both run and drop to my knees.

"Think you're wrong about that, gorgeous. Haven't been able to get you off my mind since the second you walked through my door. No forgetting you. Wreckin' my mind the way you did."

I inhaled a shattered breath. I should shut him down. Push him off. Tell him he was being wildly inappropriate.

But a fire roared.

One he'd lit.

Somehow, his voice lowered further. "Can't stop thinkin' about what would've happened had I actually asked you to stay. What it would have been like if you'd let me take you right on my chair. Wondering how good you'd taste. How good you'd feel."

A hurricane of need whipped through my body. Something brand new and terrifying.

My tongue darted out to wet my suddenly dry lips, and my voice had gone haggard. "That wouldn't have happened. I don't sleep with strangers."

He didn't need to know everyone was a stranger.

His touch danced over the ink on my arm again, though this time he'd shifted his hand to play all of his fingertips over it as if it were written in Braille. Flames lapped at the contact point.

He inhaled deeply like he was drugging himself on my scent. "Smart girl. Not the kind of guy a girl like you should go mixin' with."

He shifted from my arm and dragged his thumb down the side of my face when he said it.

A jagged rasp climbed my throat.

"You ready, Daddy-O? I'm all done!" The tinkling voice that suddenly filled the room froze us both solid, and it took a second before River was able to tear his attention from me to look over his shoulder.

Shaking, I looked that way, too, toward the adorable little boy who was doing jumping jacks in the doorway, thankfully oblivious to what his father was implying.

My heart squeezed painfully as I looked at his precious cherub face.

"Yup. Definitely ready, buddy."

River peeled himself back, slowly as he took a step away. My body bowed forward from the loss of support.

He suddenly shoved his hand into the back pocket of his jeans, and my eyes widened when he pulled out a wad of cash.

I was pretty sure it was the money I'd left on the counter at his shop.

Something wry played in the shadows of his turbid gaze as he reached out and tucked it into the left breast pocket of my scrubs.

He patted the spot, nearly sending me into cardiac arrest.

"There. Now we're even."

Then he turned on his heel and strode across the room, taking the little boy's hand in his.

"Bye, Miss Charleigh, see you next time I take a tumble!" Nolan called over his shoulder as River led him out.

The man never looked back as he went.

Chapter ELEVEN

RIVER

Sixteen Years Old

HIS BABY SISTER WOULDN'T STOP TREMBLING WHERE SHE SAT in the front seat of his crummy car. She was wrapped in a blanket and curled into a ball. Shivering and shivering.

He tried to breathe while his heart ran manic. His mind still spun, and his body throbbed from the blows he'd taken.

One after another.

But he'd gladly taken them for her before he'd retaliated, turned the full force of his strength on the piece of shit who was supposed to love and protect his sister but instead had tormented her for years.

Their mother was too fucking gone over the bastard to ever stand for what was right. Turning a blind eye to the abuse. Accepting it for her children. Accepting it for herself.

Over the years, River had tried to stand against him, but he'd been too young and too weak.

Not this time. Not this time.

He drove under the cover of night, having no fucking clue

where they were going, but knowing there was no chance in hell he'd ever return his sister to that hellhole.

A whimper rolled out of her, and he reached out to set his hand on her knee. She flinched, and he had to fight with everything he had against the urge to turn the car around and go back and end the motherfucker once and for all.

The thirst for it crawled through him, so compelling he didn't know how he resisted it, other than knowing he had to get his sister to safety.

Permanently.

"Where are we going?" she finally whispered into the flickering dimness.

He glanced at her as they passed beneath the lights that lined the city street. "Someplace safe," he promised her.

Somewhere he could protect her.

Somewhere that piece of shit could never get to her again.

Only he had nothing. Nothing but his hands and his determination to survive. His determination to see his sister thrive.

He rented them a room at a crappy motel in Hollywood, more than an hour away from their house in the suburbs, and when he went to look for a job the next day and came up short, he snagged a loaf of bread and two apples from the store on the corner.

He felt like shit about it, but he didn't have much choice. There was nowhere to turn. No one he could trust.

He knew if he went to the cops, his sister would likely end up right back at that motherfucker's house.

He skidded to a stop when he came out of the store and rounded the corner, catching the eye of a guy who was leaned up against the wall of the alley. He was likely close to River in age, dirty and definitely on the rough side.

He pulled in a long drag of his cigarette as he lifted his chin at River. "You want to steal somethin', you shouldn't walk in looking like you're already guilty of it."

River grunted and started to move around him.

The guy pushed from the wall, his attention dropping to the bulge in River's shirt where he'd stuffed the food.

"You hungry?" the guy asked, eyeing River in speculation.

"It's for my sister."

The guy nodded like he got it, and he angled his head. "Name's Theo. You should probably come with me."

Chapter
TWELVE

RIVER

"**W**HOSE FUCKIN' TERRIBLE IDEA WAS THIS, ANYWAY?" I grumbled from where I sat at the back of Kane's booth at the festival, nursing a lukewarm beer from a disposable cup.

He'd rented one of those large canopy tents like you'd see at a wedding since there'd been no question that his was going to be the most sought-after attraction. The sides had been left open, and long tables lined the front where five of his staff filled beers from the rows of kegs as fast as they could.

No one was surprised the lines were unending.

We sat tucked back from the mayhem, a ring of low-slung fabric folding chairs set up in a circle.

Raven's booth was right next door. Hers was maybe a tenth of the size of Kane's, though the girl was probably bringing in double of anyone else since she just had a way of charming the pants off anyone who came by.

Kane clapped me on the shoulder as he plopped into a chair, scratching his fingers through his perfectly trimmed brown beard. "What are you complaining about, brother? You've got a beer in your hand and this gorgeous scenery all around. What could be so bad?"

He waved a tatted hand around the park where the festival had been set up in the fields. A slew of evergreens grew high, surrounding the park, steepled tips stabbing into the blazing blue sky.

A band played on a stage across the field, and a makeshift dance floor with lights strung between the trees had been set up below it. It was basically empty at this time of day except for a group of what looked to be eight-year-old girls doing cartwheels on it, but it was likely to be packed once the sun went down.

Behind us, the park rolled right up to the edge of the lake, and a ton of kids and families were playing on the beach.

The water glinted and sparkled with the rays of sunlight that slanted down, the rambling expanse dotted with ski boats that left white waves in their wake.

Beyond it the mountain range rose high.

It was gorgeous, but it was also hot as fuck, and it didn't help things that I was still sweating from the unfortunate encounter that I'd stumbled into yesterday afternoon.

Skin sticky and slick at the memories of the way Charleigh had felt when I'd been pressed up against her in the breakroom.

At the way she'd smelled. At the way I'd almost been able to taste her.

Cinnamon and clove.

I swirled the tepid beer in my red Solo cup. Yeah, it was not close to cutting it.

I wanted something stronger. Whiskey on my tongue.

I'd been the dumb fuck who'd pushed up against her boundaries, wondering if she'd break, if she'd give, unable to resist her lure.

Shocked as hell to find her in the doctor's office, thinking it was kismet or some kind of bullshit.

I should've been relieved that she'd shot me down because I had the sinking sense that one bite of her was not going to be enough.

No way to sate whatever the fuck was roiling inside me.

I wasn't relieved, though.

I was irritated. Annoyed. Itching like a fiend.

"And it's all for a good cause," Kane added with a smug-ass grin, wearing jeans and a blue tee.

"Yeah, and we know what kind of *good cause* that's going to be," I grumbled.

My attention drifted to where Nolan had set up shop at the animal shelter's booth that was on the other side of Kane's tent. He was inside the short fences they'd put up to house a bunch of puppies that were up for adoption. Otto was keeping an eye on him as he romped and played, and the kid squealed every time one of the puppies jumped up and licked his face.

Nolan had already been over three times begging me to take one of them home.

Had no fuckin' clue how I'd managed to resist.

Theo laughed at my expense. Dude was tall and lean, dark haired and cunning as fuck.

When we'd come here, he'd purchased the old motel on the far side of the lake near my house.

He'd named it The Sanctuary, and people came from all over to stay at the reclaimed motel that was hugged up close to the lake, though no one had any fuckin' clue what its name really meant.

The only one of us who wasn't here was Cash.

Surprise, fucking surprise.

He was basically a recluse, hiding out in his cabin high on the mountain, never trusting a soul. Not that I blamed him after the shit he'd been through.

"Thousand bucks says you go home with a puppy tonight," Theo razzed.

"Thousand bucks says I'm gonna kick your scrawny ass if I do since it'd be because of all you fuckers encouraging it."

I pointed an accusatory finger between him and Kane.

They both laughed like they thought this shit was funny.

Thing was, I didn't need any more responsibilities on my plate. This life was already a balancing act, and I was trying my hardest to give Nolan the most normal childhood that I could.

"Nah, brother. I think what's really clear here is that kid has made you soft," Theo said, pointing a finger at me.

Might have given Theo shit that he was about half the width as the rest of us, but the guy could strike you down so fast you wouldn't know what hit you.

He lifted his cup and took a swig of his beer, flashing the tattoo made of the stacked Ss on the back of his left hand that he had in the exact same spot as the rest of us.

I scoffed though it was true. Other than Raven, Nolan was the one person in the world who could turn me to a hapless pile of putty that he held in the palm of his little hand.

He was the one ounce of goodness I carried. A shock to the purpose I'd found.

"All while he acts like a total prick to the rest of us," Kane ribbed, grinning from behind his cup. "Our brother here is nothin' but rainbows and sunshine."

"Have more riding on the line now," I grunted, voice low, watching the child run in a circle within the fence.

I used to only have Raven to worry about, which was fucking stress enough, plus the rest of the guys.

My crew was an entirely different thing, though, since there wasn't one of them who couldn't stand for himself, but we never hesitated to jump and help each other.

God knew what we'd been through together. What we'd done to survive.

There'd never be an instance when I didn't have my crew's back.

But a kid?

Dread pulled through my chest. It was terrifying, and there wasn't a day that passed that I didn't wonder how the hell I was going to manage it.

When it was all going to fuckin' crumble.

Made me sick to think of what might happen to him then.

"Heard you had to take him in to see the good doctor yesterday." There was the hint of a question in Theo's voice.

A bolt of angst rocketed through me at the thought. "Yup."

Nearly crawled out of my skin any time I had to.

Kane raised a brow. "He still on board?"

My chest squeezed tight. "Always seems to be."

"He's being paid well enough." Theo scratched a finger against his clean-shaven jaw.

"I think it's more than the money. I think he gets it." Kane dipped his head in a gesture that encouraged us not to worry.

Our voices were low, held between the three of us, though the decibel of the festival echoing around us was loud enough to ensure there wasn't a chance that anyone could overhear.

Music rolling on the warm air was intermixed with the dull drone of conversations.

But what I couldn't miss was when my baby sister squealed, her voice carrying as she shouted, "Oh my God, you're finally here! I was beginning to think you weren't going to show and I was going to have to make good on that whole kidnapping threat."

I swiveled to look over my shoulder to find out who she was talking to.

Couldn't be blamed that I was still on edge by her claim that someone had asked her out. All too ready to interrogate the clown so he'd have it clear really damned fast there would be no fooling around.

My sister might look like she was all fun and games. Up for a good time. But I knew her better than anyone. She'd get her heart tromped, she'd be crushed, and the parts of her that were finally healing would be ripped right back open.

I wasn't going to stand aside and watch it fucking happen.

But no, it wasn't some douchewad with a hard-on standing next to my sister.

It was Charleigh Lowe.

And my sister was hugging her tight.

Chapter

THIRTEEN

Charleigh

I'D CHANGED MY MIND THREE TIMES ABOUT COMING HERE, wavering, the mental pros and cons list stacked so high against each other that it'd weighed me down. I'd changed my shoes just as many times, waffling between cute sandal wedges and comfy sneakers and the ultimate *this is not a big deal* pair of flip-flops to pair with the shorts that I'd pulled on.

Then I'd glimpsed that gorgeous bouquet on my table, and my spirit had squeezed with the truth that it would be rude if I didn't show. I'd figured I should put in some effort since Raven had for me, inviting me here, making me feel welcome, treating me as if I might mean something to someone.

And the truth was, I was lonely. So lonely that I ached. So lonely that I could feel the proof of it carved out in me.

A throbbing, misshapen hole.

Wearing a cute flowy blue floral top, I'd shoved my feet back into the wedges, buckled them, and stared at myself through the mirror and told myself I was going to march out the door and have a good time.

So, I'd walked the half mile to the park beneath the warm, caressing rays of the sun, convinced that I would. Still, I sucked in a shallow breath when I rounded the corner and saw the horde of people gathered at the park.

Rows of white-topped canopies lined the edges of the fields, and strains of country music floated on the breeze, laughter woven in between.

A rush of disquiet gusted, that tremor that warned me to slink away and hide.

The words on my inner arm blazed their reminder.

In grief we must live.

I forced the scatter of fear down, lifted my chin, and walked the rest of the way to the park.

I felt a little semblance of calm when I stepped into the mass and blended in with the crowd.

Becoming one with the families, the conversations and the smiling faces.

I wound through, peeking at the displays at each of the booths. There were crafts and organic vegetables, drinks and art, jewelry and handmade soaps and candles.

Each was donating a portion of their profits to the Moonlit Ridge Animal Shelter.

I kept moving, searching until I finally found the small booth with a banner claiming *Moonflower* across the top.

There was a small line wound around the display, but I could see Raven's black hair piled on her head with a bunch of flowers sticking out of it as she chatted with a customer.

I held back, browsing a display of hair clips and ribbons at the booth to the right of hers.

Once the last customer walked away with an armful of fresh flowers, she turned to rearrange the bucket of lilies behind her that was almost empty.

I eased up to the display table that separated us.

When she turned back around, she did a double-take when she saw me standing there before a screech of excitement flew from her tongue.

"Oh my God, you're finally here! I was beginning to think you weren't going to show and I was going to have to make good on that whole kidnapping threat." She waved her hands in the air as she hurried to squeeze through a small opening she'd left between her display tables to get to me.

She threw her arms around my neck, hugging me as if she'd known me her whole life.

A breath of surprise punched from my lungs as she tightened her arms, rigid in her hold as she rocked me back and forth. It took a second before I finally gave into the embrace, letting go of some of the fear I constantly held at being seen—terrified that one day someone would recognize me—and I hugged her back, trying to allow the tease to wind into my voice. "You warned me I didn't have another choice."

I exhaled at the warmth that rolled through me as she gave me one more fierce squeeze, like her spirit knew mine needed soothing, before she edged back and gripped me by the outside of the arms. "You're lucky you listened because five minutes more and you would have found yourself in the trunk of my car."

A teasing smile pranced across her lips that today she'd painted blood red. "Come on, you need to meet my brother and his friends."

I didn't have time to renounce the idea and tell her I was only swinging by to see her before she had me by the hand and was dragging me between the small section separating her booth and the enormous one next to it.

I struggled to keep up, my wedges sinking into the soft grass beneath me as she hauled me along the side and to the back where a circle of four chairs had been set up.

One was empty, and the other three were occupied.

Two men sat facing our direction, lost in conversation, emitting a vibe that nearly made me trip.

Each covered in ink and radiating a foreboding ferocity that I was sure had to steal every eye, no doubt garnering attention and scrutiny and curiosity in this small town.

So out of place they stood out like menacing beacons you couldn't look away from.

Brutally beautiful and screaming of trouble.

Exactly like the man who sat with his back to us with his attention fully focused on his cup that he held between two tattooed hands. The one who made the oxygen punch out of me on a wheeze when I was slammed with the recognition of who was sitting there.

There was no missing the crop of black hair and the tattooed tendrils of what looked like smoke that rolled up the back of his neck and disappeared into his hairline at the back of his skull.

I could feel that intensity radiating from him. Tension gripped hold of his bulging muscles and bunched his wide shoulders as he slowly swiveled around to look at me.

A blister of darkness streaked across the afternoon air. Arrows that impaled as those storm-ridden eyes devoured me from across the space.

Couldn't get you off my mind…

His words from yesterday spun around me like a dream.

Raven only tugged at my hand when I faltered to a stop. "Come on, they're right over here."

She pulled me right up to where they were sitting.

"Hey guys, this is my new friend I've been telling you about, Charleigh Lowe."

She waved a hand over me like she was presenting them a prize. I could feel River's eyes penetrating me, so deep I thought they might cut through to the soul.

"Charleigh, these are a couple of my brother's friends. Kane…" She pointed first at a man with short-brown hair and a full but trimmed beard. Tall and muscular, arrogance came off him in waves.

Raven gestured at the man sitting next to him. "And this is Theo."

Theo jutted a sharp chin at me, his cheekbones harsh slashes that contoured his face in a way that promised he could likely seduce anyone into their destruction.

He was completely covered in tattoos, black ink that swirled and curled over his lean, packed muscle. My head dipped in a small hello.

"And this is my brother, River."

Of course.

River was her brother.

My heart hammered as I tried to figure out how I was going to get out of this. Because I didn't think I could handle being in his space. Not when he made me feel as if I was unraveling.

My mind twisted and my thoughts skewed.

Dangerous ideas slipping through.

Releasing my hand, Raven stepped up to River and ruffled her fingers over the super short black hair on his head, as if she was certain he wouldn't bite when he looked like a viper ready to strike.

Coiled and rattling.

She looked back at me with a sly wink and mouthed, *told you*, like she was doing me the favor of introducing me to her brother's friends when the only thing I wanted to do was turn and flee.

But no.

I was pinned.

Chained by those menacing eyes that ravaged me where he sat. So powerful that I had no defense.

No resistance.

"Good to meet you, Charleigh."

The scruff-laden voice knocked me out of the stupor, and I looked to where Kane sat. His long legs were stretched out in front of him and he had one arm draped around the back of the chair like he might be lounging on a throne.

"Nice to meet you, too." Somehow, I managed the sparse, shaken words, but my stupid regard was climbing right back to the pillar of a man whose tongue stroked over his plush bottom lip.

My stomach twisted, thoughts back to the words he'd whispered yesterday.

Temptation and a threat.

"*Smart girl. Not the kind of guy a girl like you should go mixin' with.*"

A smart girl would run.

Run far and fast.

And there I stood as if my feet had grown roots.

"Welcome to Moonlit Ridge," Theo said, the man sitting low in the chair, his eyes appraising me as if he were searching to see if I should be trusted.

Which was kind of hysterical when he oozed nothing but sin.

"It's nice to meet you, Theo."

His attention snapped to River before it snapped back to me, and something amused lit at the edge of his mouth. "Oh, I think it's definitely going to be *nice*."

I couldn't quite make sense of whatever sound rolled from River's throat, but I was looking that way again, unable to stop myself, then silently scolding myself for acting crazy.

This was stupid.

I didn't need to cower. Didn't need to let this guy affect me this way.

He'd given me a simple tattoo, for God's sake. It wasn't a big deal. Not at all. Except the problem was I couldn't seem to dodge him, whatever I did.

Not in my thoughts or my dreams or my actual days since he kept popping up everywhere I went.

I guess I should have known this would be a small-town problem when I'd come here, but it wasn't like Moonlit Ridge was that tiny. I'd thought it'd be the perfect size to both see fewer people and blend.

"Watch out for these two," Raven said with affection in her voice, pointing between Theo and Kane. "They might be pretty, but they'll have you out of your panties so fast, you won't know what hit you. Unless, of course, that's what you're looking for."

She smirked back at me, eyes widening with the innuendo.

Her brother grunted again.

I was pretty sure it wasn't going to be *these two* who were the problem.

"Hey, wait, I know you!" A little voice suddenly cut through the tension, and I looked up to find Nolan racing through the backside of the tent, his arms in the air as he came, that sweet, adorable smile on his dimpled, freckled face.

It lanced through me again.

Javelins of pain and adoration.

Adoration that shouldn't be mine, but there was something about the little boy that had made an impact.

"What are you doin' here, Miss Charleigh? You got a doctor's tent?"

There was no stopping the affectionate giggle that rippled out with my words. "No. I came to say hi to your aunt Raven."

His brows jumped toward the sky. "You know my auntie?"

"That's right, she does. Charleigh lives in the apartment above my store, and she's my new bestie."

Raven hooked her elbow with mine, and my nerves fluttered, both in a thrill of gratitude and a dose of worry. I wasn't sure how I was supposed to be her friend when River was her brother. Wasn't sure I could handle being in his vicinity.

But I didn't know how to move from the spot, either, when Nolan kept bouncing my way. "It's really good you got a new best friend and she's my auntie because she's AWESOME!"

He jumped and punched for the sky when he said the last.

I choked over his sweetness.

"She is awesome." I sent her a soft smile before I turned back to him. "How's your mouth today?"

"It doesn't even hurt a bit! And look it!" He came right up to me, clenching his jaw and twisting his mouth in what appeared close to a grimace though it was anything but, and he used his finger to pull down his bottom lip to show off the gap where his tooth had been. "I got a big boy *toof* right there, so it wasn't even nothin' that I knocked the little one out. And I can eat and everything."

My chest squeezed.

"Well, that's really good news."

"Yup, I always got the good news, and my uncle Otto said things always work out for the best, so I don't got nothin' to worry about. And we got a bunch of puppies right over there." He pointed to the big canopy on the opposite side that was closed in by a short fence. "I'm thinkin' I'm gonna keep four or five if my Daddy-O says yes, but he keeps sayin' no because gettin' a puppy is a really way big responsibility."

A giggle rolled up my throat, and I attempted to ignore the way his father ran a flustered hand down his face.

I couldn't do anything but reach out and run my fingers through the baby soft curls of brown on the little boy's head. He beamed up at me and leaned into my touch.

That vacancy inside me moaned. But it was different this time. It was as if looking at him and a piece of myself was soothed.

"And this one is Otto." Raven's voice lowered when she said that, and I looked up to see a giant of a man strolling up with a confident kind of casualness. His messy brown hair glinted in the sunlight, and a massive grin played on his handsome face.

"Hey, Ravi Girl. This your new friend?" The man's startling blue gaze flitted between us. I was pretty sure my new *best friend* was shaking.

"Yup, this is her. Charleigh. She lives right upstairs from the store."

The man's grin deepened. "Good to meet you, Charleigh. This one won't stop talking about the new resident of Moonlit Ridge she met. Welcome to town."

He waved a flourished hand, and it was the first time I realized all four of the men had the same tattoo on the backs of their left hands.

Two stacked Ss with an eye in the middle. Though I'd noticed each varied a bit.

River's had a knife that cut through the middle.

"I'm glad to be here." I wasn't sure right then if I was being honest or not. If it was the ultimate lie or if the truth of it would be my demise.

I'd been running for years.

Hiding.

Putting one foot in front of the other because it was the only thing I knew how to do.

But coming here, I'd thought…I'd thought I'd try to lay down roots. It was hard to grow when you were simply moving.

Surviving.

Five years was a long time to be stuck in the same agonizing moment.

And I thought maybe…maybe I was ready.

In grief we must live.

I could feel the burn of the words that had been imprinted on my arm.

Molten black eyes flamed as River stared at me, and I wondered if he could feel them, too.

Raven took my hand again and swung it between us. She glanced over at me with a wistful expression on her face. "The only one who isn't here is Cash because he doesn't come around much, but this? This is my family. And I'm really excited for you to get to know them."

Chapter
FOURTEEN

Charleigh

"**O**H MY GOD, WHY IS THIS SO GOOD?" RAVEN GROANED AS SHE wiped a big glob of whipped cream from her cheek. Shocker since she'd just stuffed half a deep-fried Twinkie into her mouth.

A soft laugh climbed from my chest.

My chest that felt lighter than it had in a long, long time.

After she'd made introductions, she'd suggested we browse the festival since she was nearly sold out of flowers, anyway. I'd jumped on it since I'd needed to get away from the dark, dark eyes that had tracked my every move.

Spending this time with her had been…fun.

Incredibly fun, and I liked her so much that it was scary. The way it felt like I could slip right in with her, be at ease when I knew that I could never truly be that with anyone.

"I'm pretty sure you're confusing delicious with disgusting," I told her.

She feigned a gasp. "I'll have you know I have the best taste in the world. I mean, have you seen me?"

She spun in a little circle. The fifties-style pin-up dress she wore hugged all her curves. Raven was all sass and pure sweetness, and I'd never met anyone like her.

"Okay, the dress is cute, but the Twinkie…" I drew it out like I was calling her judgement into question.

She giggled and looped her elbow with mine, our gait slow as we meandered the displays. "Okay, fine, I might be developing a stomach-ache, but that first bite? Delish."

The sun had begun to set, and the soft breeze that rolled over the lake dimmed the temperature to perfection. Overhead, string lights had just blinked to life, and the crowd had slowed. It was as if everyone there had become partners to the peace.

I slowed even more as I noticed a display to my right, and I dragged my fingertips over a hand-knitted stuffed animal.

A blue puppy.

A wave of wistfulness rushed over me, and a smile pulled to my face. I glanced at my new friend. "Do you think Nolan would like this?"

Raven inhaled a soft breath as we stopped in front of the table. "Aww, he would love it. You know, since his dad is being a big grump and won't let him get an actual puppy, but since my brother is a big grump ninety-nine percent of the time, it's no surprise."

She rolled her pretty eyes, her lashes thick and dark, though her face was full of affection. "I mean, I really hope he wasn't rude to you yesterday at the doctor's office when he took Nolan in. The guy gets so spun up when he's worried."

I bit down on my bottom lip, wondering if I should confess that it wasn't the first time we'd met. It shouldn't be a big deal, but I'd already made it weird that I hadn't said anything.

"He was fine."

Okay, *fine* wasn't anything close to what River Tayte was. He was a shock of chaos to my sanity.

A compulsion.

Raven chuckled with a lift of her brow, clearly agreeing with my internal thoughts. "Fine? I don't think that's a description I've ever heard given to him, unless you're talking about how *hot* he is? Because he might be my brother, but it's not like I could miss the way women stumble all over themselves the second he comes into a room. Tell me he's not the type that gets your cute butt all hot and bothered."

She knocked her shoulder into mine, slanting me a big grin, prodding me for details.

"No," I murmured what I hoped she didn't know was a blatant lie. "Of course not."

She tightened her hold on my elbow as she giggled. "Good call, bestie. He's not exactly the type to stick around for morning cuddles, if you know what I mean. And I wouldn't want to have to kick his ass for breaking your heart."

It was all a ramble and a tease while my chest suddenly felt heavy.

I wanted to ask her so many things. Where Nolan's mother was. If he saw her. If they'd been together or had even been married.

No doubt, it was a bad sign that jealousy clutched my spirit at just the thought of it, and I knew I should try to put some distance between these two guys who'd taken possession of nearly every thought.

Still, I picked up the stuffed puppy and paid the vendor.

Raven's voice was gentle as we walked away from the booth, though her tone had gone almost questioning. "That is really nice of you."

"Maybe this will remind him he doesn't need to be scared of going to the doctor in the future." I shrugged like it didn't matter. Like that had even been close to what I'd been thinking when I'd seen it.

"Except now he's going to think he needs a gift every time he falls and scrapes his knee, but I pretty much do, too, so he can't be blamed. He is basically his auntie."

She was all soft teases before she tugged my arm. "Come on, let's get back. I'm starving."

She drew it out, groaning toward the twilit sky.

I sent her a look. I wasn't sure how that was possible since she'd sampled about every treat we'd walked by.

She laughed. "What? This girl likes her food."

By the time we made it back to the big tent where we'd left her family, they were standing, and Nolan came bounding our way. "It's time for dinner, Auntie and Miss Charleigh! I just got to go on the jumping castle and now my belly is all the way empty, and my dad said I can get a special treat if I eat all my food. Hey, what's that you got?"

He hadn't paused for a breath before his big blue eyes went wide when he saw the stuffed animal.

Kneeling in front of him, I held it out between us. "I thought you might like it."

"Is it for me?" he squealed, his little shoulders popping up to his ears as he threaded his tiny fingers together and brought them to his chin.

"It is."

"Really? Thank you, Miss Charleigh!"

He didn't take the puppy. Instead, he threw his little arms around my neck.

A surprised gasp rushed out of my lungs. Grief clutched then unfurled inside me, though it whispered differently as I curled my arms around him. His warmth was a balm that spread through my being.

Hugging him tight, I inhaled the sweet bubblegum scent of his hair.

"You are really the nicest because I really wanted a puppy, but my dad said I gotta wait for a real one, so it's really good I got this one," he gushed.

"I'm glad you like it."

Jumping back, Nolan grabbed the stuffed animal from my hand and twirled it around. "Like it? I love it, and his name is gonna be Lucky!"

He turned without saying anything else, and he ran back toward the group who'd gathered at the back of the tent with the stuffed animal lifted over his head. "Dad, Dad! Look it! Miss Charleigh got me a puppy!"

That unfathomable gaze found me, spearing me to the spot, making my heart race.

Erratic and thready.

I didn't know how long I stood there, just staring at him as he stared at me, before Raven leaned in and muttered in my ear, "Not hot and bothered, my ass."

Twenty minutes later, we were all sitting at a picnic table on the lawn closer to the lake. The night grew thicker with each minute that passed.

I'd tried to leave, but Nolan had begged me to stay to eat with them, and there was no chance that I could say no.

So, there I was with a plate of street tacos in front of me, tucked between Nolan and Raven.

The man who trembled the air with every move he made sat directly across from me, spinning my world into disorder.

"Here we go," Kane called as he sauntered up, setting plastic cups brimming with margaritas in front of me and Raven.

"Ugh, you are a godsend, Kane. What would we do without you?" Raven teased.

"Cry." He touched his chest.

"For joy," Otto called, grinning from where he was eating an oversized piece of pizza at the other end of the table.

They'd all been giving each other crap nonstop since I sat down, though I could tell it was done in good fun, the group obviously close.

"Yeah, I'm going to remember that the next time you drag your ass through the door of my bar."

"Come now, man, I'm your best customer."

Kane shook his head, chuckling under his breath as he sat down next to River. "And look how he says it with pride."

"Say everything with pride considering I'm an overachiever at all things." Otto wagged his brows, gaze jumping around all of us as if he were begging for confirmation.

I could almost feel Raven catch fire beside me, her attention downturned as she inhaled a shaky breath.

"Overachiever? You didn't even get a touchdown yesterday, Uncle." Nolan mumbled it around a big bite of corndog. "Me and my Daddy-O left you in the dust."

Otto cracked up, and River chuckled from across us, the sound smooth and rippling on the warm, night air.

I couldn't help but let my attention drift that way. To his viciously handsome face, even darker where the shadows of the night crawled overhead.

Drawn to the sound.

If I wasn't careful, I could be enchanted by it.

"That's right," River grumbled, affection in his gaze as he looked at his son.

"Well, those were special circumstances," Otto said, still grinning, his blue gaze slanting to Raven. "Just like when my baby sister over here beat me in poker last week. Girl gets me every time."

I wondered if I was the only one who noticed how she cringed when he called her that, though she was flashing him a bright smile. "You never learn your lesson. You always show up begging me to swindle you out of all your money."

"Can't help it if you're a sneaky little thing." His smile went soft, and I turned my attention to my plate, nibbling at a taco as I listened to the conversation go on around us. Laughter ringing and this comfort abounding.

I wanted to settle into it. Float on its warmth. All of which were ridiculously reckless.

But I allowed myself to do it for a little while as everyone ate and joked. Allowed myself to get lost in the lightness and the love that so clearly stretched between these people who looked so hard and rough.

Once everyone finished their food, the guys got up to help Kane with something at his booth, and Raven took Nolan to the restroom, and I found myself alone at the table.

It didn't bother me.

I couldn't remember a time when I'd felt so relaxed, and I closed my eyes and lifted my face to the heavens.

My spirit squeezed in a bid of gratitude.

For almost an entire evening, I hadn't felt alone. Hadn't ached.

"That was fuckin' sweet of you, buying that stuffed animal for my kid." The gruff voice broke me out of the drifting, and my eyes snapped open to find River standing on the opposite side of the table with his hands stuffed in his jeans pockets.

Moonlit.

His face cast in bare, silvery light.

"Well, I came into a little extra money recently."

My lips tweaked at the side, and my stomach nearly toppled over when a smirk lit on his.

"That so?"

"Mm-hmm," I hummed, not even sure what I was doing talking to him like this. He'd basically ignored me the entire evening, all except for the piercing stares he'd tossed my way.

"Don't want your money," he told me.

A frown furrowed my brow. "And what is it you want?"

I wasn't even sure what I was asking him or why it felt imperative to know.

To understand this confusion.

This…thing that was so unfamiliar to me that I couldn't process it.

His tongue swept his full bottom lip, focus firmly on me. "Told you…for you to do exactly what that tat said and live."

Nonsensical laughter rolled out of me. It was so quiet I wondered if he'd heard it. "I don't even know what that means anymore."

"Most of the time, I wonder if any of us do." His words were gruff.

Hollow.

Like he might be haunted, too.

"Until I see Nolan smile. Then I get it."

I could barely manage the nod. "He's amazing."

"Kid stole my heart right outta my chest."

I was sure the child had stolen a piece of mine, too, the way it fluttered when he was suddenly bounding up to my side. "Miss Charleigh, we're going to go dance now because dancin' is what sets you free."

A surprised giggle rippled out of me as I turned that way, and

Raven was hiding a laugh since I was pretty sure he'd taken the words directly from her mouth.

He grabbed my hand. "Come on!"

"Oh, I think I'd better call it a night and get home."

I'd far overstayed my welcome, and every molecule in my being warned that I was getting too close.

"No way! It's a dance party, Miss Charleigh. Don't you hear the music? And my auntie has to have her best friend if she's going to have a party."

"Yeah, I have to have my best friend if I'm going to have a party," Raven parroted, eyes wide. "Besides, I told you I was going to make sure you had a blast, and we're just getting started."

"Please?!" Nolan tugged at me again, his sweet little face pinched up in the plea.

Air puffed from my lungs, affected and light, and I swung my legs out from under the picnic table, whispering, "Okay, just for a little while."

"Yay!" He jumped, brown curls bouncing around his cherub face, and Raven was locking her elbow with mine again.

I glanced back once as we strolled over to the dance floor that was about a hundred yards away, at this man who screamed volatility and still was so dangerously sweet.

Lights swayed above the dance floor, and I let go of the tension as Raven turned and took my hand. She shimmied her hips as she dragged me onto the edge of the floor. "I told you that you were going to have the best time. I mean, what could be better? Margaritas and tacos with your bestie and the most handsome little man on the planet?"

"That's me!" Nolan shouted, right as he slid on his butt and spun himself around.

I laughed.

Laughed and laughed as Raven twirled me and Nolan spun on the floor around us.

The music alive and pounding through my senses.

Hypnotizing.

Mesmerizing.

One song played out and then another.

I knew right then that my heart was in danger of overflowing.

I swore to myself it didn't have a thing to do with the man I could feel watching us in the distance where he'd moved back to Kane's tent.

And for a little while, I fully let myself go.

Dancing and dancing.

The beat of the music rolled through me in decadent waves. Vibrated through my veins and thundered through my body.

My laughter was unending as Raven kept trying to get me to copy her goofy moves.

"Like this, Miss Charleigh!" Nolan was back on his feet, his hands waving over his head as he twirled.

Raven twirled, too, and so did I.

Only I stalled out halfway around when I felt a disorder billow through the air.

The hairs prickled at the back of my neck.

Awareness thick and sticky and crawling over me like a bad, bad dream.

I was facing the lake that had darkened, and the bare light of the moon glittered on the surface. There were still a few people out on the beach area, though they were little more than silhouettes, their faces obscured.

There was nothing in particular that I could make out, but I couldn't stop the cold dread from slicking down my spine.

Intuition kicking in.

I was such a fool. Such a fool. Getting complacent like this.

"Charleigh?" Raven's voice was filled with concern, and I jumped when she took my hand. I turned back that way, trying to smile, but knowing it was faltering.

Panic sped beneath the surface of my skin.

I tried to swallow around it as I forced myself to speak. "I need to go."

A frown marred her brow. "What do you mean? We just got out here."

"I'm sorry."

"Miss Charleigh?"

Pain splintered my chest as I looked down at Nolan who was peering up at me in confusion, and I couldn't do anything but run my fingers through his hair before I started to step around him.

Raven grabbed me by the wrist, worry taking over her expression.

I wrangled myself free, regret curdling the words as I whispered, "I'm sorry," before I turned and fled.

Chapter
FIFTEEN

RIVER

I couldn't look away as Raven and Nolan dragged Charleigh to the dance floor across the field.

Night had descended and covered the earth in a blanket of stars, and the lights strung up over the dance floor twinkled, as bright as the diamonds that played along the surface of the lake that were compliments of the silvered rays of the half-hung moon.

"You comin' or what?" Kane hollered from his tent, and I forced myself to move since I was standing there like an idiot, staring at a girl that I knew better than to touch. Too bad right then I was having a really fuckin' hard time remembering why.

I ambled back to the tent and plopped into the chair I'd inhabited earlier. Theo and Otto were already there, kicked back and sipping from the bottle of whiskey Kane had broken out.

His tent was still the rage, people lined up for a mile in their goal to imbibe, the laughter and volume of voices growing in time with the level of the music that played from the stage.

He poured me a finger into a plastic cup.

Super classy, but none of us gave a shit about any of that.

"Here you go, brother."

"Thanks."

I took a sip of the amber liquid, and I relished in the spice on my tongue and the fire that rolled down my throat. Immediately, my gaze was drawn back to where Raven and Nolan had hauled Charleigh out to the edge of the dance floor.

The three of them were laughing as they took turns spinning Nolan around by the hand, the kid fucking mesmerized by the woman, not that I could blame him.

"Damn, Raven's new friend is wicked hot, isn't she? Shy as fuck, but I'm pretty sure I could coax her out of that." Kane said it sly, nothing but an insinuation. Took all I had not to reach out and wrap my hand around his throat, and instead, a warning growl was coming out of mine.

"How about you don't chase the poor girl out of town since she barely got here?" I gritted, trying to play it cool when it felt like I was splintering apart. Had no fuckin' clue what it was about her that was making me crazy.

Felt like I was teetering on something that was going to leave me unglued.

"Poor girl?" Kane's brows rose for the sky. "Says the guy who's been staring at her like he's going to rip her to shreds with his teeth for the last three hours."

He tossed it out with a cock of his head, really fuckin' proud of himself with that smirk.

And I was finally catching on to the fact that he was setting me up, the fucker.

Theo laughed, nudging the toe of his boot against my leg. "Yeah. Anyone ever seen River here so spun up about pussy? I mean, she is fucking gorgeous, but it's not like he's not accustomed to the *finer* things in life. And there he sits, dude about to crawl out of his skin, foaming at the mouth."

"Rabid," Otto agreed.

"Bullshit," I rumbled.

Otto cracked up. "Really, brother? Thought you were going to go right over the table every time she shifted in her seat. Two more seconds, and you were going to blow."

"None of you know what the hell you're talking about."

Kane took a sip of his whiskey, grin playing all over his cocky face. "Well, since you aren't interested, then I guess I might as well be the one to add a little icing to her cake."

"Not one of you are touching her." The words were nothing but gravel. Scraping in possession.

Kane laughed like it was hysterical, and he wagged a finger at me. "Ahh, that's what I thought."

I shrugged like it didn't matter and I wasn't itching to fly out of my seat. "She's Raven's friend, so I'd appreciate it if you assholes didn't ruin that for my sister, yeah?"

My sister was finally spreading her wings. Meeting people. Having fun. And while I might have been protective as all hell when it came to her, it filled me with relief that she was stepping out.

I told myself the command that had grated from my tongue didn't have a thing to do with the woman herself or the way my guts had been in knots of need since the second I'd seen her standing next to Raven earlier this afternoon.

"You know, with the life he leads, I'd think he'd be a better liar." Otto hooked a thumb in my direction.

"Fuck you, man," I grumbled, and he laughed one of his jovial, easy laughs before he reached out and jostled my shoulder with his giant mitt. "Thought we just discussed you finding a way to let loose? A place to put all that aggression that's got you bound? It's a beautiful night. Get up and have yourself a little fun, brother. What do you think this whole thing is about?"

He waved a hand over his head to take in the festival.

What this whole thing was about was not getting suckered into taking home a puppy, that was what.

Which the thought of it sent my attention slanting back to the three of them dancing, not that I had been able to keep my focus away from that spot the entire time they'd been on the floor.

Nolan was on his feet and twirling in a circle with his hands thrown high, Raven doing the same. Charleigh went to mimic the move, though she stumbled when she was facing out toward the lake.

Just fucking freezing.

Swore I could feel the cold streak through the air. Mood dumping to dim while she stood there facing out toward the darkened beach of the lake where there were still a few people, though they'd become shadows and silhouettes.

She stumbled a fraction, and her ankle twisted to the side since she was wearing those high wedged heels, blown back like she'd just seen a ghost.

She wasn't so far away that I couldn't make out the terror locked on her face, though she was doing her best to pretend it wasn't there when she turned back to Raven and quickly rambled something I couldn't hear, though clearly it was some kind of excuse.

Raven frowned like she knew it, too.

Charleigh's fingers brushed through Nolan's hair before she started to push into the roiling crowd. Raven reached out to take her by the wrist like she was hoping to convince her not to leave, but Charleigh was backing away, shaking her head, smile so fake that I felt it crack.

Heading in the opposite direction of the lake and disappearing into the night.

I was on my feet in a split second, and I punted Otto a glance with a jut of my chin. "Get Raven and Nolan home safe, yeah? I've got something that came up."

"Ah, we know what's up, brother," Kane taunted, white teeth flashing. Dude might as well have been thirteen years old.

I only grunted at him.

"Don't sink your teeth in too deep," Theo called behind me, and I tossed him a finger from over my shoulder as I wound out of the tent and started across the field in the direction she'd gone.

Boots pounding the ground, this pull she had me under something I couldn't resist.

Worry clutched me by the throat.

There'd been something about her that had held me since the moment I'd met her. Something about her that made me want to look closer.

Something that compelled.

Something that I recognized.

She was in trouble.

Scared.

I'd seen it enough in my life that I could spot it clearly, though the first couple times I'd seen her, it'd wafted around her in silken, disorienting tendrils, this sorrow and tenacity blotting out the part that I'd had trouble putting my finger on.

But I felt it now.

Stark and distinct.

No chance I could sit idle and watch her traipse alone through the night. Not when I could scent her panic in the air.

That warm spice sparking like intoxicating fuel.

A wave of something I shouldn't feel rose up inside me.

A vat of protectiveness swilling high and completely overpowering.

I gritted my teeth as I pushed through a couple groups of people huddled around, vendors breaking down their canopies and packing their goods, and I hurried through the dirt parking lot that took up that side.

I scanned the area, ensuring there wasn't anyone creeping in the fringes, making sure no one was fool enough to go after this girl.

They were certain not to like the consequence if they did.

Since Raven had been going on about the new girl living above her shop for the last two months, I knew which way she was going, not that I wouldn't have been able to track her, anyway.

Strikes of chestnut hair glinted around her as she hurried under the cover of night.

Stars blinked from above, and the ground was bathed in the soft glow of the moon.

I could feel when whatever she was running from turned into me. When awareness shocked through the atmosphere, and her body rocked forward in a bow of confusion when she realized I was following her.

Got the sense she didn't know whether to slow or run faster.

"Charleigh," I called. When she only increased her pace, I called her name again. "Hey, Charleigh."

Ignoring me, she made it to the intersection, and her head swung both ways to make sure it was clear before she darted across the road.

I was near enough that I could hear the soft thwack of her shoes against the concrete echo against the brick buildings that rose up on each side.

My boots thudded above them, and I grew closer and closer with each purposed stride that I took, unable to stop myself from erasing the space between us.

No logic for what spell this woman had me under.

Fascinated.

Enthralled.

Most of all, I couldn't ignore the compulsion to ensure she was safe.

She hurried past Raven's shop, and she'd already rounded the building and was halfway up the stairs by the time I turned the corner. She gasped like she didn't already know I was there, like she was shocked at seeing me at the bottom of the stairs as she threw her attention over her shoulder.

The flecks of cinnamon in her eyes sparked beneath the light, and she kept climbing, though she'd turned to face me, taking the stairs backward as I climbed toward her.

My hand was on the railing, trying to keep myself steady rather than doing something insane like rushing her and dragging her into my arms.

"What do you think you're doing?" she rasped, words shards. As choppy as her breaths.

"Good fuckin' question," I rumbled, taking another step up. She kept backing away and I kept climbing, and she stumbled away when she hit the landing.

When I got to the top, she was frantically digging into the little purse strapped across her body to pull out her keys.

"I'm not going to fuckin' hurt you." I growled it as I took another step toward her, blood pumping with unfound rage, no clue who the hell I was supposed to be directing it at.

Needing a name.

A face.

A body to maim.

I enclosed another foot.

Tension ticked and flexed through my muscles.

She choked out a disbelieving sound, and her back made a soft *thunking* noise as she knocked into the door behind her. "Oh, I'm pretty sure you would."

I wanted to. I wanted to peel her apart and put her back together. Problem was, I'd always leaned more on the destroying side.

"What happened back there?" I demanded.

Surprise flashed through her expression before she shuttered it in feigned confusion. "What are you talking about?"

I eased forward, getting so close that I could hear the rushing of her pulse, the careening in her veins, the clanging of her heart.

She panted short, shallow breaths, and I inhaled every single one.

Cinnamon and spice.

Like the whiskey that still coated my tongue.

I angled in, words tremoring with fury. "I won't pretend I didn't see whatever the hell went down out there."

"And what was that?" She lifted her chin in that fiery defiance, with a challenge, like she was physically raising a metal shield in front of her spirit.

Refusing access.

A barricade.

My hands burned with the need to bust right through it. Fingers desperate to sink in.

I edged forward until there was only an inch separating us.

I towered over her, eclipsing her in my shadow. Shivers rolled through her body.

"I saw you run. You were scared." Could barely force the words out around the rage.

She seemed to swallow over the barbs that tremored her throat, and she shook her head and huffed. "I wasn't scared. I was ready to leave."

Didn't believe her for a minute.

"Is that so?"

"Yes."

"It seemed to me you were having a good time."

The laugh she released was riddled with disappointment, and she dipped her attention toward the ground. "And then I remembered who I am."

Felt like I got scalded when I reached out and took her by the chin to force her to look at me. "Yeah, and who's that?"

She rocked her head back on the wood, gazing up at me with that disorienting, enthralling gaze, the subject clearly shifting from whatever had sent her running to *this*.

To the tension that strained and the desire that flooded.

Lust so full in the air I was pretty sure both of us were suffocating on it.

This *thing* about her so intense there was no making sense of it.

"Someone who doesn't do this," she breathed.

I needed to shun it. End it. Step back and walk away.

Instead, I was dipping down and murmuring my lips along the soft edge of her jaw, whispering, "Maybe you should."

An earthquake rocked her, and I nearly fucking came at the force of it.

"You already warned me you aren't the type of guy I should be mixing with," she rasped.

"I'm definitely not. But I can't stop thinking about you. How's it you got under my skin?"

My mouth traveled the delicate column of her throat when I said it, there but not quite touching.

"How's it that I was the one supposed to be marking you, and you're the one who left the imprint? And now I can't stop thinking about marking myself all over you. Writing myself on every fuckin' inch of this sweet little body."

She inhaled a sharp, needy sound, her shoulders hitched to the door as her chest bowed out like she was begging for the connection.

"And I'm terrified that you make me want anything at all," she whispered.

She should be.

She should be terrified.

She should shove me off and tell me to stay the hell away from her.

While the only thing I wanted to do was wrap her up. Slay whatever fucking demon had chased her here.

"What is it you want?" I rumbled at her jaw.

Her nails sank into my shoulders. "I don't know…to feel good. To forget for a little while."

"I'd make you feel so good, sweetheart. So good you'd forget your name."

A whimper rolled out of her, and her scent was invading.

Cinnamon and spice.

I gripped her by the waist, and my palms rode up her sides, following the ripple of desire that rolled through her body.

"You want me to make you forget?" I grunted, kissing along her jaw.

"Yes."

My hand curved around the back of her neck and glided up to tangle in her hair.

Angling forward, I took that sweet, sweet mouth in a possessive kiss.

Energy crashed between us, and she whimpered as she sank her nails deeper into my shoulders.

My dick grew fat and hard as lust kicked up a path through my veins.

I needed more. I needed all of her.

I licked at the seam of her lips. She gasped as she opened, and I stroked my tongue into the hot well of her mouth.

I inhaled, and fuck, she was the sweetest thing. Soft against all my hard. I pressed myself closer, needing to disappear into the goodness of who she was.

Wanting to forget for a little while, too.

Who I was and why I could never really have her.

Except she suddenly froze beneath me.

Brittle, shattered stone.

Then she started fucking shaking.

Shaking and shaking.

Getting slammed by some kind of panic attack. Her terror was palpable as it zipped across her flesh.

I ripped myself back, and I pressed my hands to the door on either side of her head as I searched her face. She squeezed her eyes closed in an effort to keep me from seeing.

From seeing the tears and the grief.

"Charleigh."

That violence hit me anew, but I tried to keep it tapped, to keep from scaring her more, though I couldn't keep my voice from cutting like razors as I set my cheek against hers. My words were panted into the straining air. "Need you to tell me one thing…are you afraid of me or are you afraid of being touched?"

I edged back so I could see whatever was written in her expression.

And this sweet fuckin' girl blinked up at me through bleary eyes and whispered, "I'm afraid that I want you to touch me."

Fuck. I wanted to go on a rampage. Start a fucking war. Destroy the bastard who'd put that look on her face.

Because I knew.

I fuckin' knew.

I stepped back enough that I could take her by the left hand and raise her arm above her head. The willowy fabric of her shirt gave, and the sleeve slipped down and revealed the nearly healed tattoo that she'd kept concealed there the entire afternoon.

I brushed my lips along the line of words, like I might be able to carry a little of what they meant.

Then I stepped back and murmured, "Go inside and lock the door, Charleigh."

She stared at me for one long beat of indecision before she turned away from me, her body trembling as she finally found her keys in her purse, metal clanging as she fitted it into the lock.

She didn't look back when she slipped inside, and I didn't move until I heard the metal click back into place.

Chapter
SIXTEEN

Charleigh

TREMBLING, I PRESSED MY BACK TO THE INTERIOR SIDE OF MY door, my breaths rasping from my aching lungs as I tried to orient myself. To steady the fear that continued to pump through my bloodstream.

My fingertips found my lips that felt seared.

Branded by his kiss.

A kiss that had ripped through me on a torrent of flames. Flames I wanted to burn in before they licked deep enough to ignite the old fears.

Wounds opening and threatening to swallow me whole as the terror had slicked through my veins.

Poison that would always be there to consume.

What was I doing? How had I let myself go that way? Let him touch me? Especially after I'd gotten the sense that someone had been out in the shadows, watching me.

Frantic, I looked around my little apartment, unsure of what to do with myself.

It wasn't odd for me to have moments when I felt as if I were being watched.

Tracked.

Whenever I did, I'd pack my things and get out of town because there was no chance I was going to stick around to find out if my worries were valid.

My only constant had been moving. Staying one step ahead of the peril that would forever haunt me.

Paranoia pushed me to run from one city to another, even though I doubted there was any real reason to keep doing it.

No one knew I existed, but it didn't stop the slick of ice that would slip down my spine when I'd get the sense that someone was there. Didn't stop the dread. Didn't stop the anxiety that one day it would all catch up to me.

Right then, self-preservation urged me to run into my room, drag out my suitcase, toss my few meager belongings into it, and disappear into the night.

It was the first time in over five years that my spirit constricted at the thought of doing it.

Of leaving.

Hope oppressed by the idea of giving into the prompting.

The other part of me warned of how careless I was being.

Reckless.

Slipping into a false sense of security that I would never truly have.

But worse? My mind hinged on River who I could feel lingering outside my door.

That dark, violent energy battered against the wood and slipped through the cracks.

It crawled over me like vapor that had the power to pin me down.

This man who'd…followed me. Followed me when he'd noticed that I'd freaked out.

And there I was—terrified for entirely different reasons.

Terrified of what he made me feel. Terrified of what he made me want. Terrified that for one beat of a second, I was surrendering to him.

God, what was I supposed to do?

It was only made more complex because of his little boy who

had just slipped right into my heart—no resistance to be had from his beaming smile and adorable lisp.

From his sister who'd reached out and made me feel important. Made me feel as if I might want to connect for the first time in years.

But it was this menacing, volatile man who really made me want to *connect*.

Stretch out my fingers and dip them into something that would cause me more harm in the end.

I knew better.

And still, I couldn't move from where I was chained as I listened to the buzz he emitted from the other side of the door. I could feel the echo of his reticence before his heavy footfalls finally retreated down the steps, growing quieter with each one he took.

When the thudding finally evaporated into the night, the man taking his intensity with him, I exhaled a shattered breath and did my best to gather myself.

I needed to process what course to take.

Run or stay.

Run or stay.

Sorrow billowed at the thought of the first.

I was so tired. So tired of running. So tired of being alone. But it'd been a consequence I'd long accepted, a part of the sentence that I would carry out for the rest of my days.

When I'd stepped off the bus in Moonlit Ridge, I'd been set on *trying*. On trying to forge some semblance of a satisfactory life. To try to make this place my home.

In grief we must live.

But I was afraid I'd been a fool to hope for any of that. I already felt the complications rising around me, the truth that I'd barely allowed someone into my life, as faked and superficial as it was, and they were already butting against the boundaries.

Pushing up against the secrets I could never give anyone access to.

On shaky legs, I pushed from the door and trudged into the little kitchen, tossed my purse and keys to the counter, and dug into the cupboard for a glass. I filled it with water from the faucet and took a sip, hoping it would cool the fire that burned my insides.

If only I had someone here who could splash it in my face to bring me back down to reality.

My heart spasmed when my phone dinged from my purse, and the glass clinked on the counter as I set it aside. My fingers were still trembling as I dug into the bag and pulled out my phone.

Unbidden, a smile pulled to my face when I saw the text.

> **Raven:** We already miss you! Why did you leave us?

A picture was attached. Raven was kneeling and wrapped around Nolan from behind, both of them grinning with goofy faces toward the camera. The lights of the dance floor tossed glimmering streams around their heads, striking like halos, the child such a little angel it made my heart hurt.

> **Me:** Sorry. I didn't realize how late it was and I need to get up early.

It didn't take her long to respond.

> **Raven:** And what could be so important that you'd take off like a bat out of hell when we were having a blast? And don't forget it was the BLAST I'd promised you.

She ended it with two shooting fireball emojis.

There were flames, all right. Ones licking up my insides and threatening to leave me ash.

I struggled for the right lie. It wasn't as if I could tell her I was contemplating leaving or tell her I'd been spooked. That would only conjure all the questions I could never answer.

I typed out the first thing that came to mind. I'd already pressed send before I realized the excuse was out of left field.

> **Me:** I'm going on a hike in the morning, right at daybreak.

Raven: 🐾 With who?

I bit down on my bottom lip, slipping down the spiral of the lie.

Me: By myself.

Raven: By yourself?! Do you have any idea what kind of horrible idea that is? A bear might eat you.

Me: I like to hike alone. It gives me time to clear my head.

Okay, I hadn't been on a hike in years.

It took her a little longer to respond that time, and I could feel her contemplation.

Raven: Well…be careful, okay? Call me if you need me. I'm not much of a hiker, but I'd make the exception for you.

My chest squeezed. Of course, she would.

Me: I will.

Another lie.

My spirit sank with the plunging realization that this was the way it was. I could never really allow someone to know me. Could never truly let someone in.

It would always be a sham.

A façade.

Every word I gave counterfeit.

My phone buzzed again, and I expected it to be a response from Raven, but I froze halfway to my room when I saw it was from an unknown number.

Unknown: What are you running from?

A shiver rocked through my middle, and I glanced around the dimness of my apartment like I might find River pressed against the wall and hiding in the shadows.

Warily, I turned back to my phone, gnawing at my bottom lip where his had been.

I could still taste him.

Leather and ink and wicked things.

I shouldn't even respond, but I was typing out words that would only invite him in.

> **Me:** Who is this?

> **Unknown:** You know exactly who this is.

I could almost see the glower of his face through my phone as I read his words.

> **Me:** How did you get my number?

Did he come right out and ask Raven for it?

> **River:** I looked up the information you filled out in my shop.

I blinked, shocked that he was admitting it.

> **Me:** That is a blatant invasion of privacy.

> **River:** Don't care.

My chest clutched, and I didn't know if it was out of fear or exhilaration.

But that's what happened when you'd hardly talked to a soul in close to five years. So isolated that you're desperate for any connection.

> **River:** Not going to turn a blind eye when I know something's up with you.

My throat constricted, and I stood there in the middle of my living room staring down at my phone. Having no clue what to say.

I knew what I *should* say.

I should end this. Put him off. Block him.

Forget that stupid kiss had ever happened.

Still, my imprudent fingers were moving across the screen.

Me: You don't know me.

River: Nope, but that doesn't mean I can't see what's written all over you. As defined as the words I forever marked on your skin.

Me: Why do you care?

So foolish, letting that question free, but I'd sent it to him before I could reel it back. Not sure if it was in defense or a plea.

Begging for a breaking.

But there was something about this man that compelled me toward his gravity. A magnet so strong it could rend me apart. Tear me to shreds.

But it seemed it was the raw, tender pieces that were reaching out.

River: That's the whole problem, isn't it? Why I haven't been able to get you off my mind? Why I can't look away? Why I feel like I'm going to go mad if I don't get next to you?

Me: You should stay away from me.

River: I should stay away from you?

I swore, I heard his dark chuckle rumble through the air. A warning cut through the atmosphere.

River: Make no mistake, Little Runner, it's you who should be running from me. I'm the last person you should get close to. Know it as well as you do. Yet here I am, standing across the street watching your apartment.

Chills flash-fired across my skin, lifting far and wide, and my stomach tilted as my attention lifted from my phone to the French doors that overlooked the street.

Compelled, I slipped across the floor, keeping my footsteps light, like I was worried he could hear my approach. I peeled back the sheer drape. Streetlamps shined over Culberry, and I could see a handful of people meandering the sidewalk and a few cars traveling back and forth.

It didn't matter.

He might as well have been the only thing out there.

A silhouette on the opposite side of the street that had me stuck. The man a pillar in the night.

He leaned against a plate-glass window with a single hand stuffed into his jeans pocket.

Even in the distance, I could see his violently beautiful face was tipped upward, and his stormy eyes raged where they were pinned directly on me as if he knew exactly where I'd been standing.

My heart beat manic, a brutal pound in my chest, and I realized right then I'd taken this too far and had placed myself in too precarious of a situation.

Toeing a line I couldn't balance.

Gathering all my strength, I forced myself to type the words.

> Me: Tonight was unlike anything I've experienced in a long, long time. Your son and your sister are amazing.

I didn't tell him that there was a part of me that knew that under all the aggression he wore, I was sure he was, too. Instead, I told him what needed to be said.

> Me: But I don't have space for any more pain in my life. This needs to end here.

Then I pulled away from the drape, letting it drift closed behind me, and fumbled into my bedroom and flicked on the light.

It illuminated the small space. The queen bed sat against the wall and had a white metal headboard. I'd covered the mattress with a white and pink floral coverlet and pink sheets. Pink pillows in different sizes and shapes accented it, and small lamps glowed from the nightstands on either side.

I'd hung some floral paintings on the wall, making it comfortable and cozy, though there were no real traces of me.

Those were hidden in the top drawer of the white dresser that rested on the right wall.

The emotions I'd been trying to hold back hit me all at once, and tears began to fall as I crossed the room and slowly pulled open the drawer. I took out the small, lidded box, carried it to the bed, and crawled on top. Crisscrossing my legs, I set the box in front of me.

My spirit thrashed when I opened the lid.

I had so few things other than the memories I kept shored in my mind. But these two pictures? They were the only tangible things remaining.

Treasures that I protected at all costs.

I pulled out the stack. My mouth tweaked in love and sorrow as I looked at the picture of me with my parents. They both were standing on either side of me at my high-school graduation. They'd been so proud. So excited. So unaware.

If only I'd been brave enough to tell them then, but I'd thought what I'd been doing was protecting them.

I set that one down so I could look at the next.

A grief so severe slammed me that my entire being swayed to the side. Dizziness washed me through as my heart gripped and bled with looking at the image.

My tiny baby boy was smiling back at me.

Only two teeth on his bottom gums.

The whitest blond hair was sticking up all over his head.

Fisted in his hand was a tiny plush stuffed animal that he held in the air. It had been his favorite toy, one he hadn't been able to sleep without.

A blue puppy.

And I knew what I'd been doing tonight. I'd been trying to fill a hole that couldn't be filled. Trying to cover a void that would forever ache.

I could never truly have this.

Love and home and a family.

Because I'd already lost that a long time ago.

Tears streamed as I stared at his precious face before I finally gathered myself and stood, quickly coming to the only logical decision I could make.

I couldn't stay here.

I'd allowed myself to get too comfortable. To want things I couldn't have.

Another rush of sorrow hammered me at the thought of leaving here, but there was no other choice.

Ignoring all qualms, I tucked the pictures back into the box, then knelt and pulled the suitcase out from under the bed.

I filled it with my sparse belongings. Clothes and toiletries and three pairs of shoes. I carefully tucked the box in the middle so it would be safe.

I did it systematically.

Robotically.

Rhythmically.

There was almost a comfort in it since it was an action I knew so well.

Then I curled up on the bed on top of the covers and slept restlessly, still wearing my clothes and shoes, so when the dawn broke on the horizon and the dark of my room turned to a murky gray, I was ready to leave.

I'd waited until I was sure River was long gone and any threats from last night had melted away.

I waited until the last minute that I could.

Then I stood, inhaled a steeling breath, and wheeled my suitcase to the front door. I forced myself to walk out of it and lock it behind me, then I knelt to leave the key under the mat.

I'd text the owner tomorrow to let her know I'd vacated the property.

Awkwardly lifting the heavy suitcase, I let it bang against the side of my leg as I hurried down the exterior steps with the cool of the morning brushing across my heated flesh.

Only I stumbled to a stop when I started to round the building.

Gasping.

Because River Tayte stepped out in front of me, blocking my path.

Chapter

SEVENTEEN

RIVER

I T WAS EXACTLY AS I THOUGHT.

The little runner was getting ready to bolt.

I should have minded my own fucking business. Stayed away when she'd told me things needed to end right where we'd left them last night.

I'd tried.

I fuckin' tried.

But she'd left me a twisted knot, disquiet ripping through me, unable to sleep a wink because my gut told me things weren't right.

She was in trouble, and there was no way I could just ignore it.

Not after the things she said.

And sure as hell not after that kiss.

So there I stood like a twisted fuck blocking her path.

Cinnamon-kissed eyes went wide in surprise as she stumbled to a stop, body bowing back at my proximity.

"What are you doing here?" The words wheezed from her mouth.

I tucked my hands in my pockets because I didn't trust myself not to reach out and touch her.

Last thing I wanted was to freak her out. Make her feel afraid when I knew whatever was going down in her life had her terrified.

"Came to check on you."

Emotion crested her features, like she was torn between being angry and relieved. Torn between ignoring whatever boiled between us and reaching out and dipping her fingers into it.

I watched her try to put the walls back in place.

"Why would you do that?" she asked as if she hadn't pared herself open for me last night.

I got it. The need to try to barricade who we really were. Too bad I wanted to bash through every barrier she tried to put between us.

"Because you were upset last night. Because I knew you were afraid. And once I finally pried myself away from where I was standing across the street and went home, Raven told me she was worried about you since you'd told her you were going hiking first thing this morning. By yourself."

Such bullshit.

I knew what kind of *hike* she was planning on taking.

A permanent one.

"Think we both know that excuse doesn't quite add up," I pushed.

Charleigh shifted her weight from foot to foot, and she looked around like she was hunting for the best lie to tell. My stomach kicked when she finally returned her gaze to me.

"I don't see how that's any of your business."

"Yeah, Charleigh, I think it is. You solidified it when you begged me to make you forget last night."

I watched her flinch and twitch, and I was pretty sure she was contemplating pushing right around me.

I should let her go. It was insane doing what I was doing. Shoving into her space like I had the right to be there.

When she didn't say anything, I pointed to her suitcase. "It's clear to me you aren't intending on a hike. Where are you headed, Little Runner?"

Unease had her gusting out a breath, and she ran a flustered hand over her face. Sorrow filled the movement. "I'm just…leaving."

"Why?" I pushed in closer.

I got smacked in the face with her scent.

The warm, sultry spice. I was never going to get it off my tongue.

"Because it's time for me to go." It was a whisper of helplessness.

She went to angle around me, and I sidestepped her, a protective rage blocking her escape. She startled, and her attention snapped up to my face.

"Please get out of my way," she gritted.

My mouth dipped down close to her ear. "Tell me you're not running scared, and I'll be happy to."

The happy part was a fuckin' lie, but I'd do it.

The flash of turmoil that moved through her expression told me everything that I needed to know, even if she was prepared to let a thousand untruths slip from between her lips.

When she remained silent, I pushed in closer. Pressed in deeper. "Don't be afraid, Charleigh. Don't give in to whatever you're thinking. Don't *run*. Can feel that you're supposed to stay."

I didn't know why, and I didn't know how.

But I did.

She heaved a disbelieving sound, and those enchanting eyes flicked up to meet with mine. "How could you possibly know that?"

"Not sure. Only thing I do know is I can't stomach the thought of watching you leave right now. Don't know what it is or why, but there's something about you."

My insides were knitted with the need to wrap her up and promise her I'd never let anyone get near her.

That whatever she was running from wasn't too big for me.

I'd pull the stars from the sky if it meant it'd erase the fear that had overcome her last night.

Emotion swam through her eyes, lashes fluttering as she blinked. "I told you last night this needed to end."

"Why?"

I had a thousand reasons myself, but I couldn't listen to one of them right then.

"I…you don't know anything about me." There she went, throwing up more barriers that couldn't quite stick.

"Then how about you let me? Show me who you are."

She searched my face. "You warned me last night I should stay away from you."

My stomach fisted. "Might not be able to have you the way I want…the way I've been aching to do…but everything about you tells me I'm supposed to be here, right now, in front of you."

The lure she emitted thrummed, stretching tight between us, keening like the roll of a tightly wound drum.

Yielding to it, I edged forward, unable to stay away.

I got near enough to her that I could reach out and run my fingers along her trembling jaw. The words fell low as I murmured, "And if you need someone? If you get scared or want to give into whatever the fuck happened last night? If you want to run like I know you were planning to do? Then you come to me. You understand? You don't have to be afraid."

A shiver streaked through her body, rocking her feet and nearly pitching her into me. Took my all not to loop my arm around her waist and hold her up. Bury my face in her neck.

Take a little more of what I knew better than to be taking.

This woman was dangerous. I couldn't let her slip through the cracks and the fractures lined inside me. But I wasn't sure how to stop it when the only thing I wanted to do was slip through hers.

Invade.

Possess.

Her veil slipped, and her expression turned wholly vulnerable. "And what if being afraid is the only thing I know?"

"Then you give that fear to someone who can hold it."

"Is that what you want? To hold it for me?" It was half a plea. Half a challenge.

I didn't get the chance to respond before a shrill squeal pierced the air.

"Charleigh! What are you doing? I thought you'd already be out on the trails like the masochist you are, contending with the bears with your bare hands!"

My sister's voice rang through the morning air, a full tease, and both of us jerked to look that way. Raven was striding up the sidewalk with Nolan trotting along beside her, their hands twined and swinging between them.

Looking of light and life.

Hope for the hopeless.

Charleigh tried to straighten herself out. Hide the evidence of the trauma I could see stamped all over her.

Concealed but in plain sight.

I shoved my hands back into my pockets to keep myself from making some brazen move like slipping an arm around her waist, staking a claim, and I let a scowl take to my face so Raven wouldn't be getting any ideas in her pretty little head with the way she was looking between the two of us right then.

"Hi, hi, Miss Charleigh!!!" Nolan shouted as they approached. "What are you even doin' here? I woke up and my auntie said my Daddy-O went to the bakery to pick up some goodies, but I told her I wanted to go with him, so we had to leave really, really fast."

It was just then I was noticing my son was wearing his pajamas and slippers, and he was waving that knitted puppy over his head.

It still fucked my head all up that she'd been so thoughtful.

Raven lifted a casual shoulder as she glanced at me. "I tried to text you to let you know we were going to meet you here rather than you picking up breakfast since my favorite little man woke up, but I didn't get a response."

At that, my sister tipped her head like she was making an accusation. The mess of black hair that she had tied up high on her head flopped to the side. She had mascara smeared under her eyes, and I realized she had on slippers, too.

Fuckin' hell. My sister was a damned disaster.

"But I see you might have gotten distracted," she prodded.

Raven didn't need to know Charleigh was the only reason I'd even come down here. Didn't need to know I'd toiled the whole damned night. Set on edge by her fear and her kiss and her words. I hadn't been able to sit still for a second longer, so I'd tossed out the excuse that I was going to run to the café to grab breakfast.

"Oh, yeah, I was heading out and stumbled into him, so he stopped to say hi." Charleigh's words were flustered.

Raven's gaze narrowed, zeroing in on what Charleigh was holding onto. "Why do you have a suitcase?"

"Oh…I…this?" Charleigh tripped all over herself, one worried glance cast at me before she turned back to my sister. "I'd decided not to go on a hike since my feet were hurting from all the fun we had dancing last night, and instead, I cleaned out my closet and took some stuff to donation."

She jostled the suitcase like it was empty.

"At six in the morning?" Raven's brow arched.

"Yeah?" Charleigh issued it like a question.

Raven shook her head. "You really are a masochist."

"Well, you're up, aren't you?" Charleigh punted back at her.

Raven giggled. "Fair. Fair. But there aren't bears around here. I was worried about you taking off into the mountains by yourself, so I have to admit I'm relieved to see you standing here."

Yeah, I was relieved, too.

Relieved I'd been here.

Relieved that I'd made it in time.

She and Nolan made it the rest of the way up, and the kid was beaming his precious smile at the woman, bouncing on his toes. "Well, I think it's really good you woke up so early because that means you gotta have breakfast with us. My belly's been growlin' for twenty hours. Is your stomach growlin'? And look it, I got my favorite puppy."

He waved the dog over his head again.

Charleigh looked down at him, and there was just something about the way she did it that flayed right through the center of my chest.

Something that both soothed the sting and made me altogether petrified.

And I thought I might fully come apart when she reached out and brushed her fingertips down his cheek and whispered, "I'm glad you like it."

His megawatt grin bloomed. "I like it the most!"

"We'd better get to the café then," Raven said.

She covertly glanced between me and Charleigh again, and I was pretty sure my baby sister didn't buy our lie for a second.

Then she grinned directly at Charleigh. "Now get your cute butt over here with us."

Chapter
EIGHTEEN

Charleigh

I STRUGGLED TO FIND MY BREATH. THIS LITTLE BOY WAS NOTHING but a landslide. His sweetness so overpowering it nearly knocked me from my feet.

I attempted to suck the emotion down and act normal, but I wasn't sure what that was supposed to look like when five minutes ago I'd been set on boarding a bus and never looking back, and now I was supposed to be having breakfast with the very people I was worried I was getting too close to.

A pendulum shift that made the ground tremble beneath my feet.

"Okay, just let me take this suitcase back upstairs really quick." I needed a minute to wrap my head around what was happening.

To come to terms with what River had asked of me.

To stay.

Could I? And if I did it, was it only because of them?

River grunted and wrangled the suitcase out of my hold. "I'll do it."

"I can—"

"Said I've got it. You all go on and get us a table, yeah? I'll take a black coffee." With that, he looked at his sister.

"Bossy," Raven teased.

"That's because he's the dad and the boss, Auntie," Nolan told her.

"At least he likes to think so." Raven's words were a razzing barb, shouted at her brother's back.

Rumbling a non-response, River ambled up the steps like the suitcase didn't weigh anything, and I was cringing when he leaned down and snagged the key from beneath the mat.

So, he hadn't missed that.

But I didn't have time to contemplate it because a little hand was taking mine and giving it a tug. Warmth spread through my being. "Come on, Miss Charleigh. We gotta go get a table."

Raven sent me a questioning smile over his head, and I was pretty sure she hadn't bought the whole donation bit. Caution and curiosity blazed from her, and I tried to play it off like I didn't notice it as we passed by Moonflower to Cup Café next door.

She opened the door and ushered us in.

The café had just opened, and there were only a couple customers inside. It was decorated similar to Moonflower. Rustic, whitewashed woods, and each small round table had a spray of fresh flowers in the middle.

The counter was straight ahead, and the wall behind it was a black chalkboard that showcased the menu, letters swirled and written in colored chalk. Tables ran down the side and toward the back, plus there were a few up front next to the window.

Nolan went bounding up to the display case, chattering about all the different flavors of doughnuts, while I tried to look busy staring at the menu.

Raven sidled up to me, her voice held low. "Do you want to tell me what that was about last night?"

I wasn't surprised she was pushing it.

"I already told you what happened." I injected as much innocence as I could muster.

"Um, you gave me some story about going hiking, which as your new BFF, it's my duty to call bullshit. You took off like you were the silly blonde in a slasher flick, and don't think I don't know that my brother went after you."

There was a hint of lightness to it, but more prominent was the worry in her eyes as she appraised me from the side.

My nerves were fried, ripped from one reality to another.

Leaving then staying.

The fear.

That kiss.

With all of it, I wasn't sure I could keep the mask on right then.

So, I gave her the little bit of honesty I could. "I'm trying to start over. Start a new life. Build a new foundation. But there are a lot of times when it feels like my past won't allow me to do that."

Understanding passed through her features, and she gave a slight nod. "You don't have to hide that from me, Charleigh. Believe me, I get it."

Her expression dimmed, and I wondered if there was a reason I'd been drawn to her in the first place because I recognized something in her gaze that would always be in mine.

"I'm not used to trusting in anyone. I've been on my own for a lot of years."

I couldn't believe I was admitting this, standing there in a café whispering my secrets like offering them might not come with a risk.

Raven took my hand and squeezed it, and she leaned in close, her voice as quiet as mine. "Maybe you don't have to be that anymore. Alone. You know I felt it the first day you walked by my store. Your spirit aching to find what it's been missing."

Emotion crested, and I struggled to breathe around it.

The softest smile pulled at the side of her mouth. "And maybe what it's been missing is us."

Air whispered from my nose, and I squeezed her hand tighter. I wanted to hold on. To believe what she was saying.

Before I could say anything, she leaned in closer, and the gentleness in her voice shifted to pure suggestion. "Besides, it looks to me like my brother wants to claim you. That is if he didn't already."

Speculation raised her brow.

I released a shattered scoff, and my mind spun through the bare moment when his mouth had been against mine.

The heat that had nearly razed me to the ground.

The terror that had come barreling in on its heels.

"That's not going to happen."

The door swept open behind us, and that energy came blistering back in, so strong it nearly swept me from my feet.

I attempted to guard myself against it, though there was no stopping the ragged exhalation, the way goosebumps lifted on my skin as I felt his approach.

Raven looked behind me before she was grinning back my way. "I'm not sure I would bet on that."

Chapter
NINETEEN

Charleigh

"That was delicious," Raven said as she pushed out the door into the wash of the sun that was steadily climbing the eastern sky, the pinks and blues and purples giving way to the fullness of blue.

"It hit the right spot, didn't it, Auntie?" Nolan agreed in his adorable lisp, the child holding my hand as he led me out as if we'd always shared this connection.

Raven glanced back with that big smile on her face. "The best spot."

Nolan giggled and glanced up at me. "Did it hit all the right spots for you, Miss Charleigh?"

Emotion trembled, this piece inside me that pulled me one direction and pushed me another. The entire breakfast I'd had a hard time rectifying the shift. The decision I'd made last night to run when I'd been gripped by grief and sorrow and fear.

Fear of so many things.

Of what might be lurking for me in the shadows and what had seemed to be waiting for me right here.

Friendship and a semblance of belonging.

I had no idea what to make of it or how to embrace it. But as

Nolan held my hand, trotting along at my side as we all stepped out onto the sidewalk, I didn't want to let go.

"How about you, Daddy-O?" Nolan asked from over his shoulder toward where River followed us.

River who'd seemed too large to be contained by the small café.

"Pretty danged good way to start the day." River's voice was a coarse scruff.

The whole time, he'd sat a bit away from the table, slung back in the chair with his massive legs stretched out in front of him.

So cruelly casual that I'd barely been able to eat or drink, my mind unable to stop whirring with the memories of the way it'd felt to have his lips against mine. Big, big hands touching me. The way I wondered if…

I'd put a lid on the dangerous thoughts that had begun to boil, hoping it might be enough to extinguish them. Though with the way I trembled when he edged closer behind us, I feared the only thing trying to suppress them did was stoke the need.

"I'd better get back upstairs. I have a lot to do today," I said.

You know, like stew and fret over my decisions the entire day.

"I'm so happy we ran into you. I love these kind of BFF surprises. Best way to start the day." Raven's voice might have been light and rimmed in playfulness, but she hugged me hard.

Hard enough that I was pretty sure she was trying to send a message.

Gratitude spun with the apprehension. "I loved it," I told her, knowing at least that was the truth.

"I loved it as much as I love my puppy since you got it for me and that makes it even more extra special," Nolan rambled, so sweet, still holding onto my hand and beaming my direction.

I shifted so I could run my fingertips over his plump cheek that was smattered with freckles, the curls of his dark brown hair waving in the gentle breeze.

My heart fluttered. "This morning was definitely extra special."

He grinned his crooked, dimpled grin. "That's because we're all special together."

My fluttering heart clutched, and I leaned down so I could wrap my arms around him. I hugged him for the longest time before I forced myself to stand.

I barely glanced at River as I mumbled toward the ground, "It was nice to run into you, too."

He didn't respond. Instead, he looked at Raven. "Go on and take Nolan home, yeah? I need to make sure I put Charleigh's suitcase in the right place."

I went red. Talk about blatant bullshit excuses. Couldn't he have come up with something better than that if he wanted to talk with me? Because Raven's smile shifted to suspicion. Pinging between concern and salacious glee.

She took Nolan's hand. "Of course, no worries here. We'll just head on home while you check out her *suitcase*."

She clearly was implying my *suitcase* was my vagina.

River's dark eyes ripped over me like he might be imagining it was.

While I stood there mortified and stammering, "Oh no, that's not necessary. I'm sure it's fine wherever you put it."

"River should definitely make sure. Just in case."

"Yeah, definitely should," he grunted.

"Bye." Raven lifted her free hand and wiggled her fingers, and Nolan was hollering, "Bye, Miss Charleigh! Have the very best day you've ever had," as she led him down the street.

River just stood there, his energy severe.

An earthquake that rolled beneath my feet.

When Raven and Nolan disappeared around the corner, I turned on my heel and moved around the side of the building and started up the exterior stairs.

I knew he'd follow, and with each step I took, he took one that matched.

A shroud that covered from behind.

With shallow, uncertain breaths, I stopped at the door, facing it.

River reached around me and slid the key into the lock. His big body burned into mine, so close that I could feel the thunder of his heart beat into my back.

"Go on in." The words bristled across the sensitive skin of my neck, and I reached out with a shaky hand, turned the knob, and stepped into my apartment.

River came in behind me, and I kept my attention forward for a few seconds, trying to gather myself—to find what to say and how to handle this man—before I slowly turned around.

But there was nothing I could do to prepare myself for the way he looked standing within my doorway.

A vicious fortress that writhed in the threshold as if he were a sentry who'd been fated to protect it.

Muscles rippled and bunched beneath the ruthless designs that thrashed over the top of them.

Cloud-ridden eyes dragged over me. I shivered beneath the perusal, and he took a step forward and let the door drift closed behind him.

"Suitcase is in your room. How about you plan on leaving it there, yeah?"

I glanced that way to find it sitting at the base of the bed.

"Thank you," I muttered, fiddling with my fingers when I turned back to him. "But you coming up here wasn't necessary."

He took a step closer. The ground tremored. A shockwave. "I think it was very necessary, Little Runner."

"Why's that?" I managed, lifting my chin and trying to play it casual.

"Because I don't think we quite settled things."

"And what things are we supposed to be settling?" I was letting myself get played right into his massive hands, but I couldn't stop myself from wanting to find out exactly what he was thinking.

What he was imagining.

If I'd possibly left him as unsettled as he'd left me.

"That you can trust me."

My head shook, and I glanced to the French doors to buy myself a second before I swung my attention back to him. "How could I trust you when you told me you're exactly the type of person I shouldn't?"

And it wasn't only the warnings he'd given.

It was everything about the man that warned he was dangerous. Hell, I could feel the threads that held me together fraying with his presence.

The man clearly held the power to pull me apart.

He moved, coming to within a foot of me. Electricity sparked in the bare space that separated us, that magnetism he possessed reeling me forward as if I were on a hook.

A flounder flapping around on the sand.

Desperate for a breath but the only oxygen I could find was him.

"Might not be the kind of guy to fall for and I sure as hell am not one to love, but I am absolutely the kind of guy to come to if you're in trouble. And I know it, Little Runner, that you're in trouble."

He dragged the fingertip of his index finger down my cheek.

A shudder rolled through me.

Before I could find the words to respond, he angled down to make sure I was in his line of sight. "And I felt the way you wanted to let go last night. The way you were aching to be touched. The way you needed to be shown that you deserve it so you can move on with your life and find the lucky bastard who's the match to this sweet, beautiful heart. I see what's inside you. I see what you need. And I know what you've been missin.'"

Raven's words pummeled me. *"And maybe what you've been missing is us."*

But I couldn't have them. Couldn't keep them. At least that much was clear.

River set his palm over the organ that was battering at my ribs, flailing with the very need he'd been referring to, his fingers splayed wide as if he could cover the entirety of it.

"You said I don't know you, Charleigh, but I'm asking you to give me that chance. Let me get to know you, then you can decide if I'm worthy to be the one you come to."

"I'm terrified of trusting anyone that way." Without my permission, the truth whispered from my tongue.

River removed his hand from my heart and cupped it around my left cheek. The soothing of his thumb stroking across the flesh was at odds with the words that dropped from his mouth. "I want to destroy the bastard who hurt you."

My spirit quaked. A convulsion of the instinct to run and the impulse to sink into what he said. The way he knew without me confessing the details. I wanted to let him hold it when I'd never been brave enough to allow anyone else to.

Except for that one time. That one time I'd gone to my parents and given them the truth.

Sorrow rushed through my being, stunned again by the horror of what it'd caused.

I should warn him away, but River had started brushing that thumb over the ridges of my lips, tracing them as he watched me. His eyes had turned to pitch.

Black flames that lapped.

"I want to erase every scar he left. Kiss each of them away. Help you heal them so you know you have the strength to go on. So you know you don't have to hide anymore. Because hiding who you are is a fuckin' tragedy, Charleigh. Tragic when I can feel the goodness trying to shine out of you."

"River…" My eyes dropped closed. I wasn't sure I could keep looking at him when he made me feel like this.

I was struck with a wave of possibility.

With that hope I'd felt the first time I'd stepped off the bus and into Moonlit Ridge.

He kept brushing his thumb over my lips. Back and forth. Back and forth.

Mesmerizing.

Hypnotizing.

"Give us twenty questions, Charleigh. Twenty questions of getting to know each other. As simple or as deep as you want them to go. Then you can decide if you trust me. If when you're in need, you feel safe enough to come to me."

If I were being logical, if I had my bearings, it would have been clear that I had to tell him no. I could never agree to something so ridiculous or reckless.

But I found myself nodding and whispering, "Okay."

His expression flashed with something dark and resolved, though his touch remained tender.

Careful, even.

"Good." His tongue stroked out to wet his plush bottom lip, and his eyes darted all over my face, as if he were searching me for answers to something he hadn't yet asked.

"I'm going to kiss you now," he murmured, words raw. "That is as long as it's good with you?"

It was a question.

A proposition.

One I knew would ultimately wreck me.

I could already feel my heart swinging wildly in the man's direction. Wanting to make the leap when I knew he'd never truly be there to catch me.

But maybe I did need this.

Maybe I did need a buoy.

A life raft.

Someone to support me for a little while until I made it to shore and could stand on my own two feet.

It was time.

It was time.

I swallowed around the reservations and the skitter of fear that streaked through my being. I didn't want to bear it anymore.

The fear.

The terror.

The nightmares.

"Does that count as one of your twenty questions?" It came out breathy and with the tweak of a smile at the corner of my mouth.

He touched the spot where my lips fluttered, attention dipping there before the force of it returned to my eyes. "Considering it's one of the most important ones, then yeah, gorgeous, it does."

My nod was erratic. "It's good with me."

"Yeah?"

"Yeah."

His hand slipped from my cheek, and he glided it up until his fingers were notching into my hair. His other hand came to my hip, and his fingers barely curled around my waist.

Heat sheared through my middle, while a ripple of anxiety spread within it.

I struggled to breathe around it.

River curled his hand around the back of my neck, and his forehead dropped to mine.

"Promise you, these hands will never hurt you, Charleigh. They'll only ever bring you pleasure." His words came out in short, heated rasps, panted a hairsbreadth from my lips. "Protect you. Do you understand?"

"I think so."

I wanted to.

I wanted to believe it.

Did that make me a fool?

More so, did this?

The way his big body towered over mine as he kept me close. The way his fingers felt as they slipped up my neck and to the base of my skull, barely kneading and sending little bolts of that pleasure he'd promised ricocheting through my body.

But it was his lips pressing gently to mine that sent an inferno racing far and wide.

It was a tumult to my senses.

The feeling of safety that swept through me clashing with the need to press myself against him and take everything that he might be willing to give.

The urge to fully place myself in his hands.

He kissed me softly. So soft I wasn't sure how it was possible for a man like him.

Little nips and sucks of my lips, his head shifting back and forth as he plucked and pressed, nibbling my lips between his.

Then his tongue barely swept across the seam of my mouth. I fisted my hands in the fabric of his tee as I opened to him.

His tongue swept against mine.

Need barreled through me, making me weak in the knees and throbbing between my thighs.

A gush of air ripped from my lungs at the onslaught of sensation, and he inhaled it.

Sucked it down as if he were the one who'd demanded it.

He pulled me closer, and he fully looped his arm around my lower back just as the fingers of the other hand tangled in my hair.

My hands were pinned between us as I hung on, and I could feel the intensity increase.

Could feel the desire curl through his massive, vibrating body.

The way he wanted to take it deeper.

Devour me. Ruin me. Wreck me.

Part of me wanted to let him do it.

The other was relieved when he peeled himself away. Relieved when he made the choice because I wasn't sure if I could have stopped myself.

The man's eyes were a toiling mess of greed.

Body twitching in volatility and restraint.

"Still have every intention of makin' you forget, Charleigh. I'm just not sure you're ready for that yet."

With that, he turned on his heel and walked out. He left me gaping behind him, wondering what I'd gotten myself into.

Maybe I shouldn't have been surprised when my phone buzzed from my back pocket one minute later, and I found River had already sent a text.

> River: Favorite color? Tell me it's pink like those sheets I got a peep at on your bed. Pink like those distracting scrubs you always wear. Same as the pink that flushes your cheeks when you're turned on. Because I'm pretty sure that exact color just became my favorite.

And I was the fool who wandered into my bedroom, grinning down at my phone the whole way as I tapped out a response.

> Me: Pink is my favorite color.

River: Favorite food?

Me: Pizza. You?

River: Steak.

Why was I not shocked?

River: How old are you?

Me: Twenty-six. You?

River: Thirty-two.

These ones were easy, though on the next, I tripped.

River: Did you always want to be a nurse?

I hesitated for a moment before I responded.

Me: No, I wanted to be a doctor, and I'm not really even a nurse. I'm just a medical assistant.

River: Why didn't you go for it?

Me: I did.

River: What happened?

Me: I got trapped.

River: Want to elaborate on that?

Me: No. Did you always want to tattoo?

River: Not sure, Charleigh. Only thing I'm sure of is I just wanted to survive.

The tattoo on my inner arm burned its reminder. And I wondered if I was more like the man than I ever could have thought.

Chapter TWENTY

Charleigh

Eighteen Years Old

S HE WAS IN THE SMALL ALCOVE MAKING COPIES AT THE MACHINE, a mindless job that she hated, as if her intelligence was offering anything to the company the way Frederick Winston had implied when he'd suggested she intern.

It was boring, tedious work that she could have done asleep.

But there she was, stuck for the summer. What was she supposed to do when Frederick had returned to the dining room proclaiming she was going to be joining them, and one minute later, he'd announced her father was getting the promotion?

She knew with the look Frederick had cut her that it was subject to her complying.

Why?

That was what she wasn't entirely sure about, although she figured the guy liked wielding his power. Tossing it around like a game, pulling strings and finding out who was happy to play his puppet.

One thing for certain?

She wasn't *happy*.

Not in the least.

She was supposed to be shadowing a pediatrician for the summer.

But this? This was her lot, but it was only for a couple months. She could handle it if it gave her father that extra nudge toward his own goals and dreams.

He'd sacrificed everything for his family, worked like crazy to give them anything they needed and more, and if she was happy about one thing, it was that she could give a little bit of that back to him, even though he had no clue he was working for a creep.

Everyone thought Frederick was this great guy. Constantly donating money to charities. Coming into the office and showering his staff in compliments and bonuses when they met their goals.

Running things *right*.

Tech's Man of the Year.

But there was something about him that set her on edge. Something that slithered like sickness beneath her skin whenever he came into the room.

He'd never been outright inappropriate with her, but she hated the way he looked at her. As if he were devouring her innocence. Like he could tell she was inexperienced and shy and wanted to feed off it.

Where he fell short is he assumed her inexperience made her weak.

She wasn't, though.

Her mother had always told her she had a quiet strength, and she gathered it up when she felt the sticky presence enclose on her from behind.

She blew out a strained breath, focusing on her job and doing her best to pretend like Frederick Winston wasn't there, which was impossible considering the tiny room she was boxed in left him three feet away from her where he hovered in the doorway.

"How is it going in here?" he asked.

"Fine," she said. She didn't think the mundane task warranted a deeper explanation.

"You're doing great. A true benefit to the company."

She was glad she was facing away from him so he couldn't see the roll of her eyes.

Was he serious?

When she didn't reply, he took a step forward, and his voice lowered a fraction. "A true benefit."

He dragged his fingertips down the back of her neck, and she gasped as she whirled on him. "What do you think you're doing?"

He smiled an arrogant, casual smile. "What exactly are you referring to?"

"You know what I mean. I don't appreciate you touching me."

His chuckle was amused. Mocking even. "Oh, I haven't begun to touch you, *Sweet Pea*."

Shock speared her to the spot before dread went sailing through her spirit. Her chest grew heavy, heaving with disbelieving breaths as awareness pulsed through her system.

Did he really think she was going to succumb to this? Yield to him because he was what? Powerful? Rich?

She shook her head because she wasn't going to put herself through this bullshit. "I don't think so. I quit."

She moved to wind around him, only he snatched her by the wrist to stop her. His mouth was at her ear, and the easy tenor he normally spoke with had disappeared. In its place was malignancy. "I would reconsider the choices you make."

She jerked her arm free, muttering, "Screw you."

She hurried out to her cubicle and grabbed her things. She hoped this didn't reflect poorly on her father, but she wasn't about to put herself through this.

Not for anything.

So, she walked out without looking back.

A light tapping sounded at her bedroom door before her mother cracked it open enough to pop her head through. "Are you decent? I have some mail for you."

She straightened where she was sitting with her legs crisscrossed on her bed, doodling in a journal, trying to figure out how she was going to break the news to her father that she'd walked out this afternoon.

She gave her mother a playful grin. "If I wasn't decent, would it matter?"

Her mother chuckled. "Sorry, sorry, I was used to barging into your room for years, and I keep forgetting that you're basically grown, and I need to give you some privacy."

"It's honestly fine. You know I don't mind."

It wasn't like she was hiding a boy under her bed or in the closet, though she'd been texting with this guy Scott who'd been in one of her classes last year, and she was hoping something might come of it.

Her mother pushed through and handed her a small stack of mail. "Here you go."

"Thank you."

"No problem. Your father is grilling if you want to join us for dinner, unless you have plans?"

"No plans other than hanging out in here. Does he need any help?"

Unease rippled through her at the thought of having to face him, but she figured she should just rip the Band-Aid off. And she'd be doing it in a big way.

She intended to tell her father what had actually happened and then make a complaint to HR about it.

It sucked, but she knew it was the right thing to do. She doubted she was the first intern or employee that he'd harassed that way. She couldn't ignore it.

"No, he should be fine. It should be ready in about ten minutes."

"I'll be down soon then."

"Okay, love you, Sweet Pea," her mother said as she walked out and pulled the door shut behind her.

Once her mother left, she turned to the small stack of mail. She didn't get a lot of it, and it was usually junk mail, which most of it was.

She flipped through the pile. A coupon for a free coffee at a local café that she'd signed up to receive discounts from and an invitation to attend an event at the local library.

But there was a big manila envelope at the bottom that caught her attention.

She frowned since it only had her name and address on it, and she realized it wasn't even postmarked. Whoever had sent this had put it directly in their mailbox.

Trepidation needled into her consciousness, but she ignored it and ripped into it, and she spilled the contents out onto her bed.

It was a bunch of documents.

Documents from Pygus Software.

She scanned them, uncertain of what they meant or why she'd received them.

Only it became clear very quickly.

Her heart clutched in disbelief.

It was a paper trail of her father's embezzlement.

Hundreds of thousands of dollars.

She felt sick. So sick.

She was trembling when she found the note at the very back, this one handwritten and unsigned, though she immediately knew who it was from.

It would be a shame for this to make its way to the authorities, wouldn't it? Your father would be seventy before he was eligible for parole. Half his life wasted. Your mother alone.

And the only thing it costs to stop it is one night.

One night.

One night.

Lightheadedness swept through her brain, bile climbing up her throat as she tried to process what the man was propositioning.

She understood extortion.

Blackmail.

She could call Frederick's bluff. Toss it back in his face as bullshit.

Ignore it altogether.

Or she could go to the authorities with it. But Frederick had power and reputation. She knew it could easily be swept under the rug.

And if this was real? If the proof he was showing her was true? It would expose her father. His sins.

She didn't go down that night. She couldn't look at her father and question what he'd been involved in. Couldn't stomach the truth. Couldn't fathom the way it would tear apart their family.

One night.

One night.

A war waged inside her as she flopped uneasily in her bed, horrified by the proposal. By what it would mean. At what she'd be giving up. The disgust she would feel.

But if one night could protect her father...

She gulped as she came to a decision, tears leaking out of the edges of her eyes as she succumbed to what she felt was the only choice she could make.

But maybe she was naïve, after all.

Naïve to the extreme because she truly didn't know what Frederick Winston was capable of.

Chapter
TWENTY-ONE

RIVER

H AD YOU EVER TAKEN A TURN DOWN THE WRONG ROAD AND traveled it anyway just to see where it would lead?

Knowing the path was treacherous and riddled with pot-holes and cracks, and you'd already received the warning that there was a dead-end up ahead, but you continued on because the scenery was so awe-inspiring you'd convinced yourself it wouldn't hurt to take a detour through paradise?

Guessed it was so as I sat like a dumb fucker with his first crush grinning at my phone at just after seven in the morning.

Maybe that's exactly what I was.

A dumb fucker who had his first crush because I wasn't sure that I'd ever felt this way before. Fucking antsy as hell, anticipating her next text. Wondering exactly what she'd say and how it was gonna feel, but knowing every time her words did come through, I felt like I was flying.

We'd been texting back and forth for the last week, and with each one, I felt myself getting more caught up.

I glanced back at the text I'd sent her five minutes ago.

> Me: You thinking about runnin' today?

It was the same one I'd sent her every morning for the last seven days, though I'd told her it didn't count as one of my twenty questions.

I'd used up to question nine.

Mostly I'd kept it pretty light because I didn't want to spook her, and I sure as hell didn't want to be the reason that her shining eyes went dim.

Besides, the bantering with this girl was fun.

No doubt, I was going to have to take it deeper, knock some bricks out of the wall she kept erected around her.

Fortified battlements around a castle, the girl in a tower and staring down, too fucking high for me to reach.

It also meant I was going to have to give her some of me, which was so goddamn reckless, the way I was contemplating giving her a glimpse when doing it should have been absolutely out of the question.

The rules had been set in place for a reason.

Still, I was grinning when a response finally blipped through.

Little Runner: Not today.

Me: Good girl.

Swore, I could almost feel her blush through the phone. The way she always got all shy and affected. Loved that about her. The way she was shuttered. A flower hidden behind her pains and fears.

But I could feel her, aching to bloom.

Me: How'd you sleep?

It didn't take her long to respond.

Little Runner: You sure are using up those questions on silly things for someone who was hoping to get to know me better.

Me: Checking on you doesn't count. You already know that.

I would have used up those questions on the first day if that was the case.

Little Runner: And how's it you get to make the rules?

Me: Because I'm the big boss, like Nolan said.

Little Runner: Why am I getting the sense that you always get your way?

Me: I learned a long time ago that I have to push for the things I believe are right.

Little Runner: To survive?

I hesitated, tongue stroking my lip before I tapped out a response.

Me: Yeah. You have to fight to make your way through this world, whatever that looks like. No matter how ugly it might be.

Me: That counts as one for you.

You know, since she managed to get under my skin and make me reveal another piece that I was an idiot to give her. My crew would have my ass if they knew the way I was getting sucked under.

Little Runner: Not fair. You tricked me into that one.

Me: You're the one who asked.

She sent me a slew of pouty face emojis, and I rumbled a chuckle as I typed out a response.

Me: Going to sign off. Know you need to get ready for work, and I'm going to need to feed my little dude. He'll be up any minute.

It took a second for her text to blip through.

Little Runner: Give him a kiss for me?

Me: Yeah, as long as you're sending along one for me, too.

I was surprised when a response came right through.

> Little Runner: Kisses like this feel a whole lot safer.

My heart stalled out for a beat before I let my fingers fly across the screen.

> Me: Because you're afraid of me?

> Little Runner: No, because I'm afraid every time a text comes through from you that I want to reach through the screen to touch you.

> Me: Believe me, gorgeous, the feeling is mutual. Have a good day at work. Be safe.

Tossing my phone to my bed beside me, I flung myself back on the mattress. I crammed the heels of my hands into my eyes and wondered exactly what it was I thought I was doing. What I hoped to achieve.

Wondering most when I needed to put an end to this thing. Exactly when we'd hit that dead end.

The one thing I knew was I had to stop it before I got her tangled in the consequences of who I was.

Shame gusted in from the sacred place where I kept it shored, and that gutting failure that had changed the course of my life throbbed from within. Reminding me of the commitment I'd made.

I needed to remember that was the one I was charged to protect at all costs.

Apparently, there was no heeding the warnings I'd given myself. Not when our texts continued through our days.

Between clients.

Before I picked up Nolan from the sitter.

Sending them quick then tucking my phone away, over-eager to get to her answers and returned questions that would be waiting for me when she got to them on her breaks.

It was the girl who was pushing us deeper right then. Wanting to know me the way I'd invited her to do. I wanted to reveal every element that made me up, even though I tried to keep things as vague as I could, toeing a line that couldn't be crossed.

> **Me:** What's the one place you've always wanted to go but never have been?

Little Runner: Greece. Have you always lived in Moonlit Ridge?

> **Me:** No.

Little Runner: Where did you grow up?

> **Me:** LA.

Little Runner: Why did you leave?

> **Me:** To give Nolan a better life.

It was at least the truth even though there were a thousand secrets wound in it.

It was the text that came through hours later that nearly dropped me to my knees, blipping through right after I'd pulled into the garage with Nolan chattering away from the backseat.

Little Runner: Where's his mom?

I glanced in the rearview, at his precious, innocent face.
And there I went, such a fucking fool, laying it out.

> **Me:** She's dead.

I felt pinned to the seat as I held my phone, waiting for what would come next. Nolan was halfway through telling me about what he'd had for lunch when one finally popped up.

Little Runner: I'm really sorry.

> **Me:** Yeah, me too.

When nothing came through after a couple minutes, I finally forced myself from the driver's seat, and I rounded to the back and quickly unbuckled Nolan. I swung him into the air before I set him on his feet.

He cracked up like it was the most fun he'd ever had, before he went running through the door and inside the house, shouting for his *auntie* as he went.

We'd just finished up dinner and I'd told Nolan to head upstairs to grab a game for us to play when I finally received another text. Warily, I turned my phone over where it was face down on the table.

Little Runner: Did you love her?

Her question felt like a blade was slowly being driven through the center of my chest.

Hands shaking, I tapped out a reply.

Me: No.

Raven was casting me a speculative glance. "Who are you texting?"

"No one," I grunted.

She laughed, though it wasn't an agreeable sound. "Sure, sure, big brother. Do you think I haven't noticed you sneaking around like you've got a dirty secret for the last week?"

She shocked the shit out of me when she plucked my phone from my hand and jumped out of her chair.

"What the hell?" I demanded as I pushed to standing, the legs of my chair screeching on the hardwood.

My baby sister danced away from me, spinning it over her head the way she used to do when she wanted to torment me when she was seven. "If you aren't keeping secrets, then you won't mind if I take a little peek. I mean, we don't keep anything from each other, do we?"

I went to snatch it out of her hand, and she ducked the other direction.

"Ah-ha, just what I thought," she said at my reaction, and from where she was halfway across the room, she turned her attention to my phone.

"Oh," she murmured quietly as she realized who I was talking to.

I scraped an agitated hand over the top of my head. "It isn't what it looks like."

She lifted her dark eyes to me. "What does it look like?"

I sighed, not sure how the hell to phrase it to my sister. "Like I'm sweet on your best friend," I settled on.

The two of them had been hanging out a ton over the last week. It was rare that Raven didn't stay at the flower shop after closing, coming home an hour late and telling me she'd grabbed a drink with Charleigh or had gone on a walk or just roamed around doing whatever girlie shit they did.

Had to admit that I loved it. Loved that the two of them were finding companionship in each other.

Loved that my sister was spreading her wings.

Loved that Charleigh wasn't alone.

But this? I didn't fuckin' love it. Didn't love the way my sister was looking at me at all.

"Are you?"

Another sigh. "No."

Because I didn't get to be *sweet* on anything. I didn't do love or connections or strings or any of that bullshit.

But I felt tied to Charleigh in some intrinsic way.

In a way I shouldn't.

"Are you lying to me or are you trying to lie to yourself? Because this looks like you're *sweet* to me, River."

She waved the screen at me as proof.

I roughed a palm over my face. "It's not that…"

Okay, it was all those things. I wanted to take this girl in a way I'd never wanted to take anyone.

Fuck her.

Touch her.

Keep her.

But most of all, I wanted her to realize she was free. Wanted her to know that she didn't have to be a prisoner to whatever nightmares had occurred in her past.

I knew that's what they were.

Nightmares.

Even if she hadn't let me get that deep yet, I could feel them.

"What is it then?" Raven pressed.

"It's me being a stupid prick and fuckin' around where I shouldn't."

Raven's expression grew intense, and she slowly came toward me, her voice growing soft. "I know what you look like when you're fucking around with a girl, River. And it doesn't look like this."

I cringed at what my sister was implying. Cringed at the suggestion that was written all over her face.

"You like her. You care about her."

"I don't get to have that, Raven."

"Why not?"

"You know why."

She huffed like I was in the wrong. Like my sins weren't stacked against me.

I'd made a trade. I'd long since accepted that.

"That's bullshit, River. Total bullshit. Do you think I don't know what you sacrificed for me? What you've sacrificed for the others? You deserve to be loved more than anyone I know."

My chest squeezed, pain eating me alive.

"You know the rules."

And above that, I'd given Nolan all that I was. Everything I had to give. He was my priority, and I couldn't lose sight of that.

Emotion ran thick in Raven's mahogany eyes. "Screw the rules, River. What's this life if it's not worth living?"

The raucous stomping of footsteps echoed from overhead, and I reached out and touched my sister's cheek. "Got plenty to be living for, Raven."

Adoration filled her features, and she set her hand over mine. "That doesn't mean you don't deserve more. After everything you've done for me. After everything you've done for them."

Unable to answer her, I backed away. "I need to get upstairs and play that game with Nolan."

I turned on my heel and started up the stairs. My sister's words stopped me in my tracks. "If you don't care for her? Then you need to let her go, River. Let her live her own life. She doesn't need to be toyed with. She's been broken enough."

I could barely nod with the lump constricting my throat, but I did, and I hurried to climb the stairs. I moved directly to Nolan's room where he was already on the floor with the game set out on the carpet. "Hey, yo, Daddy-O! Are you ready to play? I got it all ready for us. Get ready to go down!"

He hopped on his knees and pumped his fists, like we were getting ready to throw down in the ring rather than play a game of Trouble.

Affection pulling fierce at my chest, I sat down across from him and ran my fingers through his hair. "Yeah, buddy, I'm ready to play."

Darkness had fallen, and the house had grown quiet. I'd tucked Nolan into bed two hours before, and Raven had retreated to her room to read one of the smutty romance novels she was obsessed with.

I lay there, staring at the ceiling, unsettled as fuck. Struggling with what Raven had said. She was right. I shouldn't be messing with Charleigh if I had no intention of being the kind of guy she needed me to be. When I knew I *couldn't* be him.

Should have ignored it when my phone vibrated on the mattress beside me, but I picked it up, heart clamping like a fist when I saw who it was from.

Little Runner: Have you ever loved anyone?

Fuck me.

She really was trying to do me in. But I was the one who'd come up with this asinine idea. Begging her to trust me when I knew full well that I couldn't be.

Me: My sister? Nolan? My crew? Yeah. With all of me. But not the way you're asking. You?

Even though I was coming apart inside, I kept up with our typical cadence and asked her the same.

Little Runner: No. Not in that way, either.

Me: How's it possible someone like you has never been in love before?

Couldn't stop myself from asking it, unable to imagine a lifetime where someone like Charleigh hadn't had that. I'd figured that was a big piece of her grief. Of what that tattoo I'd marked on her had meant.

Little Runner: Because I've never had anyone that I've ever wanted to love like that. Have never had anyone to love me back.

My fingers flew in their disbelief because who in the fuck wouldn't fall in love with this girl?

Me: Have you not been in a relationship before?

It took her forever to answer, and I was fuckin' itching by the time it came through.

Little Runner: I was married.

What the fuck? Charleigh had been married?
Jealousy knocked me upside the head.

Me: And you didn't love the guy?

Fury lashed out with the force of my fingers.
Why it pissed me off so bad, I didn't know.
No doubt, we were way past the twenty questions. Far past the agreement we had made. But I wanted to go deeper. Get so deep that neither of us would be able to figure out where our histories started or where they ended. Where our days blended.
Tangled.
Tied.
I was too fucking foolish to realize the hazardous direction my thoughts had taken.

Little Runner: No.

I could feel the pulse of sadness come with it. The horror. Awareness sank through me with the weight of a boulder toppled into the sea.

This was the fucker who'd hurt her.

My teeth gnashed.

> Me: Who is he?

> Little Runner: It doesn't matter.

She was putting me off. No doubt about it. Maybe this girl understood me better than I thought because the only thing I wanted right then was to go on a rampage.

> Me: Oh, it matters. This who you've been running from?

It felt like a lifetime passed before she responded, and I didn't miss that she didn't answer but instead asked me another question.

> Little Runner: What's your biggest regret?

Had two of them. Only one I could give her access to.

> Me: That I didn't stop my stepfather from hurting Raven soon enough. That she didn't get a real childhood.

I wasn't sure what Charleigh knew about it. If Raven had shared with her any of those things in the many times they'd hung out. Things that still made nausea swirl in my guts and rage spiral through my system.

I had ended that motherfucker a long, long time ago, but that didn't mean the sting of it wasn't there. Didn't mean the regret didn't remain. The vengeance enacted would never truly cover what he'd done.

But I didn't give her time to respond. Instead, I asked her the one thing that had plagued me since I'd marked those words on her flesh.

> Me: What's the grief you have tatted on your arm?

I stared at my phone for the longest time, willing a text to come through. Ten minutes passed, then fifteen, and I finally slumped back on the mattress, wondering if I'd pushed her too far.

It felt like forever as I lay there toiling with thoughts of this woman who had lodged herself somewhere in my spirit, wedging out a section for herself. This care too much.

An actual hour had passed, and I was about to drift when my phone vibrated beside me. I scrambled to grab it, lifting it high so I could read what she said.

Little Runner: I had a son.

Grief hit me so hard I rocketed upright, and my teeth ground like it could staunch the shearing pain I instantly felt for her.

Because I could hear the finality in her words.

Had.

I wavered for one second, unsure of what I was doing, before I put through a FaceTime call. I doubted much that she would answer, and I didn't know what the fuck I would even say if she did, but I felt the compulsion to see her right then. Actually look at her face and understand what she was feeling.

I wasn't prepared for it, though, when she did. Wasn't prepared to see the tears running down her cheeks, those cinnamon eyes somber in the dull light. She was curled up against her headboard, knees tucked to her chest, all that sweetness colored in pain.

"Charleigh." I mumbled her name like it could convey everything I was feeling for her.

She choked a soft sound, and I murmured, "I'm so fuckin' sorry."

She gave a sorrowful shake of her head. "He's been gone for a long time, but I don't think this pain will ever go away."

"No. I doubt that it will."

It might dim and distort, form calluses and scars, but it was something she would always carry.

"The only thing you can do is live in it." I repeated a semblance of what she'd written. The truth that the only thing she could do was put one foot in front of the other. Find the joys of today. Peace in the midst of it.

I wanted to be the one to help her do it which was so fucked up, I didn't know how to make sense of it. I knew better than delving into any of this because there was no changing who I was, but there I sat, staring at this girl through the hazy light and wondering how it was that one person could swing into my life and make such a disorder of it.

Crack this foundation that'd been set years ago.

"What happened to him?" I finally asked after I'd given her some time to just sit there and cry.

She flinched at the question, silent for the longest time before she whispered, "Car accident."

Fuck. Didn't know how to process the information she'd trusted me with throughout the day. The fact she was married, and I was sure this person had done her wrong, treated her bad. I mean, fuck, she still felt the need to look over her shoulder in fear that he might be coming after her.

That horror was far more than enough.

But this?

It was too fuckin' much, and I hated that this girl'd had to bear that much grief.

I wanted to reach through the screen and hold a part of it for her. Promise her it would be okay. That there was joy waiting all around for her.

"That's awful, honey." The words were raw, coarse and littered with this feeling she'd lit inside me.

Sniffling, she wiped at her face with the back of her hand before she nodded, "Yeah, it's awful."

Her mouth twisted in a mournful smile, one riddled with eternal, broken love.

"See now why you look at Nolan the way you do."

Her nod was soft. "I just see him for the treasure he is."

A gift.

That's what Raven had always said.

"He is," I agreed, voice low and raw.

"Do you like it? Being a dad?"

My chest tightened.

A storm of ferocity.

"Yeah. Scares the fuck outta me most days, but I do."

This kid that little bit of joy that I'd stolen. Didn't deserve it, but there he was, sleeping down the hall, filling this house with all his happiness.

"You're a good dad." Her lips gave a soggy tilt at the side.

I grunted. "Not sure about that."

"I am," she murmured, and she was watching me in a way that no one had ever watched me before. Like she saw something deeper.

But that was because she didn't have access to everything that was buried beneath.

Hidden and concealed.

"I'm trying to be," I admitted.

"That's all we can do, right? Do our best? It's no different than the words on my arm. We have to live each day for what it's worth. Pour ourselves into those around us. And I've been so scared of doing that—so scared of getting close to others—that I've almost forgotten what that means."

She readjusted her arm, and it brought her into better view.

"Fuck, you're so pretty." I couldn't stop the confession from sliding out.

So fuckin' pretty. But I knew whatever I was feeling right then had little to do with that. This was far more than the base attraction I'd felt for her when she'd come through my shop's door.

That shyness crept through her features, though she continued watching me as if maybe for the first time she wanted to be seen.

"You make me feel that way, River. You make me want to let you look at me that way. I never thought I'd want a man. Never thought I'd want to be touched again because that was ruined for me. I'd never felt a hint of it until that night when I first met you, and now…"

She trailed off, and a hurricane of possession whipped through my body.

The need to hold her. Take her. Keep her.

The last was the most dangerous of all.

"What *now*, Charleigh?"

"Now I can't stop imagining what it would be like if you did make me forget."

Lust reverberated through my insides, need coming on thick. "You been imagining it, gorgeous? What it'll be like when I send you flyin'?"

Even in the dim light, I could see the flush crawl up her neck and hit those cheeks. "Yes."

"And what do you do while you're imagining it?"

"I burn."

Fuck me.

"Do you touch yourself?"

Wasn't sure I should admit right then that I'd been spending an inordinate amount of time fucking my hand. Envisioning her face and that mouth and that body. Fantasizing about what it would be like to possess all that sweetness.

Timidity hit her face, but she didn't look away. "No. I've never allowed myself that…had never wanted to until now. I want you to be the one to take me there the first time."

A growl rolled through my chest.

Need.

Possession.

A shout so fuckin' loud inside me that I felt lightheaded.

I didn't have time to respond before she continued, "You asked me to give you this time…to get to know you and decide if I trust you. And I do. I trust you, River."

Her words tore me up and stitched me back together.

Flayed and saved.

Because she fuckin' shouldn't. She shouldn't, and she sure as hell shouldn't be looking at me the way she was looking at me right then.

I was all wrong.

No good.

And more than that, I was held by this pact.

Didn't seem to matter right then, though, because I was gripped by the need to be whoever she needed me to be.

"I think I just need a little bit of time," she added quietly.

"You've got no obligation to me, Charleigh. Don't owe me a thing.

But it will be my fuckin' honor to be the one to show you that you're a treasure, too. To show you that you deserve to be loved and touched and adored. Only thing I ask is if you get scared? If you feel like runnin'? Then you run to me."

Her nod was soft. "Okay."

I wanted to keep her there, on the phone forever, but a text popped up at the top of my screen.

One from the group text labeled SS.

Swore, the tattoo on the back of my hand throbbed. The searing truth of who we were.

> SS: We have a situation. Midnight.

It was all the information I needed to know what had to be done. I glanced at the time. Fifteen to twelve.

I looked back at the girl who was gazing back at me. "Sleep well, Little Runner. I'll talk to you tomorrow."

She nodded again before she lifted her hand and brushed her fingertips over the screen like she was physically trying to meet with me before she whispered, "Goodnight."

I ended the call before I got stupid and said something else, and I scrubbed both palms over my face to break up the disorder the girl had left in me then sat up on the side of my bed.

I was still dressed, so I quickly worked to put my boots back on, and I crept from my room and out into the bare light of the hall. I paused at Nolan's door, peered in where the kid was fast asleep, the lion he used to sleep with replaced with the stuffed puppy Charleigh had given him.

My heart squeezed. Squeezed so fucking tight I couldn't see. Couldn't see anything but the two of them.

Forcing myself to move, I pulled his door closed, leaving it open a couple inches, before I crept farther down to Raven's room. I quietly tapped at the door with my knuckles.

"Yeah?" she called from inside.

I nudged it open. She was sitting up against her headboard, under the covers with her tablet on her lap. She looked up and smiled, though the smile fell off her face when she saw whatever must have been written on mine.

"What's wrong?"

"Got a call."

Worry flashed through her expression. "You have to go now?"

"Yeah. Can you keep an ear out for Nolan?"

Her brow pinched. "Of course."

"Thank you."

She bit down on her bottom lip and gave me a slight dip of her head. I went to back out, but the tremor in her voice stopped me. "Be careful, River. We need you."

Blowing out a strained sigh, I pushed her door open a fraction. Enough that she could see me and understand that I meant it. "Told you I would never let anything happen to me. Not when I need to be here for you and Nolan."

I needed to remember that. My duties. My calling.

I tried to as I hurried downstairs, grabbed my keys, and strode into the garage to my bike.

But the thoughts of Charleigh remained strident in my mind.

Chapter
TWENTY-TWO

RIVER

MY BIKE RUMBLED AS I TRAVELED THROUGH MOONLIT RIDGE beneath the cover of night. Stars blanketed the sky, so many that it felt as if the town were shrouded in a blanket of silver glitter.

Hardly a soul was out, and the air was cool as the wind whipped across my face and stirred my heart into chaos.

My pulse thudded hard, a thunder that rolled as I roared down Vista View. Heavy metal vibrated beneath me, and the pavement passed by in a blur. I slowed and made the left onto Culberry, and I wound my way up the road until the area became more congested as I hit downtown.

Kane's was packed, as per usual. A mess of cars and trucks and bikes littered the huge gravel parking lot, rolling from the front of the old building all the way out to the street.

I pulled in, the engine chugging low as I made my way up the middle aisle to the bikes parked in a row at the front. Slowing to a stop, I put my feet out to balance the bike, and I used my heels to back myself in between Kane and Cash's motorcycles. Otto and Theo's were there, too, sitting front and center.

I killed the engine and swung from the bike, and I strode for the front door where Ty and Jonah were manning the door.

The two of them were brutes, ensuring that anyone who came through the doors playing the prick immediately found their asses tossed to the curb.

Ty jutted his bearded chin at me, dude covered in tats, a ton of them compliments of me. "River Tayte. Good to see you out and about. Rest of the boys are already inside."

I gave him a clipped nod. "Thanks, brother."

"Not a problem."

He stepped aside so I could wind my way into the crowd.

Kane's was set in an old church, the walls brick and the ceiling steepled. Long, slender stained-glass windows rested high on the walls, and the strobes from the stage where the band played struck against the glass and sent sparks of color glinting over the space.

A long bar ran the far-left side, and there were a slew of stools set up along it. The dance floor was in the middle with the stage at the back, and along the right side were a bunch of tables and booths tucked within the dim light and dancing shadows.

The place appealed to both locals and tourists alike, the club exuding a sexy, posh vibe.

Trent Lawson owned a killer club in Redemption Hills, and he had helped Kane set it up. Kane had been happy to take his advice of bringing in rotating bands of different genres, and the roster never failed to keep the place swarming night after night.

I cut through the left, and people parted as I went, no doubt sensing the energy that crashed from within me. Instinct warning them of the barely hinged violence that skated through my veins.

Five bartenders took up different sections behind the bar, slinging drinks as fast as the orders were tossed out to them.

Mallory caught my eye, this gorgeous chick who'd come to us and had decided to stay. The only one here who knew what these meetings were all about.

She angled her head toward the swinging door that led to the back of the church where the kitchen and offices were located.

I didn't slow to acknowledge her. I edged right through, boots eating up the floor as I took purposed strides down the long hallway.

I passed by the kitchen and the breakroom and a few other offices before I made it to the very back where I pushed through the door to Kane's office.

Inside, the light was muted, the floors the same rustic wood as the rest of the building, furniture to match.

My crew was already there.

Theo stood leaning back on the edge of Kane's massive wooden desk, his arms crossed over his chest, and Kane was behind it, rocking in the executive chair.

Otto was pacing, roughing an anxious hand through the long pieces of his hair.

Cash loitered in the corner to my right, mostly out of sight, though I could feel the severity radiating from his being.

Stepping forward, I locked the door behind me, and upon my entering, Kane stood and moved to the wall of bookshelves on my right. He shifted a couple old books aside so he could get to the keypad he'd installed and tapped in the code that made the latch give.

Then he pulled open the section of bookcase that hid the passageway.

Kane ducked through it first, and all of us moved, following him down the narrow, cramped stairwell to the basement below. Cash was at the tail, and he closed the bookcase behind us. It was musty down there as the space had assuredly been used for storage back in the day, the floors nothing but raw concrete and the walls rough, exposed brick.

A big, round table sat in the middle of the room, and five chairs surrounded it.

We each took our spots, our hands stretched out in the middle of the table with the matching, swirling crosses marked on our flesh.

And I called to order the meeting of Sovereign Sanctum.

Chapter
TWENTY-THREE

RIVER

Seventeen Years Old

"Y OU SURE YOU WANT TO DO THIS?" THEO ASKED IT, AND OTTO
roughed an agitated hand down his face. Kane and Cash were
leaned back against the wall of the abandoned building that
they called home. River'd been with his crew since the day he'd met
Theo outside the store when he'd made his first theft.

There'd been a fuckton of them since.

But this was the first true crime he was going to commit.

"Yeah. Don't want to involve any of you, though. Just need you
to keep an eye on Raven when I go."

Raven was technically supposed to be living with their grandmother. He'd taken her there a couple days after they'd run away,
thinking it'd be the best situation for her since he couldn't imagine
a nine-year-old girl growing up on the streets. Sure one day they'd
get caught and she'd be sent back to her parents. Their grandmother
had promised she was going to call CPS and get Raven permanently
placed with her.

Only their grandmother had called their mother instead, and her
father had come for a *visit*.

A month ago, Raven had taken five city buses across town to find him. He'd never forget her standing in the doorway to that abandoned building, tears on her face.

She'd begged River to never make her go back.

He'd sworn he wouldn't.

Theo shook his head. "Nah, man, if you're going to do this, I'm going to have your back about it. Raven's our family, too."

It's what they'd become.

Family.

And now it was going to be written in blood.

The lights from the SUV parked down the street flashed once.

A sign.

A go.

He moved, a wraith who crept through the darkness under the cover of night. Crouching low to keep himself concealed as he hustled across the manicured yard. His back pressed against the exterior wall of the brick house to make sure it was clear. Quick as he accessed the door where the lock had already been cracked so it'd look like it was an actual break-in.

Silently, he slipped across the house and down the hall to the room.

He didn't slow or hesitate.

The bastard was exactly where he knew he would be.

Asleep.

Deep, rattled snores lifted from the right side of the bed.

Unseen, he coasted to the side of it, a shadow that loomed high, and he released a low, vengeful growl.

The piece of shit startled, the whites of his eyes blowing wide in the murky pitch of the room.

But the monster had no time.

No defense.

Not when he'd earned this punishment.

There was only the satisfying flash of recognition in his expression before River's hand clamped over his mouth, and he tipped his head back right before he dragged the blade across his throat.

Then he was gone.

Without a sound.

Without a trace.

TWENTY-FOUR

Charleigh

> River: You thinking about runnin'?

I BIT MY LIP TO WARD OFF THE RUSH OF EAGER ANTICIPATION THAT gushed through me when I opened my phone to find the waiting text from him.

It'd been three days since things had gotten heavy between us. Three days since I'd cut myself open and allowed him to see a piece of me that I'd thought would be forever unexposed.

Three days since I'd given a view of the most broken, fractured pieces of me then had turned around and offered him the hope he'd sparked inside me.

The need.

This…this…expectancy that had bloomed and filled my aching chest with something new.

I had the sneaking suspicion that what I was feeling was joy, but it'd been so long since I'd experienced it that I couldn't be sure.

During the last few days, he'd gone back to playful, and God, I loved it. Loved when I woke up or took my lunch break or powered up my phone after work that there was always some message waiting for me.

Constant reminders that he was there. That maybe…maybe I didn't have to be alone anymore after all.

Grinning as I pushed through the front door of the medical office, I tapped out a reply.

> Me: Not today, Guardian Angel.

I could almost feel his scoff ripple through the distance.

The first time I'd called him that, he'd warned me that he was no angel, but I couldn't help but tease him about it, anyway.

Even though I meant it. There was something about him that made me feel protected. Watched over.

I blinked rapidly as I stepped out into the bright rays of the late afternoon sun. It'd be hot if it wasn't for the breeze that whispered through the woods that surrounded the town.

Easiness billowed, and I felt it.

The fact that this place was becoming a sanctuary.

A refuge.

I wouldn't try to deny that it didn't have everything to do with the people I'd met here.

Raven and Nolan gliding into the vacancy. Assuaging it with their care and their laughter and their friendship. It was a rare day that Raven wasn't standing at the door of Moonflower after I got off work, waiting to drag me inside so she could flick the lock and pull me into the back so we could share a bottle of wine.

We'd giggle and chat and goof around, though we both seemed to skate over the more substantial topics. Each tiptoeing, seen and understood without actual confessions to support it.

But River? River was an entirely different story.

He was a riot to my senses and a whisper to my soul.

There was no doubting it when another text blipped through as I walked across the parking lot.

> River: Good girl. You wouldn't want me to have to hunt you down.

Giddiness rushed, bounding through my system, and there was

nothing I could do to curb the affected smile that tugged at the edge of my mouth.

> Me: Stalker, much?

> River: You have no idea.

My stomach twisted in a bout of greed and a fluttering of anticipation.

I could still feel him against my lips. Could feel the tingles that remained even though it'd been close to two weeks since he'd kissed me the second time inside my apartment.

My stomach fisted in that throbby, achy sensation that felt oh so sweet but wasn't even in the range of being enough. This want that burned.

But it was my heart that squeezed in fierce affection that warned that I was veering into the treacherous.

I knew I was only setting myself up to get destroyed again. Getting attached to a man who'd made it clear that this was only temporary. But there was no stopping the way I felt pulled in his direction.

The man a magnet.

Gravity.

I was still staring at my phone when I hit the sidewalk that ran along 9th Street. My attention was tipped down at my phone, though I made sure to watch where I was going in my periphery, my fingers loose as I played along.

> Me: Oh, but I have plenty of ideas.

> River: That so?

I could almost see the arch of his menacing brow, the way the stars tattooed on his hairline would dance as he did, everything about him so cruelly beautiful, though those stormy eyes would be softened with the tease.

> Me: Yep. This imagination is wild. I should be an author.

River: You know what they say, truth is stranger than fiction.

Another warning. The man was forever pushing me away all while drawing me in. He might as well have had a leash around my neck.

I had my fingers poised on the screen when something tripped me up.

A creeping awareness that rustled through on the breeze. The breeze that suddenly felt hot and sticky.

I glanced around, trying to pinpoint what it might be that had made me uneasy. Uneasy enough that I couldn't do anything but slow to a complete stop in the middle of the sidewalk.

A few people moved around me, casting me curious glances, while I tried to steady myself.

Apprehension gusted, coming at me in waves, and the fine hairs lifted on the back of my neck.

Spiky pinpricks that raised like defensive quills. Licking out for whatever had caused the shift in the air.

I felt caught in the middle of it, though I put my head down and forced myself to keep moving.

Covertly, my gaze darted all around as I walked, searching every direction.

The cars.

The sidewalk.

The buildings.

Nothing seemed out of order, but the sense wouldn't abate. It was the same sense that normally would send me packing my things and leaving town. The same sense I'd gotten a couple weeks ago at the festival.

Was it paranoia?

Nothing less than a coping mechanism that clicked into action when I slowed for too long?

When my spirit warned I'd spent too much time idle?

Demanding I put one foot in front of the other since it was the only way I knew how to survive?

Except I didn't want to leave. Couldn't.

Drawing in a steadying breath, I kept my head down but my attention keen as I hurried down the sidewalk.

At just after five, the street was busy with those leaving work, and a ton of people were coming in and out of the buildings I passed.

I could find no comfort in the numbers, though.

The safety I'd been feeling a moment ago had been ripped out from under me.

I increased my pace, hustling by the commercial buildings that surrounded on each side.

Medical clinics, the lab, and a few offices.

They soon fell away as I headed in the direction of my apartment.

When I got to the intersection, the crosswalk light was red, and I paused, keeping my head low but trying to inconspicuously glance around at my surroundings. I scanned through the faces, over the cars, trying to understand what it was that set me on edge.

The problem was, the tiniest thing could do it.

Only this time, I swore I saw the shape of someone duck behind the wall of the building just in the distance.

Dread washed through me on a current, a crashing of desperation that dumped into my stomach. The red light changed, and I rushed across the crosswalk to the other side.

Though rather than continuing down the block to my building like I normally would do, I hurried across the intersecting road.

If someone was there? After me? I couldn't lead them back to my apartment. Raven would be at Moonflower, watching for me out the window.

There was no way I'd bring danger to her door. And if it was nothing? I couldn't stomach the idea of her seeing me this way again.

Shivering and afraid.

Running.

I kept peeking over my shoulder as I hurried by the buildings that ran along Broadway, which was the street that connected 9th and Culberry.

I silently chanted, praying that I was only making things up.

Letting panic set in the way I'd done for years.

For so long, I'd allowed it to own me.

But I didn't want that.

Not anymore.

I wanted to stay.

I wanted to stay.

But how could I do that if there was a chance I'd been found? Discovered?

I looked again, peering through the mass of people who were traveling the streets.

I glimpsed him again.

A man loitering back about a hundred yards, though I was sure it was the same person who'd hidden themselves behind the wall a minute ago.

A shadow.

A wraith.

A ghost catching up to me.

No.

No, no, no, no.

Panic rose in a tide of stinging bile, filling my chest and climbing up my throat. Breaths panted from my spasming lungs, and the air wheezed in and out.

I glanced again.

He was there.

A man wearing a khaki jacket and brown pants.

He'd grown nearer, though I still couldn't fully make out his features with the glare of the sun.

But I was sure of it. He was tracking me.

Terror tore through my bloodstream, setting fire to my nerves, and I started to jog. Pushing between people, jostling them aside in my haste.

"Hey, watch where you're going," a man shouted as I knocked into him from the side.

I didn't slow to apologize.

I couldn't.

I had to get away. I had to get away.

I made it to the next street.

Culberry.

I didn't wait for the light to turn, I darted across it. A car horn blared and tires screeched. A startled scream burst out of me, and I whirled that way, my hands pushed out in front of me like they might protect me from the impact.

I gasped as the car careened to a stop an inch away.

The woman driving was shouting obscenities, gesturing her frustration and fear through the windshield.

"I'm sorry," I wheezed through a haggard cry, my hands in supplication as I stumbled the rest of the way across the street to the sidewalk on the other side.

I went right.

Drawn.

Fumbling through the mass that roamed the trendy street.

People shopping.

Browsing.

Laughing as they chatted.

Unaware that I was certain my life was slipping out from under me.

Anxiety hit me in a full-fledged attack, and I wheezed for air, for oxygen, choking over the sob that was stuck in the middle of my throat.

By the time I tore through the door, tears were streaming in hot waves down my cheeks.

The security system beeped, and one second later, River was towering in the opening of his station.

Dark, dark eyes a toiling storm. A protective rage instantly in his stance.

"Charleigh?"

And at the sound of my name, I dropped to my knees.

Chapter
TWENTY-FIVE

RIVER

I FELT HER BEFORE I HEARD HER. FELT HER IN THE WAY THE AIR suddenly turned volatile right before the door blew open. I was on my feet and rushing to the opening of my station, my heart leaping from my fucking chest when I saw her come stumbling in.

"Charleigh?" Her name ripped off my tongue, and the second it hit the air, she crumpled to the floor.

Face full of tears and terror radiating from her being.

I tore off my gloves and tossed them to the floor as I raced to her. I had my arms around her in a flash, panic searing me through at the sight of her like this.

"What happened? What's going on?"

Tried to make it soothing, but the words were shards as I tried to hold back the aggression that pounded through my veins.

I'd just texted her not five minutes before, and she'd been fine. Flirting with me the way we'd taken to doing.

And now she was falling apart in the middle of my shop.

Jagged, rasping cries ripped up her throat, and I curled my arms tighter around her as I pulled her against me. My mouth went to her temple. "It's okay, Charleigh. It's okay. I'm not going to let anything happen to you."

She heaved over a sob, and she pressed her face into my neck.

I curled around her like I could be her shelter when I murmured, "Tell me what happened. Need you to tell me what's going on."

"I…I thought…I saw…"

"What did you see?"

"I—" It cracked as she shook.

She couldn't even get words to form around the panic that had her tongue tied, her heart racing mad, girl logged with horror and grief.

But I got enough from it that I rumbled, "Stay right here."

Otto had come in to get a piece worked on, and I tossed him a look where he stood in the doorway of my station.

Watch over her.

In understanding, he gave me a jut of his chin, and I turned and flew through the door and out onto the sidewalk that ran in front of my shop.

Sure she'd been running.

But this time she hadn't been running to flee, she'd been running from someone, and she'd come runnin' to me.

So fuckin' terrified she couldn't stand.

My eyes scanned the faces of the people who rambled by for any hint of depravity. Searching for the corrupt. I'd known it enough in my life that it wouldn't be difficult to sift out. Spot it in the rambling throng that rippled by.

I couldn't nail down anything amiss. Couldn't pinpoint one single person who was going to pay.

I could feel it, though.

Could feel it ride on the atmosphere, floating on the rays of warmth that filtered through the late afternoon day.

Evil.

The kind you could taste like an oil slick.

I moved in the direction of where I sensed it, shouldering through the crowd that was thicker at this time of day. Their grunts of annoyance and disapproval did nothing to slow me down.

And still, there was nothing there.

No hint or innuendo.

No phantom or shadow.

Whoever this fucker was had turned to vapor.

Frustrated, I roughed a palm over my face, and I cast one more vicious glance around before I gave up and stormed back down the walkway to my shop. Nearly pulled the door from its hinges when I tore it open.

Second I stepped back inside, I was slammed by her turmoil, a fucking tsunami that almost knocked me from my goddamn feet.

Fuck.

This woman possessed a power that could annihilate me.

She was still on the floor, though she was surrounded by Otto and the two other artists who were in the shop working today.

Each kneeling around her in a circle in an attempt to give her comfort.

I tore through them, gritting, "Everyone get the fuck back."

My heart ran jagged and my spirit staged an all-out assault.

A furor of protectiveness lined my insides in liquid steel.

Otto tossed me a wide-eyed *who do we have to kill* as he pushed to his feet, and I just sent him a look that promised we'd talk later as I pulled the girl from the ground and stood with her in my arms.

Charleigh felt too fucking light where she was pressed to my chest, her flesh burning into mine, though there was still something about her that made me feel like I bore the weight of the world as I swiveled on my heel and carried her through the lobby and down the hall that led to my office in the back.

She was quivering. Quivering so hard that each tremor rocked through me, and she gulped over these little sobs that she couldn't quite fully emit.

Each bottled and suppressed.

"I've got you, Charleigh. Shh, I've got you." I tried to soothe her as I moved, my boots thudding hard against the floor. "I've got you."

She needed to understand that as long as she was with me, she wasn't in danger.

I'd raze anything or anyone who dared to get close to her.

At my words, she only choked and cried harder, like my voice had been the hammer that had finally made all her fractured pieces crack.

Or maybe she was just letting go.

"I've got you," I promised again, muttering the truth against the crown of her head where she was tucked tight against me.

I angled to the side so I could get to the handle of the office door. I pushed it open and kicked it shut behind us to give her privacy.

I carried her over to my desk. The top was littered with papers, different sketches that I'd been working on, random ideas and notes and thoughts, and I swept them aside with my forearm before I carefully set her on the edge of it.

I didn't step back. I stayed close, an arm around her waist and the other up high on her back.

Refusing to let her go.

Couldn't have if I tried.

Not when I felt this overpowering need to hold her forever.

Keep her close.

From here to eternity.

And I had no fuckin' clue how she could make this mark on me, like she was the one who'd forever etched her soul somewhere on mine rather than the other way around.

I ran my hand from the back of her head and down her back.

At the contact, electricity crackled.

"Breathe, Charleigh. Just breathe. That's all you've got to do. Nothing else matters. Just breathe." I forced it out through the chaos that raged in the middle of me.

She hiccupped and wheezed, and I kept caressing down her back.

Softly.

Slowly.

Praying the placid strokes of my hand and the tranquil tone I was trying to coerce my voice into would cut through the anxiety attack that had gripped her.

"That's right, just breathe. You've got this. You've got this."

She finally inhaled deeply, fully inflating her lungs, and that was enough to have me shifting a little farther back so I could take her by the chin.

I gently prodded her to look up at me.

Though rather than letting me see, she threw her hands over her face.

Obstructing the beauty.

"You don't have to hide from me, Charleigh. I already see you."

She stayed that way for the longest moment, soft cries still getting loose, before she finally allowed me to pry her hands away.

The sight of her this way punched me in the gut. Gorgeous face stained with tears, cheeks red and chapped, cinnamon-flecked eyes swollen with desperation.

Another wave of protectiveness slammed me, limbs shaking with the violence I wanted to enact.

But I tucked it down, saving it for the motherfucker who I was going to hunt. The one I was going to end. And when I found him? I was going to do it slow. "Look at me, Charleigh. Look at me and know."

She tipped her face fully toward me, those eyes doing wild, wild things, crashing between old fears and the trust she'd given me.

"Tell me what you saw."

Her jaw trembled, and I brushed away the tear that streamed down her cheek with the pad of my thumb. "I…I thought someone was following me after I left work."

Aggression churned, but I forced myself to keep it cool. To show her I could be her rock. That she'd come to the right place.

"Who?"

Her head barely shook. "I never got a good look at him. I just… felt it. This…" Her eyes squeezed closed for a beat, and I knew exactly what she'd felt.

The same evil I'd scented in the air out on the sidewalk.

"I thought I was only being paranoid because that's something I do. I get paranoid and I run, even though I don't have any proof that anyone is even after me. But I just get this sense…"

Charleigh pressed the tips of all the fingers of her right hand to the center of her chest. "I get this sense right here that someone is watching me. And today when I did, I swore I saw someone duck behind one of the medical plaza buildings. I kept going, and when I looked behind me again, the same person was following me in the distance."

My teeth ground, and I itched to race back out the door. Track the bastard. But I didn't know who the fuck I was looking for.

"Would you be able to describe them?"

Sniffling, she shook her head. "No. It was a man, I'm pretty sure, and he was wearing a khaki jacket and brown pants, but other than that, he was too far away to make anything out."

"Would you recognize him if you saw him again?"

She blew a heavy strain of air through her nose. "I'm not sure."

"It wasn't your ex?" She'd already told me she didn't recognize the person, but my gut told me that's who it had to be.

Despair shook her head. "No. I think I would have known if it was him."

I wanted to demand his name. Didn't matter if it wasn't him. I knew he was responsible for her fear. Wanted to fuckin' gut him for whatever he'd done to her in the past.

She laughed a demoralized sound and turned her gaze away. "Maybe it was nothing and I was imagining it. It wouldn't be the first time."

I tugged her forward a fraction, leaving an inch of space separating us. My voice was a hushed roar as I muttered, "You and I both know it wasn't *nothing*, Charleigh. If you've been runnin' all this time, then you've been runnin' for a reason. You can trust me with that, too."

I dragged the pad of my thumb up over her cheek and gathered the glittering moisture. "There is no shame in fear, Charleigh. There's no shame in trying to protect yourself. You've been carrying this on your own for a long, long time, but you need to know that you don't have to do that any longer."

"I don't want to. I don't want to be scared any longer." She whispered it before she reached out and curled her fingers in my shirt, nails scraping through the thin fabric like the lick of flames.

This girl with the power to burn me to ash.

"I don't want to be this way any longer. I want to live, River. I just want to live."

In grief we must live.

"You are, Charleigh, you are. And I'm going to see to it that you continue to. That you don't have to live this life afraid. Promise you, I won't let you go until you're flying free. Until you're no longer looking over your shoulder. Until we're sure you're safe."

Issue was, I wasn't sure I was ever going to want to let her go. This thing she'd lit in me was something bigger—something more powerful—than I'd ever felt before.

I could almost see the words form on her tongue, a confession, before she retracted them and instead leaned forward and set her cheek on my chest.

And she just…breathed me in.

Like I was her peace.

Her solace.

Fuck, how desperately I wanted to be.

I gently ran my hand up and down her exposed neck, lifting chills on her delicate skin.

My voice splintered when I told her, "I can handle your truth."

The problem was I could never give her mine.

I dropped my lips to the top of her head. "Don't need you to hide. I can handle your burden."

When she only tightened her hold on my shirt, I murmured, "Whenever you're ready, you say the fuckin' word, and I'll end this."

Knew I was exposing more about myself than I ever had before. But I wouldn't keep it from her. Not if it could set her free.

A shudder rolled through her, the woman getting the meaning, only she pressed herself closer, shifting so she was burrowing her face up into my neck.

She took in the deepest breath, like she was trying to draw me in, bring me closer.

Fuck, I was already there.

"Going to take you to my place now."

She jolted back, and she was instantly shaking her head. "That's not—"

I had her back in my arms in a flash, plastering her against me, my mouth at her jaw. "Please don't fight me on this, Charleigh. No fuckin' way could I send you back out on your own after this."

She peeled herself back so she could stare up at me. "I'm not your responsibility."

I dipped down until my lips were a breadth from hers. "Yeah, baby, you are. The second you ran through my door? That's what you became. My responsibility. So, thank you, Little Runner, for runnin' to me."

Chapter
TWENTY-SIX

Charleigh

I TRIED TO GET MY BEARINGS, TO STEADY THE WORLD THAT WAS whirling and whipping, canting to the side.

My foundation no longer felt like my own.

River gripped me by both sides of the waist and rumbled, "I've got you," as he lifted me from the desk to place me onto unsteady feet.

"You good?" he asked, trying to keep the aggression out of his voice, but there was no mistaking it. The way his big body vibrated with that same ferocity I'd felt in him when I'd come in here the first time.

When I'd been sure the man was dangerous.

Only I'd never been so sure of it than right then.

I didn't know whether to be terrified or comforted that his words were clearly not an idle offer.

Okay, I'd be a liar if I said I wasn't comforted.

That was absolutely what I'd been as I burrowed myself into his hold because I'd carried this fear on my own for so long, it'd felt like the greatest relief to rest in someone else.

I gave him an erratic nod, and he reached around me and pulled a tissue from the box, and he dabbed it all over my face.

Gently.

Tenderly.

Watching me with those stormy eyes the entire time.

God, how could this menacing man make me feel so important?

"Let's get you out of here," he rumbled as he tossed the tissue into the trash, and I swallowed down the emotion that still roiled, sniffling and straightening myself out as I prepared to go back out into the lobby.

I'd never allowed anyone to see me this way before, and part of me wanted to hide it, but the other knew there was no shame in it the way River had said.

This was real.

My trauma was real.

My loss was real.

And I think it was the first time since everything happened that I'd begun to allow my grief to truly come out. To process who I wanted to be on the other side.

"Okay," I told him.

Satisfaction flashed through his expression. Heat spread through me when he weaved his fingers through mine, and he lifted my hand and brushed his lips over my knuckles.

My knees wobbled. This man was going to do me in.

He was all terrifying confidence as he led me out of the back office, down the hall, and out into the middle of the tattoo shop.

The man and woman I'd never met before who'd come running out to my aide were still there. The man appeared cautiously confused while the woman ran her hands up and down her heavily tattooed arms as she gazed across at me in worry.

But it was Otto who tossed out one of his enormous grins. "Ah, there she is. You good, darlin'? Had me worried there for a bit."

"I'm fine," I managed, feeling ill-at-ease as I stood there shifting beneath the weight of the attention the three of them had on me.

"Of course, you are. You just needed a little breath, and it looks like you came to the right place to get one."

His blue eyes gleamed, the focus of them dancing back and

forth between me and River as if he were trying to calculate what had transpired between us.

Why I was there all while he seemed satisfied that I had been.

River still held my hand in his big paw.

Unwilling to let go.

He grunted in response to Otto's words. "We're gonna split. Lielle, you closing up?"

The woman with bright turquoise hair sent him a nod. "Yeah, I'll be here with a client until ten."

"Good. If anything comes up, give me a call."

"I will."

Then River lifted his chin at Otto, and Otto did the same.

It was a negligible demonstration, but I swore the two of them had shared a secret, covert conversation in the half second it'd taken.

"Will check in, brother. You two be safe." Otto's gaze was fixed on me when he issued it, eyes making a quick pass over my body as if he were evaluating if I was really okay.

As if my scars might be visible.

River pulled open the door, and he released my hand and swiveled around to hold it open so I could pass through, but rather than taking my hand again, he splayed his palm over the small of my back.

Fingers wide as if he could cover me whole.

Only the second I stepped out in the light of day with people all around, I had to fight against the current of anxiety that threatened to take me hostage again.

Run. Run. Run.

My rationale chanted it, urged me toward what had been my creed.

River's mouth came to my temple, his voice a rumble that tumbled through the center of me. "Let me be your shield, Little Runner."

I barely nodded against it, and I could feel the tension wind him in a fist as he sent glares shooting through the atmosphere as we walked down the sidewalk. A clear warning for people to stay out of his way.

He never allowed his scrutiny to wane, the man a steel barricade that surrounded me, completely vigilant as we hurried down the sidewalk.

Groups of people parted before he even got close enough to touch them, the power of his being dividing them as he barreled through.

We passed by the couple businesses that were housed in the same building as River of Ink before we made it to Broadway.

It was the same intersection that I'd come running up from mere minutes ago, where in my panic I'd nearly gotten hit, but rather than heading back that direction, River took my hand and wound around the building to the right.

He dragged me along until I was standing at the side of a vicious looking motorcycle that was parked in an angled spot facing out.

Completely matte black and low to the ground.

River didn't let go of my hand as he swung a leg over the machine, straddling the metal, before he patted the minuscule seat behind him. "Hop on."

Incredulous, I gaped at him. "Excuse me?"

He let go of a low, scraping laugh. "Said, hop on."

My head shook, and I tried to pull my hand from his hold. "I don't do motorcycles."

Those wicked eyes glinted beneath the rays of sunlight that streaked through the tops of the trees. The man was so cruelly beautiful that I felt like I was being impaled every time I looked his way.

"You do now."

"Oh, I don't think—"

River was off the motorcycle and towering over me before I could make sense of his sudden movement, my hand released in favor of him gripping me by both sides of the face.

I gasped, the rake of air drawing his presence into my lungs.

Leather and ink and wicked things.

He dipped in close, and I could feel the whisper of his lips as he rasped, "Do you not get it yet, Charleigh? I'm not going to let anything bad happen to you." He tightened his hold and brought me even closer, his words a command, "I promise you, you're safe with me."

How reckless did it make me that for once I felt that way? After getting this sense twice in the last two weeks? One that I was being tracked? Hunted?

And there I stood, a trembling, brittle leaf that wanted to float in the security of his hands.

A smirk cracked at the edge of his menacing, beautiful mouth. "Now, are you goin' to climb on the back of my bike or am I goin' to have to make you?"

Chapter
TWENTY-SEVEN

Charleigh

AIR WHIPPED ACROSS MY FACE AS WE TRAVELED THROUGH Moonlit Ridge, and the sunlight that slanted from the blue-spun heavens was warm on my cheeks.

My arms were wrapped around his waist, my front plastered against his back, clinging so tightly I was afraid I might be causing him physical pain. I was afraid if I gave even a fraction, I'd go toppling off onto the pavement that blurred beneath us.

Heat blasted from his body, a blaze against mine, and I did my best to focus on holding on rather than burrowing my nose in the back of his tee to inhale his intoxicating scent.

I needed to be careful. I was already distracted enough.

Tiptoeing so far out of bounds there was no chance I wasn't going to get caught.

As if he felt the unease ripple through me, River splayed his right hand over my trembling arms that I had locked around him. I knew it was supposed to be some show of comfort, but it only served to freak me out, and I was shouting over the howl of the wind and the roar of the heavy engine, "Two hands!"

I could feel the roll of his dark, deep chuckle, and he squeezed my arm a little tighter before he reclaimed both handlebars, and he shouted over the battering of the wind, "Told you that I've got you."

River took us all the way to the end of Culberry where it came to a T at Vista View. He made a right onto the two-lane road that wound around to the west side of the lake.

Here, the scenery was gorgeous.

Breathtaking.

What tourists flocked to the mountain-side town to experience in both summer and winter.

A bunch of cabins and homes ran alongside the smooth, crystalline waters, the colossal, peaked mountaintops their backdrop.

Slowing, River took a right, and I held my breath as the bike dipped to the side before he accelerated, the engine a loud grumble, and the motorcycle righted again.

He traveled maybe a quarter of a mile before he slowed even more so he could make the sharp left onto a tree-lined driveway.

I blew out what could only be construed as surprise when I saw the house sitting on what appeared to be about an acre of land.

It gave off a cabin vibe, fronted by dark wood planks and accented by stone. It was two stories with a pitched roof, and abundant, colorful flowers grew from pots situated around the elevated wraparound porch.

River somehow managed to get his phone from his front pocket, and he spread out his legs to support the bike with his booted feet as he punched a code into his phone and the garage door slowly lifted.

He pulled the motorcycle up beside a dark SUV and killed the engine.

In an instant, we were surrounded by a thick, tacky silence.

Uncertainty billowed as strong as the breeze. I kept my arms locked around him because I had no idea what to do at this point.

It'd been different exposing myself through the texts and calls we'd shared over the last two weeks. Coming to the place where I'd felt so comfortable with him that my secrets had begun to pour from the reservoir where I kept them dammed.

My hurts and griefs and fears.

My wants and needs.

I wasn't sure what to do with it now that he possessed those truths. Now that he was here, in the flesh.

After the panic had melted away and now it was just the two of us. Beating hearts and murmuring spirits.

"Wasn't so bad, was it?" I could hear the amusement in his voice. The soft care that shouldn't be possible.

I kept holding on, though playfulness had drifted into my voice. "I don't think my arms or legs work anymore."

"Not a problem. I'll just carry you." He said it low, with a hint of that suggestion that spread through me like flames.

How it was possible I was thinking about him touching me after what had just happened was beyond me, but there it was, that shivery, throbbing sensation coursing through my body.

"I'm not sure I'd survive that, either." It came out both timid and wry.

The truth that I wasn't sure how to handle what he made me want.

But it was there. Burning like a beacon inside me.

River grunted. A low sound that hit me like seduction.

My thighs trembled where they were still tucked up close to his hips and my heart drummed wildly against his back.

"The way I'm going to make you feel might knock you out for a minute or two, but believe me, Charleigh, pretty sure it's me who's not going to survive you."

He was still facing forward, balancing us with his big boots planted on the ground, and he let go of the handlebars with his left hand and set it on my knee.

The contact hit me like a lightning strike.

Then thunder rolled as he let it slide upward until he was squeezing my upper outer thigh.

His big, tattooed hand hot and heavy.

"Mutually assured destruction." I mumbled it at his spine as I held on.

A laugh rumbled through him, his voice just as dark and low. "But we're sure going to have fun while we're doing it."

I wasn't even sure how he maneuvered it, but he'd swiveled around on the bike to pull me into his arms, and he lifted me at the same time as he swung off the bike.

He had my front pressed against him, my feet dangling, tips of my toes barely brushing the ground as he held me in the security of his arms. "Want you to know this is a safe place, Charleigh."

I couldn't speak around the lump lodged in my throat, so I nodded, my cheek brushing against the solid expanse of his chest.

"Good. Let's get you inside."

He set me on the ground, and he guided me forward by placing his hand against my lower back again. The scent of him invaded. His aura profound.

Leather and ink and wicked things.

It whispered around me like a drug.

Intoxicating.

Soothing and healing and terrifying.

We stepped inside and moved through a laundry room to a short hallway that led into the main area of the house.

"This is it," he said as we stalled at an opening that led into the kitchen. It was French country style, the cabinets a teal blue and the floors old wood and rustic. It was quaint and charming and had Raven written all over it.

I couldn't hide my smile. "I take it you weren't the one making the decorating choices."

He chuckled. "My sister gets her way ninety-nine percent of the time."

Affection billowed. "She has that way about her, doesn't she?"

"She won't stop until she does." Dark eyes swam, tracking over me where I had moved into the middle of the kitchen, a thunderstorm brewing. "Though I guess when my mind gets hooked on something, I don't stop, either."

"And what did you have in mind?" My teeth clamped down on my bottom lip as I played into his hand, wanting him to take me there.

Elevate me to a place I'd never been before.

Tease and play and explore.

I wanted to be made new.

Or maybe I just wanted to become who I was always meant to be. And maybe...maybe now I had a chance.

"You." It was a greedy stroke from his tongue, and he crossed the space in a flash. A whorl of energy bashed against the walls in his wake.

He had me by the waist and propped on the high island in a flash.

The breath whooshed out of me, and my hands shot to his shoulders to keep myself steady while his nearly completely circled around my waist.

The span of them enormous.

That big, big body towered high, and he'd wedged himself between my legs.

"It's you on my mind. You who has me hooked. You who has me wanting to do things I don't do."

His hands splayed wide, stretching out over the entirety of my back, his front pressed close. I got the sense he could cover every inch of me at the same time.

Envelop and consume.

I breathed out a shaky breath as he studied me in the glittering rays of light that streaked in through the windows, evening slowly approaching and casting the air in pink, misty hues.

He pulled the strap of my bag over my head and set it aside, and I reached out with a trembling hand and let my fingertips play along the contours of his face. Over the harsh lines and defined edges. The man was carved like a blade. Hewn in severity and shorn in brutality.

My fingers drifted, brushing over the sharp angle of his brow and dancing over the stars tattooed at his hairline, dragging down his jaw before they were caressing over his full, plush lips that were the only thing that was soft about him.

Those lips barely moved with my touch, just soft puffs of air that felt like murmured kisses.

"Can't fuckin' wait to show you what it feels like to be touched by me. Can't wait to adore this body. I'm going to explore every inch of you. Show you that bastard no longer has any control over you."

Goosebumps lifted, and a gluttonous sound rolled through him as he leaned in and chased them up my neck.

"That sound good to you, Little Runner? You want me to show you what it's like to have so much pleasure you won't be able to think of anything else but me? Gonna write myself so fuckin' deep."

A tremble rolled through me.

An earthquake of need.

He groaned like he could feel the way my center throbbed. The way I wanted to melt into him and disappear.

"I want that," I whispered, too turned on to be flustered or shy. "I want to feel everything."

Experience it.

On my own desire, on my own volition.

Not because I'd been coerced or manipulated.

"I'll give you everything you want and more than you've ever dared to imagine."

I was right.

I was never going to survive this.

But I wanted it, anyway.

So, I murmured, "Show me."

Begging him for his kiss.

For his hands and his touch.

For him to do me in.

I wanted to be wrecked. Destroyed. Rebuilt.

He obliged with a growl, taking my mouth in a possessive, mind-bending kiss.

One hand spread all the way across my back to yank me against the hard planes of his body, and the other gripped me by the base of my neck at my skull so he could angle me the direction he wanted me.

This kiss wasn't careful the way the last had been.

This one was a ravaging.

A plundering.

His tongue stroking deep as I opened to him.

Need rolled up his throat and a whimper danced through mine, and I struggled to get closer, to rub myself against the hardness beneath his jeans that I could feel pressing at the thin material of my scrubs.

Normally, I would shrink and cower. Fold in on myself. Close my eyes and pretend I wasn't there.

But I was just as famished as him.

Kissing and kissing him.

My hands rushed to touch him everywhere.

His back. His shoulders. His arms.

Raking down his chest and his abdomen.

"River." I moaned it, this desperate sound that came from a place I didn't know existed.

"I know, baby, I know. I've got—"

We both froze when the sound of the garage door whirring open echoed through the house.

"Shit," River hissed as he broke the kiss. Panting, he dropped his forehead to mine. "That will be Raven and Nolan. I shot her a text and asked her to pick him up from daycare for me."

I struggled to get my bearings.

To come back down from wherever River had lifted me.

I swallowed hard, and River picked me up from around the waist and set me on my feet just as car doors were slamming. One second later, the interior door busted open to the sound of Nolan's voice carrying, "Hey, yo, Daddy-O! I'm here. Did you miss me?"

He came barreling around the corner and into the kitchen, and he skidded to a stop when he saw me. It took all of one beat for his confusion to flash to a beaming smile.

A smile that speared through me and made the haggard breaths I was breathing grow thick with affection. "Miss Charleigh?! What are you even doing here?"

"Oh, well, I…" I stammered it.

Brilliant.

I couldn't even speak.

Then a rush of self-consciousness came barreling through when Raven rounded the corner.

On a gasp, she halted in her tracks, and her dark eyes widened in surprise as she took us in.

My flushed skin and mussed hair and swollen lips. Not to mention River who was a vibrating ball of energy beside me.

And well…just the fact that I was there. Because I'd denied anything was going on with her brother over the last two weeks like I was denying committing murder, and there I stood, pretty sure I was wearing his kiss like a brand.

I shifted on my feet, uncertain of what I was supposed to say or do.

"Charleigh?" She muttered it like a question.

"Hi." I awkwardly fluttered my fingers at her.

Could I be more obvious?

"Did you even know Miss Charleigh was goin' to be waitin' for us here, Auntie?" Nolan bounced, his fingers threaded together like he was issuing a prayer.

Her attention volleyed between the two of us.

"Um, no, I did not even know that Charleigh was going to be here waiting for us."

"Well, surprises are really good. I like surprises. Do you like surprises, Miss Charleigh?" The child was a perfect whirlwind. It wasn't so hard to force a smile to my face.

"As long as they're the good kind," I told him.

He giggled like mad. "Well, I think you're a good surprise. What do you think, Daddy-O? Do you think Miss Charleigh is a good surprise?"

River's gaze swept to me. So intense it nearly bowled me over.

Redness splashed my cheeks, and I couldn't look away from him as he stared at me before he said, "Yeah, I think she's a really good surprise."

Chapter
TWENTY-EIGHT

RIVER

SHIT. I'D ALLOWED MYSELF TO GET CARRIED AWAY, WHICH WASN'T all that shocking considering I'd had the girl propped on the counter, her sweet little body tucked up close to mine.

Woman making me insane with the greed pounding through my veins. So out of my head with my desperation to have her that I'd let it slip my mind that Raven and Nolan would be right around the corner.

Should've given Raven a heads-up that Charleigh was going to be here when she arrived, but I hadn't had the fortitude to think it through.

I was too fucking wrapped in the need to hold her. Protect her. Please her.

So, there I stood with my cock straining so fucking hard I thought I might pass out while my sister stared daggers at me like I'd stolen her favorite plaything.

Considering she'd chosen Charleigh as her best friend, I was pretty sure she was worried that I had. That I was going to do something stupid and fuck it up.

No question, I would.

Made it worse that she'd asked me to leave her friend alone if I didn't plan on actually pursuing something real with her, warning me that Charleigh had been hurt enough and she didn't need me adding to that.

And fuck. It was the last thing I wanted. To hurt Charleigh more.

Raven cleared her throat, shucking off the surprise as she waltzed the rest of the way into the kitchen. "Well, I'm glad to find you here, Charleigh, you know, since I waited for you at the shop and then texted you to let you know I needed to leave and then I didn't hear from you. I was getting worried."

She sent me another cutting glance.

Yeah, I was in trouble with my baby sister.

"I'm sorry. I didn't even check my phone." Charleigh patted her pockets while she looked around like she'd misplaced it, her attention landing on the purse that rested on the island right next to where I'd had her propped.

Redness heated her cheeks. No doubt, she was instantly picturing me having her there.

"It's fine. I really was worried for a minute, but it looks to me like things are handled."

Another searching glance my way as my sister set the two shopping bags she'd carried in onto the counter. "So, what are you doing here?"

"Did you come over for dinner?" Nolan shouted it right behind Raven's question, the kid completely missing the implications swirling through the room.

"I was going to—"

"Yeah, she is staying for dinner, Nolan. So why don't you guys hang out for a bit, and I'm going to do a quick errand, then I'll bring dinner back. How's that sound?"

"It sounds like you've got a smart plan, Daddy-O."

Nah, was probably the biggest fool who lived with the things I was planning to do, but I knew I'd do whatever it took to give Charleigh the life she deserved.

The one she was begging for.

Uncertainty pulled through Charleigh's expression, and I knew if we were in private, she would demand to know where I was going.

I reached out and touched her hand, the girl the flame that licked through my senses.

"Gotta handle something. I'll be back soon. Chill with my sister and Nolan."

"Yeah, you should probably go. It seems Charleigh and I need to catch up." Raven pulled a bottle of wine from a reusable bag and waved it in the air. Unquestionably, Charleigh was about to get the third degree.

But what Charleigh wanted to divulge to her was between them, and I didn't want to stand in the middle of it.

A small smile tweaked Charleigh's mouth, and she whispered, "I could definitely use one of those."

"Good." I started across the kitchen, ruffling my fingers through Nolan's hair and tilting my head at Raven's questioning expression as I passed.

"I'm going to set the alarm to *stay*," I told her, which wasn't exactly that rare since I always wanted them to have extra protection whenever I was away, but I could see it only conjured more questions.

"Okay," she said.

I dipped out into the garage, opting to take my SUV. The second I pulled out of the driveway, I reached out to the screen and pushed the button to dial Otto's number.

Knew he was going to be in a stir over what had happened.

It took all of one ring for him to answer. "You want to tell me what the fuck that was about?"

His voice was hard as it filtered through the speakers. Blowing out a sigh, I came up to the stop sign at Vista View, attention darting both ways to make sure it was clear before I made the left and headed in the direction of town.

"Charleigh thought someone was following her." The words were gravel, aggression coming back on the second I addressed it.

"Yeah, it was clear she was freaking the fuck out. Suffering a full-blown panic attack. Thing I want to know about is why it sent you bolting out the door like a beast ready to tear someone limb from limb right out in the light of day and with an audience. Looked to me a whole lot like you already knew she was in trouble. Want to tell me why that is?"

Otto was always as cool as they came. He wasn't acting so *cool* right then.

A harsh sigh raked from my lungs, and my hands clenched down on the steering wheel as I fought the wave of violence that threatened to suck me under. "When I went after her that Saturday night a couple weeks ago?"

"Yeah?"

Roughing a palm over my face, I let go of a heavy expulsion of air. "It wasn't because I was lookin' to get my dick sucked like the rest of you assholes were implying. Followed her because I could tell that something had her spooked."

Okay, it was only partially a lie. Because I wanted that girl's mouth wrapped around my cock almost as badly as I wanted to sink it into her pussy. Wanted it as badly as I wanted to go on a rampage to hunt down whoever was causing her this threat.

Wanted it more than I'd probably wanted anything in my life, which was so fuckin' twisted I knew I was teetering on a quickly crumbling cliff.

No chance was I letting that on to Otto.

"She'd frozen right in the middle of a spin out on the dance floor," I continued. "Like she'd run smack into a ghost. Then she'd panicked and taken off. Think you and I have seen that kind of fear enough times to know what it means, so I followed her home."

"Ah, shit," Otto muttered. Dude was instantly on guard, ready to step in. I knew he'd be. The whole crew would be.

But Otto and I both knew this was different.

She was here.

Friends with Raven.

And the girl had come running to me, not because she thought I was some obscure, faceless lifeline, but because she'd known she'd be safe in my arms.

And that was exactly where I wanted to keep her.

"I have no idea who it is, but I know enough to know she's afraid of someone. Apparently, she'd gotten the same sense she might be being followed earlier today, and that's when she came into the shop."

"Came into the shop? That's putting it mildly, River. That girl was in straight-up distress."

I sighed. "Know it."

"And?"

I didn't hesitate when I said, "And I took her back to my place."

Disbelief gusted out of him, and his tone lowered in concern. "You took her back to your place and not to the motel?"

It was against protocol. So against it, I deserved to get my ass beat. But there'd been no stopping myself from making that choice. Knowing there'd be no letting her out of my sight until I knew she was safe behind the walls of my house.

"You know I can't just roll up there without a plan," I defended.

"Oh, I think you had a plan, River, and I'm pretty sure that plan was to get that sweet little thing all to yourself."

"Like you don't go around getting attached." My words were barbs.

He scoffed. "I get attached because I'm worried about them. Because I care. Because I want to be sure they get on with their lives and they have the resources to do it. I still follow the rules and I follow them to a T, and I've never once dipped my dick in any of them."

"She came to me, not to Sanctum." I flexed my hand with the stacked Ss tattooed on the back.

Sovereign Sanctum.

My gut twisted. The rules were there for a reason, and I was the one who'd written them.

"Sounds to me like you're making excuses," he said.

Maybe, but they were still valid.

"She doesn't know anything about us. Who we are. Besides, I don't know what she's up against."

"And you've taken it upon yourself to find out?" It was a partial accusation.

"Yeah, you could say that."

On the other end of the line, I could feel Otto warring, unsure of what to say. Finally, he exhaled and muttered, "Just be careful, man. You know what we have riding on this. You start straying from the purpose, and the waters get muddied. It puts all of us in a precarious situation."

"Know it. I am being careful."

Nah, I was being fuckin' reckless, but I couldn't admit that.

"So what's your plan?"

"Going to call Cash. See what he can dig out."

"Without her knowing?"

"She's not ready to give me details, but I need to be prepared."

"Fuck, River, you're in deep, aren't you?"

I didn't try to fuckin' deny that one.

"Fuck," he wheezed before he continued with a sigh. "You have that job, man. Next week."

A boulder formed in the middle of my chest.

It was an extraction. We'd tried the normal avenues with her, trying to get her to safety without it getting messy, but her plans to leave had been uncovered by her piece of shit husband.

Now, there'd be no avoiding the *mess*. These jobs were the most dangerous. Ones where any number of things could go wrong. Ones where my special *skills* were often required.

"I'll be ready," I told him.

"Good."

It wasn't *good*, but we did it because it was right. No matter the consequence. No matter the price. I'd become a monster if it gave someone else a better life.

My ribs clamped around my heart as I thought about the woman who was back at my place. Wondering what treacherous shores she was battering against. If it was possible I could protect her from them, all while wondering if who I really should be protecting her from was me.

Silence traveled between us before he finally said, "You know, I've never seen you this way before."

It was both curious and a clear insinuation.

I shouldn't even honor him with a response, but I was taking his bait, anyway. "Seen me like what?"

"Smitten."

A scoff jumped right out of me. "Smitten? Believe me, brother, guys like me don't get *smitten.*"

"Well, I guess some people call it obsessed."

Irritation blazed through my system. "I'm not fuckin' obsessed."

He laughed hard. "Call it what you want, man, but I saw it written all over you this afternoon. Girl's got you."

My chest tightened. "That's bullshit, and you know it."

"Is it?"

"Just leave it, man," I warned him.

We both knew the rule.

We could fuck and play, but we could never make attachments. Could never get too close or allow anyone to really know who we were.

We had to go this life alone because we couldn't afford to have someone relying on us. Couldn't afford to take them down the precarious path we'd chosen.

Most of all, we could never risk being exposed.

Raven had already been my responsibility…and well, Nolan? He'd come into my life wholly unexpected, and he was the one exception I could ever make.

"Just wonderin' if it might be time to change up the rules a bit is all," Otto said, his musing taking on a benevolent tone.

Guilt constricted, knowing the line I'd already crossed by bringing Charleigh to my place. I scrubbed a palm over my face as I made it back into the main area of town.

"You know we can't do that."

"But how long can we really go on living this way?" he asked, a bit of longing filling the words.

The truth that we'd been living thin, even though we'd promised that having each other's backs would be enough. This mismatched family that had been forged through the flames. Through desperation and treachery.

Just a handful of fucked up kids living on the street who'd come to rely on each other to survive. And once we'd become members of Trent's MC, Iron Owls, we'd taken it full fledge.

Out of it, we'd discovered the one thing we had to offer this world.

"Don't know," I told him honestly.

"Do you ever wonder what would happen if we made this thing legit?"

Surprise jolted through me, disbelief at what he'd implied.

We'd started this thing crooked because that's what we'd been, and we kept it that way because we were a whole shit-ton more effective without having laws and chains and parameters to hold us back.

Thing was, it also made us criminals, and he and I both knew there was no going back.

"Maybe you need a break." I struggled to keep the dread out, the way my pulse had gone offbeat at the implication.

Otto sighed. "Nah, man, I'm just rambling. No need to worry."

A frown pulled at my brow. "You sure you're good?"

"Yeah."

"All right then. Take care, brother."

"Yeah, you, too."

The line went dead just as I was making the turn into the parking lot at the side of the building where Moonflower and Charleigh's apartment were housed. I pulled into a spot, looking up at the white bricks, wondering what the fuck I thought I was doing.

Did it anyway, though, because I couldn't sit back and be complacent, and I dialed Cash's number.

He answered on the second ring. "What's up, brother?"

"Need you to dig something out for me."

"Yeah?"

"Need all the information you can get me on Charleigh Lowe."

Chapter
TWENTY-NINE

Charleigh

"Is there a restroom I can use?"

Call it deflection, but I needed a second to gather myself. My body still burned from River's overpowering kiss, burned from the direction I'd been sure we'd been heading.

Then River had just left without an explanation, and I wasn't quite sure what to say or do with the way Raven was studying me right then.

"Right this way, Miss Charleigh!" Nolan sprang into action, grabbing my hand and hopping backward as he hauled me past Raven and back through the kitchen archway, down the hall, and to the door across from the laundry room.

"Here you go!" He pulled me inside the small powder room. "There is toilet paper and soap and a towel and every single thing you need but if you can't find somethin', you just let me know because I'm always at your service. I gotta take good care of our special guest."

He said it in his adorable lisp, and my heart rattled in my chest, taken by this child.

"I'm very happy to be your special guest," I told him, unable to do anything but run my fingertips over the dash of freckles on his chubby cheek.

"It's not even a little problem because I'm really glad you're here."

A clogged chuckle climbed up my throat. "I'm glad I'm here, too."

Without saying anything else, he went bounding out, and I closed the door and moved to the sink. Inhaling a steadying breath, I turned on the faucet and splashed water on my face, hoping the cold water would put out this fire.

I wasn't sure it was possible when I shut it off and looked at myself in the mirror. My cheeks were flaming red, and I was pretty sure the scuff of River's big hands was written all over me.

I grabbed one of the hand towels that were perfectly rolled on a shelf. I had it pressed to my face when the door suddenly burst open. I gasped, whirling that way to find Raven pushing through. She shut the door behind her, boxing us in, her voice dropped when she pressed, "Do you want to tell me what's going on?"

No. I absolutely didn't. I'd revealed enough today, hadn't I?

I placed the hand towel on the pedestal sink, focusing on it for a second before I turned to my friend who had her head cocked to the side.

Both curious and impatient.

My first friend I'd had in so long that she almost didn't seem real. One I'd been afraid of making for this very reason.

Because it exposed me.

Made me vulnerable.

Or a liar.

But I didn't want to be one of those. Not after she'd been so kind. Not when she'd come to mean more to me than I'd believed she could.

I blew out a sigh. "I thought I was being followed after work today, so I went to your brother's shop."

"What?" She screeched it as she flew forward and grabbed my hand, then she cringed and lowered her voice as she continued, "Someone was following you? Who?"

This was the part I didn't know how to answer. "I'm not sure. I just…got a sense that someone was watching me."

Her brown eyes widened as she was hit with the realization. "Is this what happened a couple weeks ago at the festival? You got that same sense when you were giving me that ridiculous line about going hiking because hello, who would go hiking when you could be hanging out with me, instead?"

I gave her a wary nod, and in return, hers was affirming. "I thought something more was happening than you were letting on."

I wasn't surprised.

I thought both she and her brother could see right through me.

Concern twisted her brow. "Is this something that's been going on? Is someone stalking you?"

I warred before I was whispering, "I got out of a bad relationship a while ago. It messed me up pretty badly, and I've always been afraid that it is going to catch up to me."

It was the truth without revealing too much.

Sorrow pulled through her expression, and I swore I saw her own ghosts flicker through her eyes. "I've been worried that's what it was. The reason you've been alone and afraid of trusting anyone. But you're not anymore. You're not alone."

She reiterated what she'd said at the café a couple weeks ago. Then speculation crowded into her expression. I couldn't tell if it was glee or disapproval. "And you ran to my brother so you wouldn't have to be alone."

It wasn't even a question.

My teeth clamped down on my bottom lip. Undoubtedly, the action served as a confession. And admission.

Her voice shifted in emphasis. "Good. My brother and his friends are exactly who you should turn to if you're in trouble. But the question I'm wondering is how it was that you felt comfortable to go to him?"

There was the prodding. Her expression hinting at the same thing she'd implied at the café. That River was wanting to claim me.

The problem was, that claiming would only be temporary, and I was afraid if I had too much of him, I was going to want it forever.

I inhaled. "We've been...texting."

Her nod was slow. "Yeah, I know."

"You do?"

She crossed her arms over her chest. "Like he could hide the way he's been slinking around here, acting all covert as he checked his phone every two minutes."

He was?

I wanted to smack myself that my chest glowed at the thought.

Her chuckle was low and overflowing with wry disbelief as she shook her head.

I scowled at her. "Why are you laughing like that?"

"Because it's just as it seemed."

"What is?"

"My brother wants you. Really wants you. Like…*really* wants you."

My skin tingled in all the places where he'd touched me.

"He's just being kind."

She laughed. Fully laughed. "Um, sorry to break it to you, Charleigh, but *kind* probably isn't something most would attribute to my brother. And if my brother brought you here? He might not admit it, but I'm pretty sure he plans on keeping you."

My heart fluttered. Damn it.

"No. We're just…friends."

"Friends?" she challenged.

I nodded with as much innocence as I could muster.

She didn't buy it for a second. "Has he kissed you?"

I might as well have been twelve with the way my cheeks flamed.

She gasped. "Have you two gotten naked?"

I had the urge to bury my head. "No, of course not."

"But he kissed you?" she prompted.

In unease, I shifted on my feet. "Are you mad?"

A frown cut through her features. "Why would I be mad?"

"I don't even know," I admitted. But whatever River and I were doing, it felt like a secret. Maybe because every element of my life had always needed to be that way.

She took my hand again, and her voice softened. "Of course I'm not mad, Charleigh. I love you both and I want you both to be happy. But my brother…"

She trailed off, hesitating, as if she wasn't sure she should admit whatever she'd been thinking.

"He has issues," she seemed to settle on.

I choked over a small, self-deprecating laugh. "Don't we all?"

"Oh yeah, the issues run rampant around here. Believe me. But River?"

I peered over at her, wondering what she would say. If she'd give voice to the ferocity that blazed from him. The viciousness. The danger.

My gut promised it wasn't superficial. Promised there was something hazardous woven in his layers.

Her voice whispered in stark affection. "His go deep, Charleigh. He doesn't believe he deserves to be loved or even happy, but he does. He deserves it more than anyone I know. If you understood the sacrifices he's made? What he did for me? The ones he continues to make for others? The only thing I've wanted is for him to find his joy."

She paused then tilted her head back a fraction. "Maybe you're the only one who can show him he deserves it."

"It's not like that with us." It rasped out of me. Our relationship had already been written. He'd vowed to be there for me, but only for a little while. It had to be enough. "I'm in no position to fall in love with anyone."

She reached out and ran her thumb over the outer edge of my eye. I didn't realize there was a tear there until she wiped it away. "You know, it's funny that he feels the same way. Life has a way of convincing us that we don't want something, or we don't have space for it, or we believe we're not even worthy of it. And sometimes what we need finds us, anyway."

There was suddenly a wild pounding at the door. "Hey, what are you guys doin' in there? You better not be havin' a party without me. I been waitin' out here for the whole day, and I almost don't have any of the patience left. And patience is somethin' Miss Liberty says I gotta have."

A small shot of amusement rolled off my tongue, and Raven snagged me by the hand as she whipped open the door. "What? Have a party without you? That would just be rude."

"The rudest." Nolan said it with a resolute jut of his chin.

Raven took Nolan's hand and started to haul us both back in the direction of the main house. "Since you mentioned party, I'm thinking that's exactly what we should have."

"Because I have smart ideas like my dad?" Nolan asked, jumping in the air with each step he took, his mass of curls bouncing around his adorable head.

"Um, heck yes, you have all the smart ideas like your dad." She shifted to look at me with a mischievous grin on her mouth. "You know, like bringing you here."

Chapter THIRTY

RIVER

I PUSHED OPEN THE GARAGE DOOR TO SOME KIND OF MAYHEM going down in my house.

Though it wasn't summoned by the wicked or iniquitous.

Nah.

There was no question this mess was compliments of my baby sister. Should have known better than to have left her to her own devices.

Taylor Swift was blaring from the built-in speakers, and a riot of laughter carried above it.

Raven's.

Nolan's.

I was pretty sure there was a spot of it from Charleigh, too. That sultry sound rolling through the air and aiming right for me.

It speared me straight in the chest when I rounded the corner of the opening to the kitchen and found the three of them in the middle of it, dancing around like fuckin' loons.

Nolan was on the ground, shouting, "Watch me!" as he spun on his butt, the kid's signature move, while my sister twirled with a glass of red wine lifted over her head, singing, "Go, Nolan, go, Nolan, go!"

And fuck me…Charleigh was laughing and giggling and being

adorable as shit as she was engaged in this awkward dance, trying to keep time yet totally off beat.

Still wearing those pink scrubs that shouldn't be sexy but never failed to send a bolt of electricity straight to my guts.

My sister grabbed Charleigh's hand, attempting to spin her, though the two of them got all tangled up as Charleigh tried to dip low enough to duck under my sister's arm.

Cracking up, Raven stumbled to the side like she'd already downed a whole bottle of wine, and Charleigh was giggling all over the place as she got taken with her.

Her smile radiant and wide.

My heart squeezed, as fucking unruly as my dick that jumped at the sight.

Nolan was the first to notice me, and he popped up off the floor and threw his hands over his head. "Hey, yo, Daddy-O!! You got here already? We're having a dance party, so you'd better get your booty over here."

With Nolan's welcome, Raven whirled my direction, her expression contorted in suspicion and delight. "That's right, get your cutie patootie over here and join us!"

She shimmied her hips, sloshing a bit of wine over her glass and onto the floor.

I grunted at her from where I loitered at the entryway.

She knew that shit wasn't about to happen. I didn't dance.

Charleigh had slowed to what was mostly a stop, and those cinnamon-flecked eyes widened a fraction, the caramel molten. They couldn't seem to sit still, and they took a little joyride, roving over my body like she'd forgotten my shape in the short time I'd been gone.

"Oh, come on, River," Raven whined like she thought her little pouty face was actually going to convince me to start dancing around in my kitchen.

I grunted again as I set the bags from the Chinese takeout place onto the counter.

"Whelp, even if he doesn't wanna dance with us, Auntie, he at

least brought food, and we gotta have food if we're gonna have a party."
There was my kid. Always sticking up for me.

"Guess he has to be good for something." Raven said it with all her sass, still shimmying her hips around, while Charleigh kind of just swayed back and forth, like she might be trapped in that spot.

Raven groaned and reached over to her phone she'd left on the counter and turned off the music. "Oh, fine, I see the dance party is officially over since the two of you are just standing there drooling over each other."

"You droolin', Dad?" Nolan peeped, oblivious to what Raven was implying. "You must really be hungry."

I couldn't pry my attention from the woman who remained rooted, skin flushed from dancing and wine, lips still swollen from my kiss.

Yeah. I was fuckin' famished.

"Oh, he's hungry, all right." Raven laid it on thick, her gaze keen as she strutted across the floor where she started to pull plates out of the cabinet.

I didn't even give my baby sister the benefit of an eyeroll.

"Well, I'm definitely hungry," Nolan hollered, skipping over to the bags of food. Holding onto the edge of the counter, he tried to jump high enough to see what was inside. "What'd you get me?"

Finally forcing myself to suck down the insane reaction the girl had over me, I turned to start unloading the white take-out containers. "Your favorite, of course."

"Orange chicken?" He might as well have won a million bucks with the way he shrieked it.

"Yup."

He threw himself at my leg, fully wrapping himself around it with his arms and legs, hanging off me like I was a jungle gym. He tipped his head back, looking at Charleigh upside down. "Told you I got the best dad in the whole wide world, Miss Charleigh. Except that he won't get me a puppy, but you got me one, so now I got everything I even need."

God. The way this kid managed to make my mangled heart throb.

"Yeah, I can see you have a really good dad." Charleigh murmured it in that raspy voice, emotion thick, and fuck, I didn't know what to do with her standing in my kitchen like this. Being here within my walls.

Never had brought anyone back to my place. Not once. It was our safe place. These walls were here to protect only those who meant the most to me.

And my knee-jerk instinct had been to bring her here.

I sucked the implications of it down, refusing to give it too much thought, and instead gave a little shake to my leg.

"All right, Little Dude, go sit down and I'll bring everything over."

He jumped off and went scampering over to the big island where we always ate.

Charleigh cleared her throat. "Is there anything I can help with?"

"Nah," I told her, gesturing toward the row of stools. "Take a seat. We'll take care of it."

"Sit right here, Miss Charleigh." Nolan smacked at the counter-top in front of the stool to his left. "We don't hardly never have any special guests unless my uncles come over, but they don't count as a guest because they are my family."

A soft laugh rippled from Charleigh as she slipped onto the stool next to him. "Thank you," she murmured.

"Did you know I got four uncles and one auntie?" Nolan told her, offering up his life story the way he always did.

"It sounds like you're a lucky boy to have so much family."

"I'm the luckiest! How many you got in your family?"

I didn't think I was the only one who felt Charleigh flinch when he asked it because Raven also slowed as she'd begun to set plates at each spot.

Sorrow swelled, flooding from the woman who tried to keep a smile on her face, though she failed, and the words were barely audible when she muttered, "I don't really have a family."

"What do you mean, you don't got a family?" A compassionate sort of horror rippled out with his question. "How come?"

Charleigh hesitated then whispered, "Because I lost them."

"Well, I guess you'll just have to be our family since you don't have any," he said, spilling his innocence.

Charleigh fought to plaster a smile to her face, though it was brittle, and that glowing, pretty skin had turned a pale, sallow white.

Didn't like much the way it slayed me seeing her that way. Way it made me feel like I was getting flayed alive, taken down to bare bones where the rot and decay was exposed.

The way it took everything I had to remain standing where I was and not go running to her and taking her in my arms.

Giving her false promises that it would be okay.

So fuckin' reckless.

But the urge was there.

Charleigh fully shifted on the stool, turning to face him as she touched his cheek. "That is the sweetest, kindest thing anyone has ever offered me, Nolan, and I think you might be the sweetest, kindest boy that I've ever met. But I don't want you to be sad when it's time for me to leave here. You have your family, and I may not be a part of it, but I promise, I'll always be your friend, even when I'm not here any longer."

"Family's just the people you love the most." Nolan shrugged. "And I love you, so that's gotta mean you're my family, too."

He said it nonchalant, like it was the simplest thing in the world, when it was nothing but profound.

Emotion crested the room. The overpowering kind. The kind that made it feel like you couldn't move.

Raven was the one who broke it by grabbing the bottle of wine and refilling Charleigh's glass before she lifted her own and said, "Now, I will drink to that."

Chapter
THIRTY-ONE

Charleigh

I WASN'T SURE HOW I WAS SUPPOSED TO SIT THERE AND SHARE A meal with them after what Nolan had said. How I was supposed to sit on that stool wedged between the little boy who'd wrecked my heart in the biggest way and the man who vibrated like a beast on the other side of me.

How I was just supposed to sit there and eat Chinese food as if this were just another day.

Not to mention Raven who was on the other side of Nolan, perched on her stool, though she had it angled so she could see both River and me as she chatted on like I hadn't just gotten the rug ripped out from under me.

Tossed from my feet.

Though rather than crashing to the unforgiving ground, I felt as if I was floating. Floating on clouds and rays of sunshine and an aurora of hope.

But I should know that I couldn't stay there.

I should know I would fall.

And I was terrified when I did that I was going to fall hard.

So hard and fast that when I did finally strike the ground, it would be rock bottom. Because right then I couldn't fathom a scenario when I wasn't right here, surrounded by this care and easiness.

By the laughter and the teases.

By the heat that radiated from River on hot gusts of air. The way it'd crawl over me each time our legs brushed under the stool, and I felt like I couldn't breathe.

"Do you like the orange chicken, Miss Charleigh? I bet you like it as much as I do!" Nolan asked, wholly immune to the fact that each word that came from his mouth knitted me in comfort.

Each one weaving through my loss and pain, stitching the pieces back together as if they could become one.

I took another bite and struggled to swallow around the thickness in my throat. "I think it's delicious."

"You think we got the same taste buds?"

A soggy giggle escaped me.

I guessed I was enraptured.

Taken.

Mesmerized.

"We might."

"One thing's for sure, I have amazing taste because I picked you for my best friend." Raven enthused it around a big bite of Lo Mein before she pointed her fork in my direction.

"Hey, I picked her, too, Auntie."

"Not even, Nolan. I was the one who saw her passing by on the sidewalk, and I chased her down so I could meet her. That means I picked her first."

"Well, I picked her second," Nolan mumbled around a bite of eggroll.

An almost inaudible growl emanated from River, and I nearly came out of my skin when he set his hand on the top of my thigh and squeezed. He leaned in and pressed his mouth to my ear, words so low as they raked across my cheek. "Nah. I saw you first. Wanted you first. Think that means you're mine."

There was no shaking the single word from my brain through the rest of dinner.

Mine.

I couldn't be.

He'd already warned me it would never be that way, and I knew I would likely never stay.

But God, I wanted to sink into the idea. The idea of doing this every night. Sharing a meal with these people.

With this *family.*

Nolan had climbed to his knees on his stool, and he straightened, rubbing his belly while he pushed it out as far as he could. "Look it, Miss Charleigh. I ate all my dinner and now I'm all the way full."

I could do nothing but poke it with my finger. "What? I think you could fit way more in there."

He gasped and shrieked and grabbed at my hand. "Well, I gotta save a little spot because it's movie night, and I gotta have popcorn with my movie. Right, Daddy-O?"

I glanced over at River. My stomach tilted. The man was so viciously handsome it was painful to look at him.

"Thursday night is movie night, yeah."

I glanced between them all. "Every Thursday?"

"Yep! Because I really like movies but I gotta limit my screen time."

My spirit swam, and I tried to make sense of how this man who was lined in brutal bone and written in grisly ink made sure that this little boy limited his screen time.

Raven pushed her stool back with a screech of the legs and a chuckle from her throat. "River likes Disney flicks more than any of us. He'll never admit it, but he's nothing but a big softie."

His dark eyes narrowed. "Nothin' soft about me."

Giggling, she waltzed over, carrying her plate and wine, and planted a kiss on top of his head. "Nothing but that melty heart of yours."

Another grunt.

She cracked up like it was hysterical. "See. So sensitive."

Irritation flashed through his expression, and I tried to hide the laugh that rolled up my throat.

"Watch yourself," he said. That warning was for me, stealing the air from my lungs.

Raven tittered, enjoying the show too much. "All right, I'm going to toss these plates into the dishwasher really quick, then we can do this thing."

"Yes!" Nolan shouted, and he climbed onto his feet and jumped off the stool, landing in a chaotic thud on the ground. "Let's do this thing!"

"Nolan, you know the rules. No jumping off the furniture. You forget the last time you took a tumble and knocked your tooth out?" River asked him as he wiped his mouth with a napkin.

Nolan shrugged. "Well, I got to meet my Miss Charleigh that day, so I think it was a good sacrifice. That's what love's all about, right, Dad? Sacrifice? My dad told me that."

On the last, the child looked at me.

My stomach ached.

My heart ached.

My body ached.

Ached in the best of ways.

God. I was being an idiot. Getting so cozy like this. Acting as if I might be able to carve a spot for myself in their lives.

Giggling, Raven lifted her brows at River. "How are you going to argue with that?"

River was shaking his head as he stood and began to gather the empty boxes, the man so big beside me, the muscles of his arms bristling as he leaned around me to reach for a box in the middle of the island.

His chest brushed my shoulder.

I wanted to turn and press my face into his shirt. Breathe him in. The leather and the ink and the masculinity.

"Kid's a master manipulator, that's for sure," he grumbled.

Nolan tsked. "Hey, Dad, you gotta know I just got important things to say."

A chuckle rumbled around in River's chest, warm and filled with adoration. "Yeah, buddy, guess you just have really important things to say."

River moved around the island and pulled out a drawer where the garbage was located and started tossing boxes into the compost bin, while Raven began piling dishes into the dishwasher.

Standing, I wound around to Raven's side and nudged her to give me some space. "Let me help."

She swung her attention to me, and the softest smile played on her pretty face. "Told you." The words were hushed.

I frowned.

She angled her head. "That we're what you've been missing."

Twenty minutes later, the kitchen was cleaned and popcorn was popped.

Apparently, the thing River had needed to take care of when he'd left was going by my apartment to ensure no one had been there, though he'd returned with a duffle bag full of my things.

I hadn't known whether to be angry over the clear overstep—the invasion of privacy—or be grateful, though I could say for certain that it didn't surprise me.

He wasn't exactly the kind of guy who played by rules and boundaries.

I'd gone upstairs to a guest room he'd said was mine for as long as I needed it and had changed into a pair of sweats and a tank before I'd come back downstairs.

Raven was still up in her room, changing, too.

Nolan had a big plastic bowl tucked against his chest, his little arms barely able to circle around it. "All ready! I get to pick the movie."

"You always do," River mumbled from behind me, though there was nothing aggravated in his tone, just that gruff support he always seemed to carry when it came to the child.

"Dad," Nolan drew out with a longsuffering sigh. "Thought we already figured it out that I have really good taste."

Amusement rippled through me as I followed Nolan out of the kitchen. The floors were cool on my bare feet, and the very last vestiges of the light were getting sucked away by the darkness that crawled across the sky.

I was surprised when Nolan bypassed the oversized sofa in the family room and instead carried on down the hall that ran to the other side of the house to a set of double doors on the left.

"Open it up, Daddy-O," he called, kicking out a foot since both of his hands were occupied with the popcorn.

"Yes, sir," River teased, those murky eyes gleaming when he angled around and let his gaze wash over me. He opened the door and stood aside.

Nolan rushed in, and the little guy shifted around to shower me in his excitement. "Look it, Miss Charleigh! We got our very own movie theater. What do you think?"

Okay, it wasn't quite a movie theater, but it was impressive.

An enormous black leather sectional faced a giant screen that covered the entirety of the wall on our right, plus about six different beanbags that looked like they were made for two people were tossed randomly on the floor in front of it. Throw pillows and blankets were strewn all over the place.

Movie posters lined the walls.

All cartoons.

Nolan had started for the couch when he whirled around. "Oh, wait, I forgot somethin' really very important."

He came beelining back my direction, sending kernels of popcorn slinging over the sides of the bowl. "Hold this for me for only one minute. I'll be right back so fast."

He shoved the bowl into my hands before he went blazing back through the door, and I could hear the pounding of his little feet as he clambered up the hardwood stairs to the second level above.

In it, the air shifted, and I could feel River's presence swell behind me. The second we were alone, his being rising high and taking over.

A pillar in the darkness that towered over me.

Warily, I turned to look back at him, trying to school my nerves that went sailing through me at the sight of him.

Standing in the doorway, shoulders so wide that they nearly touched each side. His expression fierce and indulgent.

"How are you feeling?" he asked, voice scraping in that gruff way as he took a step deeper into the enclosed, dimly-lit room.

The thud of his boots reverberated the ground and sent a shiver rolling through me. "Better."

His stormy gaze raked over me as if he were searching for proof. "Good."

How that one word could make me tremble, I wasn't sure. "Did you see anything when you went to my apartment?" I asked.

We hadn't gotten the chance to discuss it. He'd only given me the bare details when he'd led me upstairs to the room, though Nolan had been with us, so he'd kept it short.

His exhalation was weighted. "No. Not a fuckin' trace."

I bit down on my bottom lip, not sure if I should find comfort in that or be worried. But being here? Within the safety of his walls? The fear of this afternoon felt distant.

My worries unwarranted.

So, I whispered, "I probably was making it up."

A harsh sound rolled in his chest. "Don't fuckin' minimize it, Charleigh. If there is someone after you, I swear to God I'm going to—"

His words cut off when Raven suddenly burst into the room, wearing a pair of baggy sweats and a tight tank, her black hair twisted into a wild knot on the top of her head. The makeup she'd been wearing had been cleaned from her face. "Are we gonna do this or what?"

She was all grins.

A clatter of little feet came banging in behind her.

"Got it!" Nolan was waving the stuffed puppy I'd gotten him over his head, excitement blazing from his sweet soul. "We can do it now!"

"What are we watching, Little Dude?" River asked as he pushed a couple buttons on a console on the wall closest to the door.

"Super Pets!" Nolan sent a fist sailing for the air, then he was grinning his sweet grin in my direction. "Because I'm gonna get me one of those real puppies one day, Miss Charleigh. Or maybe five of 'em."

That time he held up five fingers.

River groaned, and Raven laughed.

"What did you think was going to happen, taking him to that fundraiser?" she goaded.

River sent her a glare. "And who forced me into going?"

She shrugged innocently. "It was for a good cause."

"Yeah, Dad, it's for a good cause. The puppies gotta have a house."

"Thought we talked about this, yeah?" River tried to defend. "We need to wait a bit before we get a dog. It's a big responsibility."

"I already waited two whole weeks, and I got really mature."

River gave him a look and Nolan dropped his head, scuffing his little feet on the floor. "Okay, fine. Least I got my favorite blue puppy."

I pressed my fingers to my mouth like I could hide the laugh gathered in my chest, but it got loose, anyway.

Raven sent me a winning, knowing smile as she crossed the room and plopped onto the far side of the couch. She grabbed a fluffy blanket, brought her knees to her chest, and curled up under it. "Now bring me some of that popcorn, bestie!"

"Yeah, bring us some of that popcorn, bestie!" Nolan mimicked as he climbed up beside her.

River just shook his head, and God, I couldn't help the smile. The smile that bloomed somewhere deep inside and erupted on my face.

I was sure this was the most genuine emotion I'd felt in a long, long time.

The speck of joy that pulled at my spirit.

And that was terrifying.

River reached out and flicked off the lights, and the only illumination in the darkened space was the screen that flickered to life.

I shifted on my feet, unsure of what to do as River started across the room, his enormous body a silhouette in the lapping shadows. He barely brushed his fingers over my hip as he passed by, eliciting a shock of electricity.

When he got to the couch, he scooped Nolan up and planted

him on his lap, the man a giant sitting there with the tiny child tucked against him.

"You comin' or what?" he issued in that deep, low voice, eyes on me.

I gulped and crossed the space, then I handed the bowl of popcorn to Nolan before I decided to play it safe and went to sit on one of the beanbags.

"No, Miss Charleigh, you gotta sit by us!" Nolan cried.

I should have resisted.

Refrained.

Claimed one of the beanbags.

Retreated upstairs.

Or maybe—maybe I should have run in the first place.

Maybe I should have never run to River.

Because I was certain there was no chance to stop the fall when I sat down on the other side of River and Nolan.

I tried to press myself as close to the armrest as I could, desperate to put some distance between me and the man who was emitting a thousand degrees of heat. To put some distance between the memory of our kiss from earlier.

To just make sense of what it was that I thought I was doing.

Did I really think I could withstand another breaking?

Apprehension billowed through me as the consequences of the choices I'd made since I'd come here caught up to me. The hardest part was figuring out what to do with the hope that had bloomed within it.

A chill rolled through me, and River reached back and grabbed a throw blanket from the back of the couch and handed it to me, and he leaned in close to my ear and whispered, "Get cozy, Little Runner. You aren't going anywhere."

Chapter
THIRTY-TWO

RIVER

Twenty-Two Years Old

HEAVY METAL REVERBERATED THROUGH THE WALLS OF THEIR MC's club where River was slung against the wall in the side alley. He inhaled a deep drag of his smoke before he rocked his head back and exhaled toward the blackened sky. He watched the vapor twist and curl before it disappeared into the nothingness above.

The sound of the city night shouted all around. The howl of the sirens and the blare of horns and the random gunshot that ricocheted through the air.

When he felt the movement, he shifted to cast a glance at the door to find Trent stepping out. Trent was their VP, though River respected him a thousand times over their actual Pres, Cutter, who was a fuckin' psychopath. River had come to the quick realization that he couldn't be trusted.

But Cutter was Trent's father, and since River's loyalty was to Trent, he didn't say much. He kept his fuckin' mouth shut and did his duty. Trent was the one who'd given him and his sister and the rest of his crew shelter when they'd been little more than kids running the streets.

Now they *ran* the streets.

Taking another drag of his cigarette, he lifted his chin toward Trent. "How's that tat, brother?"

River had been dabbling in the art, taking the sketches he'd drawn for as long as he could remember and bringing them to life with ink.

He had to admit, he found some kind of satisfaction in the work.

Trent dug into his pocket to pull out a smoke, and he leaned against the wall next to River. "It's good fuckin' work, man."

He wiggled his right hand where he'd gotten a skull and rose. "Seems you've got some prospects outside of this life."

River shook his head as he exhaled. "Nah, man, you know this is in my blood."

"You do good at that, too. Ride was clean last night."

It was the one part of this that had never sat right. Running drugs. People were fucked as it was without them being blitzed out of their minds. Families ruined.

His gut twisted, thinking how he'd feel if his baby sister got tangled in something like that.

Trent hesitated, itching as he looked around before he started to speak toward his boots. "Wanted to warn you that I think there might be a shift coming."

Uncertainty squeezed River's chest. "What kind of shift?"

"Some shit's going down. Think my brothers and I are gonna have to split."

"Fuck," River mumbled toward the ground as he ran an agitated hand through his hair. Knew what that meant. The implications.

Last thing River wanted was to be under the thumb of Cutter Lawson.

Trent was the only reason he was there.

"Keep it on the low, yeah? Not sure what's going to happen. Just wanted you to know so you can prepare."

"Of course, brother."

Trent squeezed his shoulder. "Know I can count on you."

Then he pushed from the wall and disappeared back into the club.

River blew out a frustrated sigh, dread pounding through his bloodstream. He straightened and started out of the alleyway and headed out front. He bypassed his bike that sat among the thirty-odd others lining the front of the club.

He needed to walk.

Think.

He shoved his hands into his pockets as he took to the sidewalk. It was after one in the morning, and that seedy drone had taken to the atmosphere. The drone of trucks as they passed on the freeway in the distance, the barking of dogs, those sirens that never ceased.

He took a left and headed down a narrower street. It was lined by shitty apartment buildings and bowed in poverty.

Guilt constricted again. Knowing he was a part of the problem. He did his best to ignore the begging he heard through an open window above.

A woman pleading, "No...please stop...I didn't do it."

He heard the slug that was undeniably a punch.

She wailed. Wailed and begged.

River tried to keep moving. To mind his own business. But he was scaling the fire escape on the side of the building. One second later, he was inside the crummy apartment, looming behind the piece of shit who towered over a battered woman on the floor.

The man went to kick her in the face with his boot, and River was on him without him knowing, his knife drawn from his pocket and flicked open. The man flailed and tried to whirl, but River outsized him at least by double. River pulled the bastard's head back by the hair and he dragged the knife across his throat.

Not one fuckin' hesitation.

The woman screamed and screamed.

River let him go, and the man slumped to the floor.

He turned to the woman who was scrambling back, her screams turning to whimpers as she begged, "Please, no."

Terror blanketed her eyes, and he carefully knelt in front of her as he murmured, "I'm not going to hurt you."

"The fuck are we supposed to do with her?" Theo's voice was hushed where River and his crew were huddled in the corner of the abandoned building down the street. "We can't take her to the fuckin' cops."

She was across the room, shaking where River had wrapped her in a blanket.

"Obviously," Otto said, frustration dripping from his tone.

River dragged both hands over his head. Knowing the situation he'd put his crew in, but that didn't mean he felt any regret.

He'd do it a thousand times over.

Even if it meant he was going to jail for the rest of his life.

"How the fuck we're going to keep her quiet is the question we should be asking," Kane said.

It was Cash who spoke up from where he leaned hidden in the corner that halted the conversation. "We need to get her a new identity. She can't exist anymore. She needs to disappear."

"How the hell do we make that happen?" Theo asked.

Except we all knew.

Cash was Iron Owls' hacker. The one who made whatever he wanted appear…or disappear.

Money.

Cars.

Mostly records of people the club had put in the ground.

"You can do that?" Otto's brow twisted. "Fully do that, and she can start a new life?"

"Yeah. But that means she has to go all in. Accept that it means she is no longer Angela Burkin. And she can never say a fuckin' word otherwise."

"And you trust her to do that?" Skepticism poured out of Theo, and he was looking at River when he asked it.

River hesitated then moved. The woman flinched at his approach, though there was something in her expression that made him press forward. He dropped to a knee in front of her, his voice soft. "You want a new life?"

She laughed like it was absurd. "What do you mean, a new life?"

"To start over. As a different person. We get you someplace else. Set you up. Angela Burkin no longer exists, and neither do we."

He let his eyes convey what that meant.

His life was riding on this, too.

Her gaze dropped then she said, "I had no life. Maybe now, I can."

Chapter
THIRTY-THREE

Charleigh

I BLINKED MY EYES OPEN TO THE FILMY DIMNESS OF THE ROOM, nudged awake by the quieted movement in front of me.

During the movie, Nolan had slipped off his father's lap and had climbed over to me and had snuggled into my side. I'd wrapped my arm around him, covered him with the blanket, and had held him while we'd watched the movie play out.

At some point, we'd both drifted to sleep, and I woke to him sleeping in my arms, his little breaths panted into my neck.

My heart beat steadily, slow and full, and I hugged him to me for a moment before I realized it was River who'd stirred me from sleep.

Carefully, he pulled a slumbering Nolan out of my arms and into his, and the child made a happy, unintelligible sound as he was picked up. River's voice was a mere breath in the quiet as he spoke to me. "Stay right there, I'll be right back."

He rose high, covering me in a wedge of his darkness, appearing so massive where he was backlit by the screen that had been running credits.

A fortress.

A tower.

Stony, majestic beauty.

Looking at him right then was like standing at the edge of a cliff in the middle of the night and peering into the depths of a raging, toiling sea below. Fear drumming through my senses because I knew I was in danger, all while there was a heedless part of me that urged I take a step forward and fall into the abyss.

Holding Nolan, he crossed the room, and in the hazy grogginess, I drifted off again in a comfort I shouldn't possess, but instead felt wholly cocooned in the sanctuary of it.

I didn't know how much time had passed before my eyes were blinking open again and River was there, on his knees in front of me.

So big that even on his knees he loomed.

Shorn hair distinct in the night, the outline of his rugged, gorgeous face hidden in the shadows that eclipsed the room.

He pulled the blanket off me, tossing it aside before he slipped his hands beneath me so he could pull me into his arms.

He stood, and a breathy sigh whispered out of me as I curled my arms around his neck.

Trusting him the way I'd told him that I did.

Still, my insides quivered. Both in trepidation and anticipation. My stomach in knots and my heart battering wildly at my chest.

"Got you," he rumbled, and he carried me out of the room. The thud of his boots was muted as he slowly climbed the stairs. At the landing, he went right down the hall, though he passed by the guest room where my things had been left and carried me all the way to a set of double doors at the end.

He shifted enough that he could undo the latch, and he led us into the lapping shadows of an enormous bedroom. There was a giant bed covered in black linens in the middle of the far wall, but rather than take me to it, he crossed to the left side where a loveseat sat against the wall near a rock fireplace.

My body trembled as he placed me on the soft, velvety leather. The man so tall. Obliterating reason and sight.

My nerves scattered when he slowly eased down onto his knees, and he planted his hands on either side of me as he leaned forward.

His devastatingly beautiful face was an inch away, and I stretched out a trembling hand and set it on his cheek. Heat blistered at the contact, a fire that flashed through my system. The words were craggy when I spoke. "Thank you."

"You don't have to thank me, Charleigh." His voice was gruff as ever. Low in the room, as if we weren't alone and we were trying to keep from waking someone.

Energy glinted, tying the oxygen in knots that I had to squeeze in and out of my lungs.

"Why not?"

His head barely shook. "Because this is what I do."

"What? Rescue damsels in distress?" I tried to play it a tease, but the air was too heavy for any lightness to stick.

His scoff was soft. "You're no damsel in distress, fighting me every step of the way."

"It's all I've ever known how to do."

River covered my hand that still rested on his cheek with his and pressed it closer. "Going to show you that you don't have to do that anymore. You don't have to run. You don't have to be afraid. You can stand in the beauty of who you are. And you, Charleigh Lowe, are the epitome of beauty. Inside and out. Everything about you makes me want to lose my mind. Gonna drive me out of my head, Little Runner."

My spirit shuddered in strained affection. In the feeling that this man summoned in me. He'd stoked the ashes and brought long-dead pieces to life.

I wanted to revel in them forever.

"I think you're the one who's made me lose mine. I still can't believe I'm here. That I spent tonight with you and your family."

The threat of a smirk hinted at the edge of his mouth. "If you talk to Nolan, he'd insist you were a part of that, too."

Family.

I was shocked he would even mention it.

"But we know that can't be, don't we?" My fingertips were still brushing his face, gliding over the scruff that lined his sharp jaw.

"How about we don't talk about me having to let you go and instead focus on this."

"And what is this?" It was a breath.

"It's me showing you that you are in control. Me showing you that you deserve pleasure. Me erasing that motherfucker from your being and writing myself on it instead. Gonna mark myself on you as deep as that tat on your arm. Permanently. Make you remember exactly what you want. What you need."

Need raced through my body. "I'm afraid you're going to break me."

He brushed the pad of his thumb over my lips. On instinct, my tongue stroked out to lick it.

His eyes flamed as he released a surprised growl that reverberated through the room, and he pressed his thumb into my mouth.

I sucked, and a moan got free.

A storm roared in his gaze before arrogance kicked up at the edge of his mouth. "Nah, I'm not going to break you, Charleigh, I'm just going to ruin you for anyone else."

The man rose higher on his knees as I sank deeper into the couch cushions.

Anticipation made my limbs heavy. Laden with want.

"Did you know how fuckin' bad I wanted you when you came through the door of my shop that first night?" he asked. "Did you know how badly I wanted to peel you out of your clothes and take you right on my chair? I've spent weeks fucking my hand to thoughts of you. Thinkin' about every way that I'm going to have you."

The vision of it blazed through my mind, and my thighs quivered as I was rushed with a current of desire.

He inhaled heavily as if he smelled it coming off me, and he pulled his thumb from my mouth and ran it over my lips, coating them with my saliva.

My throat went dry, but still, I managed to force out, "I haven't wanted anyone to touch me in years, for so long that I'd forgotten what it's like. And my breath was gone the second you came to stand in the doorway to your station. Though it might have had something to do with the way you terrified me, too."

River's expression went predatory. "You should probably still be scared."

"Part of me is. Of this. Of what you make me feel."

His eyes turned to pitch, greed dancing in their depths, prancing with the shadows that played on the walls. His thumb moved to my jaw as the rest of his fingers splayed out to hold me by the side of the neck.

My pulse beat frantically against his touch.

"I don't let my mind go there when I'm tattooing, not ever, and there you were, making me break every rule I've ever set, and I've been wanting to break them ever since."

"What rules?" It was a rasp, wispy thin air that no longer seemed to exist.

"I don't get numbers, I don't stand outside women's apartments, and I sure as fuck don't invite them to my house." Leaning in close, his mouth just barely brushed the angle of my jaw. He rode it all the way up until he was murmuring at my ear, "And most of all, I don't fuckin' get attached."

My spirit flailed, and logic screamed. We already knew what this was. He was a safe place. Sanctuary. A place of healing.

But right then, my heart was veering into dangerous territory.

He edged back and pinned me with the viciousness of his stare. "Gonna warn you right now, I'm not a good man, Charleigh. Need you to know it so you don't mistake me for something I'm not."

"I already know who you are, River. I know who you are right here." I let my fingertips wander down to the ravaging in his chest. "I don't care about the rest."

"Fuck," he groaned, and he wound his hand up in my hair and pulled me toward him until our noses were almost touching. "But you should. You should. I've done terrible fuckin' things."

Turmoil played through his features. His ghosts. His shame.

"But you've also done wonderful things."

I knew pure evil. I recognized it. Had lived it. And while there was no question that something brutal lived within him, I still understood *this*.

I had witnessed him with his son and his sister and felt it with the way he had treated me.

The quiet laughter he emitted was malignant, fully directed at himself. "If you really knew, you'd go running so far and fast there'd be no chance of me catching up to you." Then his voice dropped to a seductive threat as he edged in an inch. "And even knowing it, I still think I'd chase after you."

"I wouldn't get very far because you already have me on my knees."

An offering.

Or maybe I wanted him to be an offering for me.

Give this part of himself because I needed it so desperately. To feel something other than the grief. Other than the loneliness. Other than the fear.

A puff of hot air shot from his nose, and the man turned all beast. Muscles rippled and flexed beneath the tight fit of his tee, and in the muted light, the colors and shapes and innuendo crawled like monsters over his flesh.

I could almost see the demons writhe.

River unwound his hand from my hair, and he edged back and placed both hands on my knees.

A shiver rolled, yet still, I felt as if I were being burned alive. His eyes were flames that licked over every inch of my body. I arched from the couch as if he had me chained by his gaze and he'd given my shackles a yank.

"You gonna let me touch this tight little body the way I've been dyin' to?" His words had gone fierce.

My center throbbed, and my knees spread.

His tongue swept out to lick across his lips. "That an invitation, Little Runner?"

And there was nothing I could do. I whispered, "Yes."

Chapter
THIRTY-FOUR

RIVER

Yeah, my little runner was going to ruin me. I knew it. I felt her breaking me apart as she sat there gazing up at me with so much trust and desire in her expression that she might as well have cut me open with a knife.

Wasn't sure how either of us were going to survive this, but the one thing I was certain of was neither of us were going to be the same.

Guessed I hadn't been since I'd seen her standing inside my shop's door.

Girl wrecking my world and turning it upside down.

A roll of greed rumbled in my chest as I edged back enough to take the entirety of her in.

The woman was wearing these fitted black sweats and this tight white tank that fit her in all the right ways. Chestnut hair mussed from where I'd been gripping it. Her lips were still pink and plump from our kisses earlier.

Body just barely beginning to writhe as desire slowly wound her into desperation.

"Looking at you is like looking at the sun breaking on a new day and wishing I could hold onto that moment forever. That's what I'm going to give you, Charleigh. A million new days where you get to wake up and shine all your light. Shower this world in your beauty because there's so fuckin' much of it, it's a disgrace to keep it hidden. Gonna make you shine, Little Runner. Fuckin' glow."

Her thighs trembled, need throbbing so heavy that I could already taste her arousal on my tongue.

My cock was stone, pushing painfully at my jeans, and I ran my palms up the inside of her legs. She arched as I went, though her fingers were gliding into the short pieces of my hair at the top of my head like she was looking for something to hold onto.

For a way to keep herself from floating away.

I could feel her anxiety, too. Nerves rattling her to the bone as she shivered and shook, right as my name dropped like a plea from her delicious mouth. "River."

"I've got you, Charleigh. I've got you."

"Please."

"I've got nothing but pleasure in store for you."

Her hands on my head urged me forward, and I let my lips press to the curve of her jaw as I inhaled.

Cinnamon and clove.

Might as well have been taking a deep, sating drink.

Except I didn't think I could ever get close enough. Didn't think I could ever *get* enough.

I let my mouth wander down the slope of her neck, lips barely suckling as I edged downward.

On a wispy sigh, Charleigh tipped her chin back, granting me better access. My palms slid up, moving from her thighs to circle her waist. My mouth kept progressing south, devouring all the flesh I could get to as I moved over the exposed skin on her chest.

"You nervous?" I rumbled as my lips caressed down to the scooped neckline of her tank, kissing over the thrashing of her heart and dipping just below the fabric to inhale the sweet skin of her cleavage.

Her nod was erratic. "A little. But I want you more than the fear."

"I would never hurt you." The promise dropped out of me without permission, and I prayed to fuck that I wouldn't. That I could see her through this without dragging her into the depraved depths of who I was.

"I know." It was a wheeze as she arched forward, baring more of herself, her fingers tugging at my hair.

Hard enough that it pricked.

And fuck. I liked it. This girl clamoring for what she wanted.

"If it's good with you, I'm going to take your shirt off because I'm goin' to need to see these pretty tits." Had been dreaming of them since that first night, when she'd been panting on my chair, just like she was doing now.

Body quivering in a need that had taken her whole.

"I think I'm good with anything. I trust you. I trust you." It whooshed from her mouth, and fuck, my chest squeezed tight.

With greed.

With lust.

With that thing that was so much bigger than just the want. This compulsion. This overwhelming reaction she elicited in me.

Like the girl was wielding magic.

Making me dream of things that were never meant for me.

But for a little while, I was going to pretend I could be every fucking thing she needed.

My fingers slipped under the hem of her tank, and I eased back and slowly peeled it up.

Chills lifted in its wake, and her hair tumbled around her shoulders as I tugged it over her head and dropped it to the floor.

She heaved a breath as she sat there staring at me.

Vulnerable and bared.

Most stunning creature I'd ever seen.

She had on a pink, satiny bra, the cups pushing up her small tits.

"Fuck me. You're a vision, Charleigh. A fuckin' fantasy that I don't ever want to stop dreaming."

I circled my thumb over her left breast, right over her satin-covered nipple.

She gasped and arched. "River."

"Look at you, already imploring, and I've barely begun. Going to make you feel so good, Little Runner, so good that every time this needy little pussy starts throbbing, you're always going to come running back to me."

Fuck. I kept saying things I shouldn't. But they poured out like a well that could no longer contain life-giving water.

I tugged the left cup down and exposed her nipple that was just as pink as her bra. Puckered and pebbled and peaked.

Begging for attention.

I leaned in and nipped it with my teeth before I curled my lips around it, giving it a suck.

Charleigh rasped an incoherent rush of words, and her hips jutted from the couch.

Yeah. Her pussy was begging for attention, too.

I suckled and licked while I pulled the opposite cup down and pinched that nipple between my thumb and forefinger, rolling it as I rolled the other with my tongue.

Her fingers were yanking at my hair to the point of pain, and fuck, I liked it. Liked her trying to claw her way to get close to me. The zings that were ripping down the back of my skull and shooting straight to my dick.

Her hands moved, nails raking down my back and fisting in the fabric of my tee, struggling to drag it up.

A rough chuckle skated free as I edged back a fraction. "You wanna take a look at me, Little Runner?"

She gave me an erratic nod, that mesmerizing gaze doing wild, wild things. "Yes. I want to see you."

"All yours, gorgeous."

Was pretty sure it was true. I was all hers. This girl could ask anything of me, and I'd give it to her.

She pulled up the tee, and I helped her by winding out of it, and she nudged me back by the shoulders until I was hovering two feet away from her.

Hungry eyes raked my torso.

Taking in the atrocities I'd carved on myself. The graphic scenes. Life and death and obscenity. Gnarled, twisted faces, phantoms and wraiths, a haunting written across my body because it was the only thing I'd known.

Her regard darted all over, as if she were taking stock, reading me, and stowing the information away.

She should be repulsed, but she let go of a ragged breath as she let her fingertips drift from where *No Mercy* was tatted on the front of my throat, all the way over the five demons I'd marked on my pecs, down to my abs that were hard as stone with the amount of restraint it took me not to dive in and devour.

"How are you so beautiful?"

My chuckle was raw. "Not sure what you're seeing, baby."

"I'm seeing you."

I should have rejected it, the way she was looking at me like she could see through the years of hardened scars that covered me like armor. Like she was witnessing my sins play out on a reel, had direct access to my memories, and she might still want to be there with me, anyway.

"It's you who's beautiful. You who knocks the wind out of me every time I look at you." I dipped back in, kissing across both of her nipples, before I kissed up her chest and to her jaw. Then I dove back in and took that delicious mouth.

Cinnamon and spice.

Girl knocking through me. Pure intoxication.

Fingertips sank into my shoulders, raking and ripping, urging me closer.

Our tongues tangled, mouths clashing with the desperation of the kiss, and I angled back enough that I could get hold of the waistband of her sweats. I ripped myself from her mouth so I could pull them down her long, lean legs.

A tremble rocked her as I took her in where she squirmed on the couch, and I reached out and dragged the tip of my finger through the crotch of her panties.

"Pink," I grunted.

Yeah, it had definitely become my favorite fucking color. A pretty flush rolled across her flesh. "Just the way I like it," I told her.

"Would you have been disappointed if I was wearing blue?" The slightest tease edged her raspy words.

A chuckle was slipping free as I wound my fingers in the sides of her underwear. "Don't think there's a chance you could ever disappoint me, but I do have to admit, I'm pleased."

Charleigh glowed, this fucking sweet, desirous smile taking to her stunning face. "Maybe I want to please you the way you promised to please me."

Couldn't stop the hitch of a grin at the corner of my mouth. "You won't catch me complaining."

I hooked my fingers in the edges of her underwear, and I slowed. "You still good?"

Her throat bobbed as she swallowed hard. "Yes. Please."

There wasn't any hesitation in her.

She lifted her ass from the couch to help me, then she shivered as I began to wind them down.

Her thighs.

Her knees.

Her ankles.

Girl so sexy I was finding it difficult to breathe.

I edged back as I pulled them from her feet, then I took her by the ankles and pressed a kiss to the inside of each one before I propped her heels on the edge of the couch.

Exposing her fully.

My heart nearly seized, cock so hard I couldn't think.

Her cunt was swollen and *pink*.

The woman drenched.

Lust hammered through my veins. My mouth watered as I slipped my palms up her legs until I had her by the knees, spreading her wider.

"You have any idea what you look like right now, Charleigh? Spread out for me? Soaking wet and pussy swollen? Never seen a more delicious sight. I'm in fuckin' ecstasy, and I haven't even had you yet."

I dipped in and took a good, long lick. Tongue sweeping through her lips before I rode up to her engorged, throbbing clit.

She jerked, and those fingers sank deep into the back of my head. She pressed me closer as she whimpered, "Oh, God."

I eased back a fraction, blowing a soft puff of air against her nub, a clash with the heat.

She twitched and drove those needy fingers deeper into my skin. "Don't tease me, River."

"No teasin' to it, baby. Just taking my time so you know what it's like to be cherished."

A soft gasp rolled her throat. "That's what I feel like. Like with you I might be."

I dragged lazy kisses along the inside of her thigh as I murmured at her flesh, "You're going to get it now, what it's like to be someone's queen."

More promises I was a fool to make, but it didn't mean that it wasn't true. I was going to lift this girl up high.

Adore her.

Worship her.

Show her the perfection that she was.

Her chest arched from the couch when I dove in again, this time lapping and sucking, stroking my tongue through her pussy.

I moved to spread her lips so I could get better access to her clit. I swirled my tongue around it.

Charleigh was instantly losing her mind, squirming and thrashing as she tried to get closer.

I had to wind my arms under her legs and hold her by the thighs to keep her seated as her body sought to rise toward the sky.

And my name was chanting from her mouth, "River. River. River."

Licking her in long, hard strokes, I let go of her leg and brought my fingers to her cunt.

I shoved two deep inside the hot well of her body.

She arched as pleasure twined her in a bow.

I could feel it gather in every one of her muscles. The way ecstasy was knitting through her, building to become something so powerful she wasn't ever going to be the same.

The threat of rapture rasped from her mouth, air jutting from her lungs and those nails digging into my flesh.

I liked rough, and I wasn't going to mind a bit if this girl tore me apart.

I stroked deep and hard, tongue lapping in time. My cock strained as I listened to all the desperate sounds she was making. Couldn't wait to get inside her. Wreck her the way I'd promised, the kind of wrecking she was going to be begging me to do again and again.

I coiled her so tight that I could feel the second before she split. Every nerve ending in her body zapped and flickered with the coming of bliss.

"Want to feel you come on my tongue and around my fingers. Then the next time, I'm going to feel you come around my cock."

I grumbled it against her clit before I started to lick.

That was all it took, and my girl was going off. My name ripped up her throat as she came, her body fully arching, rapture so full I thought she just might levitate.

Pleasure streaked across her flesh, a bright glow that spread with the ecstasy shooting through her body.

Her walls throbbed around my fingers and her cum spilled across my tongue.

I ate it up.

Her sounds and her heat and her spirit that I could feel reaching out for me.

"River, oh God, River."

Barriers stripped, no walls left.

Like she was offering me her loneliness. Offering me her fears. Asking me to own all the parts of her that had become too burdensome to hold.

And I wanted it.

I wanted her good and her bad and her everything in between, and I knew that made me nothing but a bastard because she didn't have the first clue who I really was. She hadn't heeded the warnings I'd given her because her mind and heart were too good to endeavor that far into depravity.

Too *right* to fathom that type of immorality.

But right then, I couldn't consider it because she was twitching and shaking as I held her in the palms of my hands, slowing my movements as the aftershocks ticked through her body.

One second later, she was throwing herself at me, her arms around my neck and her mouth pressing against mine.

I groaned, surprised for the shortest beat, before I was splaying a hand across the back of her head so I could control the kiss, my tongue licking deep into the scorching welcome of her sweet, sweet mouth.

Charleigh whimpered, and her nails were raking down the front of my chest as she murmured against the kiss, "Now I get to feel you come against my tongue."

Chapter
THIRTY-FIVE

Charleigh

RIVER REACHED OUT AND BRUSHED HIS THUMB ALONG MY cheek. The tenderness was at complete odds with the ferocity that twitched through his muscles.

"You don't owe me a thing, Charleigh. We take this thing as fast or as slow as you want."

"I want it. I want to taste you. Please you."

A deep growl rolled in his chest, a riddle of possession.

His thumb slipped to my lips, and he tapped them right in the middle.

"You going to let me fuck this hot little mouth?"

"I want to make you feel as good as you made me feel." The confession gushed out of me like a plea.

Black eyes raved. A storm in the night. "Ah, tryin' to do me in, huh, Little Runner?"

I placed my palms flat on his pecs and pushed him back as I slipped off the couch. "I'm pretty sure it's me who's done in. Pretty sure it was you who had me splintering apart. What you just did to me…"

I wasn't sure I could form the words to express the way he'd made me feel.

As if I'd been elevated.

Removed.

Soaring.

Or maybe what I'd really experienced was being grounded for the first time.

Rooted.

And right there, with him, was the only place I wanted to be.

My fingers shook as I struggled to get to the fly of his jeans, my face upturned toward him because I couldn't look away from his glorious, brutal face.

He swiped the pad of his thumb over my tingling lips. "What I just did to you I plan on doing again and again. I'm going to wring so much pleasure out of you you're going to be begging me to stop all while you can't help but beg me for more. I'm going to make you *forget*."

I wanted it. I wanted to forget.

But also…I wanted to remember. I wanted to start anew. I wanted to cling to this hope that had burst inside of me.

I inhaled a trembling breath when I finally got the button of his jeans undone, and it skated the air in a shock of electricity.

River exhaled, and I drew him in.

Leather and ink and wickedness. Only it was more. It was the woods and the earth and possibility. It was the sun and light and the life I'd been missing. River slowly pushed all the way to standing. He towered over me where I trembled on my knees.

Completely naked except for my bra that was twisted, the cups still pulled down beneath my breasts.

Wholly exposed.

But I wanted to be.

I lowered his zipper and began to pull down his jeans. I took his underwear with them.

I struggled to get them over his hips, and he helped me, pushing them low enough that his cock sprang free.

A rush of dizziness slammed me with the sight. His enormous cock pointing for the sky, hard and fat and pierced at the tip.

Redness flushed, and my mind sped back to when I'd first been in his shop and had seen the jewelry in the case, how I'd been too embarrassed to even imagine someone being pierced this way.

And there he stood in front of me with a metal rod that ran through his engorged, bulging head. It ran from top to bottom, and two balls were fitted on each side.

A choked sound crawled up my throat and I wheezed, "Oh…"

River smirked. "Told you I was going to wring every ounce of pleasure out of you. Wait until you feel me filling you up so full you actually feel like you're going to break."

"As long as you make me feel half as good as you made me feel two minutes ago, then I'm okay with it," I rasped, squeezing my thighs together because I suddenly needed him all over again.

"Oh, gorgeous, I promise you, it's going to be good. Now suck me like a good girl, and then I'll show you."

Surprise jolted out of me, followed by another rush of arousal. I couldn't imagine that I'd like being talked to this way, but his voice traveled through me on a torrent of desire.

I refused any self-consciousness, and I reached out and brushed my fingers down his length before I curled my hand around him.

River hissed, and I leaned in and dragged my tongue over the tip of his cock, letting my tongue come out to play with the ball at the bottom of the rod that pierced his dick.

He jolted and rumbled, "Fuck me. You're barely touchin' me, gorgeous girl, and I'm already about to blow. What I'm going to do to you, Charleigh Lowe," he gritted.

There was no stopping the grin that pulled at the edge of my mouth before I wrapped my lips fully around his tip and sucked. Big hands fisted in my hair as he let go of a growl.

It turned into a long moan when I drew him deep into my mouth, so far that his crown hit the back of my throat.

I struggled not to gag around the size of him, my lips stretched so wide that drool dripped from the edges of my mouth as I tried to take him as deep as I could.

I hummed with the sensation, vibrating on my knees, shocked at how much I enjoyed it.

His fingers splayed out over the sides of my head, and they tangled in the long pieces of my hair. He curled them into fists as he guided me back.

Then he plunged back in deep. "Just like that, Charleigh. Take it."

I moaned and he grunted when he pulled out then drove back in.

I had to reach out to grab onto his thighs to support myself as he began to fuck my mouth.

I wanted him to.

I wanted him to take control.

I wanted to surrender.

I wanted to give and trust.

"You're so good, baby. So good the way you take me."

A bunch of tiny sounds climbed my throat, the feel of him overwhelming as he pushed in again and again.

"Couldn't have dreamed up a fantasy better than this. You on your knees for me with my dick stuffed down your throat. Perfect girl."

He withdrew then thrust back in.

Hard.

I whimpered and clung on tighter as he began to work in long, deep strokes, driving in a little farther with each rut.

I took him like I was made to do it. Like I might do it forever.

Pleasure him the way he'd pleasured me. Like the two of us could go on for an eternity.

"Nothing has ever felt better than this sweet, dirty mouth."

His praise elicited a whimper, and I couldn't help but look up to his face. His eyes were a storm at midnight, a howling of wind and rain and greed.

Desire tumbled in my belly, rolling through me in a wave of lust. I writhed, pressing my thighs together in search of friction. Energy swirled and grew each time he stroked into my mouth.

Shimmery and overwhelming.

Emotions I couldn't comprehend flashed across the beautiful edges of his face as I stared up at him. Emotions that gusted and crushed. As if maybe he might feel a fraction of what he made me feel.

Needing to show him, I gripped him by the base of his cock and took over. Drawing him deep into my throat, swallowing around him as I stroked what I couldn't take of him with my hands.

I could feel the pleasure blaze in him. The way every muscle in his body was flexed and bowed, coiled and ready to be set off.

"Fuck, Charleigh, what are you doing to me? This mouth, baby, this mouth."

I garbled a sound, needing him to know that I felt it, too. That he was wrecking me just by showing me that I could do this. That I wanted this. That I deserved this.

His hands tightened in my hair and he growled, "I'm gonna come in this sweet mouth."

He jutted and rocked before he split. Coming apart, twitching and jerking as he poured down my throat.

I took it all, swallowing him down as he roared my name. Clutching me tight as he came and came.

He slowed, wheezing for breath as he pulled out, and one second later he was on his knees, too. My face in his powerful hands as he muttered, "Yeah, Little Runner, seems you're here to wreck me."

Chapter
THIRTY-SIX

RIVER

I WAS ON MY KNEES STARING AT THIS GIRL, UNABLE TO PROCESS the way she had me tied.

Trying to process the way my chest was stretched tight to the point of pain. That numbed, frozen place inside me sparking to life. The place I could never let her go.

I had the anguished sense that she might be able to carve herself out a place there, anyway. That she might already be infiltrating it.

My teeth grated as I tried to hold back the surge of emotions that wanted to rush.

This woman who shouldn't be more than a fuck who'd swept into my life and threatened to change everything.

"You good?" I asked because the last thing I wanted to do was cause her more distress.

She nodded against my hands, still gasping for breath, though one side of her swollen lips quirked. "I don't remember a time in my life that I've felt this good."

Satisfaction burned through my insides. "Plenty more where that came from."

A hint of that shyness flushed her cheeks, but she glowed beneath it.

Fuck, how badly I wanted to carry her to my bed and sink deep inside her, but I knew I needed to be careful with her. Careful that I didn't push her too far or too fast.

So, I wrapped my arms around her and pushed to my feet, taking her with me. Her naked flesh burned into mine as I brought her flush to my chest.

She curled her arms around my neck.

Her legs were dangling, and she gave me a soft, sultry giggle that reverberated through the middle of me as I hugged her close. "Don't think I remember a time in my life when I've felt this good, either," I rumbled at her temple.

She sighed and hung on.

"I'm going to put you on your feet and you're going to get dressed, then I'm going to take you back to your room and pretend like it doesn't kill me thinking about doing it, but I don't think you're ready for what I have in store for you yet."

Maybe it was me who needed a fucking minute to get my head on straight. To remember what this had to be. To stop the things that Otto had suggested earlier tonight from invading. Things about making this legit and finding joy for ourselves.

But even if I went clean, I could never undo what I'd already done.

So, I reluctantly placed Charleigh on her feet. Feet that wobbled a bit, her knees weak.

No doubt, she needed a minute, too.

I leaned down to snatch my jeans and underwear from the floor, watching her the whole time as I shoved my feet into them. She peeked over at me as she bent to gather her clothes from the floor.

She'd shifted so she could grab them, and it gave me a bare glimpse of her back.

Her back that was scarred from the middle to the base. Scarred with a thousand gnarled lashes that I was pretty sure had been stacked on top of each other over a period of years.

There'd been no question that she had been abused, but I'd had no fuckin' clue the severity of it, and I was wholly unprepared for the rage that went sailing through my being.

Unprepared for the riot of violence that shot through me like the spray of a thousand bullets.

Impaling.

Ripping and shredding.

Destroying.

Couldn't fuckin' see through the need to bring blood. I moved behind her, my hands in fists as the words scraped from my mouth. "Who the fuck did this to you?"

Because whoever they were? They were going to die.

Chapter
THIRTY-SEVEN

Charleigh

I FROZE AT THE BRUTAL FORCE OF HIS WORDS.

A shiver rolled through me as I felt the energy shift in the room. The bliss we'd been floating on evaporated, and in its place was a hostility so severe it clogged the air in toxic venom.

I should have known this would be coming. Should have known he wouldn't ignore it the way I needed him to.

I shook my head to clear the stupor, my brain foggy from the perfection of his touch, and I hurried to grab my clothes, then turned to face him as if I could hide my back. I doubted it did anything but emphasize it with the way I had to bend over while I fumbled to get on my underwear, then my sweats.

"Who?" he demanded, still towering.

I readjusted the cups of my bra and tugged my tank back over my head, voice haggard. "It's nothing."

What bullshit.

He knew it.

Of course, he knew it. He'd known it all along.

Alarms blared at the back of my head, that part of me that had always kept myself shrouded.

Hidden.

Because I couldn't expose myself like this, but what had I expected when I'd let him touch me like this? See me like this?

"Nothing?" It was pure malice.

I glanced up at him. I shouldn't have looked. Should have known his stricken expression was going to cut me even deeper.

"It doesn't matter, River. It doesn't matter because it's in the past."

And I was here because he promised to show me what it was like to move on from that. It's what I needed so desperately. But maybe I really was a fool to believe that I could ever truly have it.

A ball of grief threatened at the base of my throat.

His face pinched in disbelief. "It doesn't matter? It fuckin' matters, Charleigh. It fuckin' matters because you've been running scared for years. Running because some monster inflicted that kind of pain on you. Running because I know you're afraid of him finding you. And you came running to me. Believe me, it fucking matters."

He slammed his fist against his bare chest. His massive chest that vibrated with an aggression so severe I was sure it couldn't be contained.

Dread sank like a stone to the pit of my stomach.

Terror trembling through me.

Not for my own safety.

But because of what I saw written all over this man. I think it was the first time I truly saw what he was capable of. The lengths he would go to when he promised that he would protect me.

And I couldn't…I couldn't…

Panic bubbled inside me, and I gulped around the fear and desperation. He couldn't get involved in this. I couldn't let him.

"I'm here for you to show me this, River." I flung a hand out to where he'd sent me soaring on the loveseat. "Here for you to make me *forget* everything else but *this*. This thing that you make me feel. But I can't give you what you're asking me for."

"Because you're afraid."

I choked an aggrieved sound, and the words hitched on a sob. "Of course, I'm afraid." My hands spread over my heart that was battering against my chest. "I'm afraid. I will always be afraid. Why do you think I can't do this with you?"

The truth of it hit the room like a bomb, and I shook my head as the realization struck me.

Struck me with the force of a landslide.

"I never should have come here."

It destroyed me, but it was true, and I wound around him and headed for the door. I had to get away from him before he convinced me that I could give him this. I should have known he'd be right behind me. I went to turn the knob when a hand slammed down on the door over my head, blocking my escape.

"Where are you going?"

"I need to get out of here. Away." I yanked at the knob.

"You think I can just ignore what I saw? After what we just did? After everything?"

My head dropped, and I could feel his harsh breaths panted at the nape of my neck.

"I need you to let me go," I whispered.

I could feel the battle that went down inside him, every muscle in his body trembling with malice.

With violence.

Finally, he peeled himself back.

I felt the movement like a loss.

A cold slick that slipped down my spine.

I swallowed down the urge to turn to him, to confess it all, to give him exactly what he'd demanded, and I opened the door, silently berating myself for even thinking of being so reckless.

I'd allowed myself to stumble. To become distracted. I started to duck through the door when the rumble of his words vibrated the air, stopping me in my tracks.

"Fine. Fuckin' run because we both know that's what you do best."

I stalled for two beats before I hurried on my bare feet down the hall and to the room where he'd left my things. Frantic, I stuffed my feet into my shoes, shoved my scrubs that I'd left on the floor into the duffle, slung the strap over my shoulder, and grabbed my purse. I immediately turned and ran back out.

I could feel the heat of him blister down the hall. The energy crack.

Drawn, I could do nothing but look that way.

He stood in his doorway, seething and bent on wrath.

Mammoth shoulders nearly touching each side.

But it was what I saw in his expression that nearly made me falter. The hurt and the pain.

I dropped my gaze to the floor and forced myself to turn and run downstairs.

I didn't even know where I was going when I hit the landing, but I crossed the rest of the way to the front door and fumbled through the locks and ran out into the cool air of the night.

I didn't let the tears start falling until I made it up his drive and onto the street.

They burned, streaking fast, the heat of them clashing with the breeze that rustled through the branches of the colossal trees.

The thick, lush leaves blocked out the moon, and I hurried through the murky haze toward the road that followed along the lake.

What was I doing? What was I doing?

I tried to convince myself it was better to end it this way before it was too late.

Before I fell for the man and his little boy.

It was the hacking at my heart that warned it might already be too late.

I hurried down the narrow road in front of his house then made a left at Vista View.

The night surrounded on all sides, though the cover of the trees had opened here. Rays of moonlight slanted through the atmosphere and glittered across the surface of the lake.

Everything was still.

The quiet distinct.

It wasn't until then that I realized I was alone.

Completely alone.

Again.

So alone that the fear crept in, rising up from the fringes to crowd in at the edges of my sight.

My heart thundered, and I quickened my pace as I fumbled around in my purse to get my phone. I went to thumb into a ride-share app. Frustration and a tremble of something deeper rolled through me when I saw that I had no service.

"Crap."

My attention darted each direction to search my surroundings, hating the deathly quiet, but also knowing it was the safest.

I kept moving through the fear.

I was close to a jog as I moved down the desolate road. Here, the houses were tucked back on their properties. Most glowed with lights, though they somehow felt a million miles away.

Unreachable.

I rounded the first corner, my breaths coming out of time, out of sync, my pulse careening in my veins.

I felt as if I'd run five miles even though I'd probably barely walked a quarter of one.

The sound of an approaching car grew behind me. I gulped for air as I increased my pace as the wash of headlights sprayed across the road. Terror gushed, and I scolded myself for being so reckless all while encouraging myself I was only being paranoid.

Apparently, I wasn't great at self-pep talks because I nearly dumped my bag and sprinted into the woods when the car slowed and began to inch along beside me, though I stalled when the window rolled down and the tinkling voice called from within, "Okay, bestie, get your cute butt in my car before I have to toss you in. I can't believe you'd think we'd let you go traipsing down this road alone in the middle of the night."

Raven kept inching along beside me.

I finally fell to a full stop and gave her the first stupid defense I could find. "It's ten."

Raven rolled her sable eyes. "Whatever you want to call it, it's dark and scary and there are bears in these woods. Do you think I'm going to leave you out here as bait?"

"I think there are worse things in the world than bears."

Her hazards were suddenly flashing right as her door clicked open. She climbed out, barefoot and wearing the same sweats she'd been wearing during the movie, though now her hair was undone, a wild, disordered mess.

Another piece of myself fractured when she crossed the road and took my hand.

It wasn't until then that I fully looked up at her through bleary eyes.

"Oh, Charleigh," she whispered when she saw the state I was in. She threw her arms around me and tugged me close. At her embrace, I broke, and guttural sobs erupted from my chest.

She rubbed my back and swayed me before she finally murmured, "I know you're used to doing things on your own, but you're not alone anymore."

I couldn't respond, and she eased back, keeping hold of me by one hand. "Now, let's get out of here before the bears actually eat us."

I could tell she was only partially joking.

"I don't think I can go back there." I mumbled it toward the ground.

I wanted to. God, I wanted to, and I realized I'd never been in more danger than right then. The way I felt like giving in. And with River? With his reaction? With his confession that he'd done terrible things? I could only imagine what that would mean.

Reaching out, Raven touched my cheek. "Hey, it's okay. I'm here for you, and I'll take you wherever you want to go."

I sniffled and swiped the back of my hand over my face. "Thank you."

She led me toward her car. "Um, did I not tell you I was going to be the best bestie around? Get used to it."

She opened the passenger door, took my bag, and tossed it into the backseat. "Now get in."

I guessed River was right. She always did get her way.

Chapter
THIRTY-EIGHT

Charleigh

RAVEN FOLLOWED ME UPSTAIRS TO MY APARTMENT DOOR. I FELT weak as I put the key into the lock.

I led us into the darkness, and I trudged through the small living room and directly into the bedroom. I dumped my bag on the floor and flopped facedown onto my bed.

Raven only cast me a searching look as she passed by, and a light flicked on in the other part of the house before she started rambling around in the kitchen. Dishes clanked and the microwave ran, and a few minutes later she was shuffling in carrying two cups of tea.

"Here."

"I don't think I want anything."

"Come on, get up, Char-Bug. It'll make you feel better."

I peeked at her through one eye. "Char-Bug? I see how you really feel about me."

How I managed the tease, I didn't know, but Raven laughed and climbed onto the mattress on both knees while somehow managing to balance the mugs. "What are you talking about? Haven't you ever heard the phrase cute as a bug in a rug? That's what you are."

My brow that was smooshed against the mattress lifted.

"Well, except that rug was actually you all tucked under a blanket, holding onto my nephew while you were snuggled up against my brother during the movie." It was her turn for her brow to lift, except it was both of them and they were filled with speculation. "And here you claimed it wasn't like that between you two."

She sang it like an uplifting accusation. Half the time, I didn't know what to make of her.

"Now up you go."

Groaning, I rolled over and sat up against my headboard. She passed me a cup.

"Thank you," I said.

"Best bestie ever, remember?"

"Don't worry, I won't forget," I told her, taking a sip of the hot spearmint tea.

She sat in the middle of the bed, facing me, her legs crisscrossed, and for a few moments, we sipped at our tea before she hedged, "So what happened tonight? The three of you were all cozy and snuggled up downstairs, and then you were getting loved up, and then a few minutes later, you were running out the door."

The sip of tea I was taking spewed from my mouth, and I choked a surprised, "What?"

She rolled her eyes. "Oh, come on, if you think I didn't hear what was coming from River's room..."

"Oh God." Mortification flamed on my face, and I tried to cover it with one hand.

Raven reached out and pried it away. "Don't be embarrassed. I only heard him shouting your name, but I think there's a chance the entire town heard it."

I died a slow death of humiliation. "Like that's supposed to make it better?"

A second later, she'd sobered, and her voice twisted in concern. "But then you left."

I breathed out a heavy sigh. "I just..." I contemplated for a moment before I whispered, "It all got to be too much."

"Why?" I swore, she always asked the most basic questions that never failed to shear through my defenses.

"Have you seen your brother?" I asked.

"He is kind of a brute." She shrugged.

I bit down on my bottom lip like it might keep me from letting her in, but she just kept watching me with that open expression on her face. With that kindness. I exhaled, then gave her some of my truth. "He saw some of the scars I have from when I was in that bad relationship I told you about."

Bad relationship.

There'd never been a greater understatement.

I felt so exposed right then, even though there was so much that remained hidden. This grief so big that there were some days it seemed impossible to put one foot in front of the other. Impossible to get out of bed. Impossible to keep moving.

But that *moving* was the only thing I'd been able to do.

The only thing I knew *how* to do.

Empathy and concern crawled through Raven's features, and her pretty eyes dimmed in awareness. I could feel her care radiate from her, as if she could sense everything I felt.

Experience it.

Her nod was slow. "I think I knew you'd been hurt. Really hurt. Maybe even the first time I saw you."

She paused, then pressed, "River is very protective."

Okay, maybe *that* was the biggest understatement ever made.

"You think so?" I tried to frame it a joke, but completely failed.

She wavered, looking down at her mug, before she looked back up to meet my eyes. "It's because of me that he's that way. Because of the abuse I suffered as a child."

My spirit clutched in the wash of pain that suddenly gushed from her.

Knives that impaled.

I'd felt hints of it before, had heard the implications from River, but I'd been so wrapped up in covering who I really was that I hadn't allowed myself to look close enough to really see.

I was definitely *not* the best bestie around.

Sorrow billowed, and I eased forward and touched her knee. "I'm so sorry, Raven."

She'd always been so confident and vivacious, but for a brief moment, insecurities flashed through her expression. "He saved me," she murmured so low I thought maybe she was afraid of admitting it, too. "Against all odds. At the highest cost. He saved me."

She pulled up her shirt a few inches, and a rasp of horror left my mouth when she exposed at least a hundred pockmarks and burns on her torso. Strategically placed so they wouldn't be visible.

"You can say he gets a little ragey when someone he cares about is harmed." Grief covered her words.

"Who?" I didn't have the right to ask it because she hadn't demanded those details of me, but I couldn't contain the lash of pain that cut through me at seeing the torment she'd been inflicted.

"My father. His stepfather."

"What happened?" For someone who was keeping secrets, I was asking her to reveal a whole lot of hers.

Her expression dimmed, and she reached out and squeezed the hand I'd had on her knee. "I think that's probably a story for my brother to tell."

Then she shook her head. "Anyway, this isn't about me. I just wanted you to know that I understood you from the beginning, saw something that I recognized in myself, and I think there might be a chance that my brother did, too, and maybe he deserves the chance to prove it to you."

She hesitated, then added, "He's holed up behind his own walls, Charleigh. Hiding behind his fears and secrets and scars. But sometimes, our souls know our match, and they're drawn to the only one who could really understand and accept everything we are."

I wanted to believe that. Accept it. Fall into it.

But she didn't understand that what I kept was greater than that.

"I don't know if I can give him that part of myself."

"River is strong enough to hold your burdens."

Maybe that's what I was worried about. He was too strong. Too ferocious. Too relentless.

And him seeking out that part of my life would destroy us both.

Chapter
THIRTY-NINE

Charleigh

Twenty Years Old

S HE TRIED TO SMILE AS SHE SAT BESIDE FREDERICK WINSTON at the big banquet table surrounded by the elite. The room was stuffy though filled with chatter, the clank of champagne flutes and the drone of camouflaged arrogance as the upper crust went on about their latest achievements.

She tried not to flinch when Frederick slung his arm around the back of her chair, the bare brush of him against her nearly sending her into panic. Her lower back burned with the lashes that he'd inflicted the previous night—punishment for her not texting him after she'd arrived at the store.

He had her so tangled in his web that she no longer knew who she was. His manipulation running deep. His perversion deeper.

Hooks embedded in her body and soul.

Nausea spun in her stomach as she sat listening to him go on about how great he was, in that deceitfully humble way that everyone bought into.

If they only knew…

Two years ago, he'd offered her one night in exchange for not turning in her father. Only he'd laughed when she'd tried to walk out, warning, "I'm only getting started with you."

It was the beginning of a nightmare.

Years of abuse and exploitation.

He'd long squashed her dreams of medical school, and if she was being honest, he'd long squashed her dreams of anything.

Every time she tried to get free of his chains, a threat was made against her family. Threats that had grown increasingly more nefarious. Threats she knew he would make good on because she'd witnessed his barbarity multiple times. The people who went missing. The questionable deaths.

And when she didn't cave to the fear he wielded, she was punished.

She cringed when she realized he'd felt her flinch, his presence making her want to vomit as he leaned in and whispered in her ear, as if he were a doting lover rather than a monster, "Watch yourself, Sweet Pea."

Sickness boiled at the way he'd twisted her family's endearment.

"It would be such a shame if something happened to your mother, wouldn't it? She's so innocent in all of this."

He tsked it as he stroked his knuckle down the column of her throat. He'd insisted on the strapless dress, saying he loved the unblemished skin of her shoulders.

The scars he'd mercilessly inflicted were hidden underneath.

"Show my friends how beautiful your smile is," he muttered with all the vileness he possessed.

She forced a smile, as if he'd been whispering sweet nothings to her, giggling as she turned to gaze at him. She wished with all of her that she could grab the steak knife next to her plate and drive it between his ribs.

He grinned as if he were pleased. But he never remained pleased for long.

Her hand flew to her mouth to cover the sob as she stared down at the positive pregnancy test that she'd taken in the bathroom at the store. Horror tumbled through her, a terror unlike anything she'd ever experienced before.

This couldn't be happening.

It couldn't.

She couldn't bring a child into this depraved world.

She sank to her knees, gripped in a fear greater than she'd ever felt.

She held the baby boy against her chest, ran her fingers through the soft locks of his blond hair. Tears streamed incessantly.

But in them was a newfound ferocity.

A new determination that lined her bones in steel.

Because there was no risk too great to give this child a chance at the life he deserved.

So when her mother and father came into the hospital room when Frederick was taking a call, she curled her fist in her father's shirt as he hugged her, and she begged at his ear, "I need your help."

Chapter
FORTY

Charleigh

I BLINKED MY EYES OPEN TO DARK EYES STARING BACK.

"Rise and shine, Char-Bug. It's about time you woke up. I've been sitting here poking you in the arm for the last fifteen minutes, and you didn't even budge. I'd think you'd be a little more excited to see me, but I guess you were probably hoping to be waking up to a different Tayte."

Raven wagged her brows where she lay beside me with her hands curled under her cheek, blinking wide and teasing.

I couldn't help the groggy laugh as I sat up and pushed back the matted mess of hair from my face. "No way. You're way prettier than him."

Raven sat up, too, fighting a smile. "Obviously."

Then her expression deepened. "How are you feeling this morning?"

Memories of the night before flash-fired through my mind. River kissing me. His head between my thighs. His cock in my mouth.

A burn erupted on my skin, though my stomach squeezed with the emptiness of walking away.

"Tired," I told her.

Tired of running.

Tired of being alone.

Tired of this fight that I knew I'd have to wage for the rest of my life.

Her nod was perceptive. "I get it, my sweet little Char-Bug."

My lips tweaked at the edge. "Tell me you aren't going to keep on with that."

"Um, hello, of course, I am. You should have seen yourself last night while you were sleeping. All doe-like and dreamy with these little noises you make. Talk about adorbs. But you might have also mumbled a few...words."

She slipped off the side of the bed and stretched her arms overhead.

"Do I even want to ask?"

"Well, one word," she corrected with an emphatic bite to her bottom lip as she turned back around to look at me.

"What one word?"

"River."

I groaned.

"Well, I'm not saying it was my brother's name you were saying," she said, fully razzing. "I mean, there are a lot of really gorgeous rivers around here and you might have been dreaming about canoeing or fishing or doing something outdoorsy like that. You know, since you like *hiking* so much."

I choked out a laugh. Of course, she would rub that in. Then she really started rubbing it in. "Okay, let's be real here. It was totally my brother's name."

She started moaning. "River, oh River. Give it to me."

"Oh my God, stop," I begged, my hands covering my face, voice rippling with both embarrassment and amusement.

"River," she sang as she spun around in a circle. "Come to me, you beast of a man."

"You are so ridiculous," I choked as I chucked a pillow at her.

It struck her in the chest, and she cracked up before she came shimmying back to the bed. She stuck out both hands. "Come on, we need to get a move on. You're going to be late for work."

Reluctance hummed in my spirit. I hadn't even considered going into work. Part of me had believed I'd be two states over by now, leaving their house the way I had last night.

Terrified and determined.

Now, I had no idea where I stood.

I finally accepted her hand and let her haul me off the bed.

"I'm going to brew some coffee," she said like it was her place rather than mine, not that I minded.

I liked it that she was comfortable.

That she didn't tiptoe.

My chest squeezed with the truth.

I liked her.

So much.

She headed out the door, shouting behind her as she went into the kitchen. "Do you mind if I borrow something to wear? I need to be downstairs in the shop in about thirty. My supplier will be banging at the back door, wondering where I am."

I could hear the clatter of the coffee carafe and water running, her voice still carrying through the space. "Seriously, thank God it's Friday, though, am I right? This girl is ready for the weekend and some fun. We're hitting Kane's tomorrow night for a little family celebration. Everyone is going to be there. Our friends from Redemption Hills are making the trip."

Her excitement traveled the motes that danced in the air. "Even Cash is going to be there, which means it's something special. Seriously, the guy doesn't come down from that cabin but a couple times a year. When I call him a recluse, he is a *recluse*. Love that grumbly bear with all my heart, though, so I totally know you're going to love him, too."

My head spun with what she was implying.

Like she just expected me to…go back.

My heart hurt where it pushed at my chest, that aching throb begging me to do it.

But how could I give in that way? Because I was sure River wasn't going to let it go.

Raven's voice broke through the spiral of my thoughts again, though this time, she was closer. "God, he is so hot, isn't he? Of course, he considers me his baby sister, which I personally think is gross since I really want him to put his dick in me."

Um what?

I scrambled out of the room to find her standing at the French doors that overlooked the street below.

I eased up behind her so I could peer out over the street.

Otto was out there, leaned against the wall of a building on the opposite side, a boot kicked to the bricks and his hands casually shoved in his pockets. The beast of a man appeared as if he didn't have a care in the world with the easy grins he kept tossing at people who passed him on the sidewalk.

"What's he doing out there?"

Raven glanced at me where I'd sidled up to her. "You didn't think my brother was going to send us off without protection, did you? But he knew you needed space, and he definitely needed to cool off himself, so he sent Otto."

My chest clutched. "Has he been out there all night?"

Raven looked at me as if I was still having trouble catching up.

Obviously, I was.

"Of course, Charleigh. It's what they do. And judging by the way River was looking at you last night? I'm pretty sure he's never going to stop watching over you."

She turned and headed back into my room as if the world wasn't spinning around us. She yanked open my closet door and dragged out a summer dress. "Oh, this is so cute! Don't mind if I do."

I didn't know if I should laugh or cry, so I only told her, "Don't think we're not going to talk about this Otto thing," as I crossed my room to the bathroom and shut the door behind me before I started to peel myself out of my sweats and tank so I could get into the shower.

I turned on the faucet to Raven shouting, "Don't act like you need to twist my arm, Charleigh. Otto is my very favorite subject."

Chapter
FORTY-ONE

Charleigh

WORK PASSED IN A BLUR OF NERVES AND UNCERTAINTY. Unsure of where I stood or where I was supposed to go.

Because while logic told me I should have finally packed up my things and left last night, stop this insanity, my spirit whispered its gratitude that Raven had intercepted me instead.

At just after five, I grabbed my things from my locker in the breakroom, slung my purse over my shoulder, and headed down the hall and across the lobby.

My nerves quivered where I stood at the door, the vestiges of the fear I'd felt yesterday when I'd left buzzing in my ear. Warning me that I was being careless.

Inhaling a steadying breath, I pushed out into the late-afternoon warmth of the summer, praying for peace.

For rest.

To find a way when it felt like every direction I turned brought me to a dead end where I'd have to pick up and run the opposite way.

I paused just outside the door, attention dragging across the near empty lot as I searched for any sense that I might be being watched. Searching for a monster lurking in the shadows, waiting for the perfect time to strike.

Butterflies scattered when I saw what was really waiting for me.

He might be a monster, but my heart both rattled and leapt at the sight.

This dark, dangerous demon who leaned against his bike on the other side of the lot. Tattooed arms crossed over his massive chest, wearing his signature uniform.

Black jeans and black fitted tee and black motorcycle boots.

My stomach toppled over with the memory of the way he'd looked beneath those clothes last night.

The carved, sculpted beauty of his ferocious body. Covered in ink and misery. The way he'd touched me. The promises he'd made.

And I wondered if it could be exactly as Raven had suggested. That two souls could recognize the other without really knowing the person.

He pushed from his bike, towering in the distance, that rugged, vicious face carved in possession.

I gulped around the uncertainty and slowly edged his direction. I stopped three feet away, the sun blazing down, burning me up. The knot in my throat was so thick I couldn't speak. Or maybe I just had no idea what to say.

Because the relief I felt at finding him there was staggering, but that didn't change anything, did it?

"Think we need to talk." The words rumbled over me, and I tried to swallow around the barbs in my throat.

"I'm not sure—"

His hand came out, and some piece inside myself shifted when I didn't flinch. When I realized how much I truly trusted him.

Heat blistered where he set his palm on my cheek. "Please…just fuckin' talk to me, Charleigh. Can't leave things the way they ended last night."

I wavered, fighting this war inside me.

His thumb brushed the hollow beneath my eye. "Told you if you ran, I would only chase after you. Thought it was going to have to be across the country, but you didn't seem to get very far. Think that says something, yeah?"

Gulping, I gave him a bare nod, and he took my hand and led me the couple steps to his bike. He swung over the black metal, the man looking as if he were carved from the machine, or maybe vice versa.

I guessed maybe he had the power to break me after all because I allowed him to guide me to climb on behind him, and I wrapped my arms around his powerful frame.

I pressed my nose to the fabric on the back of his shirt.

Leather and ink and wickedness.

I inhaled it deep.

He kicked the motorcycle over, and the engine grumbled, roaring as he took to the street.

He headed down 9th, and it was less than a couple minutes later when he was pulling his bike into the parking lot beside my building.

He killed the bike, and he took my hand and helped me off, and I somehow couldn't look back at him as we began to climb the stairs.

But I could feel him. His presence rolling over me from behind.

His power. His strength. His ferocity.

I shuddered beneath it, wanting to turn and sink into it, allow myself the fall.

I could barely squeeze air into my lungs by the time I turned the key in the lock and let us into my apartment.

It felt even smaller than normal with him in it.

Everything about him was overpowering.

As if he were gravity.

Everything drawn into his orbit.

Inhaling a staggered breath, I slowly turned around to face him where he stood just inside the door.

His hands were in fists, the tattooed Ss on the back of his hand clenched, the skull on the other thrashing.

"What I saw last night…" His voice was gravel. Shards of the aggression and splinters of care.

My chest tightened. "I can't give you that part of myself."

His expression raged, and his jaw ticked as he clenched his teeth. "Just need the confirmation that's who you've been running from."

I stalled, blinking at him as I toiled with what he was asking.

God, was I really giving him this? Apparently so because I couldn't stop the feeble, "Yes."

His head nodded a million times as if he already knew but still had to come to terms with the truth of it. He itched in uncertainty before he spoke.

"Is it wrong that I want to protect you?"

"I can't go back to that time, River."

"Yet you're still looking over your shoulder."

I rubbed my hands up and down my arms, my words trembling. "I can't just erase it, but I am trying to move on. I *am* trying to find a new life. Can't you understand that?"

"But you're hiding things, Charleigh."

I blinked at him. "And you need to allow me that."

His thick throat bobbed, like what I was asking him was hard to swallow.

It felt like an hour passed before he nodded. "I get you don't want to give me details, but that doesn't mean I am not going to do everything I can to make sure you're safe. Because that's all I want for you. Want you to find this new life. For you to fuckin' live and live right."

My heart battered. A banging so loud at my chest that I could hear it echo in the room.

One second later, he was in front of me, both hands on my face. He stared down at me for the longest moment before he said, "And fuck, I want to do it with you."

I gasped his name.

"I do. I fucking want to do it with you," he said. Right before he angled down and took my mouth in a searing kiss.

My mind spun with his words while my body burned with his kiss.

A fist wound in my hair, and he tilted my head back as he licked into my mouth like he wanted to taste every inch of me.

He pulled me flush, and a big hand splayed out over my back as he plastered me to his front.

Intensity swelled, brimming at the connection.

Our tongues twining and begging.

He hiked me into his arms, and on instinct, I wrapped my legs around his waist.

He grunted at my mouth. "That's right, gorgeous. This is right where you belong. Wrapped around me, either on the back of my bike or in my bed."

Then he dove back in.

My mind bent at the power of his kiss.

Possessive, dominating, and greedy.

Heat seared down my middle, and my hands curled into the back of his head as I struggled to get closer.

Kissing me and kissing me, he carried me into my room.

"Where's Nolan?" I somehow managed through the frenzy, and he edged back for one beat. "Otto's picking him up. Told him I had something important I needed to take care of."

Then he smirked, and God, my stomach tumbled with what I felt for this man.

"And what did you need to take care of?" I played into his hands. Exactly where I wanted to be.

"You, Little Runner, I needed to take care of you. Don't think I can wait a minute longer to get inside this body."

His kiss grew more urgent as he pressed me to the interior wall of my room. He let his massive hands wander.

Cupping my butt through the thin material of my scrubs and riding up my sides. He took fistfuls like he'd been tormented with the idea that he might not be able to touch me again.

"Nearly went out of my ever-lovin' mind last night," he rumbled. "Letting you walk out that door and not goin' after you. Took every ounce of willpower I possessed. Think you should know I won't be letting you go this time."

"I'm terrified of how badly I don't want you to."

He edged back and brushed a lock of my hair behind my ear, stormy eyes flitting over my face. "We're going to figure this out. You and me. But in the meantime, know you're safe with me. I promise you."

"I know."

I didn't know how I knew it, but I did.

I trusted it.

With my affirmation, he hoisted me back into his arms, and he plundered my mouth as he took the two steps to the end of my bed.

He dumped me in the middle of it.

I bounced on the mattress, and I couldn't help the bit of joy that erupted from my throat. The spark of happiness that had lit.

River remained at the end of the bed, every bit the dark destroyer where he watched down over me. The cyclone in his gaze promised that Raven had been right.

He wasn't ever going to look away.

Of their own accord, my hips bucked.

"Look at you, sweet little vixen. So needy." He was all arrogance then, sex and hunger roiling from his flesh and pounding through the air.

He peeled his shirt over his head, and the oxygen raked from my lungs at him standing there. Rays of sunlight slanted in through the window and amplified the vicious beauty that he was.

Cast him in a spotlight.

His shoulders were obscenely wide, and the designs that covered his flesh jerked and twitched over his bulging muscles, arms and chest and abdomen.

"I never knew someone could make me feel this way." My confession was breathy, riding on the motes that played across the room.

One side of his mouth hitched. "You don't have the first clue the way I'm going to make you feel. The ways I'm going to have you."

My tongue stroked out across my suddenly dried lips. "Show me."

"Exactly what I plan to do. Again and again. For the rest of my fuckin' days."

Turbulence rolled through me at his words. How he kept speaking of forever. And God, how perfect it would be to rest in his eternity.

"I trust you. I want you."

Greed emblazoned the storm in his eyes, as if my saying it was the best thing I could give him.

"You have me, Charleigh."

River reached out and pulled my tennis shoes from my feet, and he let each of them drop to the rug beneath the bed with a thunk. I wiggled my toes, then sighed when he leaned in and peeled my socks from my feet. He left little pecking kisses along my ankles as he reached up with those long arms and hooked his fingers in the sides of my scrub bottoms.

He hissed as he dragged them off. "Love these legs. Going to love them more when they're wrapped around my waist."

He rode his mouth up my left calf, kissed the inside of my knee, my inner thigh. Tingles raced, and my legs spread wide in anticipation as little juts of air ripped from my lungs.

"Going to take care of you, Charleigh," he murmured as he kissed up to my belly. To my belly that had the tiny, silvered scars that ran upward above my pelvis. I knew they were visible in the light, and I flinched a little when he paused for the fraction of a second.

"Charleigh," he rumbled. The sound of it vibrated through my body as he held me by both sides of the waist as he littered kisses all over the stretch marks before he eased back and took me by the hand, guiding me to sit up on the edge of the bed. He stood between my bent knees as he fisted his hands in my top and pulled it over my head.

He smirked when he saw the matching satin bra and underwear set that I'd put on this morning.

Just in case.

A blush rose to my flesh as he dragged a single fingertip from the side of my neck and down to the cup. "Pink. My favorite fuckin' color."

"I would have thought it would have been black." I tried to play it coy, tipping my chin up as I rested back on my hands.

River seemed to like that, too.

The way that heated gaze licked over my flesh like flames.

"Nah, baby, I think you're the perfect accent to all my dark. A light when things always look so goddamn bleak."

My head barely shook, unable to keep up the playful front. "How is it that I look at you and see the exact same thing?"

"Oh, Little Runner, I'm not the light. Already warned you about that. It's just that I'm going to stand in front of every demon and ghost so you can stand on a pedestal and shine."

He reached out and lifted my left arm, and he leaned in and brushed his lips over the words he'd marked on my skin.

In grief we must live.

Never had I felt the truth of it more than right then.

"You're going to, baby. Live. I'm going to see to it."

Then he dove in, a big hand coming to the back of my head as he kissed me hard, his tongue licking and lashing while he angled from side to side as if he couldn't get deep enough. Like he wanted to sink all the way inside and invade.

But he was already there.

Filling up all the holes and cracks.

He reached around me and unclasped my bra, and he didn't break the kiss as he pulled it free. He tossed it to the side and then both his massive hands were kneading my breasts.

I arched and whimpered as he ran the pads of his thumbs over both nipples, teasing and playing. It sent shocks of electricity sparking through my body.

Desire flooded, this need so intense, and I was rasping for air when he suddenly broke the kiss and stepped back so he could peel my underwear down my legs.

He splayed his hand out over my chest and guided me back until I was lying on my bed, bare and spread out.

The air grew thick, alive as it swirled and twisted, the energy bashing at the walls and colliding back into us. His expression turned feral, and I shivered as he stared down at me.

"How's it I have you like this? Tempting little angel I'm going to wreck?"

We both knew that he would.

And I wanted it. I wanted him to mark me. Ruin me. Most of all, I wanted him to keep me.

"I'm yours to take," I wheezed through the need that pounded through me. My heart rate was erratic, my blood so heavy I could feel it slugging through my veins.

"That's right, Little Runner. You're mine. This needy little cunt that's dripping for me."

He reached out and pushed two fingers deep inside me, stealing my breath, my sanity.

I arched as my walls clamped around him in a fit of pleasure.

"Fuck me. So ready. So eager," he grunted.

I whimpered in desperation when he withdrew, and one of those rough, brutal chuckles rolled through the air. "Don't fret. Just givin' you a second to think about the way it's going to feel when it's my cock filling you full."

He leaned down and undid his boots, those eyes on me the whole time, then he rose.

A fortress.

A mountain.

A hedge of both safety and desolation.

River ticked the button of his jeans, and the sound of him undoing his zipper echoed through the dense air.

He shoved down both his jeans and underwear, shucking them off, and he came to stand in front of me completely bare.

Every part of my being bowed in his direction, heart and spirit and body vying to meet with him.

A fire incinerated as I took him in.

His skin was a menacing canvas of ink, a vast expanse of death and depravity. Rippling, carved strength. Every muscle in his body was tight in anticipation.

His cock was heavy and huge and pointed for the sky, and I gulped all over again at the piece of metal that pierced him at the tip.

His tip that dripped with precum, his need so grave that I could taste it saturate the oxygen.

I should be afraid, but I'd never felt so safe.

He reached for his jeans and pulled a condom from the pocket, and the man watched me the entire time as he ripped it open then covered his cock. "And you're about to have me."

A tremble rocked me through when River set one knee on the bed, then the other, tattooed hands on my knees as he remained on his.

He towered over me.

"I need you. I didn't think I'd ever need anyone or want anyone, but it's you. It's you." The confession bled from my whimpering tongue, and River prodded me to move up into the middle of the bed.

I pushed myself back and he followed, and he planted both hands on either side of my head as he hovered over me. His cock bobbed and bounced between us, sending chills racing through me when the tip brushed my belly.

He leaned in so his mouth was at my ear, and he rumbled in that low, vicious voice, "That's because you belong to me."

He reached between us, and I felt the blunt head of his penis pushing at my center. So enormous and hard that a wave of trepidation skittered across my flesh, but River's mouth was on me again, kissing the panic away as his fingers played through my hair.

"I've got you," he murmured. "I promised you pleasure, and I fuckin' meant it."

The wave of anxiety rolled away, pulled back into the sea he was going to sweep me under as he slowly began to press himself inside me.

I gave and he overcame.

Tiny cries whimpered from my tongue, and my fingers scored deep into his back as I struggled to adjust to him.

To the feel of him.

To the size of him.

To the magnitude of him.

Crushing and devastating and perfecting.

While he grunted and growled as he nudged in and out, each time taking me a little deeper. Every muscle in his body was locked with barely contained control.

As if it were taking every ounce of willpower inside himself not to snap.

My head rocked back as he filled me so full I couldn't breathe, and it broke the impassioned kiss.

River buried his face in my throat with a groan.

"Fuck." It vibrated out of him in a roll of pleasured pain. "Fuck, Charleigh. You feel so good. Nothin' in this world has ever compared to you."

I gasped, panting toward the ceiling. "Nothing."

He pushed up onto his elbows. His eyes had darkened to pitch, a toiling storm ripping through a black, endless sea, and his giant frame curled over me as he held me in the security of his massive arms.

He slowly edged back before he jutted back in.

That time it was me who was emitting the whimper of pleasured pain, so perfect and extreme and more than anything I'd ever felt or experienced.

"Knew you were going to wreck me, Charleigh. Knew once I got inside you, I wasn't ever going to want to be anywhere else. Going to live in this body, baby," he grunted as he pulled almost all the way out before he rocked in again.

Harder that time.

"Do you feel that? The way you were meant for me? Your pussy hugging my cock? Made for me, Charleigh. Made for me."

His words were coarse, scraping the air with the lust that addled the atmosphere.

The next time he thrust in, my hips rose to meet him, my chest arching from the bed and my nipples brushing against his pecs.

"Yes. I feel it. I feel you," I rasped.

Pinpricks of pleasure lit everywhere. In my core and my breasts and my spirit.

Urgency was carved into every harsh angle of his fierce, brutal face.

And the energy screamed between us. Whipping and sparking.

"You're mine, Charleigh Lowe."

Our connection thrummed, a throb that drummed in the middle of us, our hearts beating wayward and perfectly in time.

When he could sense that I'd adjusted, River began to move. Rolling his hips and picking up a rhythm of deep, powerful strokes. Filling me and filling me as I met him each time.

He kept his arms around me as if he knew I needed to feel the surety of them. Like he wanted me to understand that he had me and he'd meant everything he'd promised. Never once did he look away from my face as he took me again and again.

And that pleasure grew with each rock of his body. The friction tossed flames that licked up my insides, and the metal ball on his tip hit at a spot inside me that nearly sent me sailing with each hard thrust.

"River." My nails raked at his shoulders as the feeling of him soared. Building and expanding with every rut of his hips.

River only gathered me closer as he increased his pace.

Deeper and faster and harder.

Marking me.

Owning me.

And I began to gasp, my body moving in time with his as he ushered me toward an ecstasy unlike any I'd ever known. An ecstasy I'd never dared dream existed. A place where I could surrender to the touch of a man's hands and know those hands were only meant for my pleasure.

He pushed back enough that he could reach between us, and he swirled the tips of his fingers over my already sensitive clit.

Bliss flickered and flared.

"River...I...I'm..." I couldn't get a coherent word out. Not when I was being swept away. Lifted and propelled. Taken to another plane where it was only me and him.

"I've got you, Little Runner. I've got you."

His promise skated through my senses, amplified with every stroke of his big, big body.

The buzz of bliss hummed through my being.

"Give it to me, Charleigh. I want to feel this sweet cunt come around my cock."

And I broke in his hands, the way he promised me I was going to do.

Fracturing.

Splintering.

Ecstasy erupted through the cracks, and bright bursts of pleasure speared through my body.

And it sped and sped, the orgasm that tore through me like a summer storm. As fierce and unrelenting as his eyes.

I cried his name, and he took me harder, his massive body bowing high as he thrust as deep as he could take me.

I felt when he broke apart. When every muscle in his body went rigid beneath my fingers that were rushing to touch him everywhere.

His back and his shoulders and his chest.

"Charleigh," he growled as he spasmed and jerked, the man's arms tightening even more as he came. "Charleigh."

We stayed like that. Lifted together. Elevated to a place that I was sure only existed for us.

This man my haven.

Finally, he exhaled the heaviest breath before he dropped his weight to one elbow and his other hand came to rest on my cheek. He ran his thumb along the hollow of my eye, and for the first time, his expression was soft. "You don't have to run anymore, Charleigh. You can rest in me."

Chapter
FORTY-TWO

RIVER

NOTHING COULD FEEL MORE BLISSFUL THAN BEING TANGLED with Charleigh. Our skin slicked with sweat and our bodies sated. Breaths short and shallow, breathing each other where we lie on our sides facing each other on her bed.

Legs twisted and hearts tied.

That's what this was.

I fuckin' knew it.

It was plain and clear that I'd crossed a line that I was never supposed to cross. Wasn't sure how I was going to deal with that shit. The truth that I'd broken the rule that I'd written. Guilt flared at the very recesses of my mind.

My failure.

The oath I'd made.

But somehow it no longer possessed me. No longer contained me.

Charleigh had swept in and rearranged every-fucking-thing I thought I'd known.

I brushed back the lock of chestnut hair that was stuck to her cheek, tucking it behind her ear.

"How do you feel?" Could barely get the words out, my throat was so raw.

An affected smile danced across her pink, swollen lips. "Like I was just ravaged by a beast."

A grin tugged at my face, heart going light. "That was not close to a ravaging, Little Runner. I needed to give you time to adjust before you find out what being with me is really going to be like."

Redness swept across her flesh, and she bit down on her bottom lip like she was envisioning it. How I was going to take her in every way.

Her fingertips came out and played across my lips. "Is that what I am? With you?"

"Think we made that much clear, yeah?" I pulled her closer, her bare, naked flesh plastered against mine. "It's you and me now."

"Yeah?" My fierce girl looked timid. Vulnerable. And I fuckin' loved that she felt confident enough to be that way with me.

"Yeah," I told her.

Her skin blistered against mine, and I could feel the steady thud of her heart as it beat at my chest.

Fingertips played along the designs on my arm before she took my left hand that was on her hip and ran her thumb over the Ss.

"What does this mean? You and all your friends have the same one."

She peeked up at me as she asked it before she turned her attention back to the design, barely tracing her fingers over the ink.

Unease gripped me in a fist, and I blew out the strain through my nose. "We all met in LA as teens. Each of us fucked up in our own way."

A frown carved into her brow, and I reached out with my thumb and smoothed it away as I continued, "We learned to rely on each other. To have each other's backs. It was how we survived. We became a family, and this is a sign of the pact we made that we would always stand by each other."

I left a whole fuckton out. Seemed she wasn't the only one who couldn't give some pieces of her life. I would one day. I just had to figure out how the fuck I was going to handle this.

Sorrow billowed through her spirit. "Raven told me a little about your pasts. Showed me the scars she has. She said you saved her, but it was a story you needed to tell."

I took her hand and pressed her knuckles to my lips. "Doubt that's a story you really want the details of."

Her caramel eyes were soft, the cinnamon flecks swirling as she gazed at me. "Yet I feel like it defined you."

My stomach fisted. Couldn't believe the way this girl could read me. Way she had direct access to who I was.

"Guess it did. The bastard taught me what hate really meant, and he also taught me the lengths I would go for the ones that I love."

Her nod was slow, like she was piecing it all together without needing the gory details. "And do you think that's a bad thing?"

A low chuckle rumbled out. "Whole lot of people in the world would label it that."

Taking justice into my own hands. But I wouldn't change it. Not after everything we'd been through. Not after the people we'd helped.

"I see who you are," she murmured. "The way you are with Nolan and Raven. The way you are with me."

Her fingertips fluttered over my heart like she could inscribe her belief on it.

A heavy sigh pilfered through my nose. "Love them with everything I've got."

A tiny smile tugged at the edge of Charleigh's sweet mouth. "How could you not? Your sister is amazing and wild and the most thoughtful person I've ever met, and Nolan…"

She trailed off, wistfulness climbing into her tone.

I brushed my fingers through her hair. "Kid is the best thing in my life."

Adoration swam in her eyes. "He stole my heart. I think that first day at the clinic, he stole my heart."

I pulled her closer, arms wrapping her tight. "Pretty sure he feels the same about you."

Hell, I was pretty sure she'd stolen mine, too. Ripped it right out of my chest.

I wavered, but there was no missing the melancholy in her gaze. The sadness that was there in the middle of her love. So I broached the topic that had been plaguing me in the back of my mind. "How old was your son when you lost him?"

A pained sound hitched in her throat, but she didn't seem that surprised by my asking it. "He was just a tiny baby."

My stomach clutched. "Were you in the car accident with him?"

Sorrow blanketed her expression, before she whispered out the words, "No. He was with my parents." She blinked through what seemed a thousand memories, awash in the torment I could feel lashing her insides. "They were coming to meet me. They were all killed."

Fuck.

"That's horrible. I'm so fuckin' sorry." I wanted to erase it. Erase it all. But I didn't hold that kind of power.

Her mouth was pressed to my throat when she mumbled, "It was when I finally got away from my husband. Because he had nothing left to hold over me. The only thing left was my body."

I couldn't imagine it, living with that sort of loss with the abuse on top of it. It was so much more than any one person should have to bear.

And here she was—the brightest light I'd ever felt. Spearing through me the second I'd seen her. The first person who'd ever held the power to strike me.

Nothing but a fucking lightning bolt.

Wasn't much of a believer in fate, but I had to wonder if this woman was mine.

I rolled us so I was hovering over her, and I lifted her left arm. I kissed over the skin that I'd marked.

In grief we must live.

I mumbled against it, "There is so much life left in you. You might have been stricken, cut down so low, but that fucker couldn't snuff out your light."

She exhaled, and I kissed up her arm to the cap of her shoulder and then along her collarbone.

A whimper got free of her, and her nails scratched against my scalp. "River." My name was a murmur.

A dream.

A plea.

It knocked through the middle of me like greed.

I eased back enough that I could roll her onto her stomach, and I crawled up over her. I planted my hands on the bed to keep my weight off her as I kissed along the backside of her shoulders and ran my lips down her spine.

Goosebumps lifted across her rosy flesh.

Fuck. She was gorgeous. Every inch of her.

All her scars. All her perfection.

I kept kissing lower until I was softly murmuring my lips over her scars. "Don't think I want to make you forget anymore, Charleigh. Think I want to help you remember exactly who you are."

She whimpered, then she moaned when I edged even lower, kissing at each side of her waist, up and over her hips.

My palms spread over her perfect, round ass.

In an instant, the mood shifted. Air still heavy, though it'd deepened with a thrumming density. With this thing that burned between us that I didn't think could ever be put out.

As sure as the sun that rose every day.

"Please," she whispered as her hands fisted in the sheets.

"You don't have to ask me twice." I pushed back until I was kneeling between her legs, then I grabbed her by the waist and hoisted her up onto her knees.

Her sweet little ass swayed in the air, her pussy swollen from me marking myself deep.

I dragged my fingertips through her lips. She jolted forward and rasped my name. "River."

"That's right, Charleigh. Told you the only thing I had in store for you was pleasure. Going to give it to you. Again and again."

Fuck me. She was so damned sexy. Perfect for me.

I kissed and licked along the base of her spine as I palmed her ass in my hands. Kneading my fingers in. "Don't know what you've done to me, Little Runner. Way I look at you and I feel like I'm standing on the precipice of something huge. Something bigger than me. Wanted to get lost in you the first time I saw you, and now that I've had you, I don't ever want to stop."

I kept kissing over her scars, down lower along the cleft of her ass.

She writhed and whimpered. "I don't want you to. I don't want you to ever stop."

Her words impaled me. Taking hold. This woman a snare in my soul. Everything I couldn't keep but I was set on taking, anyway.

Wasn't like I ever played by the rules.

Greed pulsed through my veins. Hot and heavy. Her scent all around.

Cinnamon and clove. Pure fuckin' spice.

I wanted to gulp her down. Glut and devour.

"Don't plan on it," I rumbled as I leaned down and spread her cheeks so I could swirl my tongue around her sweet, puckered hole.

Charleigh bucked on a gasp, rocking forward then back again. "River."

"Going to pleasure every inch of you."

I eased off the side of the bed so I could grab another condom from the pocket of my jeans.

Yeah, I'd come prepared because I'd known when she'd fled from my house last night that once I caught up to her, I wasn't ever going to let her go again. I was going to make this girl mine.

I covered myself while she rocked on her hands and knees, long locks of chestnut hair draped around her shoulders and brushing the bed.

Nearly got knocked to my knees when she looked back at me from over her shoulder. Cinnamon flecks shining with desire, caramel molten as that gaze devoured me like she felt the exact same thing when she was looking at me.

Like I was hers.

I climbed back onto the bed behind her, and I took her by the hips. She glowed at the connection, and that energy pulsed around us.

She kept watching me.

A vision wrecking my insides.

Complete ruination.

I dragged my fingers down her cleft then shoved two fingers deep inside her cunt. "Is that what you want, Charleigh? You want me to pleasure you? Again and again?"

Her head swished back and forth with the wisping plea. "God, yes, please."

"Tell me I'm the only one who ever gets to do it." My voice curled with gluttony.

"You're the only one I'd ever want to. The only one who ever could."

My chest tightened as a bolt of possession sheared through the middle of me.

"You ready to find out what it's going to be like with me?"

"Yes." She begged it.

Wrapping my hand around the base of my dick, I edged forward, and I lined my aching head up with her throbbing pussy.

Then I pushed in deep and hard.

She nearly knocked me the fuck out with the pleasure that slammed me at the feel of her.

Her walls gripping me tight. Squeezing me in a vise.

She sucked for air as she struggled to accommodate me. Her clutch almost too snug for me to fit.

She throbbed, and my balls tightened in a fit of bliss.

"Fuck me. You feel so good. So fucking good the way you hug my dick."

I let my hands slide up her sides once, trying to chase away some of the tension that had stiffened her muscles, and the second she loosened, I slipped them back down until I had them cinched around her waist.

Then I drew out and slammed back in.

Gasping, she clawed at the bed. "River."

"You good?"

"So good," she whimpered incoherently. Her skin was flushed in that pretty pink, and a slick of sweat had begun to rise to the surface.

I tightened my hold on her hips, and I started to rock, thrusting in and out of her needy cunt time and again.

She looked so good like that, bent over, her lips swollen around where I drove into her.

"You should see what you look like, Charleigh, stuffed full of my dick. Sweet little ass in my hands." I shifted so I could grab her by both cheeks, spreading her wider so I could take her deeper.

She writhed and thrashed. Coming back to meet me with every drive of my hips.

Wanting it.

Needing it.

Taking it.

I swirled my thumb around her asshole, just barely pressing the tip inside.

She bucked and begged. "River, please...I..."

"Do you like that?"

She frantically nodded her head.

"Such a good girl."

I drove my thumb a little deeper with each thrust of my cock.

I fucked her hard and deep, winding her high.

She started making all these little mewling sounds that promised me she was getting ready to go off.

I needed to see that unforgettable face when she came, so I pulled out and flipped her over onto her back. Frustration ripped from her before I had her by the legs, spearing them wide before I surged back inside her.

Nearly blacked out with the smack of pleasure. "So fucking good, baby. What have you done to me?"

I drove in deep, watching down over her as I did. Her slim waist and her tiny tits and that face that had ruined me the first time I saw her.

Girl laid out like a fuckin' prize. Like I could ever do anything to deserve the treasure she was.

That feeling fluttered inside me again. That thing that I'd tried to ignore from the start. Something that was more powerful than anything I'd felt before.

I felt desperate to wrap her up.

Hold her.

Love her and fuck her and keep her.

Bliss gathered fast, stalking up and down my spine. "Charleigh."

She lifted her hips from the mattress with each thrust, and I slammed into her, quickening my pace. I let go of one of her legs so I could bring my thumb to her swollen clit.

I swirled it around her nub, and the air gushed from her lungs, every ragged pant filled with a plea.

"Please…I need…I can't…"

"Told you I've got you. Told you I have everything you need."

And my name became a chant, this woman who'd given herself to me. Trusted me. Let me touch her when the only touch of a man she'd known was pain.

I gathered her closer, lifting her up so I could meet her, though it was those eyes that had me tangled and caught up.

A beacon when I'd been so fucking lost.

Every cell in my body got twisted in it, struck with what she'd come to mean.

Pleasure glowed between us like the air had come alive.

Like the crash of waves on a cliffy beach. The toil of the sea in the middle of a storm.

"You feel it, Charleigh? Do you feel what you do to me?" I grunted it as I kept driving deep.

"Yes, I feel it. I feel you."

Could tell she was getting ready to blow. Way her body bowed and tightened.

I swirled my thumb faster, in time with the rock of my hips.

Her hair was spread out around her, girl this fuckin' angel in the middle of her bed.

Every element inside me wanted to crawl out and meet with her. In it, she stared up at me and she murmured, "Nothing has ever felt better than you."

I couldn't do anything but shift forward, gather her up with one arm, and drag her chest against mine.

I kissed her like it would be my saving breath while I continued to drive.

She split apart then. An orgasm speeding through her like an out-of-control train. Shuddering and jerking as rapture swept through her body. She took me with her, bliss breaking as I took her whole.

Ecstasy blistered out, reaching and seeking. Two of us sharing it, this thing that bound.

Her walls clamped around me as I poured and poured.

And when I finally slowed and edged back so I could look down at her face, I thought this bliss might go on forever.

This connection that couldn't be severed.

Because there was something about her that tied us. Something woven deep in our makeup that made her feel intrinsic.

Essential.

This woman the blood in my veins.

Chapter
FORTY-THREE

RIVER

Twenty-Seven Years Old

I T WAS FUCKING CRAZY THE WAY LIFE CARRIED YOU. How it would toss you from one point to the next. Nudge you in the direction it wanted you to go.

He was never sure if it was happenstance or if it was some fucked up predestination on how things went down.

The way circumstances and situations weaved together to create something that you never could have expected.

He didn't know if it'd been witnessing the abuse of Raven and his mother for all those years that had instigated it. If that had been the spark of this rage and hate that drove him to do what he did.

If it'd been the first life he'd taken, that monster he'd put in the ground because he couldn't take the chance that he could ever come back for his sister.

Maybe it'd been the woman he'd heard crying on that fateful night.

Or maybe each one had been required of the other to bring him to this place.

He sat in his chair at the round table that was hidden in the attic of the house they'd rented in LA, and he called to order the meeting of Sovereign Sanctum.

The beginnings of it had been bred that night when they'd made the decision to help Angela Burkin start a new life. Cash had gotten the documents together, Theo had kept her hidden in his apartment while he did, then Otto had driven her across the country to get her set up.

She'd kept her promise and never breathed a word about them, or at least they'd assumed so since they'd never had any blowback.

River guessed he'd known it immediately—that this was going to be the purpose of his life, and when Iron Owls had been dismantled, it became blatantly obvious he was destined for something different.

When the rest of his crew had climbed on board, sure it was their calling, too?

Sovereign Sanctum had been born.

A secret society that got women and children to safety.

Of course, they did it a whole shit-ton more careful than they had the first time. Safeguards set in place to protect themselves. Their identities. Cash did all the background checks when they were contacted to make sure it was legit.

Contacts were made through a chain of counselors at different shelters and doctors' offices they'd come to trust throughout the country. People like them who were willing to do anything to keep the innocent safe. Plus, there was a hotline that had been set up under a different umbrella. A couple counselors who they'd taken under their wing who then got those in the most dire of situations in touch with them, though that connection remained forever untraceable.

"Melanie Castro and her son were delivered safely," Otto said, raking his massive hands through his hair as he rocked his chair back on two legs, concern still written all over his face.

It was a rough one.

River had thought he was going to be able to slip in and get them out safely without her boyfriend any the wiser. Plan was he'd just think she had packed up her things and left him.

Only the fucker had followed her to the meeting point—the

grocery store she visited every other day—no doubt picking up the scent that she was getting ready to bail.

There'd been an altercation, and River had to make it look like the bastard had been mugged in broad daylight. It'd been messy. Hands bloodstained and dirty.

Most of the time it didn't come to that, but he never hesitated when it did.

Kane scrubbed a tatted palm over his face. "That's too close, man. Out in the day and in public like that. You're skating a thin line. Worried one of these times someone is going to see."

River clasped his fingers together where his hands rested on the table. "Did what I had to do. The way I always do."

"A bit reckless, yeah?" Otto said, still spun up.

Thing was, it was always on River to do the reckless things.

"Who knows what would have happened to her if I'd stepped back and let her act like nothing was going on and she went back to that house. If he suspected…?"

He trailed off with the truth of it.

Theo sighed. "Only thing River could do. And it's behind us now. We need to look toward what's coming up in front of us."

Everyone looked to Cash at that.

He blew out a sigh. "Got a hit last night. This one is going to be complicated. And really fucking dangerous."

And with that, all their eyes slanted to him.

Chapter
FORTY-FOUR

Charleigh

"**Y**OU'D BETTER GET UP AND GET DRESSED." HE SQUEEZED MY bare thigh in his meaty palm. My only response was a groggy giggle since I seemed to be at a complete loss of all my faculties, nothing but a pile of mush in my bed.

Wrapped up in him. Giant arms locked around me where we lay on our sides, my front plastered to the strength of his massive chest.

Our breaths had slowed, but our hearts were still thudding harder than normal, or maybe I could just feel the way his had met with mine, and now mine would forever beat differently.

"Do I have to?" I mumbled at the skin of his neck. The stubble that had begun to sprout prickled over my lips.

I loved the way it felt.

Rough and raw like the man.

But the truth was, I liked every raw thing about him. The way he'd touched me. Taken me. Spoken to me.

I loved him hard and I loved him soft. Loved him gruff and loved when his words went tender.

I gulped around the realization of what I really felt, and I wondered if it was possible he truly had changed everything. If he'd shifted the trajectory. Diverted my course.

If, when we'd collided, he'd broken this cycle that I'd believed I would spiral in forever.

Running. Running. Running.

He leaned in closer and rumbled at my ear, "As much as I like you naked and intend to keep you that way as much as possible, not sure anyone else needs to see my girl like that on the back of my bike. Though now that I mentioned it, pretty sure I'm going to have to have my way with you on it and soon."

Desire rolled in the tranquil waters where we floated.

I edged back so I could stare at the rugged lines of his handsome face. "You want me naked on your bike?"

It was half astounded. Half a tease.

"Want you naked everywhere, though it's not going to be with an audience. Not the kind of guy who likes to share." He pecked a swift kiss to my lips. "Now get that sweet ass out of bed. Nolan's going to be waiting on us."

He slipped off the bed and started gathering his clothes from the floor. Sitting up, I brushed back my hair from my face as I contemplated what he'd said.

"What?" he asked, taking in my uncertainty when he turned to face me as he shrugged into his jeans. My breath punched from my lungs again. I wasn't sure I would ever get used to seeing him this way.

"You want me to go back with you? To your place?"

He breathed out a sigh, and he shifted, climbing up from the end of the bed until he had one side of my face in the power of his hand. "I want you wherever I am. As close to me as I can get you." Then he grinned. "How else am I going to get into this tight little body whenever I want to?"

He brushed his fingers between my legs.

I gasped, though somehow I managed to remain playful. "Maybe I just want you to come to me."

His hand slipped up my torso then he curled his hand around the side of my neck. Gripping on. "I would follow you to the ends of the earth, Charleigh, if that's what you wanted. But right now, there's a little boy at my house who I'm pretty sure is eager to see us both.

He about had a fit when he found out you'd left last night without saying goodbye to him."

My heart squeezed. Expanded and pulsed. The affection I had for him was so intense I didn't think there was room for it within the confines of my chest.

"Well, I guess I'd better go and apologize, then, hadn't I?"

"Pack some things while you're at it. Want you to stay with me for a while."

And still I wavered, unsure. "Don't you think we're taking this a little fast?"

His thumb brushed the angle of my cheek. "How could it be too fast if I've been waiting on you my entire life?"

We rode through Moonlit Ridge along the two-lane road that ran beside the lake, the air cool on my face as I clung to the man in front of me. His big body vibrated as he held onto the handlebars. The roar of the engine clouded out all other sound but heightened the rest of my senses.

The scent that clung to him. Leather and ink and wickedness.

The glint of the fading sun that sparked through the dense leaves of the trees.

The taste of his kiss that still whispered on my tongue.

His skin an inferno where it blazed against mine.

Anticipation billowed when he made the couple turns it took to have us gliding down his driveway toward the sanctuary of his house.

An old, custom pickup truck was parked out front. It was low to the ground and painted jet black. River slowed, and he swung his boots to the ground to support the motorcycle while he dug his phone out of his pocket and entered the code to raise the garage door.

He pulled his bike in between his SUV and Raven's little white car before he cut the engine. Then he took my hand to help me swing off, helping me to maneuver without touching any hot metal parts.

But it was River who could scorch me. Sear me through. Those dark, dangerous eyes raking over me while I stood beside his bike.

"A man could get used to this."

"And what's that?"

He swung from the bike, rising to his full, imposing height.

A devastating warrior.

His hand slipped to my cheek, and his voice turned low. "You."

That one word seemed to hold more meaning than any before it, and he shook off whatever had held him rapt before he snagged my hand and hauled me to the interior door. He jammed at the button to close the garage in the same second as he dragged me inside, right down the hall and to the clatter transpiring in the kitchen.

It was another dance party. Like yesterday's, only Raven and Otto were swing dancing, like they'd stepped straight out of another era. Raven squealed and screamed when Otto flipped her.

Nolan howled and clapped where he sat on the island watching them. "That one was a ten! Or even an eleven even though we aren't even supposed to have one of those, but it was really perfect, so I think you get extra credit."

Then he screeched and kicked his feet when he noticed me and River in the archway. "Miss Charleigh, you came back to me!"

He popped off the counter, hit the stool, and was on his feet in a flash and barreling over to me. I didn't have the time to prepare myself before he launched himself into my arms.

I lifted him. Hugged him to me. Breathed him in.

Peace whispered through my being, this child a balm to my soul.

I held him that way for the longest time, relishing in the feel of his perfect weight.

Then he edged back. "You are in so much trouble that you didn't even say goodbye last night. I thought you were supposed to be sleepin' in the guest room right across from me, and I went right there in the morning, and the bed hadn't been slept in or nothin.'"

I didn't know whether to laugh with the amount of joy his sweet, demanding words brought out in me, or weep from the truth that I'd been so close to never seeing him again.

Weep that I'd been inclined to run.

And I would have missed *this*.

I splayed one hand over the back of his head, holding him so close that I could feel his spirit knitting with mine. "Well, that was completely rude of me, wasn't it? Which is why I had to come back here to make sure you knew I was thinking of you."

He angled back, hanging onto my shoulders with both hands. A hopeful twist pulled to his brow. "You were thinking about me?"

"All day," I told him.

I realized then that three pairs of eyes were on us, and the music had been turned down. It was also when I noticed River's spine had sprouted a rod of steel where he stood beside me looking at Otto.

All the lightness in Otto had disappeared, and the two men shared what appeared to be some sort of silent argument.

Worry and questions strained between them.

My stomach twisted in uncertainty, but it was Raven who cleared her throat to break up the tension. "It's about time you two got here. Work was crazy busy today, and I'm starving. I made fettucine."

The tightness in my stomach turned into a growl. I hadn't eaten all day, unable to tolerate food with the way I'd been riddled with indecision. And then after my evening with River...

Nolan inhaled as he rubbed his belly. "Do you smell it, Miss Charleigh? Deee-licious."

"It does smell delicious."

"Um, that's because your auntie is the best cook around." Raven turned her attention to me. "Prepare to have your mind blown." Then she quirked a grin. "Never mind. Cleary, it's already been."

She exaggerated the last with the blink of her long lashes.

Redness flushed my entire being, and River grunted in some kind of warning.

Otto laughed this low laugh that promised whatever he'd been thinking had been proven correct, and he shook his head before he smiled at me. "Good to see you again, Charleigh. How are you tonight, sweetheart?"

I was still holding Nolan. Refusing to let him go. I cut a glance at River. Between the two of them, my heart swelled to overflowing.

"I'm better than I've been in a long, long time." I saw no purpose in hiding it.

"That's because she didn't have any family, Uncle Otto, so she's gotta be in ours because we got a lot of love around here," Nolan said, so matter of fact, as if he didn't wreck me a little more with each adorable word that dropped from his mouth. "Family's just who you love most."

Otto rumbled a satisfied sound. "Yeah, it sure is, isn't it?"

He looked at River again, though this time, there was something emphatic in his expression. Trying to drive a point home that was invisible to me.

I didn't know how much time had passed before Otto cleared his throat. "All right, I've got to get out of here."

"What, you aren't staying for dinner?" Raven pouted. I wondered if he had any idea that she was actually disappointed or if he believed she was only playing it up.

He curled an arm around her shoulder and tucked her close to his side. "Got plans. But don't worry, baby sister, I'll see you tomorrow at Kane's."

He planted a kiss to the top of her head.

She placed a hand on his chest as if to steady herself. I was pretty sure what she was steadying was her heart. "Can't wait."

"Whole crew is going to be there," Otto said with a blaze in his blue eyes that he directed at River.

Nolan bounced in my arms, exuberance riding into his expression. "You know what that means, Miss Charleigh? My best friends Gage and Juni Bee are comin' to see me! We're gonna have a sleepover at Miss Liberty's house and it's going to be the most fun I ever had."

"Wow. That sounds amazing."

"The most amazing," he said with a jut of his chin.

My heart squeezed again. Unsure how I'd been given this. Wondering if I could really truly be a part of it.

Wondering if I could really stay.

"All right, I'm out of here." Otto came striding across the kitchen, so enormous I wasn't sure how the room contained both him and River. He plucked Nolan out of my arms and swung him high, making the child shriek and giggle and clamber to get ahold of his head.

Otto was chuckling as he flipped him before he settled him onto his feet. "There…just to show you've got as good of moves as your auntie Raven."

"Was it an eleven?" Nolan asked, his brows shooting for the sky.

Otto poked his belly before he looked back at Raven. "Just about, Little Dude, just about."

He swung his attention to me and River.

"See you two tomorrow night."

A surprised sound peeped out of me when he pulled me into a massive hug and leaned in close to my ear. "It's really good that you're here. Really fuckin' good."

Then he gave River a clap to the shoulder before he angled between us to head to the front door.

It rattled shut behind him.

Raven clapped her hands. "Let's eat."

Chapter
FORTY-FIVE

Charleigh

"**C**OME ON, MISS CHARLEIGH, I GOTTA READ YOU A STORY AND then you gotta tuck me in because it's already thirty minutes past my bedtime. Dad says I keep tryin' to break the rules, but I really just need to have some fun. He's gotta know that."

Affection tugged at my spirit as Nolan hauled me upstairs. He climbed backward, jerking hard at my hand like I wasn't capable of taking them on my own.

River climbed behind us. His aura battered against me with each step. That dark ferocity that rolled and whipped, though the grunt he released was tender as he said, "Yeah, that's because you'd stay up the entire night if I didn't have somethin' to say about it."

"He's got a lot to say about everythin', Miss Charleigh." Nolan shook his head as if he couldn't believe the audacity his father had at setting rules.

I couldn't stop the ripple of a chuckle that crawled from the crevices of my spirit. Rising up from where all the pain had been trapped, but now it felt as if some of the pieces held there were being freed.

"I think your dad just wants to make sure you get a good night's sleep so you have plenty of energy to play with your friends tomorrow."

Through all of dinner, Nolan hadn't stopped going on about Gage and Juni Bee coming to visit.

"Well, he does got a lot of smart ideas, too, and I try to get all the smart ideas like him, but sometimes I just make bad choices." He cupped his free hand around his mouth and lowered his voice like it was a secret. "Like staying up way past my bedtime."

From behind, a rumble echoed from River. It skated my skin like a caress. Like joy unfound. Purposed and right.

I still couldn't quite believe that I was here like this. Sharing another evening with these amazing people who'd weaved themselves so deeply inside me there was no chance I could ever get them out.

Treating me as if they…as if they just expected me to be there. As if I belonged.

"But you aren't going to be doing that tonight, are you?" River said in that low voice.

"Nope. Like my Miss Charleigh said, I got to have my energy to stay up the whole night tomorrow. We're gonna party until the sun comes up."

I choked on a laugh as I glanced back at River whose expression had shifted to pure exasperation. Not sure what to do with the precious child who was definitely a little whip.

We hit the landing, and Nolan led me into his bedroom. Releasing me, he went sailing for his bed. He planted his hands on the edge of the mattress and propelled himself into the air.

His legs flailed, and half his body bent to the side as he attempted the flip that was basically him toppling and crashing onto the middle of his bed.

"Oomph," he cried when he landed on his back. "That was definitely not an eleven. But if you don't make it, you gotta try and try again, right, Dad?"

He grinned at River who hovered in the doorway. The man didn't have time to answer before Nolan was hopping up onto his knees, words spewing from his mouth. "That was another one of my dad's smart ideas. If you want something and you fail, you just gotta try, and try again until you get it."

"First person who ever said it." River's tone was dry.

I pressed my fingers to my lips as if it might be able to stop the amusement that kept tumbling out.

"Well, it is really good advice," I told him as I peered back at him. His storm-cloud eyes were different tonight.

The grays lapping soft within the darkness that they always held.

Nolan plopped onto his butt and bounced off the side of the bed before he was on his knees in front of a bookcase that sat on his wall. "What's your favorite, Miss Charleigh? Dragons or fairies?"

"Um…dragons."

"What? You got the same favorite as me?" Nolan jumped onto his feet, waving a book over his head. "I got a really good one for us!"

He scrambled back onto his bed.

"Sit right there." He pointed to a spot on the floor beside his bed.

I climbed onto my knees. "How's this?"

"I think it's pretty good," he said with a shrug, and then he tossed open the first page and started speeding through the book. Clearly, he'd memorized every word.

River remained hovering just inside the door, leaning against the wall as he watched his son read me a story.

I was enraptured by the child's sweet voice. The tinkling lilt. The way he dipped his voice when the villain came on the scene. The giggles. His expression that enthused each spot where he was supposed to be surprised, even though there was no question he had heard this story a hundred times.

"The end! What did you think?"

"I think it was my favorite story I've ever heard."

"Really?"

"Absolutely. Because I had the best storyteller reading it to me."

He was on his knees in a flash, throwing his arms around my neck. He squeezed so tight that I could hardly breathe, his cheek smooshed against mine.

"Because you love me as much as I love you?"

The cavern inside me trembled. As if it were threatening to cave in, and all the brittle boulders inside were getting ready to dislodge and tumble into the pit. As if the crater stood a chance of being filled.

"I do, Nolan. I love you as much as you love me."

More, I was sure, because I doubted a child could feel the magnitude of what I felt right then. The way I wanted to become a part of something so brilliant and right.

"That's good because family is who we love most, remember?" He leaned back, his shining blue eyes searching my face to make sure I understood the importance of what he was saying.

Reaching out, I touched his cheek because I understood it more than he could ever comprehend or imagine. "I remember."

"Guess you're pretty smart too."

He said it casually as he plopped back onto his butt, shoving back his covers so he could get under them. He wiggled around as I drew them up to his chest.

He wore a matching pair of children's pajamas—pants with a short-sleeved tee with moons and stars all over them. He reached up again to hug me, and it was the first time I noticed the birthmark on the inside of his left arm.

A frown curved my brow, and I lifted my hand so I could tremble my fingers over it. Nostalgia whispered through, my mind blinking through memories I'd done my best to keep at bay.

But River was right.

I didn't want to forget anymore.

Not any of it.

So, I let it invade, as much as it hurt, all while I was soothed as I traced the mark on his skin. It was nearly heart-shaped, though it was a bit distorted and longer on one side.

I blinked through the joy and sadness when I turned back to his beaming face, and I ran my fingers through the locks of his warm brown hair. "Goodnight, Nolan."

"Night-night, my Miss Charleigh. You better be here in the morning, but if you gotta go, you gotta wake me up and tell me that you're leavin'."

"Okay, I promise." I leaned forward and swept a kiss to his forehead.

"Your turn, Daddy-O," he shouted toward the ceiling.

River approached, a rippling mountain from behind, covering us in his shadow.

A shroud of fortitude.

I scooted over as he knelt down beside me, and River readjusted Nolan's covers, tucking them beneath his little body.

"Sleep tight, Little Dude." River's voice was hushed. Full of devotion.

"Always, Dad, because you tuck me in the best."

We started to stand when Nolan grabbed his father's hand. "Don't forget my puppy! I sleep even more the best since Miss Charleigh got me my Lucky."

River chuckled, and he reached for it where it was on the floor halfway across the room. He tucked it in with him. "There."

"Perfect," Nolan said, beaming.

I stared down at him where I stood, and I gave myself over to the overwhelming presence of the man beside me.

Yeah.

Perfect.

River led me out, and he pulled the door shut behind us, though he left it open a couple inches.

I wavered, unsure of what to do. I ran my hands up my arms before I murmured quietly, "I should get ready for bed."

I started for the guest bedroom where I'd deposited my things once again after dinner.

I'd barely made it a step before River swept me up and off my feet, surrounding me in the sanctuary of his arms. "Where do you think you're going, Little Runner?"

A shiver raced, as sure as the ecstasy that pounded through my veins.

"To bed?" It peeped out of me like a question.

"Yeah, that's exactly where you're going, only you're headin' the wrong way."

And I didn't mind at all when he carried me to his room.

Chapter
FORTY-SIX

RIVER

I STOOD AT THE BIG GLASS-PANED DOORS THAT OVERLOOKED THE backyard, unable to move as I watched Charleigh and Nolan playing on the lawn.

Laughing.

Teasing.

Chasing.

Running, except Charleigh wasn't running anywhere. Instead, she was here and present, like she'd been a fixture all along. Was weird watching the two of them playing beneath the bright afternoon sun, their beautiful faces flashing beneath the shade of the leaves that hung low over the yard.

Normally, I freaked the fuck out when strangers were around Nolan. Protectiveness so acute that I didn't know what to do other than to keep him hedged in, but I didn't think I'd ever felt so satisfied than right then.

Watching on what my gut told me was meant to be.

Didn't mean I wasn't completely rattled when my sister eased up beside me and asked, "What are you going to tell her?"

Apprehension gusted, and every muscle in my body flexed. Didn't need to ask my sister what she was referring to. Still, I couldn't tear my gaze from outside as I mumbled, "Don't know."

Raven scoffed. "What do you mean, you don't know? You can't invite someone into your life like this and expect that you're going to keep them in the dark."

"I thought you wanted me and Charleigh together?" It scraped up my suddenly raw throat like I was dueling my sister in some kind of challenge. Knew she was only concerned, but shit.

She smacked me on the side of the arm with the back of her hand. "Of course, I want you two to be together, you big dummy. You two are perfect for each other. I knew it the first time I saw you together. Like, hello chemistry. There was this whole...*thing*...going on between you two."

She waved her hands around when she said *thing*, like she was trying to encompass whatever *this* was in the flail of her hands.

"I mean, it was so intense, there wasn't anyone there who didn't see it for what it was. But that doesn't change who you are, River. What you've done and what you continue to do, and the only reason I have been concerned about you two being together at all is because I know the lengths you go to conceal those parts of yourself."

"What do you expect me to do, Raven?"

She widened those dark eyes at me like it should be obvious.

When I didn't answer, she let go of a disbelieving breath and pushed, "Tell her."

My insides shriveled. Balking at the thought. Stomach dumping out on the floor, already anticipating the coming loss.

If she had even the slightest inclination, she'd go running so far and so fast that I'd never be able to catch up to her. Sure, she'd acted like it was no big deal when I told her I'd done terrible things, but we had a way of minimalizing warnings in our minds if we wanted something bad enough.

Ignoring every danger sign.

She'd probably chalked it up to me committing some petty theft. But if she knew? There was no way she could ignore it.

"Tell her?" The words came out on a bitter laugh.

Crossing her arms over her chest, Raven cocked her head. "Um, yeah. What, you think you can invite her into this family and just act like you're someone you're not? I know you're scared of what she'll think, but you can't start a relationship based on secrets, River. You know those secrets will only eat away at anything you build, and that foundation is going to crumble. And I can't stand the thought of that for either of you. Both of you deserve so much better than that."

My head shook. "My whole life is a fuckin' secret, Raven. You know it's not safe for anyone if she knows. It's bad enough I brought her here. That I'm doing *this*…"

This came out of me like I was confessing a mortal sin. Maybe that was exactly what it was.

"What exactly are you doing, River? Loving someone who needs to be loved? Allowing yourself to be loved?"

I blanched, spirit trying to refute it. My transgressions so dark and ugly there was nothing I could ever do to eradicate the blemishes. Nothing I could do to wash the stains from my hands.

I'd always had the terrible sense that having Raven and Nolan in my life was only temporary. That I got to keep them for a little while only to know exactly what it was like to love with all your heart, and my punishment was going to be getting them ripped away.

Which I guessed was why I'd always spoken of the temporary when it came to Charleigh. Unwilling to believe that I could have anything permanent, even though the promise of its permanence kept getting free of my heart and lips, anyway.

Unable to imagine letting her go.

My attention drifted back out the window. Charleigh and Nolan were both cracking up where they'd toppled to a pile on the ground, rolling around and giggling as they played.

My heart that kept telling lies climbed up to take residence in my throat.

Raven laughed a sorrowful yet glacial sound. "You can't even admit it, can you? That you love her?"

"I don't…" I turned my attention to the ground and ran a trembling palm over my face.

Fuck.

Apparently, I couldn't deny it, either.

Raven sighed, took a step closer, then reached out and took me by the outside of both arms and turned me toward her.

Her hands curled tighter around my forearms and her voice dipped in emphasis. "You think you live a life unworthy of love, River. I know you do. I've seen it. I've watched it. I've felt it. Do you think I haven't always known how you meet any bit of joy you receive with reticence? How you're terrified of it? Like it makes you a bad person for accepting it?"

"In case you've forgotten, I *am* a bad person, Raven."

Disbelief shook her head. "Why don't you go back and ask any one of those women…any one of those children…if they think you're a bad person?"

"Raven…" How the fuck did I answer that? Yeah, it meant something, what we did. I'd never regret it, but it didn't change the rest of it.

"Ask *me* if I think you're a bad person," she goaded.

My sister was always goofing around. Radiating light. But there wasn't anything light about her right then.

I watched the old ghosts play through her eyes.

The kind of demons you could never fully outrun.

She turned me to face out the window. "How about her, River. Why don't you tell her and ask her if she thinks you're a bad person. I'd bet my life that she won't."

She paused for a moment before she murmured, "I think she might understand you better than anyone else. More than anyone else could."

It was right then that Charleigh looked our way, as if she felt the weight of our gazes peering out at them. They were still on the lawn, but she had Nolan on her lap, and she was rocking him back and forth as he pointed at something in the sky and prattled on about something the way he did.

Sun shining all around them, faces lit in the glitter of the day.

I could feel Raven peer up at me. "I told her that you were strong enough to hold her burdens…and I'm willing to bet she's strong enough to hold yours, too."

She gave a small shake of her head. "I know what you tattooed on her arm, River, and I have to wonder if that might not have been meant for you, too."

We stayed like that for the longest time while her words banged around inside me.

"Now if you'll excuse me, I'm going to start getting ready. I plan to look extra amazing tonight. I have a date."

She'd crossed the room and had started up the stairs by the time I was able to process what she said.

My stomach fisted, and I sent her a glare as she climbed the stairs, her hand gliding on the handrail as she did.

And Raven? She fuckin' cracked up.

I pounded at Raven's closed door.

"The hell is taking you two so long?" I shouted at the wood. It was getting close to ten. Nolan had been dropped at Miss Liberty's hours ago for his big sleepover with his friends.

The kid had to have been the most excited I'd ever seen him. Fuckin' bouncing off the walls and asking me if it was time to leave every three seconds.

Raven had organized it with Miss Liberty, setting it up that Trent and Eden and Jud and Salem could leave all their kids with her for the night, along with Nolan.

It was all to celebrate the fourth anniversary of Kane's opening, though what we were really celebrating was the coronation of Sovereign Sanctum from years before.

Trent and Jud had been intrinsic to its birth, and it was only fitting that they would be here for it.

Miss Liberty was being more than well-compensated for her going over and above, though I imagined she might be having second thoughts with the fucking mayhem that had to be going down at her house right then.

I'd gotten back what felt like five hours ago to Raven and Charleigh locked behind Raven's door. I'd knocked then and had been met with Raven telling me to go away as a shit-ton of giggles echoed through the wood.

Now, I was fucking itchy, and some douche-nod wearing a goddamn suit who I'd never seen before was downstairs waiting on my sister.

Fuck my life.

I started to knock the back of my fist on her door again when it suddenly burst open. It sent me stumbling back a step when Raven came strutting out.

Yeah, fuck my life.

She was dressed far too scandalously for my comfort, in leather and looking like a straight-up biker chick, and I had half an inclination to point my finger and tell her to go back into her room and change, except my jaw unhinged and hit the floor when Charleigh came out behind her.

And well…fuck me again. She had on this itty-bitty skirt, white and puffy, so goddamn short I'd barely have to slip my hand under it to get to that tight pussy I'd come to the swift conclusion I was addicted to.

Way my dick leapt in my jeans, lust punching me straight in the gut, even though I'd already had her three times this morning before everyone got up and twice during Nolan's nap.

She had on a red tight-fitted tank that was tucked into the hem, and that sweet little tat was exposed on her inner arm. My goddamn heart fisted because it felt like a brand.

Like she might really be mine.

Her hair was done in big, fat waves that floated around her precious, perfect face. Those lips plumped and coated in shiny pink.

"Tryin' to do a man in, yeah?" I grunted, my tongue coming out to stroke my lips as I moved her direction, unable to stop myself.

Charleigh gasped as I pinned her against the wall, and her hands fisted in my tee.

Raven squealed and clapped. "I knew that outfit would make you irresistible. My designer skills are on par. You're welcome. Xoxo, your bestie."

I barely peeked at my sister from out of the corner of my eye since I couldn't look away from my girl. "She's always irresistible."

It was the goddamn truth.

"Aww," Raven sang as if it was the cutest thing in the world, though she was looking at me with those sharp eyes that warned me not to fuck this up.

And I swore to God right then that I wouldn't.

Chapter
FORTY-SEVEN

Charleigh

I held on to River as we traveled beneath the night. The blanket of stars were low and eternal, and the lake was moonlit, ripples of silver that glittered beneath the expanse.

River's back burned against my chest as I clung to him tightly, though I didn't feel afraid where I sat on the back of his bike.

Not this time.

I wondered if I would ever again.

The heavy engine vibrated the metal, and my thighs shook where they were wedged on either side of River's hips. Wind whipped and blew, and I was pretty sure the waves that Raven had meticulously curled into my hair were a hot mess, but I couldn't find it in myself to care.

I felt free.

Free for the first time in so many years.

River took the few turns it took to get us onto Culberry Street, and five minutes later, we were pulling into the overflowing lot of Kane's.

It was the most popular bar in Moonlit Ridge, known for designer drinks and live music. It brought in different genres of bands to play each week, not that I had frequented the place, but Raven had filled me in on every detail while we'd been getting ready.

She'd told me about the people we were going to meet and some of their backgrounds, which all seemed to be pretty traumatic and dark, although I could tell she was being careful not to be gossipy, hanging onto more intimate details that I only knew were there because of the reticence in her eyes.

The one thing I knew for certain was they had a ton of history together, and her affection for them all was clear.

My stomach tumbled as River wound around to the front where a slew of bikes were parked facing out. He slowed to a stop, then he used his boots to glide us in backward. He shut off the engine, and the loud grumble of the bike gave way to the sound of music thrumming through the walls of the club.

Voices and laughter carried within it, and I could almost taste the chaos in the air.

River took my hand and guided me off. Stormy eyes raked over me as I tried to keep my skirt down so I didn't give everyone loitering in the parking lot a peek at my underwear.

Maybe this skirt had been a bad idea, but Raven had insisted I looked crazy hot, and well…that's exactly what I wanted to be.

For him.

Because that's the way he appeared to me.

So hot I felt as if I were getting burned alive as he swung all the way off his bike, rising high and so damned mighty where he stood over me. Wearing his signature uniform. Black tee and black jeans and worn motorcycle boots.

The man pure intimidation.

Pure fascination.

Color swirling out from beneath his sleeves and up his throat, his muscles bulging against the fabric.

My stomach twisted in need.

"How the fuck am I supposed to think straight tonight with you lookin' like that?" he said as he took a step forward. The ground trembled beneath my feet.

He leaned in close, his big body concealing me from the group of people who walked past, the soles of their shoes scuffing on the loose pavement as they headed for the entrance.

He only edged closer. "How am I supposed to keep my hands off you when the only thing I'm going to be thinking about is this sweet little pussy right here?"

His hand wedged between my thighs, and he cupped me over my underwear. Pleasure sparked, and my head tipped back on a whimper.

River wound his arm around my waist to support me, and he burrowed his face in my neck, the words a growl as he muttered, "How am I going to get through the night without being inside of you?"

His fingers pushed against my sex. My vision went fuzzy.

"Maybe we should just go home." It was an incoherent ramble from my mouth.

River chuckled against the sensitive flesh of my neck, and he kissed along the column as he whispered, "Eager girl. Just the way I like you. My fuckin' perfection. Don't worry, I'll be taking this time to think up all the delicious things I plan to do to you once I get you home."

I whimpered, and when he suddenly straightened, my knees were weak, and I was barely able to remain upright on the four-inch stilettos Raven had insisted on.

My wild new BFF had squealed yesterday morning when she found out we were the same shoe size when she'd been looking for something to wear while she was getting ready to go down to the shop. She'd claimed we really were meant to be. Tonight, she had been all too excited to dig around in her closet for the perfect shoes to wear with the outfit she'd picked.

River slipped his hand around my waist and pressed his mouth to my ear as he led me out of the shadows and into the spray of light that shined from the entrance. "Want you wet the whole night...thinking of all the ways I'm going to have you."

I tried to press my thighs together as we walked, only my heels scudded on the gravel, and I nearly tripped.

Chuckling a sexy sound, River clamped his palm down on my ass and squeezed. "Oh, Little Runner, what I'm going to do to you."

It was me who couldn't think straight as he bypassed the line and led me directly to the door. A bouncer tipped his head in River's direction. "Ah, River Tayte. How's it going tonight?"

"Better than I deserve," he told him, dragging me closer like I was the reason for it.

The man appraised me, and a smirk tugged at the edge of his mouth. "I can see that."

He stepped aside to let us in, and I snuggled into River's side as he led me into the throng.

It was much louder inside. Music blared from the overhead speakers, compliments of the country band that played on the elevated stage on the far side of the bar. The middle area that made up the dance floor was filled with couples doing a quick two-step.

White lights flashed and strobed where they hung from the vaulted ceiling.

A tremor of disquiet rippled through me, that old fear of being in large crowds, worried that someone would see me.

Recognize me.

It was that gut instinct that warned me to slink away and hide.

The words on my inner arm blazed their reminder.

In grief we must live.

But the real reminder was when River shifted and took me by the hand, his grip so firm, a promise that I wasn't alone.

Not anymore.

So, I shoved the dread down, refused the ghosts that threatened to drag me back into their depths, and chose to be here in the present as River began to lead us through the crush.

People parted, quick to get out of his way, and we angled along a long bar that ran the entire left wall. A bunch of bartenders worked behind it, filling drinks for the slew of patrons who'd gathered around, vying for their attention.

We kept going until we were at the far back left wall where a large, round, high-backed booth was hidden in the corner. It was the only booth on that side, and a few high-top tables were situated around it. That entire area was sectioned off by a velvet rope.

It was just as packed as the rest of the bar, but in an entirely different way. Filled up by the enormous men who were hanging out behind the boundary.

Giants that had found sanctuary in this small town.

Otto, Kane, and Theo were there. Otto and Theo were quietly chatting between themselves where they stood around a high-top table, and Kane was stretched out in the booth.

There was a man I didn't recognize next to him, the guy a mountain where he was wedged into the seat. A stunning woman with jet-black hair was tucked in next to him.

There was another couple on the opposite side.

That man I recognized. He'd been getting a tattoo the night I'd gathered the courage to go into River's shop. A petite blonde was pasted to his side, and his massive arm was holding her plastered against him, as if he could never get her close enough.

My nerves rattled again.

"Don't be nervous, gorgeous. These are the best group of people you'll ever meet. Loyal to the fuckin' bone, willing to drop everything to help those in need. Promise, if you can trust anyone, you can trust them."

I gave River a wary nod, and he unhooked the rope and ushered me through. When she saw me, Raven squealed from where she had been talking with her date.

"Oh my God, you're here! I was worried my brother had dragged you back to his room and tied you to his bed." She basically shouted it as she sauntered in our direction, her hips swaying from side to side as she approached, all lush curves and confidence and an aura I was sure had the power to steal the breath of anyone she passed.

Raven was a rare kind of beauty.

But it also meant everyone was paying attention to her as she shouted the playful accusation to basically the entire bar.

My cheeks flamed, and I tried to hide myself behind River. Only she dragged me out from behind him and hugged me hard. "I missed you."

"It's been fifteen minutes," I wheezed beneath her crushing hold.

She pushed her mouth to my ear. "Um, yeah, that's fifteen minutes too long. My date is boring as hell. Save me." She quietly begged it as she rocked me back and forth. "If you hadn't gotten here in the next two minutes, I would have grabbed a fork and stabbed my eye out. Or his. Definitely his."

She was still hugging me tight as she said it.

Light laughter rolled out of me. "I think Nolan would tell you that would be a bad choice."

"The only bad choice I've made was agreeing to go out with him."

She was still trying to cling to me as if I could actually save her when River pried us apart. "Paws off, you've got your own date," he grumbled, though I could hear the tease woven in it.

Raven propped her hands on her hips. "And that's my bestie you're talking about. You stole her from me."

"Don't know what to tell you, baby sister. Charleigh is mine." He reached out and tugged an errant piece of her hair. She scowled while I tried not to swoon.

Shocking since I'd never wanted to belong to anyone.

River looped an arm around my waist again. "Come on, want to introduce you to everyone."

"Okay."

As he started to lead me toward the big booth, everyone piled out of it.

"Ah, River, you made it," Kane called as we approached.

River lifted his chin at him. "Like I would miss it."

"And you're not alone." Kane's gaze settled on me. A smirk played at the edge of his mouth, though there was something in his eyes that left me unsettled. "Good to see you again, Charleigh."

I wasn't entirely sure he was being genuine.

"It's good to see you, too," I managed, hating feeling uncomfortable, but God, I didn't get what was up with River's friends. He kept saying they were the best people, but they kept watching me like I might be some trespasser or spy.

Otto and Theo had joined the group, and they gave us both quick hellos.

Then the mammoth who'd been sitting next to Kane stepped forward. "River, great to see you, man."

He and River gave each other one of those quick hugs with slaps to the back. "Good to see you, brother. It's been too long," River said.

River stepped back and gestured between us. "Charleigh, want you to meet one of my oldest friends. Jud Lawson. And this is his wife, Salem."

Jud grinned. He was covered in nearly as many tattoos as River, handsome in that terrifying, biker way, though his smile was easy and kind. "Nice to meet you, darlin'," he said.

"You, too."

"Hey, it's really good to meet you, Charleigh." Salem stepped up and gave me a welcoming hug.

"It's good to meet you," I told her, overwhelmed by all the attention.

River turned. "And this is Trent and his wife, Eden."

Satisfaction played on the man's mouth as he glanced between me and River. "Ah, looks like someone really did need that spot more than I did."

"Yeah, seems she did." River let it go in that rough, raw voice, stormy gaze taking me in like I might have the power to calm it.

Nerves fluttered, joy and anxiety at being in the middle of a group this way.

"Thanks go to me then, yeah?" Trent said as he cut an elbow into River's arm.

River only chuckled.

Eden gave her husband a playful shove as she stepped in my direction.

She was the exact opposite of him. Where he oozed the same danger that River possessed, dark and menacing, dripping intimidation, she appeared wholly innocent. Sweet and caring with her gentle hazel eyes.

"Oh my gosh, I'm really happy to meet you. Trent told me about what happened that night."

"Called it, didn't I, Kitten? Thousand bucks said I was gonna see you again." With that, he jutted his chin at me, grinning wide.

"And I was the idiot who bet against him," she said in a soft, tinkling voice, fingers bouncing off her forehead like she couldn't believe her judgement. "Only because I *have* met River before, and I thought never in a million years, but now that I *have* met you…I see what's happened here."

It was all lighthearted as she pointed between the two of us.

River tightened his hold around my waist and ran his nose up under my hair, along my neck and to my ear, his words only for me. "Yeah, I see what's happened here, too. Little Runner wrecked me. Wrecked me good."

Heat erupted across my flesh, and the air tremored from my lungs, and Trent was sending us another winning grin as he slung his arm around Eden's shoulders. "Looks like we really do have a whole lot to celebrate."

Everyone turned when another man was suddenly within the boundary, a surprise rippling through the crowd. Then Raven shrieked. "Cash is here!"

She beelined his way and threw herself at him, hugging him tight, before the rest of the group pretty much surrounded him to tell him hello, though I could tell by his demeanor that the attention made him uncomfortable.

Could sense the same reluctance I often did when I was surrounded by too many people. The panic that simmered right below the surface.

River and I hung back, waiting for our turn, and once everyone had cleared out, River slowly ushered me forward. "This is the last of my brothers you haven't met. Charleigh, this is Cash. Cash, this is Charleigh Lowe."

Cash was more country than the rest of River's friends, wearing faded denim jeans and boots, though his arms were completely covered in what I now recognized was River's ink, his designs distinct. He wasn't as tall as River, but he was thick and burly, muscles corded and ripped, skin tanned a deep golden brown, as if he'd spent all his life living off the land.

He had wavy brown hair that hung down near his chin and curled around his neck, and a short beard. Keen green eyes took me in, his expression guarded. "Good to meet you."

"You, too," I whispered, hating that I felt like the man was pulling me apart. Trying to see beneath every hidden layer.

The two of them shared a look before River turned to me and slung his arm around my waist, his mouth at my jaw when he muttered, "Come on, gorgeous, let's find us a drink."

Maybe it made me a fool that I tucked the turbulence I felt radiating from his friends down. The questions and speculation. Because for a little while, I wanted to be what River claimed I was.

I wanted to be his.

Chapter
FORTY-EIGHT

RIVER

CHARLEIGH WAS TUCKED AGAINST MY SIDE WHERE WE WERE all squished in the enormous booth. It felt good being there this way, my girl at my side while my friends shot the shit.

Telling old tales of our days back in LA, though everyone strategically left out all the sordid, condemning parts.

Funny that the bar fights and late-night rides sailing at a hundred miles an hour beneath the stars were the uncorrupted parts. The wild parties and scandalous shit we'd all always gotten ourselves into was fodder for the laughter that rolled around the booth.

"So anyway, this dumb fuck pulls his car into the parking lot of the bike shop we had," Trent said, voice full of a laugh where he sat in the booth next to me. "He dumped some girl in the middle of it and told her she could find her own way home if she was going to be a cock tease. Fucker picked the wrong damned place to be spouting that kind of bullshit. So, this asshole right here, who was little more than a kid, mind you…"

He jostled me in the shoulder before he continued, "He jumped on his bike and chased the fucker down, busted his windshield with a crowbar. Was the minute I knew he was one of us."

Trent slanted me a grin, and I chuckled under my breath.

Remembering the way he'd taken us in. Given us a home. A purpose. "Don't act too proud. Just wanted to bust up some shit."

His grin deepened because he knew I was only talking shit.

Charleigh laughed beside me, half horrified and half aroused.

"What?" I asked her with amusement playing at the edge of my mouth.

She looked up at me, those cinnamon eyes doing wild, wild things. "So violent."

She had no fuckin' clue.

I tipped up her chin and pecked a kiss to her lips. "He had it comin.'"

It was basically my motto.

The band's set had ended, and a DJ had taken their place, spinning dance music and the crowd into disorder.

Raven tossed back the rest of her frilly drink before she slammed the empty onto the table. "Time to hit the dance floor. All my girls, let's go!"

"Count me in!" Salem said, and the gorgeous woman shoved at Jud's shoulder to let her out.

My sister pushed out to standing, and everyone scooched out so Eden and Salem could get out of the booth. Trent followed and so did I, and I watched as Charleigh slid around, wearing that damned skirt that was going to drive me straight out of my mind.

She climbed to her feet. Needing to get my hands on her again, my palms went straight to the back of her bare thighs as I drew her to me and kissed her deep.

Fuck me.

She tasted good.

Cinnamon and spice.

The old fashioned I'd been sipping all night didn't come close to comparing.

"You have fun out there," I told her, still pecking at her lips, wanting to lap up every last drop of that sweetness.

Jud and Trent were too wrapped up in their girls to pay me any mind, but you could be damned certain the rest of my crew did. When

Charleigh tore herself away, my eyes were hooked on her back as she joined the rest.

All the women linked their arms as they headed for the dance floor, Charleigh right in the middle as if she'd been a part of them forever.

My chest did that achy fucking thing. That pull of possession and the frantic desperation to keep her close.

My crew all settled back into the booth, and the server brought us another round of drinks.

Kane lifted his whiskey-filled tumbler, the cut glass glinting beneath the chandelier hanging from above the table. His gaze jumped between all of us before he started to speak, his voice just loud enough that only we could hear.

"Fuckin' glad to see each of you here tonight. It's been a long road for all of us, and the fact that we're all still here is a testament to our loyalty and devotion. Trent and Jud may not have Sovereign Sanctum tattooed on the back of their hands, but none of us would be here without the two of you, so first and foremost, this one is for you."

He lifted his drink higher, and Otto, Cash, Theo, and I each lifted ours and clinked our glasses together as we said, "To our brothers, Trent and Jud."

Both of them dipped their heads.

"It's always been an honor to stand at your sides," Trent said.

"Yeah," Jud agreed. "We always have, and we always will, so anything you need, if there is any way we can ever help, you know we're there."

Trent and Jud had overcome a ton of shit in their lives. Their past mistakes and sins nearly ending their chance at a good life. But they'd both triumphed over their tragedies and iniquities, fought for the good.

"We appreciate that more than you both will ever know," I said, "but we'll do our damned best to make sure we don't come dragging you two into any of our bullshit."

Jud shook his head with a massive grin. "Nah, no hesitation on our part. You need us, we're there."

"Yup. Just say the word," Trent added.

"Thanks," I said, and I could feel the intensity of my crew's eyes shifting to me. Jud and Trent must have picked up on it because they both slid out of the booth. "Think we're going to get a closer view of our women."

Kane gave them a nod, and in an instant, the mood changed. Each of my brothers stared me down like they might not recognize me any longer.

Got it because I barely recognized myself.

"Think we should take this downstairs," Kane said, and everyone nodded, slipping out of the booth and snagging our drinks. We followed Kane through the door that read *employees only* and down the hall to his office. He shut and locked the door behind us then moved to the secret panel.

When he opened the passageway, we all wound down to the room below.

Normally, I was the one in charge. The one calling meetings to order. But I had a hunch tonight that was getting flipped on me.

We all sat around the round table, and I fuckin' itched while they stared at me like I might be on trial. Finally, it was Kane cutting me what appeared an accusatory smile that broke into the dense quiet. "She seems to be something more than a fuck, yeah?"

There wasn't a whole lot of anger behind it, just steely speculation.

My chest tightened, an arrow of protectiveness spearing through the middle. "Guess so."

Issuing the response that way felt like some kind of betrayal. But I still didn't know how to handle this. What the fuck to say.

I knew I was in the wrong. Knew I was in over my head. I just didn't know how to stop it.

I pressed my fingers to the achy spot in the middle of my chest, a reminder that I didn't want to.

That I wanted to keep this feeling forever.

Possess it.

"Guess so?" Otto asked with a tilt of his head. "She's staying at your place. Pretty sure that warrants a whole lot more than a *guess so.*"

A ripple of unease rolled around the table.

Theo chuckled a low sound like the fucker he was, and Cash rocked back in his chair, frustration billowing off him in waves.

Kane sipped at his whiskey as he studied me for the longest time before he said, "Going solo is one of our number one rules. She sticks around long enough, she's bound to know there's something up with you."

My nod was affirming. I wasn't going to deny what was plain obvious. "Yeah, reason I made that rule in the first place."

"And what do you think she'll do if she finds out?" Theo asked, head cocked as he scratched at the side of his cheek.

Air huffed from my nose. "Don't know. Hasn't gotten that far."

"Are you going to let it?" Kane's brow rose.

Agitation shook my head, and I slanted a hand through the short pieces of my hair. "Don't know that, either. Only thing I do know is I can't let her walk away. Not like this. Especially when I think she might be in trouble."

I looked at Cash then, hoping he had news for me after I'd called him two days ago. It seemed like so much had happened between then and now. Charleigh going from this woman who'd captured my attention, twisted me up and made me chase after a girl for the first time in my life, to someone I wasn't sure I could live without.

"What kind of trouble?" Kane asked.

"She's been hurt in the past, by her ex. That's about as much as she'll give me, other than knowing she's been running from him for years and is afraid someday he'll catch up to her."

"So what? We take her under the protection of Sovereign Sanctum?" That was from Theo.

"No." It shot out of me like a bullet. That would mean her starting a new life. Not here, and sure as hell not with me. We never left a trace.

Couldn't fucking stomach the idea.

Aggravation rolled out of Otto as he scrubbed a giant, tattooed hand over his face. When he dropped it, his gaze ping-ponged around all of us. "Think we all know what this is, yeah? And I think we all should have been smart enough to know it eventually would come to this."

"To what?" Theo asked.

"To a change. How long are we supposed to go on living this way? In fuckin' secret?"

"Only way we can do it," Kane said. "The more people we trust, the more people we put in danger. Including ourselves. We can't take that risk."

"But what about Raven? She knows," Theo tossed out, tracking what Otto was saying.

"She's the exception. She was already with us before we started," Kane argued.

"And maybe that's what Charleigh's going to be, too, an exception." It erupted from me without permission.

Kane blinked my way. "Are you insane, brother? You really want to bring her all the way in like that?"

"Don't know how I'm going to keep her if I don't."

Problem was, I wasn't sure how I was going to keep her at all. Either way I went, I was fucked. She'd be terrified of me if she knew.

A smirk lit on Kane's face, and he cracked up as he smacked a hand on the table. "You sappy motherfucker...you went and fell in love on us."

I screwed up my face like I could refute it.

"Guess that changes things," Kane added as he looked around the table. "Say we put it to a vote."

"Think you should know something before you all go running to welcome this woman with open arms," Cash said, speaking for the first time. Everyone went silent, and his intense green gaze turned to me.

"You asked me to dig around on her. Find what she was running from. But Charleigh Lowe? The one upstairs? I couldn't find one goddamn thing on her except for her place of work and her apartment here in Moonlit Ridge. Before then? She doesn't exist." His head barely shook. "Sorry to break it to you, brother, but she isn't being honest with you."

My spirit clutched. A fucking vise squeezing the oxygen from my lungs.

I didn't know what the fuck possessed me, but I was on my feet, my hands planted on the table as I leaned his direction, words breaking off like shards of broken glass. "Then maybe you need to look deeper."

Rationally, I knew it wasn't his fault. But fuck, wasn't sure I could handle it if Charleigh had been lying to me.

"I can't give you that part of myself."

Her words tumbled through my brain. Words I'd accepted, knowing she had secrets. How deep did they go? And how could I truly protect her if I didn't know?

I was storming back upstairs without saying anything else, and the rest of my crew scrambled to keep up. The second Kane had the basement access closed, I hurried to unlock the office door and ripped it open, flying back down the hall and out into the mayhem of the bar.

It was crazy packed. A riot going down on the dance floor. There were more people here than I'd ever seen before. I started to cut through the crowd, shouldering through, the need to go to her so severe I could taste the adrenaline that pumped through my veins.

I broke through to find the girls all in a circle, dancing without a care. Trent and Jud were at a high-top table off to the side, watching over them, though none of us were close enough to intercept the fucker who came up behind Charleigh and put his hand on her hip, moving behind her like he thought he was going to rub his junk all over her ass.

I was there in a flash, winding an arm around her, sending the drunk fuck the growl of a warning as I pulled Charleigh against me.

Think he pissed himself scrambling to get away, and I breathed out the first real breath I'd had since Cash had given me the update as I wrapped her up.

Her aura all around.

Cinnamon and spice.

I started to sway, pulling her into the crowd, hugging her close and breathing her in.

Fuck. Fuck. Fuck.

I was wrecked. Ruined. Destroyed.

Because I'd never felt so much relief than when I had her in my arms.

Charleigh giggled as she looked up at the rage that must have been playing out in my expression.

"Ah, I see you do dance, after all. All you needed was a little... motivation."

I buried my face in her hair and muttered, "Think you've become *the* motivation, Little Runner. You changed everything. Every. Fucking. Thing."

It was about fifteen minutes after two when we all spilled out into the parking lot. The mood was light, everyone chatting and laughing, our women giggling from the amount of alcohol they'd slung back over the night.

I kept Charleigh close to my side. Close enough that it felt like there wouldn't be any room for secrets between us. Like our spirits could reach out and read each other's minds.

The lot had cleared out since the bouncers had ushered the rest of the crowd out at closing.

We all headed to the row of motorcycles that were lined at the front. Cash, Theo, and Kane swung onto their bikes and kicked them over. Trent and Eden and Jud and Salem walked to a blacked-out SUV so they could drive over to Theo's motel where they were going to be spending the night.

Otto said he'd give Raven a ride home since her fucktwat of a date had gotten the hint that he didn't fit and had scurried off hours before.

"Be safe," everyone called as we said our goodbyes.

Otto cut a salute in my direction as he rode off with my sister on the back of his Harley.

I led Charleigh to mine, my insides rattling like chains, anxious to get her home so I could find a way to breach whatever cavern gaped between us. Reach into the places she insisted needed to be kept hidden.

But how could I blame her when I was keeping secrets of my own? When a million untruths were scattered between us.

We both climbed onto my bike, and I kicked it over. The loud rumble of everyone's bikes echoed through the crisp, cool air, the night thick and heavy.

In it, I felt the shiver of something in the distance. A blister of the foul. This sense of foreboding that drifted through the atmosphere and became one with the breeze.

A white SUV came flying up the road only to ram on its brakes, the windows on the front and back passenger side barely cracked as it slowed to a crawl.

But it was enough to see the barrel of the guns sticking out.

I dove onto Charleigh, pushing her off the backside. We hit the hard ground with a thud. A yelp of shock ripped out of her, and I could feel the confusion and panic radiate from her, though I kept her pinned, my weight fully on her, covering her with my body as the spray of bullets flew across the lot.

Bullets pinged and dust flew.

It was chaos and confusion and screams.

Panic ravaged my heart as I squeezed my eyes closed and tried to shield every inch of Charleigh.

To keep her safe.

It lasted for all of fifteen seconds before the dust cleared and the peeling of tires screeched on the road as the SUV raced away, though it was difficult to hear with the ringing in my ears from the gunshots and the loud roar of our bikes that still reverberated.

Or maybe I couldn't hear over the rage that screamed in my brain and set fire to my veins. Couldn't hear over the alarm and the fear. Couldn't hear over the reckoning that was coming.

I scrambled back, searching Charleigh where she was on the unforgiving ground.

"Are you hit?" I gritted it through clenched teeth, and my hands were fuckin' shaking as I ran them over her body. "Baby, are you hit?"

I didn't know if she could understand me through my turmoil and the disorder that battered her senses. Her eyes were wide, and when I found no blood, I pulled her up against me, relief obliterating all reason.

"You're okay. You're okay."

"River." My name finally cracked, and she choked over a sob as the awareness of what had happened came raining down.

"Stay down," I told her as I stood, and my hands were in fists as I took in the scene.

Trent and Jud climbed out of their SUV, guns drawn as they scanned through the dust and debris, ready to dive straight back into depravity.

It was in our blood. In our bones. Wasn't sure any of us could eradicate who we were beneath it all.

"Is everyone okay?" I shouted.

A flashfire of fury burned through the middle of me.

Incinerating. Charring. Scarring.

"Everyone's okay here," Trent hollered.

"Get Eden and Salem to the motel," I shouted back.

"You sure, brother?"

"Yeah. Go. Get them to safety."

"Call if you need us." Trent and Jud hopped back in, and they took off, peeling out of the parking lot.

Kane and Theo were still on their bikes, though Cash's was tipped over and he was holding his leg.

"Fuck, Cash," I roared, and I ran to his side. "You're hit."

"It's nothin'. Someone get those bastards."

I sent a vicious glance to Theo and Kane who got the message and tore out of the lot, heading in the direction the white SUV had gone.

"You recognize anyone?" he asked, turmoil in his gaze.

The shake of my head was grim. "No."

It could be a million people. Our enemies long and deep though none of them should actually know our names. But it was a risk we ran with every job we did.

The truth that one day it was all likely to catch up to us.

"Let me check your leg," I demanded. I could see blood soaking through his pant leg.

I started to kneel, only he shook his head, his teeth gritted. "It's a fucking scratch. I'll be fine. You know I've had much worse. Get your girl out of here. I'll go back inside and clean it up while I wait for Theo and Kane to get back."

"You sure?"

"Yeah, I'm sure. It's what I fuckin' get for coming into town," he grumbled.

I would've laughed if I wasn't a second from going on a rampage. A second from hunting down the motherfuckers who dared to come at my family this way. I wanted to hop on my bike, track, and destroy.

But the twisted thing was there was a bigger part of me that wouldn't allow me to leave Charleigh. Charleigh who was still on the dingy ground, her fear and confusion coming off her in a crash of violent waves.

I started to stand before Cash fisted his hand in my shirt. "Be fuckin' careful, man," he raked through the pain.

My nod was tight. "I will."

I returned to where Charleigh was sitting on the ground on the other side of my bike. Tears streamed down her gorgeous face.

"Fuck, Charleigh."

Her eyes squeezed closed, and she buried her hands in her face as a guttural sob erupted from her chest. Carefully, I gathered her up, murmuring, "You're okay. I've got you. You're okay."

Without letting her go, I swung onto my bike, though this time I put her in front of me, her chest to mine, caging her in like I could act as a shield.

Knowing that's what I would be.

Her shield.

Whatever it took.

Chapter
FORTY-NINE

Charleigh

I CLEAVED MYSELF TO River AS HE FLEW DOWN THE ROAD, MY face buried in his shirt and my hands fisted in the back of it. It was disorienting, traveling backward, unable to see where we were going or even understand what was happening.

Trying to come to grips with what had transpired outside the club. Trying to process the horror that pummeled through my insides and spun me into confusion.

Dizziness washed through my brain and nausea roiled in my stomach.

River's heart thundered at a manic pace, a thunder at my ear, a snarl of turmoil and a clutter of wrath.

He took the right turn fast, barely slowing as the bike angled before he was gunning it again. In an instant, the air was cooler, and I knew we were on Vista View, though I could tell he'd passed by the turn-off to his house and instead was barreling farther toward the mountain in the distance.

Finally, he slowed and made a couple quick turns, and I peeled myself back enough to see that we'd hit a dirt path that wound beneath the trees. When he came to a stop, we were in a clearing up close to the lake.

Trees all around.

Soaring and shrouding.

Moonlight glinted through their abundant leaves, casting a pale glow over the wild grasses that grew at the shore.

River killed the engine.

In an instant, silence surrounded us. The only sound was the distant hoot of an owl and the lapping of the waters against the embankment.

That and the frantic beat of our hearts that refused to slow.

River curled his arms around me as another sob hitched in my throat.

"I've got you, Charleigh. I've got you."

I hiccupped as I wept into his shirt, and words started tumbling out, "It's my fault. I never should have come here. Never should have entangled myself in your family. Put you in danger. It's my fault."

That's what this was, wasn't it? Frederick had found out where I was. Had found out I was alive. I should have known I could never sit still. Should have known I could never stop watching behind me.

Could never stop moving.

Running, running, running.

River held me tighter, and I could feel the hostility bristle in every muscle of his body.

"No, Charleigh. Don't think that was about you." His voice was hoarse. "Think it's me who put you in danger. Me who's getting you entangled in my shit."

His words barely cracked through the tumult that wracked me through.

"Me," he wheezed, somehow pulling me closer.

A thousand questions spun through my mind, thoughts breaking through and penetrating the disorder.

The confessions he'd made.

The warnings he'd issued.

"I've done terrible fuckin' things."

A slow awareness crept over me. I'd been so shocked that I hadn't recognized River's reaction. The way Trent and Jud had gotten out of their SUV with guns drawn. The way Theo and Kane had taken off after the shooters on their bikes.

And no one had called the cops.

No one.

And rather, River had run with me to this secluded spot.

Trepidation clotted in me like curdled milk.

Sour and fermented.

"What do you mean?" How I managed to get it out around the rocks in my throat, I didn't know.

River shifted, edging back to take me by both sides of my face. Those storm-cloud eyes raged. A hurricane in this false calm. They flicked all over my features as if he was the one who was hunting for answers.

He swallowed hard, and the words tattooed on his throat bobbed and writhed.

No mercy.

"Warned you I was a bad man, Charleigh."

My insides quivered, and part of me wanted to hop off his bike and run. The rest of me was pinned, unable to move beneath the weight of the man that'd had me hinged since the moment I'd first met him.

I could feel the plea pinch my face. "What does that mean?"

Hesitation brimmed in him, and I could almost hear his secrets bashing against the confines of where he kept them chained.

"Please...you're scaring me, River."

He exhaled a shattered breath before his eyes dropped closed as he squeezed my face tighter. "You asked me about the tattoo me and my brothers have on the back of our hands."

Dread pooled in the pit of my stomach, and when he finally opened his eyes again, I could see all the way to the depths. To the torment and shame. All the way down to the corruption and immorality.

The second he lowered his walls, I could feel it ooze from him.

"Told you it was a pact we made. That we'd always be there for each other. Have each other's backs. But it goes way deeper than that."

"Tell me." It wheezed from my mouth.

He warred for one anxious second before I could see him come to a resolution.

See the walls drop.

This man exposing himself to me.

"You already know we started out rough. On the streets."

"Because you protected Raven." I thought I was begging it because I needed that to be his reason.

River's laugh was hollow. "Yeah, Charleigh, I got Raven to safety. Got her out of that house. Hidden from the violence. But that violence still lived in me. My hatred for the monster who'd hurt her. Knowing he was still alive after what he'd done to her? Knowing he could do it to someone else? I waited a year...a fucking year that piece of shit got to breathe when he should've been six feet underground. But I went back, and I made sure he would never get the chance to hurt anyone ever again."

Sickness coiled my stomach.

I'd known immediately, though, hadn't I?

That he was dangerous?

I'd tasted the wickedness that emanated from his being.

And still, I remained there, pinned. My eyes were wide as I watched the horrors play out through his expression.

I couldn't speak, and River continued, "After I got her out of that house, we went into the city. Into LA. We were basically homeless, staying in whatever pit we could. Met Theo, Cash, and Kane there. All of us were running from something. We survived the best way we could, doing whatever odd jobs we could find and stealing the rest that we needed to get by. That was until Trent took us under his wing. He set us up with a safe place to stay. I patched into his MC because it was clear from the start that was where we belonged. The rest of my brothers followed."

River paused, gauging my reaction. My fingers were curled into his shirt at his stomach, my breaths harsh and shallow as he finally gave me access to the places I'd known he'd kept concealed.

"World we lived in was rough," he said through the strain. "Full of crime and misdeeds. We were surrounded by it night and day. One night, I was walking the street, and I heard this woman screaming from her apartment above, and a man was shouting as he clearly was beating her. I tried to keep moving. Mind my own goddamn business, but I couldn't force myself to walk away. I climbed the fire-escape stairs and went in through the window. She was just fucking...bloody, and I knew if I left her there, she'd end up dead. Maybe not that night, but one day, she would. So I ended that fucker right then and there."

His jaw ticked, the muscle feathering as he fought a wave of aggression, while I struggled to breathe.

To make sense of what he was saying.

His voice softened as his brow pinched. "The woman, she was crying and crying, whispering that she didn't know what she was going to do. Stuck in that fucked up cycle of relying on someone who would only hurt you. So, I took her with me, and me and my crew set her up in another state. Helped her start a new life. MC was running drugs and guns at the time, so we had plenty of cash to make it happen."

My mind spun with what he was telling me.

The brutality up against the generosity.

The kindness up against the barbarity.

My lungs squeezed as I tightened my fists in his shirt, my pulse thundering with each detail that he gave.

He tilted his head back to be sure I was fully in his line of sight. The severe cut of his jaw flexed with the clench of his teeth, his carved cheeks hard, his sharp brow cut in this beautiful defiance so fierce that I wasn't sure how to make sense of it.

"That was when Sovereign Sanctum was born."

SS.

I felt the burn of the imprint on the back of his hand where he had his palms gripping my cheeks.

"What exactly does that mean?" The words wobbled.

"Means I didn't stop after that. It became my purpose. My sole reason for living. Getting the vulnerable to safety. Setting them up and giving them new lives."

Shock tore through me, and the question shook. "All of you... that's what you do?"

My brother and his friends are exactly who you should turn to if you're in trouble.

Raven's encouragement from that day flashed through my thoughts.

"Yes. Each of us has different responsibilities. Kane funnels the money where we need it, Theo temporarily shelters them at his motel until we can get them moved to their new homes, Cash creates new identities for them, and Otto gets them to where they're going to be."

My eyes searched the grave lines of his face. "And what's yours?"

I somehow already knew what his answer would be.

"I get them out. By whatever means necessary."

He didn't need to say what was clearly implied.

He killed whoever tried to stop them.

The air wheezed from my lungs, words locked, uncertainty unending.

He gripped me even tighter, drawing me toward him an inch. "Say something. Please fucking say something."

I blinked through the reservations and doubt. "I'm terrified." It choked out of me, and he started to pull away, only I dragged him back by the shirt. "I'm terrified and awed."

A frown curled his brow. "You should be disgusted."

"How could I be?" Maybe I was all wrong. It wasn't like I didn't know his actions were criminal. But even if I hadn't met him and I read about what he and his friends did? I think I would…understand it. Secretly applaud it. Because if you were exposed to the type of depravity they worked to save the vulnerable from? You understood saving them was worth it. Understood going beyond the laws that had been set to offer a justice that would rarely otherwise be found.

It seemed insane that I had tried myself. Tried to fight for what was right.

Only, I'd failed and had lost everything.

At that time, I would have given anything for someone like him. For someone to have helped me. Guided me.

My hand slipped up and splayed over the booming of his heart. "I told you I recognized what was here. Recognized who you are. And maybe that's why I was drawn to you to begin with. Because I'm no different than any of those women and children you've helped, and I knew, even though there was a part of me that was terrified of you, that I'd be safe with you."

River curled his hand over mine that remained on his chest. "We don't let anyone in, Charleigh. Because the more people who know what we do the likelier it is we're going to get caught. Because what we do is dangerous. Because of things like what happened tonight. Because of a thousand reasons."

His hand cinched down. "I'm not supposed to keep you, but I don't know how to let you go."

"Then don't."

He groaned as if my words caused him physical pain, then his hands were in my hair and his mouth was on mine.

His kiss was crushing.

Bruising.

Desperate in its demand.

His tongue was hot as it swept over mine, an anguished searching that had me whimpering into his kiss.

Pleading for it as I kissed him back.

His fingers drove into the locks of my hair, alternating between gripping and splaying over my head. Every move was wrought with the need to get me as close to him as he could.

"I won't. I fuckin' can't." He rumbled the words at my lips. "Can't let you go."

His hands clamped down on the sides of my head and he pried himself back so he could look at me. Our breaths panted between us, and those stormy eyes raged.

Torment twisted his expression. "Because I love you. I'm so fucking in love with you. So caught up I can't see a future where you don't exist in it. I can't imagine a day that I wake up without you in my arms. You fuckin' struck me the first time I saw you, Charleigh. Pierced me all the way through. Stole some part of me when I inked myself on you. But you have all of me now. If you want it. If you'll take it."

Emotion rushed, careening through my veins. It washed away every last question and reservation.

My words were a jumble of desperation. "I'll take it. I need it. Because I love you, too. I think maybe a part of me fell for you that night. Because I was dead inside. So dead, and you lit the last vapor of hope that I possessed. Stoked it and brought it back to life. And I want to live. I want to live. And I want to live it with you."

In grief we must live.

I just had never known that in it I might find joy, too.

He pulled me all the way to him until our noses were an inch apart, and he uttered, "It's you and me, Charleigh. From here to eternity."

Then his mouth was back on mine.

Chapter
FIFTY

RIVER

FUCK ME.

She knew. She fucking knew, and she hadn't run. Instead, she was in my arms, confessing her love over and over against my lips.

"I love you, I love you," she whimpered as I consumed that cherry-kissed mouth.

She knew. She knew.

Now she knew and she could rest in me. Trust me. It might take time, but I was going to show her she could give me every burden she was carrying.

No doubt, I needed to dig into the info Cash had given. But not right then. Not when I just needed to show her I'd be there to hold her, no matter what. Not when I didn't want her walls to rise. Not when I didn't want anything between us.

"You're mine," I rumbled back, guts a twine of devotion and desire. It was all tossed with the rage still roaring through my veins at what'd gone down tonight. At what could have happened.

I wouldn't let it.

I would find whoever the fucker was who'd found us and snuff them out.

"And you're mine. The first person I've ever wanted," she murmured frantically.

Lust smacked me in the face, my cock steeled in possession. "Good because you're about to have me."

Needed her right then. I couldn't wait another second to get inside this woman.

My feet were planted wide to support the bike, and Charleigh scrambled to get even closer, climbing my lap like she was climbing a tree. Pressing those sweet tits against my chest as she wrapped her legs around my waist.

Her pussy was an inferno, burning me up where she rubbed herself against my straining cock.

"Need you," she begged at the frantic kiss, her nails raking, digging into my flesh over my tee. Dragging over my shoulders. My chest.

"Know what you need, Little Runner. Told you once you had my cock, you'd keep running back for more of it. Told you that you'd never get enough."

But it was me who was suffering the ailment. Sure I might die if I didn't get to feel her wrapped around my dick in the next five seconds.

My hand slipped up her bare thigh until I was gripping at the little satin piece that covered her center.

I ripped it off.

Charleigh gasped, surprised for a flash as I yanked her underwear free. I pressed the soaked fabric to my nose, inhaled that delicious scent, her essence coating my senses in greed.

"Drenched for me," I rumbled.

She whined and rubbed her bare pussy against my jeans. "Always. I didn't know what it was to want someone. To *need* someone. Not until I met you. And I need it. Fuck me, River. Possess me. Make me *remember* who I'm supposed to be."

I growled, satisfaction ripping through me since she was long past the forgetting.

She let her hands slide down until she was jerking at the button of my jeans, and I helped her, unbuttoning the button and lowering the zipper. With my position, the denim was tight, but I was able to get myself free.

I gripped my cock, my shaft fucking stone and pointed for the sky, dripping at the tip. Head so engorged it verged on painful.

Her tongue stroked over her lips in a whispered frenzy, her legs quivering where she held herself up, hovering high. "Oh God, look at you."

I stroked myself once. "You want it, Little Runner? You want my cock filling you full?"

"Yes," she whimpered.

"Want you bare." I grunted it. "Want to feel your slick walls drenching my flesh."

She gave a rabid nod of her head, and she curled her arms around my neck as she fully straddled me, though she kept her body high and lifted.

I gazed up at her.

She was moonlit.

Rays of milky shimmer rolling over her, casting her in warmth and light. Stunning face illuminated, soul shining bright.

Heart clutching, I tossed her skirt up around her waist.

I fed her just the head of my cock, the barbell notching into her cunt. Even that was snug. So fuckin' snug I got the wind knocked out of me.

I tightened my hold around her waist, fisted the base of my cock, trying to will myself into control.

Every time I had her, it was the same. The pleasure she wrung out of me close to torture.

Her thighs shook. "River."

I gave her another inch, then another, and her nails sank into my shoulders as I took her deeper and deeper. Her breaths turned raspy as she struggled to adjust. "You feel so…it's too much."

She said it almost every fucking time when I spread her wide, her tight little body barely accommodating me. But she did.

"You can take it, Charleigh. You were meant for me. Meant to take my cock."

Meant to take every part of me. Her sweet, open soul seeing me for who I was and accepting me, anyway.

Her cunt spasmed and clutched as I gave her more. It was different this time, her arousal coating my dick, her walls throbbing as I filled her halfway.

"You're turn, Little Runner. You take the rest of me. Take my cock like you were made to do."

The cinnamon in her eyes turned to lava.

She sank down.

Hard.

Stuffing herself so full neither of us could breathe. We were nothing but gasps and moans and burrowing fingers. She stayed seated that way for a few excruciatingly blissful seconds before she eased up then propelled herself back down, using my shoulders for leverage.

"That's right, ride me, baby. Told you I was going to have you spread out on my bike. Nothing fuckin' better than having my girl wrapped around my cock, earth around us, metal beneath us."

She started rocking, rising up and driving down. Shocks of ecstasy shot up my spine with every stroke.

I shoved up her tank, exposing those gorgeous tits, and I took a hard-tipped nipple between my teeth.

Her fingers drove into my hair on a gasp, trying to grip on though there was little to hold on to, her touch wild as she started to buck.

I gripped her by the hips, guiding the angle so the metal ball of my piercing would hit that sweet spot inside her with each thrust.

I sucked and licked at her breasts, my hands gliding up and down her sides as she rode me.

She whimpered and writhed and moaned, and I couldn't do anything but edge back a fraction so I could watch over her while she let go.

The woman bounced on my dick, pitching and lurching, unrestrained. Taking it the way she wanted it.

In it, I knew she was free.

And I loved it. I fucking loved it. Loved her.

My chest fisted tighter than it ever had before.

Fuck. I loved her.

Was never supposed to have this. But now that I did? I'd never let her go.

Chapter
FIFTY-ONE

Charleigh

Twenty-One Years Old

HER FATHER TOOK HER BY THE ELBOW WHERE THEY WERE hidden in the hallway at her house. There was another function. Frederick putting on a show for his colleagues and friends. Acting the good guy the way he always did.

It meant she was also putting on a show. Entertaining their guests as if she were a doting, happy wife. All while her insides were a toil of desperation and despair.

Six months had passed since Levi was born. Six months of torment. Six months of fear.

Knowing she couldn't remain there and raise this child that she loved more than anything she'd ever loved in her life. She'd heard it spoken of—a mother's love. How powerful and unending it was. That you couldn't truly understand it until you held that child in your arms.

She understood it now, and she understood the lengths she would go to protect it.

"I have a plan," her father said, pinning on the fakest smile so it would appear as if he were having a normal chat with his daughter if someone were to notice them.

Hope blossomed in the middle of the turmoil, and she gulped around it and tried to play it cool.

She'd managed to meet with him several times over the last few months. In the few moments she'd been able to sneak away. He'd crumbled when she'd told him of the abuse she'd suffered, when she explained how she'd gotten wrapped up in the vilest of men.

Her father had wept. Had told her he'd been set up, too. That Frederick was using threats against her and her mother to blackmail him into doing his nefarious deeds. Forging his books and making his dirty business look clean.

It seemed Frederick Winston just twisted his manipulation in every direction. Using them all for his heinous will.

They'd discussed options. She knew the only thing she could do was completely disappear. Take her son and run. She just didn't know how to do it.

Trapped under the rubble of this life that was going to destroy her.

Smiling wide, she giggled, as if her father had said something funny as she set her hand on his forearm. "Oh really? And what is that?"

"Two weeks from Friday. Frederick will be out of town. Meet me with Levi, in your car, at the Starbucks on Tremont and Oak. Ten a.m. Whatever instruction I give you, you mustn't hesitate. Just do what I ask you to do."

Dread pooled in her stomach, but she kept up the smile. "I need you safe, too."

"We're all going to be. I promise, Sweet Pea, we're all going to be."

That morning, she rose with the sun. Frederick had left for a business trip the previous night.

She climbed from bed and went straight into her son's room. Her heart nearly burst when she saw his sweet face where he sat up in his crib, smiling at her with his two little teeth he had on his bottom gums, waving his little stuffed puppy in one hand.

She swept him up and into her arms. Love overflowed.

She pressed a kiss to his temple, breathed in the sweet scent of his blond curls as she tried to settle the nerves that ravaged her insides.

They were leaving.

They were getting out of there.

They were going to make it.

I'm going to give you a good life, she silently promised again and again.

She did her best to keep her same daily routine. Feeding Levi. Playing with him on his floor. Acting as if nothing was amiss since she was sure Frederick would be monitoring her on the video.

She didn't make any deviances. Not until twenty to ten when she slipped on her shoes, grabbed her son, and walked out the door. It wasn't that odd for her to leave during the day. Frederick wanted to make sure she kept up all appearances.

Doing yoga and lunches and fundraisers. Things the wife of a man like him would do.

Though she was shaking out of control as she buckled Levi into his car seat, her sweet boy babbling and waving his puppy. She kissed his cheeks, his knuckles, tried to calm herself as she climbed into the driver's seat and made the fifteen-minute drive to meet her father.

She pulled into the parking lot. Immediately, she saw her father's car on the other side of the lot. She took the spot beside it, her pulse clattering through her veins.

Her father was in the driver's seat, and her mother was in the front passenger.

Her cousin Lilah got out of a car on the other side of them.

Her stomach was a riot of knots.

Barely able to get her hands to cooperate, she unlatched her door and climbed out of her car just as her father and mother got out of theirs.

Fear and determination pulled through her mother's expression. "Grab Levi and buckle him into our car."

Confusion bound her, but she remembered what her father had requested of her. She needed not to question. They didn't have time. She had to trust that he was going to get them out of this.

She immediately did, unbuckling her son who was giggling and cooing and waving at his grandparents, no idea of what they were about to embark on.

Having no idea the danger that surrounded them.

Panic thundered, but her determination was stronger.

Her mother opened the back door of their car, and she was quick to buckle Levi into the car seat that was already there.

"What's going on?" she asked while she fumbled with the straps.

"We decided this morning it would be best for you to take Lilah's car and leave yours here. Lilah is going to come with us, just in case anyone is watching," her father rushed.

Lilah resembled her. A lot. Tall with long blonde hair. A slow, sinking feeling crept over her when she realized what her father was thinking.

"But Levi..." Her voice croaked when she said it.

"We think it's best to separate you two."

She understood immediately. Her father wanted to throw Frederick's guys off their tracks. Disorient them.

"You'll meet us here tomorrow." He shoved a folded piece of paper into her hand.

Sickness coiled in her being, and her spirit screamed at the thought of being separated from her son for even a second.

"Trust me. It's the best way," her father urged, his voice low. His attention whipped around as he searched the lot, as if he were worried that they might be being watched.

Because if Frederick had picked up a trail, if he had any idea, then...

Horror gripped her, a cyclone of fear ripping through her senses.

But she had to.

They had no other choice.

She had to take this risk.

"Go," her father gritted.

In a frenzy, she ducked back into the backseat of her parents' car, and she smothered kisses all over her little boy's face. Her hands were on his cheeks as she murmured, "I love you. I love you more than anything."

He babbled and yanked at a lock of her hair.

She forced herself to straighten and then she threw herself at her father. "Be careful," she begged.

He nodded. "You be careful, too."

She hugged her mother and then rushed to hug her cousin, murmuring, "Thank you."

Lilah nodded against her shoulder. "It's time for you to live free and without pain. I'm honored to have a small part in making that happen."

She choked over a cry and hugged her cousin harder because she knew she'd never see her again.

Then she raked the tears off her face before she tossed her phone into the bushes then climbed into her cousin's car. She fumbled to plug the address where they were supposed to meet in Columbus, Ohio into the map on the dash.

And with her heart in her throat, she sped away.

Chapter
FIFTY-TWO

Charleigh

"**H**OW ARE YOU HOLDING UP?" CONCERN FILLED RAVEN'S VOICE as she peered at me from where we sat at the island.

She had asked me that no less than fifteen times throughout the day.

"I'm okay," I told her. "Shaken for sure, but I know they'll figure out who it was."

It was strange that I was the one who was reassuring her because honestly, I was terrified.

But Raven had been extremely anxious.

Unable to sit still with each second that'd passed.

A constant diffusion of fear emanating from her spirit.

Last night, when River and I had finally returned to the house, she'd been pacing the living room, and she'd come beelining for River and had thrown herself into his arms right as she'd started sobbing.

He'd promised her again and again that he was fine, telling her he'd never let anything happen to him since he needed to be there to take care of her, but that promise hadn't seemed to soothe her.

Their bond had never been more obvious than right then. Their pasts forging an affinity that was stronger than I'd realized. It was also apparent that Raven's scars went deeper than I'd ever imagined.

Otto had stayed with her, and he'd been sitting on the couch, his expression grim when he'd finally stood. He and River had disappeared down the hall, their voices hushed snarls as they discussed what had happened.

We learned that Theo and Kane hadn't been able to catch up to the attackers, and they'd returned to the club to check on Cash, carrying only hate and hostility.

River had kissed me hard before he'd said he had to go and meet with his crew. He'd crawled into bed with me at just before dawn, had undressed me slowly and taken me quietly.

His dark, dark eyes had watched down on me.

After he'd picked Nolan up this morning, he'd brought him back here and had spent a couple hours with him before he'd said he needed to go back to the club. They were doing everything they could to weed out whoever might be responsible. To find who might have picked up on a trace or a clue.

So now, Raven and I were at the house, the alarm set, and one of the bouncers from the club was stationed outside, the same as another had been last night.

River wasn't taking any chances.

Raven looked at me with all the worry she couldn't evade where we sat at the kitchen island. We'd made an easy dinner, and the coffee we'd drank throughout the day had been exchanged for a bottle of wine we were sharing.

"I know they will find whoever is responsible," she whispered. "They're...careful."

My swallow was thick as I was still toiling with the details River had given me last night. Still unsure what to make of them. Torn though it was clear where I'd landed.

"I'm so glad you stayed," Raven said, as if she'd known exactly what I'd been thinking. "I knew you'd be able to hold his burdens, too."

She reached out and squeezed my hand.

I blinked through the reality of what River was. "It's really difficult to make sense of something that is both so honorable and depraved."

Something he could...go to prison for.

For…forever.

Her nod was slow. We both turned our attention to Nolan where he was playing with Legos on the floor in the living room. We kept our voices low enough that only we could hear.

"He only does what he has to…*when* he has to. For people like him." She softly gestured with her chin toward the boy. "Could you imagine if it was Nolan? And there are so many women and children just like him. In trouble. Desperate to get free of their situations. Trapped with no way to get out. River makes sure they can. In the moment, I believe most of us would do the same."

"I know. If someone were in danger right in front of me, and my only option was to…"

My heart hitched, unable to say the words, and my gaze returned to Nolan, sure of the lengths I would go to protect him.

He looked up at that moment with his sweet, sweet grin.

My heart nearly seized with the amount of love I felt for him.

It's you and me from here to eternity.

My spirit hummed.

It was going to be us.

All of us.

This child a permanent part of my life which made sense since I could already feel him etched in my soul.

Nolan climbed to his feet as if he felt the pull of my heart. "Whelp, I better take a bath because my Daddy-O told me I needed to be extra good today since he was gonna be gone, and I don't want to go breakin' any rules. I need a really good report when he gets back because maybe then I'll get to go get ice cream after I get picked up from Miss Liberty's tomorrow."

Blinking, I attempted to shove off the heaviness. The worry that strained on the atmosphere as we waited to hear any news. "That sounds like a really good plan."

I glanced at Raven as I slipped off my stool. "I'll take care of it."

She didn't argue with me. She just let this softness rise to her features, as if she understood the position I was taking.

She waved her glass of wine in my direction. "I'm going to polish this off and then I think I'm going to go upstairs and read. I need something to get my mind off things."

"Go ahead and polish mine off, too." I shot her a grin.

She pressed her fingers to her chest. "And here I thought *I* was the world's best bestie. I think that title might actually belong to you."

"It's the little things," I told her.

She laughed a soft laugh. "God, I really love you."

"I love you, too," I whispered, then I took Nolan's hand and let him lead me upstairs.

He rambled nonstop the entire time, telling me all about the great time he'd had the night before.

"And Gage is already going to be eight and Juni Bee is seven." Then he frowned as he looked up at me with his index finger pressed to his chin. "Wait a minute…I'm not for sure because I can't even remember how many birthday parties I've been to but I think that's pretty right."

A soft laugh rippled out of me as I followed him into the bathroom that was off the same side of the hall as his room. He started peeling off his clothes while I ran the water, making sure it was warm but not too hot.

"I like lots of bubbles, Miss Charleigh. All the way up to my chin. It's the pink bottle because it smells like bubble gum, and I love bubble gum. Do you love bubble gum?"

Amusement made its way through the worry. "I haven't had any bubble gum in a long time, but if I remember right, I think I do."

I tipped over the bottle of bubbles and squeezed it beneath the rush of water from the faucet.

The scent of bubble gum filled the room.

Nolan was not kidding.

"Well, we should probably get you some because it's really good if we have the things we love." Without warning, he hopped into the tub. He splashed a giant wave of water over the side, and his blue eyes went ridiculously wide. "Oops. I think I got the floor wet."

I couldn't stop my giggle, and I stood so I could grab a towel to sop it up, then I climbed back onto my knees at the side of the tub. The water rose, and the bubbles gathered and grew.

"There, all the way to your chin." I dabbed a bit of suds onto his dimpled chin. "I think it's because you want to look like Santa Claus."

Laughing, he kicked his feet and splashed more water over the side. "Santa Claus is my favorite, and he's probably a good guy to want to be. Like my dad except my dad doesn't got no white beard."

My spirit clutched. Because I knew he was. I knew his father was a really *good* guy while being so thoroughly bad.

"Okay, let's get that hair wet," I told him. I edged up high on my knees so I could reach him, and I slipped an arm under his back to support him while I dunked him without getting water and suds in his eyes. Then I grabbed the shampoo bottle that also was bubble gum scented and squeezed a dollop onto his head.

His head was tipped back, and he was beaming up at me as I massaged it into his hair.

Only I frowned when color started staining the suds.

A dark, dark brown. Almost black.

I pulled my hands away, staring at them and wondering if I was imagining things. I would have chalked it up to dirt, but this was...

My brow pinched.

Hair dye.

It was fresh *hair dye.*

I'd dyed my own hair enough times to recognize exactly what it was.

I was frozen, staring at it in confusion. Bewildered and perplexed. Though something more consequential nagged at the back of my mind.

"Is your...hair dyed?" The question cracked.

"Oh, yep! My Daddy-O made my hair all better a couple days ago, and that always happens and gets my water all dirty, but don't worry, Miss Charleigh, after one more bath, it's all gone and then I'll be all clean again."

He smacked his hands against the surface of the water, sending droplets splattering onto my shirt and arms.

"Your dad...dyes your hair?" I pushed out on a whisper. The words were laden, as if the disorientation made it difficult to speak.

"He says he likes it really, really dark so it can be just like his, and that's good because I really want to look like him and not Santa Claus like you thought."

He cracked up like it was hysterical while the walls spun around me.

I didn't know why it unsettled me so profoundly. Why I was shaking as I rinsed the shampoo out and repeated the process with the conditioner. Why disquiet gathered from the edges of my being, whirling together to become a gnarl of apprehension.

Woodenly, I helped him wash then rinse, then I undid the drain stopper and wrapped him in a towel. He prattled on as he brushed his teeth and hair, still going on about his favorite friends as he dashed into his room and pulled on a fresh pair of pajamas.

He read me another book while I just stared at him. Stared and stared at him through the disorder that billowed and blew through my consciousness. And when he flopped onto his back for me to tuck him in, I lifted his left arm and ran my fingertips over the birthmark on the inner side.

A tidal wave of memories crashed through me.

Nolan giggled. "That's my love mark."

"Love mark?" My voice was haggard.

"Yep. My dad said he thinks I probably got it from my mom because it's almost like a heart, and he bet she loved me a whole, whole lot."

That disorder surged, and I couldn't make sense of what I was feeling. The chaos that battered my insides.

I was going insane. Conjuring ideas that I couldn't afford to conjure. Still, my insides quaked and my spirit shivered.

I pulled his covers to his chin, and he squirmed beneath them. "Do it like my dad does it," he said through his sweet voice.

I tucked the covers under his little body while my pulse thundered through my veins.

"How's that?"

"Perfect!" he shrieked, then he threw his arms out and squeezed them around my neck. "I love you the most just like I love my dad!"

"I love you, too." It was a breath. A whisper, and I finally stood and moved across his room, looking back at the child where he snuggled on his bed.

His heart beating. Blood running through his veins.

Finally, I forced myself to flip off his light. I moved to River's room, changed into sleep shorts and a tee, and slipped under the cold sheets.

I tried to find sleep, but I couldn't rest. Couldn't stop the dangerous idea that had sprouted roots in my heart and mind.

I squeezed my eyes closed. I had to be being…paranoid. Grasping at straws. Imagining things that weren't there. My heart trying to convince me of something that was impossible.

But still, I couldn't let it go when River finally slipped into the room in the middle of the night. He crawled in behind me and pulled me into his arms, his big body a thousand degrees as it burned into the chill that had taken me hostage.

I wanted to turn to him and demand answers.

Scream.

Plead.

But no.

I couldn't force the hazardous thoughts from my tongue.

Because if I was wrong? It would destroy me all over again.

Chapter
FIFTY-THREE

Charleigh

"THE DOCTOR SHOULD BE WITH YOU IN A FEW MINUTES," I said, voice hollow as I left the patient in the examination room.

River had tried to convince me not to go in to work, but I'd refused, telling him I had no sick time to take. It was the truth, but it didn't have anything to do with the reason I couldn't agree.

I needed to move. To shuck the errant thoughts that had laid siege to my brain and had sunk their talons into my psyche.

Since I'd insisted on going in, Raven had decided she was going to go into work, too.

She'd suggested I drop her off at Moonflower and take her car since I got off earlier, and then I would go back to pick her up at the end of the day.

She'd paused when I'd pulled up outside her shop, and she'd reached out and squeezed my wrist, concern burrowed deep in her brow as she asked, "What's wrong?"

I had barely been able to toss out the lie. "I…I just haven't been sleeping well after everything. I think I just need to get back into a normal routine. Shake myself out of the fear."

She'd nodded and promised, "It's going to be okay."

I wanted it to be.

I wanted to feel okay.

To grasp back onto reality.

But I hadn't been able to escape the thoughts that had plagued me since last night here, either.

They'd followed me throughout the morning.

I moved into the office so I could get the records for Dr. Reynolds' next appointment, and I pulled out the file cabinet drawer labeled T so I could grab Francisca Thomas' chart.

Only I stilled when my fingertips brushed over the name on a tab toward the front.

Tayte, Nolan.

Nerves tumbled through my stomach. What did I think I was doing? But instead of ignoring it and moving on, I glanced behind me to make sure no one else was around and pulled out the file.

It wasn't like I didn't have access to the files or wasn't allowed to look, but it felt like what I was doing was illicit.

Wrong.

With my back to the door, I kept it concealed as I rested Nolan's file on my left arm and flipped it open.

I scanned the information. Name, date of birth, address, family contact.

The inputs in my handwriting that I'd made the first day that I'd met him.

I started to flip through the papers.

His well-checks.

A visit for a fever.

I didn't even know what I was looking for. What I hoped to find.

Until I did.

I'd flipped through the entire stack until I made it to the last page. It was a record of Nolan's very first visit. A well-check of a six-month-old baby boy.

17 lbs. 2 oz, 27.1 inches.

Blue eyes.

Blond hair.

Blond hair.

It felt as if I got socked in the gut.

But what nearly dropped me to my knees was the symbol that had been drawn in the corner.

A haphazard shape clearly drawn by an amateur's hand—Dr. Reynolds' hand.

But there was no mistaking it.

The stacked Ss with the eye in the middle.

The same as River and all his friends had tattooed on the back of their hands.

Oh God. Oh God.

Sweat slicked on my flesh and tears burned at the backs of my eyes.

"Charleigh? What are you doing?"

A gasp ripped out of me, and I whirled around to find Dr. Reynolds standing in the doorway. His hand was on the knob and his face was written in concern. Apprehension curled through his expression when he saw that I was holding a patient file.

"Oh. Nothing. I just was looking for the next patient's chart, and I accidentally grabbed the wrong one." I flipped it closed and turned, trying to get my hands to cooperate as I frantically stuffed it back into its place. I hurried to grab Francisca Thomas'.

Slamming shut the cabinet drawer, I waved the folder high as I whipped around. "Here we are."

A frown pinched tight across his weathered brow. "Are you okay?"

No. I was not okay. *I was not okay.*

I was crumbling.

Shattering.

I forced a smile. "Of course."

Warily, he nodded. "All right then. I need you to call the lab and ask about the status of Mr. Murray's bloodwork. We should have received it before his follow-up today."

"I'll get right on it."

He hesitated again before he mumbled, "Thank you," and ducked out. I waited until his footsteps retreated down the hall before I scrambled out of the office and hurried to the breakroom. Every molecule in my body shook as I grabbed my purse. I attempted to keep my cool as I crossed the lobby.

But the second I pushed open the front door, I broke into a sprint.

Running to where I'd parked Raven's car, I frantically clicked the locks over and over as I approached, and I fumbled to yank open the door handle. My pulse thundered as I jumped into the car and pushed the button to start it.

I put the car in reverse and whipped out of the parking spot, and my breaths came in shallow, jagged pants as I shifted it into gear and rammed on the gas.

I peeled out as I took to the street.

It was impossible.

Impossible.

I was terrified I was right.

Terrified that I was wrong.

Because how?

How?

Tears blurred my eyes as I flew through Moonlit Ridge. I skidded around a corner, fishtailing as I hit Vista View. But I couldn't slow. Couldn't stop to consider that I was being impulsive and rash.

Desperate was what I was.

Desperate in the truest sense of the word.

I came to a screeching stop in front of River's house, and I jammed at the button on the rearview mirror that lifted the garage. I didn't bother to pull in. I jumped out and ran inside the empty house, quick to punch in the code for the alarm system.

Silence echoed, and for a moment, I slowed, faltering in the hall, not sure what direction to go. Then I gulped the crash of confusion down, and I ran through the house and bounded upstairs.

I went straight to the end of the hall and tossed open the door to River's room.

My gaze raved as I looked around.

I made the quick decision and cut through the en suite bathroom to the walk-in closet at the back.

I tore open the door, scanning, unsure of where to start or what I thought I was looking for. Just knowing I had to do *something*.

I went to the row of shirts hung on the racks to the right, and I parted the sections, pushing them back to see if anything was behind them.

My stomach twisted when I came up with nothing.

I kept moving, digging through his things, my movements growing more agitated with every second that passed. I tossed his shoes off the shelves and pulled pants from where they were stacked, toppling everything to the ground as I searched.

I wheezed in a torrent of frustration before I moved to the opposite side of the closet and began doing the same.

Ransacking River's things.

There were a bunch of boxes on the top shelf that I could barely reach, and I jumped, knocking them free. I ripped off their lids and dumped their contents onto the floor.

One after another.

Nothing.

Nothing.

Frantic, I searched, ripping through everything I could find.

There was a small box at the back of the top shelf that I couldn't reach, and I used a hanger to drag it free. It toppled off the shelf and onto the floor, and the lid came free when it hit.

The contents spilled out, and for one fleeting second, I froze.

Then I dropped to my knees.

My heart severed down the middle.

Tears poured, so thick that it was difficult to see. But I knew what was strewn out in front of me. A little one-piece outfit. Yellow with a giraffe embroidered on the front. The tiny white Vans.

I choked and gasped as lightheadedness swept through me.

My soul screamed and my spirit wept.

Then I picked up the tiny stuffed dog, woven of blue yarn, and I pressed it to my nose. I inhaled deeply as if it could fill the cavern carved out in the middle of me from the years of loss.

I held onto the puppy as I floundered to my feet and stumbled out of River's room, my shaking hands on the walls to keep myself steady.

Tears kept falling and falling.

Terrified of believing.

The wounds inside me gaped, torn open wide, and I almost tripped over my feet as I raced downstairs and back out the garage door. Raven's car was still idling where I'd left it, and I jumped in and peeled out as I shoved it into reverse. The rear tires slid as I careened up the drive and out onto the street.

I kept trying to sweep the tears out of my eyes as I drove.

Tried to focus.

To see.

To breathe.

I swerved through traffic, driving manic and reckless. But I couldn't wait one second longer. I whipped into an open spot on the street, and I bolted out of the car and ran for River's shop. Without slowing, I tore open the door and staggered inside.

River spun around from where he'd been standing at the display case. Venom curled into his expression, ready to snap into action when he saw the state I was in. Ready to go on a rampage because he'd instantly thought I'd been harmed in some way.

Only he blanched when he saw the stuffed animal I had gripped in my hand, and a different sort of severity blistered across his face and ticked through the muscles of his body.

"Charleigh?"

My name was caution.

Reluctance.

My throat was nearly closed off, but somehow, I managed to force out the garbled words as I gripped at the stuffed puppy as if it could be an anchor.

"Tell me Nolan isn't actually your son. Tell me he's mine."

Chapter
FIFTY-FOUR

RIVER

Five Years Ago

"A RE YOU SURE WE SHOULD TAKE THIS JOB?" THEO PACED THE bedroom where River shoved a couple changes of clothes into a duffle bag.

Agitation seeped from Theo in black waves, his aggression snagged on the cloud of disquiet that covered the air.

"Think it's a little late to be questioning that," River rumbled as he dragged the zipper shut.

Theo scuffed a palm over his face. "This fucker is a billionaire. We've never gone up against someone this powerful. And Cash is getting ready to strip him of a few of those zeroes. Pretty sure he's not going to take too kindly to that."

It was the rich monsters who supported them. Cash was all too quick to hack his way into their assets and divert them to untraceable accounts. They used that money to set up their clients with their new lives.

"This guy isn't going to just sit aside and act like his wife and kid didn't just go missing...plus the millions from his accounts," Theo continued.

Unease clamped in River's chest. "We already accepted this job. There's no turning back now."

And it wasn't like he'd leave some woman and her kid stranded. Not when her father had contacted him and asked him to get his daughter and grandson to safety.

His part in this was going to be easy. The father would be delivering his daughter and grandson to him, he was going to drive along the Northern border all the way to Washington, then cut down through Washington and head south to California. Her parents were going to meet them there where the crew would then proceed to get them all new identities.

He was flying to New York where he'd rent a car, then he'd drive to the meeting point this side of the Massachusetts border. He'd drive them back to LA where they could protect them until they felt it was safe to start new lives for them elsewhere. Keep them secreted because there was no question that the rich bastard was going to be looking for them.

"Have a bad feeling, man," Theo said, grabbing River by the arm as he started to stride from the room.

River paused and looked at his friend. "Took an oath to protect, whatever that looks like."

Theo released a heavy sigh. "Just…be careful, River."

River gave him a clipped nod then walked out.

River gripped at the steering wheel where he sat tucked back just off the two-lane road. The area was wooded and secluded, pines and oaks hugging the road, their spiked tips disappearing into the heavy clouds that hung low above.

He'd only counted three cars that had passed traveling either direction in the hour he'd been sitting there.

A river snaked through to the east of him, and he kept his attention focused on the high, suspended bridge that crossed the river, prepared for any sight of the silver Lexus sedan he was waiting for.

This was going to be quick. Make the transfer and get them the hell out of there. Time sensitive. The piece of shit was away for a business trip, but that didn't mean he wasn't keeping tabs on the woman.

Men like him always did.

When he heard the distant sound of an engine approaching, River sat upright and peered through the windshield. He was frustrated as fuck that he couldn't see a thing around the trees.

Finally, a car wound the corner on the other side and came into view a hundred feet or so before the suspended bridge.

A silver car.

Anticipation lined his bones, and he sat forward even farther, squinting to try to make out the emblem on the car.

Only he realized the car was flying. Flying fast as it hit the bridge. Trepidation coiled through him when he saw there was another car behind it, some kind of black SUV, speeding just as fast. The driver of the SUV swerved into the oncoming lane, trying to pull up to the side of the silver car.

"Fuck," River spat, and he grabbed his gun where he had it hidden on the floorboards.

Theo was right.

This job was about to get messy.

He unlatched his door and started moving, running that direction along the line of the trees.

The black SUV swerved again, and the silver Lexus veered to the right, coming up close to the edge, before it swerved back to the left. It bashed against the SUV, metal sheering, and it sent the Lexus sailing back the other direction.

"Fuck, no!" River shouted it like he could stop what he could already see playing out in his mind. The driver had no fucking experience to be driving like that.

He hit the right barricade, sparks flying from the metal grating against the car.

He overcorrected, and the tires squealed as he cut left. So sharp that he cut across the left lane behind the SUV and went straight for the left barricade.

The low metal barrier wasn't enough to keep it in. He blew right through the barricade.

River's heart toppled to his stomach when he saw the car fly over the side and into the river below. The SUV skidded to a stop, whipping around and stopping for the flash of a second before the driver gunned it, flying back in the direction they'd come.

River ran at an all-out sprint, fumbling down the bank. The tail end of the car stuck up, and he dove in.

Freezing cold water swallowed him, but he swam with all he had. He got to the back door and busted the glass with his gun. He managed to get the door open, and he gulped for air before he ducked under the water.

His eyes were wild as he struggled to process. To see what he could do. How he could fix this. Save them.

Blood drifted through the water, and long blonde hair floated around the woman on the far side.

But right in front of him was a child.

A baby in a rear-facing car seat.

He fumbled to get his buckles free, and he nearly gasped when he had him in his arms.

River swam with him to the surface, lifting him above.

But he didn't think the child was moving.

Horror clanged through River, and he kicked his legs to propel them the short distance back to the bank of the river. He climbed up, gasping and shaking.

Freezing cold.

He laid the baby out on the wild grasses, his hands shaking as his fingers went to the child's neck.

A pulse.

He had a pulse.

"Oh my God."

River ripped his shirt off and tucked the baby to his chest to give him warmth, and he climbed back to his feet.

He looked back to where the tail end of the car was still tipped in the air and watched as it fully turned over and was swallowed by the river.

Guilt constricted. A death sentence. It rang in his ears and beat through his blood.

He struggled to breathe.

He'd failed these people.

Failed.

Suddenly, the baby wailed. Wailed in his arms. River choked and held him closer. "I've got you. I've got you."

River jogged back to the car, ripped open the back door, and laid the child on the seat so he could pull him out of his wet clothes. He quickly buckled him into the car seat that he'd already purchased to be ready for the extraction, covered the child with a blanket, and got back into the driver's seat.

He turned the heat on full blast.

Then he drove.

Chapter
FIFTY-FIVE

RIVER

MY PULSE ROARED IN MY EARS AS I STARED AT CHARLEIGH. She stood across the lobby, face full of tears, eyes puffy and red, cheeks chapped and raw.

My mind fucking reeled, trying to make sense of what she was saying. I kept looking between her face and the stuffed animal she had clutched in her hand.

Stones sank to the pit of my stomach as I tried to process through her demands. Wondering why the fuck she had that stuffed animal. Why she'd gone through my things.

Why the fuck she could barely stand.

She swayed from side to side, clinging to that stuffed puppy like it was a lifeline. A buoy when she was drowning in a sea of misery.

My throat thickened, and my chest stretched tight. The protectiveness I'd always felt for the child built in intensity. Steel barricades I would never let anyone through.

But this was Charleigh we were talking about. Charleigh who I'd confessed everything to.

Everything but this.

"Is he yours?" She choked the words around a sob.

I wavered, uncertainty battering my brain. My devotion to

the child had become the greatest focus of my life. My reason. But Charleigh had become that, too. I couldn't keep her in the dark. Not with this.

I minutely shook my head. "I love him in every sense of the word, but no, he's not my biological son."

It felt like a blade was driven through me at saying it.

Charleigh broke at the confession, and she flew into a fury of sorrow and grief and rage. In the span of a second, she'd erased the space between us and was slamming her fists against my chest. "Whose is he? Whose is he? You said his mother was dead. Tell me."

She kept begging it. Wheezing it over the grief that clotted her throat.

What the fuck was going on?

I tried to gather her up and stop her assault, but she was distraught, verging on hysterical. "Tell me!"

I managed to pull her to my chest, and I locked my arms around her. My thoughts were a disorder as I tried to catch up to what she was implying.

I tucked her tight, pinning her arms to my chest as I muttered at the top of her head, the grief of what I'd felt that day slamming me through.

The way I'd failed.

The way I'd made the commitment that day that Nolan would be the only person I would ever again make a commitment to.

Until her.

"She is dead." The words scraped from my throat as if they were a confession.

"No," Charleigh sobbed, her head shaking against the violent thunder in my chest. "No. You had his things. I know they are the same. It's him. It's him. And his hair...the birthmark."

"Charleigh." I tried to break into the turmoil that had her trapped.

"Levi. He's Levi."

I went cold. A slick of ice slipped down my spine, freezing every inch of me as it went.

"What did you say?" It raked out of me like the dragging of razors.

"Levi. My son was Levi."

Levi.

I started to tremble, guts a tangle of confusion and fear.

"Tell me who you've been runnin' from, Charleigh. Who?" It grated off my tongue.

Charleigh went rigid before she burrowed deeper into my chest. "Frederick Winston."

The two words hit me like shotgun blasts.

The room spun around me, and the walls closed in. I held her tighter as it all sped, coming together. The truth slammed me like a runaway train.

Charleigh Lowe doesn't exist.

My arms fucking shook, and my teeth ground as I forced out, "What's your name? Your real name?"

Charleigh flinched then hung on tighter as she breathed, "Chastity Winston."

No.

She was dead.

Chastity Winston was dead.

I'd seen it myself.

Had seen that car go over the bridge.

I'd only been able to save one person in that car.

Levi.

"Chastity died in that car wreck." The words were gravel. Shards and stone.

Charleigh trembled like razors were dragging across her flesh.

"No. It was my cousin," she choked. "She was in the car. A decoy so I could meet my parents at the right place so they could help me and Levi get to safety."

That energy that had connected us bashed against the walls. A howl that thundered and shook.

"Levi was killed," she whimpered. "The news said…"

I gripped her tighter, holding her through the hurricane that beat around us. "I got him out, Charleigh, I got him out."

A sob tore from her mouth and Charleigh lost strength. She

crumpled to the floor. I went with her and pulled her onto my lap and let her sob. My hands stroked through her hair. Again and again.

While the truth whirled around us.

Nolan was her son. Nolan was her son.

"How?" she begged. "I didn't...my father..."

She couldn't even form the questions, and I tried to fill in the pieces that loomed around us.

"Your father contacted us for help to get his daughter and grandson out of an abusive situation. We were supposed to meet on the other side of the bridge where the accident happened. I was waiting. They were being chased by an SUV. No question, Frederick's men. They were driving recklessly and caused the accident. I watched the car go over. The SUV immediately took off, and I dove in. I was able to get Nolan...Levi..." I corrected, "...out."

My tongue stroked across my dry lips, my body a fucking live wire. Zinging with disturbed energy.

"I wasn't able to save the rest of them."

Charleigh's tears seeped through the fabric of my shirt. "But my father gave me an address in Ohio where I was supposed to meet them. I don't understand."

My head shook. "I don't, either. It was supposed to be the two of you I was picking up."

"He separated us," she choked.

I kissed her head, gutted by the loss she'd sustained but realizing what he'd done. Knowing Charleigh would have died in that crash if he hadn't.

"They all died because of me," she whimpered.

My lips brushed back and forth over the top of her head. "No. They died because of Frederick."

"You saved him," she wept. "And you...you kept him? You raised him?"

"I couldn't report that I'd saved him, Charleigh. I knew the only thing that would happen was he'd go right back to Frederick. Everyone needed to believe he'd been lost to the river. So Cash created a new identity for him."

She scrambled back, that stunning face drenched with emotion, the flecks of cinnamon a toil in the depths of those caramel eyes.

"He's mine?" It was a plea.

Wasn't sure how to fuckin' believe it, but I recognized it then. This woman who I'd only seen pictures of.

Super long blonde hair. Much thinner than she was now.

I'd never gotten a close enough view to see the color of her eyes.

She was so much the same and somehow entirely different.

I reached out and brushed my thumb over her cheek. "Yeah, Charleigh, he's yours."

She gripped me by the shirt. "Take me to him. Take me to him now."

Chapter
FIFTY-SIX

Charleigh

IZZINESS SWEPT THROUGH ME AS River helped me to my feet.

I couldn't believe it. Was *terrified* to believe it.

But I knew it was true.

Knew all the way to my soul that that little boy belonged to me.

I'd felt it.

Sensed it.

This connection that wouldn't let me go.

A connection I knew had somehow led me here.

My heart flooded with emotion, and I swayed with the impact of it.

River curled his arm around my waist. "I've got you, Charleigh."

I nodded against him as he guided me out of his shop. He locked it behind us and led me around the corner to where his SUV was parked.

He helped me in, and I itched on the seat, so anxious to get to my son that I couldn't sit still.

My heart pounded violently in my chest, and I glanced at River as he climbed into the front seat. I immediately reached for him, this volatile, perfect man who kept me steady. "Thank you. I don't even know how to…"

I trailed off.

River swiveled and took both sides of my face in his hands. "There is no thanking me, Charleigh. I've been haunted for five fuckin' years that I failed you all. And I fucking hate that your parents and your cousin were killed in all of this, but I…" Storm-cloud eyes raged. "I can't believe it's you. That you found him."

My fingers brushed across his lips. "I found you both."

The harshest kind of love cut through his sharp features. Devotion and loyalty. This man who would truly do whatever it took.

One of his hands slipped into my hair and he dropped his forehead to mine. "Told you, Little Runner, this is where you belong."

I nodded against him, and he sat back and pulled out of the parking spot, then he started in the direction of Miss Liberty's.

"Miss Liberty knows. She's under the protection of the club," he said.

I gave him the jerkiest nod. Of course, he would make sure that Nolan was protected that way. The same as he'd been with Dr. Reynolds.

Anxiousness burned through me as we traveled through Moonlit Ridge. I was leaned forward, bouncing, antsy, desperate to get to him.

To see him anew.

Without the sorrow I'd been written in.

Without the grief and the loss.

With this pure joy that blistered through every faculty and every sense.

And still, I knew I loved him the same. That I'd already fallen wholly in love with this child, with or without my blood that ran through his veins.

River made a left into the modest neighborhood on the far side of town.

Tears of disbelief continued to track down my cheeks as he pulled to a stop at the curb in front of Liberty's house. A sob hitched in my throat as I looked out the passenger-side window. "I can't believe…"

It broke off.

River reached out and squeezed my hand. "Come on, Charleigh, let's go get your son."

River hopped out and was rounding the front of the SUV as I fumbled out. Unable to wait.

My nerves rattled and more questions poured through my brain. The hows and the whys.

I knew some of them would never be answered. My father had taken those to his grave.

Anticipation billowed beneath the surface of my skin, and shivers lifted when River took my hand and we walked together to the door.

But it was dread that slithered through me when I felt the alarm on the other side of the door. I thought River must have sensed it too because a frown cut across his brow and he knocked on the door with the back of his fist.

One second later, Miss Liberty ripped it open, horror drenching her face.

"Oh God, River…I can't find Nolan."

Chapter
FIFTY-SEVEN

RIVER

CHARLEIGH WAS ROCKING ON THE COUCH WRAPPED IN A blanket. Unable to sit still as she swam through the anguish. Finding out that Nolan was her biological son and losing him in the same goddamn breath.

While I stormed back and forth across the living room, trying to tamp the rage. To save it up for the fucker who I was going to carve into a million little pieces and take pleasure while doing it.

"We're going to find him." Raven whispered it where she sat next to Charleigh, rubbing her leg like she might be able to give her comfort.

Knew there wouldn't be an ounce of comfort until we brought Nolan home.

We'd warred about going to the local Sheriff. We'd been feeling him out, trying to decide if he could be trusted to be brought in, but we hadn't been able to discern that yet.

So there we'd been, weighing risks, and my crew had decided we had to continue to go this alone.

But this was my fuckin' son we were talking about.

Charleigh's son.

"We *are* going to find him," Otto grunted. His attention flashed to me. It was one of those moments when I knew the old wrath that had lived in Otto had been revived. When I knew he'd gladly go up against this monster and rip him to shreds. Make sure he suffered the gravest pain.

Fucker was going to have so much of it, he'd be begging us to cut short his last breath.

We'd searched the entire fucking town and came up empty, so my crew had gathered here at the house. Trent and Jud had come, too. Their kids were out playing in the back with Eden and Salem watching over them.

It was fucking gutting that Nolan wasn't out there with them.

An atrocity that wasn't going to go without penalty.

My hands fisted as I turned and started back the other direction, boots causing an earthquake on the floor. I dipped my head and ran my hand over the back of my neck in an attempt to squash the brutality that pounded through my veins.

Bloodlust on my tongue.

So excruciating that death was the only thing I could taste.

I wanted to. Hunt. Track him down. But just taking off in some random direction wasn't going to do Nolan any good. Not when we already knew the reason for him going missing.

This motherfucker wanted Charleigh.

Drawn, my gaze shifted to the woman who'd come into my world and obliterated my foundation.

Her hair was a mess, and her eyes were nearly swollen shut, but she was still the most gorgeous thing I'd ever seen. Most glorious kind of beauty I'd ever touched.

I'd fallen so fucking hard for her there would never be any getting up from off the floor.

I'd be on my knees for eternity.

Maybe I should have known the pull between us had to be something bigger than the both of us. Should've known the energy that compelled had drawn her to this place because she should have been here all along.

Kane, Jud, and Theo were talking in hushed tones in the kitchen, no doubt trying to come up with a contingency plan, while Trent and Cash remained quiet on the other side of the room…just fuckin' waiting.

On a shattered breath, pain ricocheted from Charleigh, and another sob ripped from her throat.

In a flash, I was on my knees in front of her.

Hands on the outside of her thighs, rubbing up and down. Hoping to give her some comfort the way Raven had been trying to do, only I wanted to crawl all the way inside her. Rid her of every ghost. Slay every fucking monster.

Fine.

One monster would do.

"I can't believe I failed him again. If I would have…" She choked over the words that had kept trying to get loose for hours. Blaming herself for not admitting to me who she was, thinking that might have changed something.

"No, baby, no. You had your reasons for not telling me your identity. You were protecting yourself the only way you knew how to do. You had no idea that Nolan might be involved this way. Not one fuckin' clue."

And we still had no idea which of them Frederick had discovered was alive first. If one or the other had drawn him here. The only thing we weren't questioning was it was him.

If only I'd have been able to sniff that bastard out that day when she'd come to me, but I had a hunch Frederick Winston wasn't acting alone. It was unlikely I would have recognized who'd been tracking her through town.

"I just…we have to find him." She looked up at me. Grief was carved on every inch of her face. I reached up and tried to wipe some of the moisture that wouldn't stop falling down her cheeks.

"We're going to. This asshole isn't going to disappear with him, Charleigh. You know that."

Charleigh nearly hit the ceiling when her cell phone rang, and she scrambled to grab it to look at the screen.

Hope and terror blazed across her face.

"It's an unknown number," she wheezed.

A wave of anxious quiet rolled through the room.

This was what we'd been waiting for.

Knowing Frederick would make contact some way.

I gulped around the animosity and hate that butted up against my own swell of hope.

My nod was slow.

Encouragement.

Charleigh was shaking as she answered and put it on speakerphone. "Hello?"

A wave of depravity rushed from the hushed silence that hovered on the other end of the line. It was the type of silence you knew without a doubt was a trap.

"Hello?" she asked again, her voice tripping on what amounted to a plea.

The man on the other end of the line tsked. The sound was malicious and cruel. "Chastity. You've been such a devious little wife."

A shiver jolted her, and the oxygen clogged in her throat.

"After all the things I gave you," he continued.

I wanted to snatch the phone from her lap and demand to know where he had Nolan. Utter all the ways I was going to torture him so he could stew and fret in the trepidation before I made the nightmare a reality.

But we'd agreed if he called, it needed to be Charleigh who did the talking.

"Where's Levi?" she whispered.

"Don't worry, Sweet Pea, he's fine. You wouldn't think I'd harm someone I love, would you? Especially after I've been mourning his death for five years?"

Horror streamed down Charleigh's face, rods of pain that drove through her middle, and her hand was on her heart like she was trying to keep it from bleeding out.

I ground my teeth. Searching for restraint. To be fucking patient so we could ferret out this piece of shit.

Frederick Winston released a discordant laugh. A clang of malice and spite. "I would have been mourning my beautiful wife, too, if

I hadn't known the second I went to identify her body that it was not actually you. I've been searching for you for years. The second I saw pictures of the two of you on that dance floor...I knew he was alive, too."

"What do you want?" Charleigh gasped it. "Just tell me what you want."

"What I've always wanted...You."

Revulsion beat against her fear, and Charleigh's expression morphed into this deep-seated sorrow, though it was cut with devotion and determination.

I squeezed her knee. A silent reminder that I was there and she wasn't alone. Not anymore and not ever again. And more than anything, I wanted to reassure her that we were going to get Nolan back.

She looked up at me. Caramel eyes shimmered with pain, though the cinnamon flecks blazed with fire.

She cemented her voice. "You can have me as long as I see Levi is whole and unharmed."

My hand squeezed again. Riddled with pride because my girl was fuckin' stronger than anyone I'd ever met. It was twisted with the ruthlessness that carved me into shards. The crushing urgency to get my son back.

"1645 Mabel Street in Keeton."

Fuck, he had him in the next town over.

"Seven o'clock. Come alone. You've heard it said it is the child that pays for the sins of his mother."

Then the phone went dead.

Charleigh shot to her feet. "I'm going."

I flew to mine, and the words ground off my tongue. "No. We already agreed on the plan, Charleigh. We find out where he has Nolan, and we go in and get him back."

I left off the part where I was going to put a permanent end to Frederick Winston. He wouldn't hurt either of them ever again.

Charleigh's jaw clenched, and a fresh round of tears slipped from her eyes. "That's my son, River. You can't expect me to sit aside and wait. I know you will fight for him...but don't ask me not to fight for him, too."

Half a second later, I had her in my arms. Plastering her against me. That sweet body burned, fire against my flesh, and her heart bashed in time with mine.

Two chaotic souls who'd give it all.

My hand wound in her hair, and I kissed her.

Kissed her hard and desperate and with every ounce of devotion I had.

Then I pulled back and murmured, "Let's go get our son."

Everyone had gathered, antsy and eager, unsure what we were going to come up against. We weren't fool enough to believe a man like Frederick Winston was just going to do as he'd promised.

And neither the fuck were we.

Chapter
FIFTY-EIGHT

Charleigh

"P LEASE, BE CAREFUL." RAVEN SQUEEZED ME SO TIGHT I WAS sure it was going to leave bruises. Or maybe I felt brittle. Fragile yet impenetrable.

As if I had been broken.

Whittled all the way down to bare bone and exposed to the marrow.

Yet in it, I'd been reborn.

Because the fear that had terrorized me for five years had been altered.

Shaved and pared down to one single moment.

This moment.

This moment that meant everything for Nolan.

And that fear would no longer own me or control me. I'd face it the way I'd regretted for years that I hadn't done from the beginning, forever wishing I'd had the courage to cut Frederick Winston down from the start.

From that first day when he sent the false information accusing my father of embezzling.

"I will," I promised her.

Eden and Salem hovered behind, anxiety thick as they anxiously shifted. Empathy and worry were etched clearly in their expressions.

It didn't go unnoticed that their husbands were putting themselves on the line for us, and I would be grateful to all of them for the rest of my life.

The way they'd rallied around us.

A promise to bring Nolan home.

To put an end to this nightmare that had started so many years ago.

"Everyone ready?" River asked. His attention was sharp as it traveled over all their faces.

A new plan had been set.

I would be bait.

An offering.

But I'd be willing to make any sacrifice if it meant Nolan could continue to live this life.

A rumble of agreement rolled through the group.

River turned to me, eyes the color of a thunderstorm. "You sure you want to do this?"

My chest clutched in certainty. "Yes."

He stole my breath when he suddenly gripped me by the back of the neck and pressed his forehead to mine. "We have this, Charleigh. I'm going to keep both of you safe, and we're going to get him back. I promise you. Whatever it takes."

I nodded against him. "I know. Whatever it takes."

Then he stepped back and jerked his head to his crew. "Let's roll out."

Everyone walked to where they'd parked their bikes out front, and a riot of motorcycle engines roared to life. Each one of the men were dressed in black. Head to boot. A tumult of dark mayhem that moved through the approaching evening.

They sped out in a rumble of anarchy.

A different bouncer stood guard outside the house, his watch wary.

I was supposed to wait fifteen minutes before I left. They had to be the most excruciating fifteen minutes of my life, though Raven, Eden, and Salem encircled me, Raven and Eden holding my hands where we sat on the top step of the front porch, Salem on the step below, rubbing my knee.

Those minutes finally passed, and I sucked in a steadying breath. "It's time."

They all nodded, and I gathered my courage, stood, and strode for Raven's car.

I opened the door, and Raven was suddenly behind me, grabbing me by the wrist, mahogany eyes grave when she whispered, "Bring him back."

I hugged her tight, my love for her greater than it'd ever been, knowing what she'd done to help care for my son over all these years.

Swallowing around the rocks in my throat, I pulled away, then slipped into her car. I punched the directions into Maps.

My hands were slick with sweat as I drove through town, and the anxiety only heightened as I hit the mostly barren two-lane road that led toward Keeton.

My heart drummed violently. I could barely hold onto the steering wheel as I traveled the half hour it took to get to the next town, praying over and over that my son was safe and unharmed.

That he was whole.

That he wouldn't fear.

I gulped when I finally saw the sign that said Keeton City Limits. It was larger than Moonlit Ridge. More commercial and the terrain was flat. A lot of the buildings were worn down, the landscape drab and dingy, as if this place had had the life sucked out of it.

My lungs compressed, and I drew in haggard breaths as I took the four turns required to get to Mabel Street. Here, it was industrial, the roads lined with metal buildings and chain-link fences. Most of the businesses seemed to be vacant at this time of evening.

I made a left onto Mabel, and I crawled along the road. Terror reverberated through my body with each second that passed.

I needed to get there. To see that Nolan was safe and whole. It was the only thing that mattered.

A tremor rocked through me when I made the right into a deserted lot. A giant metal building was situated right up front, but I could see that the gate was open on the right that led to the back.

I squeezed the steering wheel as I wound around, peering up at the surrounding buildings and praying that River and his friends were able to get into place.

It was still light out, but it was that foggy hour that tossed color through the atmosphere. Pinks and blues and grays. In it, I could feel that the air was distorted. Saturated with a vileness that slicked my skin in dread.

Nolan. Nolan. Nolan.

It chanted through my mind and surged through my heart. This child. My son. He was alive. Part of me still hesitated to believe it. To accept it. As if it were too magical a concept to put my faith in it.

The other part thought I'd known it all along. Had known that I'd felt it—this familiarity that had ached. The longing that had struck me like a blade.

I couldn't stomach the idea of him succumbing to this fate. Couldn't fathom the idea of that sweet, sweet child being torn from the love of River and Raven and given over to Frederick.

Sickness roiled. I wasn't delusional. Frederick Winston was powerful. His influence was great, and his reputation was spotless. I didn't know how we were going to manage this.

But we had to.

We had to find a way to end it.

A short gasp left me when I saw a black Navigator sitting on the far side of the lot in front of a large metal building, though the back-building was maybe half the height of the main building in front.

I slowed the car, creeping across the space until I came to a stop about fifty yards away from the SUV. Rays of sunlight slanted in from over the roof of the building, obscuring my vision, but in it, I saw shadows move.

I fumbled out, and it felt like my heart got ripped out of my chest when I saw an unknown man held Nolan. The little boy's back was to his chest, his feet and hands bound, a blindfold over his eyes. Though he seemed…limp.

Incoherent.

Oh God.

"Nolan." I whimpered it, wanting to race across the lot and pry him from the man's cruel arms.

But I held. Trying to stick to the plan to draw Frederick out so there would be time to assess the situation. The plan would need to be formed in a blink, and there was no room for error.

My gaze scanned. I spotted two more men, one on each end of the building. They were armed and standing guard, each of them wearing suits.

But it was the man who slipped out of the backseat of the SUV that made my knees wobble. Old wounds and a vat of fear dumped out in the middle of me, and in an instant, I was drowning in memories of the torment he'd put me through.

The suffering.

But the greatest suffering had been what he'd stolen.

My parents.

Lilah.

Levi.

Nolan.

My soul thrashed, and the tremor of fear that threatened was displaced by obstinacy and conviction.

Frederick shoved a casual hand into his suit jacket pocket, always the good guy when he was twisted with inhumanity.

A sadist to the core.

I'd never forget the glee he'd felt when he made me scream.

I tried not to shiver as his vile gaze raked over me, his blue eyes that were the same color as Nolan's gleaming in the type of greed that made me nauseous. "After all these years, and still so beautiful. How I've missed my Sweet Pea."

Revulsion crawled over my flesh, but I attempted to keep it at bay as I demanded, "What did you do to him?"

Frederick cast an easy smile, as if I were ridiculous for worrying.

"The little brat wouldn't stop crying, so I decided we should put him down for a nap. But don't fret…it's only temporary. At least, for now."

A warning edged into his voice on the last.

"You promised you wouldn't hurt him."

He shrugged a nonchalant shoulder. "I've promised a lot of things, but the only one that has ever truly mattered was that you belong to me. You've been mine since the first time I saw you when you were seventeen. I knew I had to have you. Knew I was going to carve myself on your flesh, so deep you would never forget me. I couldn't wait to draw your blood. I've missed it so."

Bile burned my throat, and the horrors of his depravity came rushing up from the recesses where I'd tried to keep them buried. I put a dam around them, refusing the assault.

I wanted to toss it in his face that I'd allowed another man to write himself all over me to replace him. To cover him. To eradicate him.

But I knew that would only enrage him, and it would put Nolan in more danger than he already was.

I had to play this smart.

Frederick lifted his chin and stretched out his hand. "Now, come to me. It's time for your punishment."

That must have been the breaking point for River because two men suddenly dropped off the roof.

In an instant, pandemonium broke out. Shouts and gunshots and a flurry of dust.

I watched through the vapor, wide-eyed, shock belting through my consciousness, though it felt as if time had been set to slow, as if I were taking in every movement independently.

Jud was on the left, and he fired two shots as the guard in front of him began to fire. The guard stumbled backward as he was hit, and he toppled to the ground. On the opposite side, Otto was there, though he'd come up from behind, and he rammed a knife into the man's side.

Over and over.

The guard dropped to his knees.

Oh God. Oh God.

Fury surged out of Frederick, and he ran for the man who held

Nolan. He ripped him out of his hold, and in an instant, he had a knife to the child's throat.

I lurched forward, stumbling a step, the single word a jagged stone that turned in my throat. "No."

River had dropped from the roof, too, and he was tussling with the man who'd held Nolan. Shots were fired as they struggled to get on top of each other, and horror clutched and gripped, terrified of River being hurt.

The others had gathered behind me.

I could feel their presence like the gathering of a squall.

Theo, Kane, Cash, and Trent.

Their weapons were drawn, though they hesitated, unsure of how to approach since Frederick had the knife to Nolan's neck.

But I knew.

I knew there was only one thing I could do.

My spirit screamed in resolution.

And I went racing for Frederick, running across the space, my feet pounding on the concrete.

Frederick grinned a maniacal grin as if my surrender was exactly what he wanted. Thinking he had me. That he had me on my knees.

"Frederick," I begged. Begged in the way I used to do. In the way that he ate up, hungering for my agony.

But this agony?

It was completely different. And I threw myself at him like I was throwing myself into his arms. He didn't realize until the last moment that I had a knife. I drove it into his stomach. His wicked blue eyes went wide, and he released Nolan.

My instinct was to catch the little boy. To keep him from slamming limp against the ground.

I grabbed him awkwardly, just before he hit, and I fumbled to draw him fully into my arms. As soon as I did, I curled myself around him to shield him with my body.

Frederick stumbled forward, leaning into me as he grated with pain, his mouth at my ear when he muttered, "One more time. Your blood. It belongs to me."

My eyes went wide as the piercing pain sheared through my flank. So deep I thought it went all the way through.

I fumbled back, struggling to keep Nolan in my arms. To hold him. To protect him.

Frederick started to take another step toward me, still wielding the knife that dripped with my blood.

Only River was suddenly behind him.

His storm-cloud eyes had darkened to pitch. Black lightning that struck in the middle of the night. He gripped Frederick by the forehead and pulled his head back. "You sick motherfucker. You're getting off lucky."

River dragged the blade across Frederick's throat.

Blood gushed.

Gushed and gushed as my tormentor gurgled for air that had ceased to exist.

I met Frederick's eyes as awareness befell him.

As he realized there wasn't enough money in the world to stop this.

His power no match.

No match for this love.

No match for this devotion.

No match for the truth that River and I would do anything to protect this child.

And with my own realization, I dropped to my knees, still clinging to Nolan as I slumped to the ground.

Chapter
FIFTY-NINE

RIVER

Panic slammed me as Charleigh crumbled to the hard, unforgiving ground with Nolan still in her arms. I dropped the motherfucker like a rock, his worthless body toppling to the ground, and I flew for Charleigh and Nolan.

"Charleigh. Fuck, Charleigh."

Hands shaking out of control, I rolled her over, and a shock of pain ripped from my lungs when I saw the blood that saturated the front of her shirt over her stomach. Her skin was pale and sticky with sweat, though those arms still clutched Nolan.

His support.

His sanctuary.

I gulped through the disorder, and my crew came hustling up, Otto at the helm. "Are they okay?" Otto shouted.

Anguish shook my head as I peeled back her shirt enough to reveal the wound. It was more than a cut. It was a two-inch wide puncture that went deep. So deep that the skin gaped open as blood poured from it.

"Someone get me a compress," I roared, the desperation hemorrhaging from my mouth.

Kane knelt down, already prepared as he started pulling supplies out of his pack. "Here."

I accepted the compress and pressed it against her injury, my hands pushing firm to it, praying it'd be enough to staunch the flow of blood.

I did my best to keep my cool as I shouted orders, though I could feel myself splintering apart. "Someone help me get her to the car. Get Dr. Reynolds on the phone and tell him we need him. Otto, you drive. Trent and Jud...take Nolan and follow us."

They were the only other ones who had something other than a bike.

A furor of activity rushed around us. Boots thundering. Trent scooped Nolan into his arms, and Theo and Cash helped me carefully lift Charleigh, doing our best not to jostle her so I could keep the compress held firmly to her side.

They cast me worried glances, glances that made it feel like I was the one being stabbed straight through, knowing what those expressions meant.

She was in trouble.

The situation dire.

My heart bleeding out.

We carried her to the back door of the car, and I slid in with her in my lap.

Fucking praying with all the strength I had.

"You're going to be okay," I whispered the hoarse words, my arm bound around her as I held her against my chest, my hand wedged between us to give extra pressure to the compress. "You're going to be okay. Just breathe. Breathe."

I poured my belief into her.

Otto jumped into the driver's seat and tore out of the lot. He sped back through town.

I was so close to telling him to take us to the emergency room. To get her immediate help. But I'd promised. Knew it wasn't what Charleigh would want.

Nolan would be taken from me if it was discovered what I'd

done, and she'd made me promise, no matter what, that Nolan would be the first priority.

The second we made it through the town, Otto gunned it, taking the car to its limits. Trees whizzed by on both sides of the road as we traveled the twenty miles back to Moonlit Ridge, the landscape growing denser with each second that passed.

He made the thirty-minute drive in half the time, and my heart was battering at my chest as he blazed through Moonlit Ridge. He barely slowed as he took a sharp left into the parking lot of the medical facility, and he flew around to the back of the building to the private door.

He screeched to a stop. I didn't wait, I tossed open the door and jumped out with Charleigh in my arms.

Dr. Reynolds was already there holding the door open.

"Hurry," he wheezed, and I angled around him and jogged down the hall to the private room that we'd had stocked for circumstances exactly like this, though I'd never imagined it would be quite like this. I'd always thought it'd be a stranger I'd carry in and not the woman who'd come to mean everything to me.

The one I could feel beating through my veins.

The one I could feel slipping away.

I laid her on the elevated examination table.

"Help her." I fucking begged it, I didn't care.

Dr. Reynolds shuffled forward, then he stumbled in confusion. "Charleigh?"

My chest clutched in a fit of desperation. "She's Nolan's biological mother. Help her. Save her. We can't lose her."

"Oh my God." The old man jumped into action, his concern clear as he examined the wound and then bustled to the cabinets to pull out supplies.

I knew he knew what he was doing. A retired surgeon who'd opened his own practice once he'd left the hospital in Denver. A man who'd shown his integrity and care and compassion with every victim we'd brought through his door.

Still, my insides were in knots of grief and tangles of desperation.

Trapped in the disturbance, Otto hovered at the doorway, his face a mess of sorrow and sympathy.

I turned back to my girl. My perfection. My match.

And I pressed my lips to her temple and murmured, "Don't leave, Little Runner. Don't leave. Run back to me."

Chapter
SIXTY

Charleigh

I BLINKED MY EYES OPEN TO THE GOLDEN HAZE THAT SATURATED the room. It was quiet, and the rods of sunlight that slanted in through the bedroom window appeared alive. Dancing as they played through the motes that dusted the air.

My thoughts were fuzzy and disjointed, but in an instant, I recognized one thing.

The soft pants that puffed from the child's mouth where he was fast asleep beside me. Both blue stuffed puppies were tucked to his chest, his little arm holding them close as he slept.

He was on his side, his precious face turned toward me. My fingers trembled as I reached out and brushed them down his chubby cheek.

Love swelled. Swelled to overflowing.

Nolan.

My son.

"He wouldn't leave your side." That low voice rumbled from across the room, and I jerked, then shifted enough to find River standing in the doorway. His giant body was leaned against the jamb, all that ferocity shearing through his features.

My heart that was already filled to overflowing leapt.

I attempted to sit up, then yelped as a smack of pain pierced through my middle.

River's hands shot out like he could reach all the way across the room and keep me pinned to the bed. "Don't try to get up."

I rolled until I was flat on my back and staring up at the ceiling. I gently placed my hand over the throbbing in my side.

It wasn't until then that I realized there was an IV attached to my left wrist.

I could feel the bandages covering the spot where Frederick had stabbed me. Images sprang to my mind, those last moments when I'd rammed the blade into his side, me grappling for Nolan, the knife that had impaled my side.

The moment when I would have been happy to surrender if it meant that Nolan had *this*.

I looked back at the child.

At the peace that smoothed his features into tranquility.

I was sure he had to be traumatized in some way, being taken from Miss Liberty's, and I had no idea what Frederick had put him through in the hours he'd held him hostage, but at least he was here.

In the safety of his home. The only one he'd really known.

The bed sank on the other side of me, and I slowly rolled toward River. He had his knee tucked up on the bed so he could fully face me, and his hand came to my cheek. Thunderclouds toiled in the depths of his eyes, though his thumb stroked softly along the apple of my cheek.

"How are you feeling?" The coarse words were accompanied by him searching my face, his gaze traveling down my body as if he were terrified a new injury might have sprouted in the time I'd been asleep.

I stared up at him. At his vicious beauty that etched him in severity. His sharp jaw and defined cheeks and the stars that played along his hairline.

I inhaled his volatility. The taste of violence and destruction on my tongue. This man so dangerously sweet.

My throat was tight, and my mouth was dry, but I somehow managed to whisper my truth. "Happy."

So happy I didn't know how to make sense of all that I felt.

Everything I'd known had been ripped apart like the shredding of a contract that had been made null and void.

And in its place was this.

This.

River kept brushing his thumb gently across my skin, his expression carved of possession and relief. "I was so fuckin' scared. Didn't know he'd gotten to you until you fell to the ground."

"I heard you," I told him around the thickness. "I heard you calling for me. Asking me to run back to you. Well, demanding it because I don't think you've ever asked nicely for anything."

A shaky smile pulled at one side of my mouth.

River grunted an amused sound that still was pained. "Refused to let you leave me. Refused to let you leave *us.*"

Emotion burned in my chest, and I reached out and dragged my fingertips over the scruff that lined his jaw. "I still can't believe you saved him. That you took him in. That he's been with you all this time. That you've loved him like this."

He slipped off the side of the bed and onto his knees, and he took my hand in both of his. He brushed his lips over my knuckles, his voice scraping on the hushed admission. "Sovereign Sanctum wanted me to place him with another family. With one of the women we'd helped start anew. But from the second I held him…"

His head shook as he drifted in the memory. "I knew I couldn't let him go. Knew I was bonded to him in some way. Even though keeping him made things a thousand times more difficult for my crew. At the time, I chalked it up to believing I owed him for letting you down. For not being able to bring you to safety. For failing you and your family. So, I devoted my life to him. He became my purpose."

He kissed across my knuckles again. His chest expanded as he inhaled. "But now I have to wonder if maybe I wasn't purposed to hold him for you. To protect him until you could return to him."

My nails scratched up his cheek. "And maybe I was purposed to find both of you."

"I would do anything for him. For you."

"I know…just the same as I would for both of you."

Darkness crowded his expression. "We almost lost you."

"I would have gladly made that sacrifice, just the same as I know you would have made it for us."

"Charleigh, fuck, I'm—"

I knew it was going to be an apology, as if this selfless, beautiful man was responsible for the actions of Frederick. So, I pressed my fingertips to his lips to stop him, and I murmured, "There's no room for guilt here because the only thing I have left is love. I've lost so many days, River. So many days. I don't want to lose any more."

On a heaving breath, he leaned forward and pressed his forehead to mine. His big palm splayed out over the entirety of the left side of my face.

Energy whispered and lashed.

That connection that had found us from the beginning.

And one I knew would be with us until the end.

"Don't worry, Little Runner. We've got from here to eternity."

EPILOGUES

Charleigh

COOL AIR LIFTED WITH THE GENTLE BREEZE THAT BLEW OVER the lake. The sun shone high in the vast expanse of blue above, and the warmth of its rays caressed my skin where I sat on a blanket on the sandy beach.

Voices and laughter carried from where River's family was gathered at the foldable tables we'd brought for our barbecue.

I gazed back at them.

My chest clutched.

My *family*.

It's what they'd become over the last two months since everything had happened.

Kane was giving Otto crap the way he always did, and Theo was chuckling along at their antics where he sipped from a beer where he sat on a fold-out chair.

Raven retaliated in Otto's favor. She sat tucked close to him, tiny against his massive frame, though likely not close enough if she was ever to get her way.

I thought the guy was oblivious, though, or maybe just…scared of looking at her in a way he thought he shouldn't.

Cash was missing, as I'd come to understand was the usual unless there was something important going on with their family.

And River...River was down at the water with Nolan, the two of them skipping rocks.

"You did it, Daddy-O! Did you see that? You had five whole skips!" Nolan jumped as his little hand sporting all five fingers jabbed toward the sky. "My turn!"

Nolan grabbed a giant rock and tossed it. It blobbed against the water and sank straight to the bottom. "Whelp, guess I don't got any extra points for that. I'd better take your advice and get a different kind of rock. That's because you got smart ideas, right, Dad?" he asked as he started to poke around in the line of rocks that had gathered on the beach.

River chuckled that sound that rolled through me like greed, and as if he felt it, he turned to me. That dark gaze raked over me, and his expression shifted, a promise of what he was going to do to me later.

I bit down on my bottom lip.

I couldn't wait.

That man had had me in every way. Constant and unendingly. And I knew I would never get enough.

But right then, this time was about family.

About our family, and I stood from the blanket and started down the shore.

"How about we take a break from rock skipping and take a little walk?" I asked, my nerves rattling inside me.

Nolan squealed and clapped his hands, bouncing toward me as he asked, "Like a hike? I'm really good at hikin.'"

"Yeah, like a hike."

River looked at me from over his head. Awareness pulled between us, and emotion gathered thick at the base of my throat, this heaviness that was also the lightest light.

I took Nolan's left hand, and River took his right, and we began to wind up the trail to the spot we had picked for this day.

It was no surprise that Nolan had been traumatized that day two months ago. He hadn't let me or River out of his sight for two weeks before he'd felt safe and confident enough to move around the house on his own. Once in a while, he still cried out for us in the night.

But he'd begun to heal, and I knew it was time.

We climbed up the winding trail that wound through the dense, soaring trees.

Nolan's little feet scuffed behind me. "Whew, this hike is really tough, isn't it, Miss Charleigh? You got hard puffs from your mouth, too?"

A soft, affectionate giggle rolled out of me. "I sure do. But we're almost there."

We finally broke out in the clearing where we'd climbed to the short cliffs that overlooked the lake. Beyond, we could see the cabins that lined the area, hidden beneath the swells of lush leaves.

Theo's motel, The Sanctuary, was down at the base below us.

From here, the lake appeared crystalline, a scatter of diamonds glinting over the top.

It was gorgeous. Awe-inspiring.

But not close to the beauty I saw when I turned to look at River standing there holding Nolan's hand.

"Come over here, Nolan, I have something really important I need to tell you."

He didn't hesitate. He trotted along at my side as I led him to a big rock that gave an extraordinary view of the valley. We settled down onto it, the stone worn from the weather and storms.

We were far enough back that there was no danger of falling over the edge but close enough that it felt as if you hovered right over the lake.

I pulled Nolan onto my lap and angled him sideways, and River came and sat beside us.

"So, what you gotta tell me that's really important?" He was all grins, kicking his sandal-clad feet as he beamed between us.

My spirit ached in the most blissful sort of way, and I brushed his hair back from his face that now was nearly completely blond as the coloring had faded away. "Do you remember when you told me about your love mark?"

Nolan rushed to push up the short sleeve of his shirt, flinging his arm overhead and pointing to the birthmark on his arm. "This one right here?"

"Yep. And you told me that your dad called it a love mark because your mommy must have loved you so much."

"She had to if she left a heart on me." He said it pragmatically. As if it should be plain and obvious and he'd long ago accepted it.

As if it were simple when I'd never felt anything so complex.

"She did love you very, very much. And she still does."

A frown scrunched between his eyes as he tipped his head back to peer up at me. "You know her?"

My heart fisted and my throat nearly closed off. "I am her, Nolan. I am your mom." The words dropped out of me like a plea. "I got lost for a little while and I couldn't find you, but I finally did. I found you, and I found your dad."

River and I had decided to try to keep the explanation as simple as possible. Leaving out the sordid details. The pain and the tragedy.

Plus, River wasn't sure it was safe to tell Nolan he wasn't his biological father.

Not when we were keeping his identity as Nolan Tayte. Not when we didn't want to disrupt everything the child had ever known. Not when we could never link ourselves to what had happened to Frederick Winston and his guards.

It was best if it was forever believed that Chastity and Levi Winston had died in that car wreck.

Maybe the day would come when we felt it was in Nolan's best interest to know, but for now, we were going to raise him as our own.

His little frown deepened. "Where'd you get lost at?"

Anguish twined in my spirit. The years lost. The sorrow I'd sustained. But I knew…I knew with every place I'd run to, I'd been running here.

Toward these two.

Curling my arms around him, I hugged him tight and whispered against the top of his head, "I just got lost looking for you, but I finally found my way."

"Well, it's really good you found me because I already loved you like you're my mommy because I already loved you the most, just like I love my Daddy-O."

"I love you the most, too. Just like I love your Daddy-O."

I looked at River then.

River, this storm of a man who was my calm.

My safety.

The sanctuary that had held this child in all his ferocity.

And I knew he would for all his days.

I hugged Nolan for the longest time before he hopped to his feet and tried to drag me to mine. "Well, come on then, Mommy. We should probably go tell the rest of our family the really good news."

Again, he said it simply.

As if it were rational when I knew I'd been given nothing less than a miracle.

I sniffled over an affected laugh. "I guess we probably should."

River stood, too, and he enclosed, picking up Nolan and hugging him between us, his massive arm looped around my waist as he pressed a kiss to my temple. "Little Runner...thank you for running to me."

RIVER

The sound of the tattoo machine whirred in the enclosed space of my station. It was close to eleven at night, and all the lights were cut in the shop other than the bright one that hung low from the ceiling to illuminate the area.

I was working the most gorgeous piece I'd ever done.

I might have been biased, but I didn't give a fuck.

The tattoo chair had been adjusted so Charleigh could sit straddling it, wrapped around the leather with her cheek rested on the headrest.

I was sitting low on my stool so I could get to her lower back where I was doing the fourth session of her tattoo.

A piece that covered the scars that bastard had carved onto

her lower back. Eradicating him the way I'd promised her I would. Covering her in beauty rather than the atrocity he'd intended.

It was a forest scene, an innuendo of Moonlit Ridge, though we'd taken some liberties to make it our own.

Trees rising up around the lake.

But this one…this one had a river running through.

She'd said we were the current that had led her here, and she believed she'd ridden on our energy that had called her to this small town. Hidden in the torrent was the silhouette of a blue puppy…stretched out and riding through the waves.

She flinched when I swept the needle over the ridge of her spine where I was adding a teal blue shading.

Could tell she was trying to hold her breath. Doing her best to ignore the burn that erupted on her skin as I marked her deep. Cutting into the lines and filling it with ink.

She squirmed and whimpered, and fuck me, my dick strained.

That first night when I'd tattooed her, I'd chalked the reaction I had to her up to me being a twisted fiend. Hungering for something I should never take.

I'd loved that I had been the one to etch her permanently. Loved that she had been going to walk out of my shop and forever carry a piece of me.

What I hadn't known was this woman was the one who would permanently etch herself on me.

The one who would change everything.

The one who was going to take my guilt and shame and knit it back into love.

I edged back, and I wiped up the excess ink and the bit of blood with the towel before I leaned in and blew across the heated skin to give her some relief. Didn't feel I was crossing a line that time.

Not when the Little Runner was mine.

"How you holding up over there?" I rumbled as I kept brushing the needle over her flesh that bloomed pink.

"I'm great." It was all kinds of breathy.

A rough chuckle rolled out of me. "Great, huh?"

She shifted to look back at me from over her shoulder. The cinnamon flecks in her eyes flamed. "Any time I'm with you, I'm great."

"That so?"

"Mm-hmm." There was a coyness to it. The girl playing nothing but temptation and a tease.

"If this is great, then I can't imagine just how good you feel when I'm tryin' for it." I let the suggestion wind into my tone.

A raspy laugh escaped her. "Now that is something else entirely."

"Only thing I want…to give you pleasure." I said it as I finished up the last few passes I needed to make. I set my tools aside and ripped off my black rubber gloves, then I eased back, inspecting my work.

Pride gripped me by the chest.

But it wasn't of my work. It was of this woman who'd only known running.

Fear.

Terror of what might catch up to her.

But when she'd finally found her way home…to us…she had been willing to give it all to protect it.

This home.

This place.

Our son.

"How does it look?" she asked on a whisper.

I let my gaze travel up the column of her back. "Stunning. Steal the breath straight outta my lungs *stunning*."

Goosebumps lifted on the surface of her flesh. She knew I wasn't talking about the tat.

Still, I pushed from the stool and took one step to the side so she could peer behind her to see the reflection of it in the mirror that hung on the wall.

Tears blurred her eyes as she glanced up at me. "Oh wow, River. It's…beautiful."

My fingertips slipped along her bare shoulder. "You're what's beautiful, Charleigh."

"You've always made me feel that way. I felt *seen* the moment I met you."

"Think you've been the only thing I could *see* since the second I found you standing in that doorway."

I sat back on the stool and began to clean the tattoo.

Charleigh hummed as I did, as if she found pleasure in that bare touch.

She had her shorts pulled all the way down so the band only covered half her ass, and she'd removed her tank, her bare tits smashed to the leather of the seat.

I was inundated by the way I'd felt that first night. The way I'd wanted to peel her out of her little shorts and rid her of her tank so I could get to those sweet, tiny tits.

How I'd wanted to sink my cock deep into the well of her squirming body.

Fucking her right here on my chair, something I'd never done before because it was fucking unprofessional.

I had every intention of changing that tonight.

Making sure I didn't touch any of the area I'd tatted, my hands slipped down to grip her by the outside of the waist. "You, Charleigh," I murmured. "You came into my life like a hurricane. Thought you were fuckin' it all up. Destroying the foundation I'd set. The commitment I'd made to a little boy after I'd failed his mother. My commitment to Sovereign Sanctum. And there you were…filling the hollow spaces we didn't know had been empty."

She shifted so she was looking back at me, her hands still clinging to the chair. "And there you were…showing me that I didn't have to be alone. That I didn't have to be afraid. Lighting the places inside me that I thought were forever dead. Making me fall in love with a little boy. The two of you becoming my balm. And then to find out he was mine…"

My palms glided up her ribs. "We're both yours, Charleigh. Think we would have been either way."

"Yes. I loved him, no matter what."

Energy swelled, two of us trapped, the already cramped walls of my station closing in.

Lust and possession smacked me in the face.

I pushed to my feet, rising up behind her.

"Get on your knees...I want to fuck you on my chair."

Charleigh made a choked sound in the back of her throat, though she scrambled to get up and kneel on her knees, my woman more than eager.

She panted while I slipped my fingers in the elastic waist of the tiny shorts she was wearing, and I began to peel them down.

Exposing the perfect globes of her ass.

Her trembling thighs.

She lifted each knee so I could drag them all the way free.

And there was my girl.

Naked and writhing in my chair, hanging onto the headrest while she stared back at me.

Hair that she'd let go back to blonde cascaded over her shoulders and back.

That tat I'd permanently marked on her exposed, skin still red and hot, the color bright and shiny with the cream.

Knew I needed to be careful not to touch it or irritate it, but I had to have her.

Just like this.

She arched her ass out. No doubt she needed it, too.

I reached out and dragged my fingers through her pussy. She was already soaked. "Look at you, always so fuckin' needy. I hadn't even touched you yet, and you were dripping wet."

"Because I always need you," she whimpered.

I ticked the button of my jeans then dragged down the zipper. The rip of it bounced against the walls, and Charleigh inhaled a jagged breath as she squeezed her thighs together.

I pulled myself free, cock in my hand. I pressed the blunt head to her entrance. "Do you know how hard I've been since the second you sat down in my chair tonight? Hours spent dreaming of this... driving my dick into the sweet heat of your cunt."

I took her in one possessive thrust.

Pleasure flashed in bright lights at the edges of my eyes, the feel of the girl pure, awe-inspiring bliss.

Her tight little pussy hugged me in a throbbing, greedy fist, and Charleigh gasped and writhed as she adjusted to my size.

"So good, Charleigh," I grunted. "Doesn't matter how many times I have you, I will never get enough. Will never stop feeling like I'm dreaming. Fuckin' fantasy, having you like this."

"Yes…I…please…take me." A roll of pleas toppled from her, and she pushed back, trying to take me deeper.

I was happy to oblige.

I gripped her by the hips, and I watched as I pulled out, my cock drenched with her arousal, her lips slick and swollen and perfect.

I rocked back in.

Hard.

Charleigh bowed forward before she rocked back.

I began to drive into her like that. Fucking her in hard, deep strokes.

A buzz of pleasure built around us. A burn that was only meant for us.

We were both panting and grunting, fighting to get closer to the other. This woman my ecstasy.

Praises poured out of my mouth.

"Look at you. The way you take my cock. The way you were made for me. Good girl."

Good girl.

The best girl.

My only girl.

The only one who could be meant for me. The only one who could see me for who I was.

A monster who would gladly rip the world to shreds if it meant protecting her.

Loving her.

Keeping her.

"Touch me," she begged, and I looped my arm around her so I could play with her engorged clit.

"Like that?"

"Yes," she rasped.

Her ass was jutted out as I pounded into her.

Hard and fast and desperate.

"River...Oh God...I..."

"Come for me, Little Runner. Come."

She exploded around my dick, the girl shooting off in this orgasm that ripped through her like a storm.

That's what we were.

The perfect storm.

Volatile and chaotic and perfectly right.

Her rapture set me off, bliss bursting through me as I came. I held her tight as I poured into her body.

We were both gasping as we came down, though neither of us ever really touched the floor.

We were always lifted.

Elevated.

Given to this thing that could only belong to us.

"I love you," she whispered.

Careful to avoid her back, I leaned forward so I could murmur at the sensitive flesh at the nape of her neck.

"Yeah, baby. I love you. From here to eternity."

The End

About the
AUTHOR

A.L. Jackson is the *New York Times* & *USA Today* Bestselling author of contemporary romance. She writes emotional, sexy, heart-filled stories about boys who usually like to be a little bit bad.

Her bestselling series include THE REGRET SERIES, CLOSER TO YOU, BLEEDING STARS, FIGHT FOR ME, CONFESSIONS OF THE HEART, FALLING STARS, REDEMPTION HILLS, and TIME RIVER.

If she's not writing, you can find her hanging out by the pool with her family, sipping cocktails with her friends, or of course with her nose buried in a book.

Be sure not to miss new releases and sales from A.L. Jackson - Sign up to receive her newsletter http://smarturl.it/NewsFromALJackson or text "aljackson" to 33222 to receive short but sweet updates on all the important news.

Connect with A.L. Jackson online:

FB Page https://geni.us/ALJacksonFB
A.L. Jackson Bookclub https://geni.us/ALJacksonBookClub
Angels https://geni.us/AmysAngels
Amazon https://geni.us/ALJacksonAmzn
Book Bub https://geni.us/ALJacksonBookbub

Text "aljackson" to 33222 to receive short but sweet updates on all the important news.

Made in United States
Orlando, FL
03 November 2024

53440342R10248